Sierra backed away. "I have to ask you not to do that again."

He nodded. "Agreed. It wouldn't be a good idea for you to get involved with me. I won't be around for long and, despite our little charade, I'm not very good boyfriend material."

Sierra hadn't expected him to agree with her so quickly. Disappointment filled her chest. Pushing back her shoulders, she lifted her chin. Why should she care? He'd only confirmed her desire to avoid anything sticky growing between them. Still…

He turned and walked toward the door.

Before he crossed the threshold, she asked, "Why?"

He stopped and half turned toward her. "Why what?"

"Why do you make bad boyfriend material?" She shouldn't be interested in his answer, but she was and she waited for his response.

He shook his head, a hint of a smile tilting his lips.

D1428174

9030 00005 5659 8

He shook his head and licked a smile biting his lips. "Trust me, I'm no good for you, or any other woman." With that, he walked out of the room and shut the door.

HOT VELOCITY

BY
ELLE JAMES

First Published in Great Britain 2017
By Mills & Boon, an imprint of HarperCollins*Publishers*
1 London Bridge Street, London, SE1 9GF

© 2017 Mary Jernigan

ISBN: 978-0-263-92898-3

46-0717

Our policy is to use papers that are natural, renewable and recyclable products and made from wood grown in sustainable forests. The logging and manufacturing processes conform to the legal environmental regulations of the country of origin.

Printed and bound in Spain
by CPI, Barcelona

Elle James, a *New York Times* bestselling author, started writing when her sister challenged her to write a romance novel. She has managed a full-time job and raised three wonderful children, and she and her husband even tried ranching exotic birds (ostriches, emus and rheas). Ask her, and she'll tell you what it's like to go toe-to-toe with an angry three-hundred-and-fifty-pound bird! Elle loves to hear from fans at ellejames@earthlink.net or www.ellejames.com.

This book is dedicated to my grandmother who, at the age of 97, is still fighting to stay in this world. After a broken back, she powered her way through physical therapy to make it back home from rehab for Thanksgiving. She's a fighter and I hope to have as much gumption as she does when I'm 97!

Chapter One

"Whatcha got?" Captain Rex "T-Rex" Trainor leaned toward the man sitting beside him in the helicopter, preparing to deploy into the small Afghan village on the edge of nowhere.

Gunnery Sergeant Lance Gallagher, Gunny to the unit, grinned, splitting his scarred, rugged face in two, and held up a small, shiny piece of paper with a black-and-white picture on it. "Number four is a boy!" he shouted over the roar of the rotors spinning overhead.

T-Rex nodded. "Congratulations!"

"Three girls and a boy." Gunny shook his head, his lips curling into a happy smile. "Poor kid will be out-numbered by women." He looked up, catching T-Rex's gaze, his smile fading. "That's why I'm giving up the good life of a career soldier to retire. I plan on being there to make sure Junior gets a shot at playing football, baseball and whatever the hell sport he wants."

T-Rex didn't blame the man. "Someone needs to be there to make sure he has that chance."

"Darn right." Gunny waved the thin piece of paper at T-Rex. "I want to teach him to throw his first ball, build a fort, take him hunting and, most of all…teach him how to treat a woman right." He winked.

What every boy needed—a father who cared enough to show him the ropes. T-Rex's dad had taught him everything he knew about horses, ranching and riding broncos in the rodeo. He'd taught him how to suck it up when he was thrown and to get back up on that horse, even when he was injured. Too many kids nowadays didn't have that parental influence, whether it be a mother or father, to push them to be all they could be and more.

"LZ coming up!" the pilot shouted. He lowered the craft onto the rocky ground and held steady while the team exited from both sides of the Black Hawk.

Although it was night, nothing stood in the way of the stars and the moon shining down on the rugged landscape.

They were deposited on the other side of a hill from their target village. In less than thirty minutes they climbed to the top of the ridge and half ran, half slid down the other side into the back wall of the hamlet.

This was supposed to be a routine sweep to ensure the small group of Taliban thugs they'd chased off hadn't returned. The intelligence guys had some concerns since the location was so close to the hills and caves the terrorists fled to when driven out of their strongholds.

T-Rex motioned for his team to spread out along the wall. When he gave the signal, they were to scale the wall and drop to the other side. When everyone was in position, he spoke softly into his mic. "Let's do this."

In two-man teams, they helped each other over the wall, landing softly on the other side. T-Rex led the way through the buildings, checking inside each one. The locals knew the drill, they'd been invaded so many times. They remained silent and gathered their sleeping children close.

What a life. These people never knew who was coming through the door next, or if the intruders would kill them all or let them live to see another day.

As T-Rex neared the other end of the village, doors stood open to huts that were empty of people and belongings.

The hairs on the back of his neck stood at attention. "Something's not right here," he said softly into his mic. He knelt in the shadow of a building and strained to see any movement in the street ahead or from the rooftops. Nothing moved. No shadows stirred or separated from the buildings, and no one loomed overhead from the tops of the homes.

In his gut, T-Rex knew they were walking into a trap. "Back out the way we came," he whispered.

"I've got your back," Gunny said.

"Get the others out of here. I smell a trap."

"Not going without you, sir," Gunny insisted.

"That's an order," T-Rex said, his tone firm, despite the whisper. "Move out." He glanced over his shoulder to the gunnery sergeant's position a building behind him, and on the opposite side of the road, the other members waited for the signal, hugging the shadows. At that moment, a shadow appeared on the roof directly over Gunny's head.

"Heads up! Tango over you, G," T-Rex warned, setting his sights on the man, waiting for the telltale shape of a weapon to appear. His finger on the trigger, T-Rex counted his breaths.

One...two...

The man yanked something in his hand.

"Not good!" T-Rex pulled the trigger, hitting the man in the chest. He collapsed forward, the object in his hand slipping from his grip, falling to the ground. "Grenade!" T-Rex shouted.

Gunny threw himself away from the small oval object rolling across the dirt. But not soon enough.

T-Rex lurched to his feet, too far away from his gunnery sergeant to be of any use. "No!"

The world erupted.

T-Rex was flung backward, landing hard on his back, the breath knocked from his lungs. Stunned, he lay for a second, staring up at the stars overhead, shining like so many diamonds in the sky until the dust and debris from the blast obliterated the night. Then he remembered how to breathe and sucked in a huge lungful of dust. The popping sound of gunfire came from above and all around.

T-Rex rolled toward the shadows of a building and bunched his legs beneath him. Bullets rained down around him, kicking up puffs of dirt near his feet.

Raising his weapon to his shoulder, T-Rex scanned the rooftops through the cloud of dust.

A man stood above him, aiming an AK47 in his direction.

His ears still ringing, T-Rex pinned the man in his

sights and fired. One shot. The man fell to the ground, his weapon clattering on the rocky street.

T-Rex quickly scanned neighboring rooftops and the road ahead. Nothing moved there, but the world was pure chaos behind him.

He spun and ran toward the others, his heart hammering in his chest, his head still spinning from the detonation of the concussion grenade.

His men were pinned to the sides of the building, by a single fighter wielding a machine gun from his position near to where his comrade had been standing when T-Rex had taken him out.

T-Rex knelt, aimed, but his vision blurred. He blinked, gaining a clearer shot. His finger tightened on the trigger. He fired one round, and the fighter fell, dropping the machine gun to the street below.

Farther ahead, three of his men were exchanging gunfire with two fighters hiding out between the buildings. How the hell had they missed them?

Their training kicked in and they leap-frogged, providing each other cover as they worked their way to the fighters and knocked them out, one by one.

T-Rex hurried to where Gunny lay in the rubble of the building damaged by the grenade.

The man lay so still, T-Rex's gut knotted. He bent to feel for a pulse. At first, he could feel nothing. He held his breath and shifted his finger. That was when he felt the reassuring vibration of a heartbeat. Quickly scanning the man's arms and legs, he noted the tears in his clothing where shrapnel had penetrated. None of the wounds was bleeding profusely. If Gunny had sustained an arterial wound, T-Rex was prepared to apply a tourniquet. But he hadn't.

Chief Petty Officer Miles Kieslowski ran up to him. "Sir, we got incoming enemy reinforcements. We have to get out of here while we can." He stared down at the man covered in dust. "Damn." He glanced up into T-Rex's gaze. "Is he…"

"Alive. But I don't know the extent of his injuries."

"Let's get him out of here." Kieslowski started to lift Gunny. "Kenner is on the radio, calling in for pickup."

"No. I've got him," T-Rex said. "You cover me." He handed his rifle to Kieslowski. With his hands free, he pulled Gunny to a sitting position and then draped the man's body over his shoulder. Straightening, he felt the strain on his back and legs. But nothing would stop him from bringing his man out. Never, in all of his skirmishes, had he left a man behind. He wouldn't start now.

With his burden, T-Rex hurried toward the designated extraction site. As he emerged from the village into the open, he spotted several trucks in the distance, stirring up dust as they barreled toward them. In the light from the moon, T-Rex could tell the men loaded in the backs of those trucks all carried weapons.

The thundering roar of helicopter rotors sounded nearby as the aircraft rose up over the hill behind the village and landed a couple of hundred yards from where T-Rex had stopped to catch his breath. The other marines from his team knelt behind him, firing at the village, as more enemy fighters came out of hiding.

T-Rex had one goal: to get his men to the waiting chopper and out of there before they were outnumbered.

As he reached the helicopter, he gave over Gunny's care to the medic on board and turned toward his team.

Several of them ran toward him, while the others returned fire, backing up as they did. When they were out of range of rifle fire, they ran toward the aircraft and leaped in.

T-Rex stood beside the vehicle, helping his men board. When the last man was in, T-Rex climbed in, yelling, "Go! Go! Go!"

As he settled into his seat, he noted the trucks had stopped short of the village. Several men climbed out carrying long narrow tubes. "They've got RPGs!" he yelled.

The helicopter couldn't move fast enough for T-Rex. It lifted off the ground with its heavy load of souls on board and swung back toward the hill.

They had just made it to the ridge when an explosion went off so close, it made the chopper shudder.

Instinctively, T-Rex ducked.

They made it over the ridge and dropped out of the line of sight of the truck and the RPG-bearing fighters.

The rest of the trip back to their post seemed like they were moving in slow motion. The medics worked furiously over Gunny and the other men who'd sustained injuries.

"Is he going to make it?" T-Rex leaned over his gunnery sergeant, thoughts on that sonogram photo of the man's fourth child. The boy he'd always dreamed of having. For the first time in a long time, T-Rex closed his eyes and prayed.

Chapter Two

"Time to line up," Sierra Daniels called out to the toddlers on the playground outside the Grizzly Pass Community Center. Some of the little ones headed her way. Others ignored her completely and continued to play with their favorite outside toys or apparatus.

Sierra couldn't be angry with them. They were children with the attention spans of gnats, and so adorable she loved each one of them like she would her own. If she had any kids of her own. She sighed, pushing back against that empty feeling that always washed over her when she thought about how much she'd wanted to hold her own baby in her arms.

With a shrug, she called out again, forcing her voice to sound a little sterner. "Okay, ladies and gentlemen, it's time to line up for a game." Though they were all under six years old, they seemed to have a keen sense of who they could push around and who they couldn't. Sierra was 100 percent a pushover when it came to children.

Once all the boys and girls stood in front of her, Sierra instructed, "Let's play follow the leader. Hands

on the shoulders of the one in front of you, like this."
She placed the hands of one of the little girls on the
shoulders of another. When each child had his or her
hands on the one in front, Sierra led the little girl who
was first in line around the play yard, weaving back and
forth, creating a giggling, laughing snake of toddlers.

The community center had once been a US Army
National Guard Armory. Eventually, the Montana National Guard moved its meeting location to a larger
town and turned the building over to Grizzly Pass. It
was now used as a community center for local events
and the Mother's Day Out day care program. There
were also several offices in the building rented out to
local businesses.

Sierra had been ecstatic to land a job as a caregiver to
the small children who were too young to go to public
school. Jobs were hard to come by in the small community, and she'd needed one when she'd filed for divorce.

She and the other caregiver, Brenda Larson, worked
together to corral the little ones and see that they were
happy, fed and learned something while they were at
the center.

Brenda was inside with the babies and infants. The
two women traded off between the babies and the more
mobile toddlers.

Sierra led the children around the yard one more time
and had angled toward the door to the armory when a
truck pulled up and the driver honked the horn.

Her fists clenched and she tried not to glare at the
man stepping down from the vehicle. The children
picked up on her moods more than she'd ever realized.

If she was sad or angry, tiny Eloisa would pucker up and cry her little eyes out. It broke Sierra's heart to see the tiny girl with the bright red curls shed a single tear, much less a storm of them. She refused to give in to the temptation to yell and throw rocks at the man walking her way.

She pasted a fake smile on her face and waited until he was within twenty feet of her before she said in a patient but firm voice, similar to the one she used with her class, "Please, stop where you are." Her smile hurt her cheeks, but she refused to release it.

Clay Ellis crossed his arms over his chest. "Get your things. You're comin' home."

"I don't live with you, Clay," Sierra said, her voice singsong in an attempt to fool the children into thinking she was fine and that the angry man wasn't scaring her, and therefore they shouldn't be frightened either. She glanced down at the thirteen children gathering closer around her knees.

Eloisa stared from Clay to Sierra, her bottom lip trembling.

Oh, no. Sierra wouldn't let Clay's bad temper impact the little ones. "Come on, everyone. It's time to go inside."

"Like hell it is." Clay stepped forward.

Eloisa screamed and flung her arms around Sierra's legs, burying her face in Sierra's slacks.

She laid her hand on the bright, soft curls and faced her ex-husband. "Clay, I'll have to ask you to leave. You're frightening the children."

He didn't leave. Instead, he walked up to her, grabbed

her arm and pulled. "Quit playing around with these brats and get home. I've put up with enough of your nonsense."

Sierra dug in her heels, refusing to go anywhere with the jerk. She'd put up with enough of his verbal and physical abuse. "We aren't married anymore. You have no right to boss me around, now or ever. Let go of me."

He raised his free hand as if to strike her.

Sierra braced herself, but wouldn't flinch. There had been a time she'd cowered when he'd raised his hand to her. But not anymore. She'd learned the hard way that she had rights, and she didn't have to take abuse from any man.

The children clung to her, their eyes wide, scared. Eloisa sobbed loudly into the smooth linen of Sierra's tan slacks. Once Eloisa started, the other children sensed her distress and joined the squall.

"Shut up!" Clay yelled.

For a moment, all the children stopped crying and then, as if the spigot had been opened full blast, they all screamed and cried like a dozen caterwauling cats in a back-alley fight.

Clay yanked her out of the center of the noise and dragged her toward his truck.

Sierra dug her feet into the dirt and resisted with all of her might. "Let go of me. I'm not going with you."

"The hell you aren't," he said. "You belong to me."

"I belong to no man." She clawed at the meaty hand gripping her wrist like a vise. "I have a restraining order against you."

"No one's going to honor it. Everyone knows you're my wife."

"*Ex*-wife. What part of *divorce* don't you understand?" She couldn't let him get her into his truck. Sierra couldn't go back to this man. He was a bully, a cheater and a monster. "Let go of me, or I'll scream."

"Scream. Only those brats will hear you." He snorted. "You expect them to come to your rescue?"

"I don't need anyone to rescue me." She stopped leaning back against his hold on her and let him pull her close. When she was in range, she stomped hard on his instep and raised her knee hard against his crotch.

Clay bellowed and bent double, clutching the area she'd injured. But he didn't release his grip on her wrist.

Sierra's fingers were growing numb, and the kids behind her were hysterical. She had to do something to stop this madness. But what? Clay was bigger, stronger and meaner than she was. He'd demonstrated that over and over again. She had the scars to prove it.

"Please, Clay, you're scaring the children. Let me get them into the building. When I'm done, I'll go with you."

"Yeah, right." He grunted and straightened. "You expect me to believe you?"

"I will. Cross my heart." She held up her hand as if she were swearing in front of a jury, something she'd had to do in order to convince a judge she'd been abused and needed out.

"No way." He turned and dragged her closer to his truck.

"You can't leave them standing outside. They might get lost in the woods. They're just children."

"Like the kids you wouldn't give me? Why the hell should I care?"

"I wanted children. I tried," she said. "You can't blame our problems on these little ones."

"They aren't mine. I don't give a crap what happens to them."

When he set his mind on something, there was no stopping the man. He'd refused to listen to reason when they were married. What made Sierra think he would listen now?

Using another one of the techniques she'd learned in her recent self-defense class, she twisted her wrist, jerked her arm downward and broke free of Clay's hold. Free at last, she spun and ran. She hadn't gone two feet when a hand clamped on her hair and yanked her backward.

Sierra screamed and stumbled backward. The children screamed, as well. She could see them standing there, terrified and confused. It made her mad enough she could have spit nails, and all the more determined to free herself of the madman she'd once promised to love, honor and cherish.

"Well, it goes both ways. And you didn't live up to your part of the bargain," she muttered, twisted and turned, attempting to get away. But short of letting him rip chunks of her hair out of her head, she was caught.

Chapter Three

A persistent ringing grated on T-Rex's nerves. He didn't like to look away from the road when he was driving, so he waited until he pulled to a stop sign before glancing at his cell phone.

GALLAGER

The name on the screen made his heart tighten. The man had gotten out of that Afghan village alive, barely. He hadn't lost his life, but he'd lost so much more. "Hey, Gunny, how's that baby?"

"Great. I got to hold him today. With a little help."

T-Rex swallowed hard before saying, "That's great, man."

"Did I tell you that I'm getting some of the feeling back in my fingers?"

"No kidding?"

"No kidding." Gunny sounded more upbeat than T-Rex had heard him since he'd returned to the States. The hand squeezing his heart loosened a little. "Glad to hear it."

"I'll be throwing a football for slugger before long."

"Please tell me you didn't put 'Slugger' on his birth certificate."

"No. The wife wouldn't let me. Officially, he's Lance Gallagher. But I drew the line at Junior. Nothing shoots a man's ego down more than being called Junior."

"True."

"So, how's your TDY going?" Gunny asked. "About ready to head back to home station and ship out again?"

"Past ready."

"That boring?"

T-Rex had to think about that. "Not really boring, just not what I want to be doing."

"What? Kidnappings and big-game hunters not exciting enough?"

"How'd you know about that?" T-Rex asked.

Gunny snorted. "I read the news."

"I could do without some of the excitement. I want to get back to the front line."

"You know you won't find the guys who did this to us," Gunny said, his voice softening. "You could hunt every last member of the Taliban and still not know whether you got the guys who staged that trap."

"Maybe, but if I don't try, they get away with what they did to you."

"Oh, is this about me?" Gunny laughed. "The way you blew up in front of the command psychologist, you'd think it was all about you."

T-Rex's hand squeezed the cell phone so hard, he was surprised it didn't crack. What he was feeling was in direct response to what had happened to Gunny. The man had taken the full brunt of the attack. He'd suffered spinal cord damage and might be a quadriplegic the rest of his life. The thought of the father of four spending his life in a wheelchair made T-Rex want to rage at the universe. "It's just not fair. I should have been the one injured. I didn't have a baby on the way."

"You didn't get to pick," Gunny said. "It's the way the cards fell. Or the grenade, in our case."

"Anyway, things might be settling down here. I feel like I'm spinning my wheels."

"Yeah, but I doubt the commander will want you back so soon. He was pretty hot when he sent you off."

"If he knew what a boondoggle it is, he wouldn't have sent me."

"Boondoggle?" Gunny snorted. "Sounds like another day in the life of a marine. You've got enemy hiding in the hills, you've been shot at and you've taken out some of the bad guys."

He had a point. Still, T-Rex would rather be back where his world had come apart. Then maybe he could put it back together. "I don't know which strings our team lead pulled to get a loan of highly skilled military men to work for the Department of Homeland Security." Luckily the team had been there, or there could have been a bunch of kids dead or trapped in a mine. "It's like the Wild West out here in Wyoming."

"Dude, Wyoming *is* the Wild West. Who lives there, anyway?"

"Exactly. Mostly a bunch of cowboys. There's not much more to do out here than ranching or work for the pipeline."

"What's wrong with that? You're in the most beautiful part of the country. Take in some fishing in your time off. If you get to know Wyoming, you might not hate it as much."

"I don't exactly hate it." He didn't. In fact, the area was beautiful. If he wasn't in the military, and maybe when he retired, he might consider living there. The rugged mountains were majestic and appeared serene. "I just want to get back to the real war."

"And some unhealthy fixation on retribution against the Taliban. Do you think you could do more good for the US in a foreign country than here at home?"

"There are other people who defend the home front."

"Clearly there aren't enough people with your skills in Wyoming." Gunny sighed. "Look, I'm not going to change your mind about the need for you to be where you are now. Let's change the subject."

T-Rex relaxed some of the tension from his shoulders. "Good."

"Good," Gunny agreed. "What have they got you doing now?"

T-Rex hadn't realized he'd slowed nearly to a stop on the main road until a honk reminded him he was in a truck and he should be driving to where he was supposed to go. He pressed his foot to the accelerator and the truck leaped forward. "I'm on my way to the County Records office to look up who owns property along an existing gas pipeline."

"Okay, now you're talking boring. I practically fell asleep as you talked about it." Gunny laughed. "Just kidding. Sounds like you're having to do a little sleuthing. That could be interesting."

T-Rex had to admit, after all they'd been through in the few weeks he'd been in Grizzly Pass, the need to resolve the open issues had crawled beneath his skin and stuck with him. "It's all part of figuring out who's behind the problems they've had lately in this little backwater town."

"I thought you caught the guy."

"We caught *some* of the guys we think were involved. But not the one who had enough money to purchase a couple crates full of AR-15 rifles for distribution. Nor have we found those missing rifles."

"You think you have something bigger going on? Wow. You are in up to your eyeballs."

"Maybe. Or maybe we're marking time. If someone is truly out there planning a takeover of a government facility, they might be lying low until the Department of Homeland Security releases us military augmentees. Then they'll do their damage."

T-Rex turned onto the street that would lead him to the Grizzly Pass Community Center and the County Records office. As he pulled into the parking lot, he noted a truck, with a mashed front fender, parked at an odd angle, taking up more than its share of the available parking spaces. But that wasn't all. A man was dragging a woman by the hair toward the truck. By the expression on her face, she wasn't at all happy about it.

"Gunny, I gotta go." Without waiting to hear his friend's response, he dropped the cell phone into the cup holder, slammed the shift into Park and slid out of the truck, his hands balling into fists. Nothing made him madder than witnessing a man abusing a woman.

SIERRA STRAINED HER NECK, trying to get Clay to release his hold on her hair. "Let go of me. I have a job to do. I have children to take care of."

"You have a husband to take care of, and you're not doing it here."

"We. Aren't. Married," she said through gritted teeth. The pain of having her hair pulled so hard brought tears to her eyes.

A loud crack sounded behind Sierra.

Clay grunted and dropped to the ground, taking her with him.

Sierra fell to her backside. Clay's hand loosened its hold on her hair. She rolled to the side, bunched her legs and shot to her feet, putting several feet between her and Clay before she looked back and came to a complete stop.

Clay lay on the ground, his hand clamped over his cheek.

A big man with massive shoulders and an iron jaw loomed over Clay.

"Who the hell do you think you are?" Clay demanded.

The big guy growled. Literally growled. "Your worst nightmare if you lay another finger on that woman."

Sierra watched in wonder. The children gathered around her legs, clinging to her, shaking in their fright.

"I'll do whatever the hell I want," Clay said. "That woman's my wife."

"Ex-wife," Sierra reminded him.

"I don't care if she's your great-aunt Sue." The man poked a finger at Clay. "If you ever lay another hand on her, you'll have to reckon with me. Do. You. Understand?"

"I don't have to take this." Clay rolled to his feet and came up swinging.

The big guy ducked and, in one smooth uppercut, popped Clay in the chin, knocking him to the ground again. This time, Clay lay for a moment, blinking. "I'll kill you for that."

"Big talk for a man who can only seem to push *women* around."

Clay rubbed his bruised chin. "You gonna let me get up?"

"You gonna apologize to the lady?" He tipped his head toward Sierra.

Her ex-husband's lip curled into a snarl. "Ain't got nothin' to apologize for. *She's* the one who walked out on *me*."

The big guy shot a glance at Sierra. "Seems to me she had reason."

"That's a load of bull." Clay started to rise.

Big Guy pushed his foot into Clay's chest. "Not until you apologize."

Clay's cheeks burned a ruddy red and a muscle ticked in his jaw.

Sierra held her breath. She'd never seen Clay apologize for anything.

"I'm sorry," Clay said, his voice tight and angry, not apologetic in the least.

"Say it like you mean it," Big Guy warned, his fist clenching.

The color deepened in Clay's cheeks and his lips formed a thin line. "Fine. I'm sorry," he said, his tone measured, softer this time, but just as tight, the anger simmering between the surface.

Big Guy stepped back.

Clay rolled over, pushed to his hands and knees and staggered to an upright position, glaring at the man. "Who the hell are you anyway? And don't give me that crap about being my worst nightmare. What makes you think you can get in between me and my wife?"

"Ex-wife," Sierra repeated. "The divorce has been final for months. I have the signed copy to prove it."

"Not in my mind." Clay turned toward Sierra, his gaze boring into hers, his hands tightening into fists. "I never would have signed that paper if the judge hadn't threatened to throw me in jail."

Sierra planted her fists on her hips. "Yeah, well, it's done, legal and final. I'm not going back to you. I have a life now. And it doesn't include you."

Clay shot a look at Big Guy. "But it includes him? What? Is he your new boyfriend?"

Sierra lifted her chin. "If he was, it's none of your business."

Clay's eyes narrowed and he studied Big Guy. "So, you ditched me to hop in bed with him?"

"If she did, it has nothing to do with you." Big Guy crossed his arms over his massive chest and stood with his feet braced slightly apart, like a conquering warrior. "What she does is her own business."

Sierra's heart fluttered. By all appearances, Big Guy was a man's man. He didn't need to push a woman around to make himself feel big. He was larger than life and, at that moment, a hero in her eyes.

"Yeah, well, you can't be everywhere she is." Clay faced her. "I'll see you when your boyfriend isn't around."

Sierra's cheeks heated at Clay's reference to the stranger being her boyfriend. She figured now wasn't the time to correct him. Perhaps if Clay thought the guy who'd kicked his butt was her boyfriend, he'd be less likely to target her. "Just leave me alone, Clay."

"You belong to me," her ex said. "No hulking ape takes what's mine."

"Okay, buddy." Big Guy gripped Clay's arm and marched him toward his truck. "I can take a man swinging at me and I can take some verbal abuse, but when you start calling me a hulking ape, I draw the line." He opened the door and shoved Clay into the driver's seat. "Leave my girlfriend alone, or you'll be reckoning with me." Then he slammed the door and stepped clear of the truck.

Sierra held her breath, fully expecting Clay to push the truck into gear and run Big Guy over.

Clay lowered his window and yelled, "It ain't over."

"Oh, yes, it is." Brenda Larson stepped out of the building with a phone in her hands. "The sheriff is on his way."

Clay slammed his truck into Reverse and backed up so fast, his tires spit up gravel. He swung around and left the parking lot and Sierra in stunned silence.

Brenda waved. "Gotta get back to my babies."

"Go. I'll get the kids inside." Sierra waved toward her friend. Brenda ducked back inside, leaving Sierra with Big Guy and the thirteen crying children, clutching her legs.

"Are you all right?" her hero asked, turning his full attention to her. He had reddish-brown hair, cut high and tight like a military man, and his eyes could have been brown or green depending on the way he turned his head toward the sunshine.

Sierra gulped and tried to remember his question. "Uh, yes. I'm okay." She rubbed her arm absently.

"Did he hurt you? You know, you can file a report." The man closed the distance between them and took her hand, his face darkening. "He did hurt you."

Sierra stared down at the bruises forming on her arm. She pulled against his grip. "I'm fine. Right now, I need to get these children calm and inside."

Eloisa sobbed against her leg, clutching Sierra so tightly, she couldn't move without knocking the little girl over.

Several of the children who couldn't get close enough to Sierra turned to Big Guy and wrapped their arms around his legs, crying.

Sierra laughed and gulped back a ready sob. "I'm sorry. But it seems we are trapped by a handful of toddlers." She held out her hand, forcing herself to sound normal and upbeat, putting a game face on for the children. "I'm Sierra Daniels. And you are?"

"Apparently, I'm your boyfriend." His lips curled into a sexy smile that nearly bowled her over. "Rex Trainor. My friends call me T-Rex."

Sierra raised her brows. "As in the dinosaur?"

He nodded. "That's right." He engulfed her hand with his big one.

Warmth flowed all the way up her arm and into her

chest. "Thank you for coming to my rescue... T-Rex." She glanced down at the toddlers. "Okay, gang, the show's over and everybody's okay. Let's go play in the gym."

"I want my mommy," Eloisa wailed. Sierra lifted her small body and settled the redhead on her hip.

Several other children joined in the chorus.

"Who wants a ride into the gym?" T-Rex reached down and lifted a little boy named Nathan and settled him on his shoulders.

At first the little boy's lip trembled, and then he gripped T-Rex's hair, grinned and giggled.

"Who else?" T-Rex asked. With Nathan clinging to his hair, Sierra's hero scooped up a little girl and a boy in his arms. "Follow me!" he called out in the best impression of a drill sergeant's tone Sierra had heard in a long time.

Without hesitation, the rest of the toddlers lined up behind T-Rex and marched with him into the community center.

Sierra hugged Eloisa against her chest and followed. This must have been what it felt like to follow the Pied Piper. She didn't know this man, but she trusted him with her life and those of the toddlers in her care.

And if he had hazel eyes that she could fall into and dark, reddish-brown hair she'd like to run her fingers through, that shouldn't matter in the least. He'd come to her rescue. That made him a hero in her eyes and the eyes of the children.

Her heart beat faster and butterflies fluttered their wings inside her belly. Her day was looking up. And all because of a stranger who'd arrived in time to save the day. Talk about heroes.

Chapter Four

T-Rex entered through a side door that led into an open gymnasium with brick walls and basketball goals on either end.

A woman stood in one of the open doorways off the side of the gym, a baby in her arms. "Oh!" She blinked several times. "I was expecting Sierra. Who are you?"

His lips twisted into an ironic grin. "Apparently, I'm Sierra's boyfriend."

"He's kidding." The woman he'd rescued from her ex-husband entered behind him, carrying a tiny red-haired girl. Sierra's cheeks were rosy and her blue eyes bright. "Clay assumed he was my boyfriend." She shrugged. "I didn't disavow him of that assumption."

"Like I said. I'm her new boyfriend."

Sierra's friend stared at him, her eyes narrowing. "Wait. You're one of the new guys in town working with Kevin Garner, aren't you?"

T-Rex nodded and set down the children in his arms and then swung the little boy off his shoulders to his screaming delight.

As soon as he set him on the ground, the boy reached up. "Do it again! Do it again! Please?"

T-Rex lifted the boy high into the air and swung him back to the ground.

The other toddlers all raised their hands, shouting, "My turn!" at the top of their lungs.

"Okay, children," Sierra called out over the commotion. "Mr. Trainor isn't here to entertain all of you. Let him go about his business. Go on and play." She set the red-haired girl on her feet and shooed her and the others toward the tumbling mats scattered across a corner of the gym. Once the children had moved away, Sierra held out her hand. "Thank you so much for coming to my rescue."

He gripped her small hand in his, and a shock of electricity raced up his arm. His gaze connected with hers. Had she felt it? Her eyes widened for a second, but other than that little bit of motion, she didn't indicate recognition.

Her lips curled upward in a smile. "Are you done with my hand?"

T-Rex immediately released her and jammed his hand into his pocket. "My pleasure."

"Seriously, Sierra," the woman with the baby on her hip said. "You haven't met the men from the team of military guys who helped save us when the bus was hijacked?"

She shook her head. "Actually, I haven't. You remember. When that happened, I was out with the flu."

"You're the one they called T-Rex, right?" The woman walked forward. "You might not remember me, but I'm Brenda Larson. We met in front of the Lucky Lou Mine a few days ago, after the showdown with the Vanders boys."

T-Rex shook her hand. "I'm sorry. I don't remember."

"I can understand. There was a lot going on." Brenda's lips thinned and she glanced at Sierra. "Be glad you were sick that day. I still have nightmares."

Sierra shuddered. "I'm so sorry for Mrs. Green. Her husband was such a nice man."

"Mr. Green, the bus driver?" T-Rex asked.

Sierra and Brenda nodded.

"It was a shame. He didn't do anything to deserve being shot," T-Rex said.

"Well, don't let us keep you, Mr. Trainor," Sierra said. "Thanks again." She stepped back, out of his way.

A baby's cry had Brenda moving toward the door she'd come out of. "That's my cue. Nice to see you again, T-Rex."

T-Rex shook his head and glanced around. "I understand the County Records office is somewhere in this building."

Sierra nodded. "You have to go back out to the front of the armory to get to their offices."

"This was an armory?"

"It used to house a small unit of the Montana Army National Guard. When they moved out, they donated the building to the town. Now it's the Grizzly Pass Community Center."

He swept the gym with another assessing glance. Now that she'd mentioned it, he could imagine a military unit holding formations in the gym when the weather outside was too cold, wet or snowy. A twinge of regret filled his belly. While he was pretty much playing the civilian Stateside, members of his unit were putting their lives on the line in some godforsaken country on the other side of the world. His fists clenched. "Nice that the building could be useful." As much as he'd like to talk to the pretty woman with the long, wavy blond hair, he had work to do. The sooner they figured out who was at the bottom of all the troubles in Grizzly Pass, the sooner he could be back with his unit.

Besides, it would do him no good to get close to a female. His career was with the US Marine Corps. And he'd seen the devastation a career in the military could wreak on a family. He couldn't do that to a woman, any more than he could do what Sierra's ex-husband had done to her. No, he was single for a reason. Career military men had no business dragging families along with them.

"I'll be going. If your ex gives you any more trouble, you can call me. I'll be happy to step in as the protective boyfriend for as long as I'm here." As long as that was as far as it went. He didn't say it, but he thought it, specifically to remind him he wasn't in Grizzly Pass to start anything. He was there to finish it.

He spun and walked out of the building and around to the front, where an entrance led into a hallway with what had once been the offices of the officers and enlisted men who'd run the unit. Now the doors were marked with the names of businesses. He found the one marked County Records and entered.

With the help of the clerk, he found the surveys and

plats of the properties bordering the oil pipeline running through the hills on the south side of Yellowstone National Park.

He snapped photos with his cell phone, and on a notepad he jotted down the names of the people or corporations who owned the land. When he was finished, he tucked his notepad into his pocket. "Thank you," he called out as he left the office. He'd been there for over an hour. He knew he should go straight to his truck and leave, but he couldn't without first checking on Sierra. Back around the side of the armory, he found the entrance to the gym and day care.

Sierra stood with the little red-haired girl and a woman with equally red hair who had to be the child's mother.

"She took a nap after the commotion, but she might continue to be distressed," Sierra was saying. "I'm so sorry it happened in front of the children."

The mother held her daughter close in her arms. "I'm just glad you're okay. Don't you worry about us. Take care of yourself." The woman turned and stopped, her eyes wide. "Oh. I didn't hear you come in." Her eyes narrowed and she shot a glance back at Sierra. "Do you know him? I can stay if you need me to."

Sierra smiled. "I know him. He's the one who chased Clay away. The kids love him."

As if on cue, the little red-haired toddler reached her arms up to T-Rex. "My turn."

Her mother frowned.

"It's okay." Sierra nodded. "T-Rex had them all wanting a turn."

Eloisa leaned farther out.

T-Rex grabbed her before she fell from her mother's arms. "Do you mind?"

"I guess not." Eloisa's mother gave him a confused smile. "She doesn't usually go to strangers."

T-Rex swung her up into the air and back to the ground, then up again.

Eloisa giggled and laughed. When he handed her back to her mother, she clapped her hands and held them out. "Again."

"Sorry, sweetie." Her mother straightened the child on her hip and hiked her diaper bag up onto her shoulder. "We have to get home and cook supper." She smiled, waved and exited, leaving Sierra alone in the gym with T-Rex.

"Are all of the others gone?" he asked.

"Everyone but me." She retrieved her purse from a chair and slipped it over her shoulder. "I get to lock up tonight."

"I'll wait."

"You don't have to."

"I know." He waved a hand, indicating she should lead the way.

"Really. I can do this on my own."

He touched her arm. "Look, you're giving chivalry a bad name. After what happened today, I would feel better knowing you made it home safely."

Her baby blue eyes sparkled, and her cheeks turned a pretty shade of pink. She pushed her long blond hair back over her shoulders. "Okay, then." She led the way to the door.

T-Rex's gut twisted and his groin tightened as she sailed past him, her slim hips swaying ever so slightly in her tan slacks.

He liked what he saw. Normally he would go after her and ask her out on a date. But his usual MO was to date and ditch. Based on what he'd witnessed of how her ex-husband had treated her, he couldn't do that to Sierra. She needed a man who treated her like a princess, with all the love and caring she deserved. This woman was strictly off-limits.

She led him out of the building, closed the door and locked it behind them.

"So, you're here with the others who've been loaned to the Department of Homeland Security?" she asked as they walked side by side to their vehicles.

"I am." He paused beside her older-model sedan and waited for her to pop the locks. When she had, he opened the door for her.

She glanced up at him. "Thank you for all you did today."

"You're welcome." She stood so close he could smell the subtle scent of her perfume. If he leaned forward just a little, he could capture her mouth with his. His pulse quickened and his gaze slipped from her shining blue eyes to those soft, full kissable lips.

"I…I'd better go. It's getting dark." She slipped into the car, closed the door and started the engine.

T-Rex stepped back, telling himself he was a fool to even think about kissing the woman. She was on the rebound from a bad marriage. He'd be doing her a favor to stay out of her life.

Sierra lowered the window. "If ever I can do anything for you, don't hesitate to ask. I owe you big-time."

He nodded, tempted to collect on her debt by requesting a kiss. Instead, he shook his head. "No repayment required. Just being a good citizen. I'll follow you to make sure you get home okay."

"This is a small town. It's not necessary." She smiled and backed out of the parking lot.

T-Rex waited until she disappeared down the winding drive heading away from the community center. Then he climbed into his truck and drove to his temporary quarters at a bed-and-breakfast off Main Street.

As he pulled into the parking lot, he noticed that one of the other vehicles parked at the very end looked familiar. He parked and got out. Could it be? He entered the big, rambling colonial home the owner had converted into a six-room bed-and-breakfast. Standing in the large living area was Sierra, talking to the owner, Mrs. McCall, two suitcases on the floor beside her.

She looked up as he entered, and her brow furrowed. "You didn't have to follow me."

"Mr. Trainor, I'm glad I caught you. I hope you don't mind, but I had the handyman here today. He worked on the balcony door to keep it from sticking."

"Thank you, Mrs. McCall," he said, his gaze on Sierra, not the owner of the bed-and-breakfast.

"Oh, have you met Miss Daniels?" Mrs. McCall asked.

T-Rex nodded. "I have had the pleasure."

"She'll be staying with us while her apartment is being renovated."

He nodded. "That's nice. You'll love Mrs. McCall. She makes the best scones this side of the pond."

Mrs. McCall blushed. "Oh, you're too kind. Thank you."

"No need to tell me about her scones." Sierra smiled and patted Mrs. McCall's arm. "I've been eating Mrs. McCall's scones since I was a little girl visiting her with my mother. And you're right. They're wonderful."

"Thank you, sweetie." Mrs. McCall smiled and pushed back her shoulders. "Now, if you'll excuse me, my program is coming on television and I don't want to miss it." She winked. "An old woman needs something to look forward to." She scurried away, entering a door marked Private.

"Let me help you." T-Rex grabbed the handles of the suitcases.

"I can do that," Sierra said, reaching for the cases.

"I know you can. But we've already had this discussion about chivalry. It isn't dead. At least not where I'm concerned. My mother taught me better." He headed for the stairs. "What room?"

She gave him the number, and his brows rose. It was the room next to his. He wanted to groan, but he didn't say anything. She'd find out soon enough.

For a man who didn't want to start something with the pretty day care employee, the odds were stacking against him.

"I didn't know you were staying here," she said as she followed him up the stairs.

"In a town as small as Grizzly Pass, the lack of hotels forced us to scatter out among the few privately owned establishments." He stopped in front of the door to her room and stepped back to allow her to use her key in the lock.

She entered and held the door for him to carry her luggage through.

T-Rex set the two cases on the wooden floor and turned. "Welcome to the McCall house."

Sierra giggled. "You don't look like a bellboy, but I appreciate the help." She reached her hand into her purse and dug around. "What do you require in the way of a tip?"

He laid his hand on her arm. "No money. Just this." Before he could stop to question his motives, he lifted her chin with the tip of his finger and claimed that kiss he'd been thinking about since she'd left him at the community center. One quick, toe-curling kiss. That was all he wanted and he'd be out of her way.

But it didn't happen like he planned. As soon as his lips touched hers, fire exploded in his belly and his blood ran like heated mercury through his veins, angling downward to his groin.

He raised his other hand, cupped the back of her head and deepened the connection.

She laid her hands on his chest, but she didn't push him away.

And he was glad she didn't. Because, now that he was kissing her, he didn't want it to end.

SIERRA HAD BEEN shocked and tinglingly aware of the man when he'd stepped through the front door of the bed-and-breakfast. She'd completely forgotten what she'd been saying to Mrs. McCall. All she'd been able to do was stand there and stare at the broad-shouldered hero with the reddish-brown hair and hazel eyes, and just barely been able to stop herself from drooling. He was the kind of man every girl dreamed of. Tall, dark, handsome and willing to fight for her honor.

Now he stood in her room, kissing her. Her knees trembled and she curled her fingers into his shirt, pulling him closer. She raised up on her toes, deepening the kiss of all kisses. Clay had never kissed her like this. Like she was special and the only person in the world. She pressed her body into T-Rex, loving the hardness of his muscles against her soft curves. He was a man a woman could lean on in tough times. He didn't need to have his ego stroked to make him feel more of a man.

His tongue darted out, tracing the line of her lips. She couldn't resist him, opening her mouth to allow him in. Part of her felt a little guilty. She had to remind herself she was single now. She could kiss anyone she liked. And she liked kissing this one.

He caressed her tongue with his, gliding in and out, taking her along on a rising wave of passion. The only thing that could have been better about that kiss was if they were both naked. Skin to skin.

Heat built low in her belly. An intense ache made her sex clench and her body long for more. She felt more alive than she had in years, and it was all due to this stranger, who asked for a kiss for his tip.

All too soon, T-Rex lifted his head.

Sierra dropped back onto her heels and glanced down at where her hands crumpled his shirt. She licked her swollen lips, tasting him on them. "Well, that was quite the tip," she managed to say, appalled at how squeaky her voice sounded.

"I'd apologize," he said, his tone low and husky. "But I can't. That was incredible."

She nodded and dared to look up into his eyes. Then reality set in. Having divorced only six months before, she wasn't sure she was ready to get right back into a relationship. If anything, her seven years of marriage to Clay had convinced her that she wasn't very good at long-term commitment, or was she just terrible at choosing the right man for her? Either way, it was too soon.

Sierra backed away. "I have to ask you not to do that again."

He nodded. "Agreed. It wouldn't be a good idea for you to get involved with me. I won't be around for long, and, despite our little charade, I'm not very good boyfriend material."

Sierra hadn't expected him to agree with her so quickly. Disappointment filled her chest. Pushing back her shoulders, she lifted her chin. Why should she care? He'd only confirmed her desire to avoid anything sticky growing between them. Still…

He turned and walked toward the door.

Before he crossed the threshold, she asked, "Why?"

He stopped and half turned toward her. "Why what?"

"Why do you make bad boyfriend material?" She shouldn't be interested in his answer, but she was and she waited for his response.

He shook his head, a hint of a smile tilting his lips.

"Trust me. I'm no good for you, or any other woman." With that, he walked out of the room and shut the door.

All of the starch leached out of Sierra's shoulders and she sagged, raising her fingers to her mouth. Holy hell, the man could kiss. Her brows dipped and her eyes narrowed. And what kind of nonanswer was that? *I'm no good for you, or any other woman.*

Her curiosity aroused and left unsatisfied, she yanked one of the suitcases up onto the bed and began the task of unpacking. Within minutes, she had both cases emptied and her meager belongings stored in the dresser and closet. Six months ago, she'd left most of what she owned with Clay, taking only what she could carry in the cases. The apartment she'd been living in had come fully furnished. Unfortunately, the roof had sprung a leak in the last rain. Not only had they had to repair the roof, they'd had to rip out the drywall and flooring due to water damage and mold. She wouldn't be allowed back into the apartment until they'd completed all of the repairs and mold remediation. Thus, the move to the bed-and-breakfast.

The night was still young, the sun having barely dipped below the hilltops. She could lie there and reminisce or go find something to eat.

Grabbing her coat and purse, she headed for the door, slung it open and nearly crashed into T-Rex. "Oh, sorry."

He steadied her with his big hands and then dropped them to his sides. "Are you all right?"

"I'm fine." She stepped back and willed her heart to slow.

"I was coming to see you."

"You were?" Her pulse leaped again.

T-Rex dug in his pocket and pulled out a device that fit in the palm of his hand. "I want you to have this." He reached for her hand and placed it on her palm.

"What is it?" she stared down at the gadget, her heart banging against her ribs at the touch of his hand beneath hers.

"A stun gun."

Okay, so it wasn't a diamond bracelet, but seriously, what man gave a woman a stun gun as a gift? "How does it work?"

He turned it over and pointed to the button on the side. "You switch it on here. When someone gets close enough to you, you push this button and stick it to him."

"And then what?"

"He will lose muscle control and balance and become disoriented. It will disable him for up to thirty minutes."

"Wow." She held it out. "Sounds dangerous."

"The effects aren't permanent. It gives you a chance to get away. Carry it in your hand when you're alone, like when you're locking up at the day care and walking out to your car. If your ex ever pulls a stunt like he did today you can be ready to take him down long enough to get away. One jolt from this baby and he'll think twice about harassing you."

She stared at the device and then glanced up at him. "That's about the nicest gift anyone has ever given me."

He laughed out loud. "Better than roses?"

"Much." She slid it into her purse, careful not to switch it on in the process. "I'm not sure I have the nerve to use it, but it will make me feel better knowing I have it in case I need it."

"Were you heading out?" he asked.

"I was just going to find something to eat. Normally, I fix a salad and eat at home." She grimaced. "But that won't be an option while I live in the bed-and-breakfast. I miss my apartment already."

"I was about to go to the Blue Moose Tavern. Care to join me?"

She smiled and shook her head. "So much for avoiding each other. I think it will be nearly impossible in such a small house."

"No need to. I promise—" he held up his hand as if swearing in court "—not to overstep your boundaries without your permission."

"In that case, I would love the company. I hate eating alone." She led the way down the stairs and out of the building.

Once outside, he glanced around as if looking for something or someone. "I don't see your ex anywhere, but we should probably keep up appearances." T-Rex held out his hand. "Girlfriend?"

She hesitated, staring at his big, open hand. Knowing it would only be for appearances, it shouldn't be a big deal. But as soon as she placed her hand in his, the electricity of his touch zipped through her body, pooling low in her groin. Yeah, being this close to T-Rex could only lead to trouble.

At that moment, she didn't care.

Together, they walked the three blocks to the Blue Moose Tavern and asked the waitress for a table.

Once seated across from T-Rex, her hand in her own lap and no longer touching the man, Sierra's thoughts settled from the scramble they'd been since she'd kissed him. He was just a man. The first man she'd kissed since her divorce. Surely there would be more, and she wouldn't make such a complete fool of herself over the next.

The waitress brought them their drinks—a glass of red wine for Sierra and a draft beer for T-Rex.

Sierra lifted her glass. "To new friends."

He touched his mug to her glass. "To new friends."

They sipped and stared over the tops of their respective drinks.

Sierra had to focus on staring into his eyes and not letting her gaze fall to his sensuous mouth. For a long moment, she struggled to come up with something to say that wasn't *kiss me*. Finally, she knocked back the rest of her wine and set her glass on the table. "Tell me about yourself."

Chapter Five

T-Rex felt his muscles tighten. He'd never been this uncomfortable sitting across a table from a beautiful woman. When she stared at him and demanded he tell her about himself, his pulse kicked up a notch. He swallowed the last of his beer and set down his mug. What did she really want to know?

Did she want to hear that he'd watched his best gunnery sergeant nearly get blown apart? That he wished he could have taken Gunny's place in that explosion? That he loved women but avoided relationships because of the profession he'd chosen to dedicate his life to? He didn't want to talk about himself, so he stalled. "Like what?"

"Not going to make this easy, are you?" Sierra nodded, squared her shoulders and launched. "You can start by telling me which branch of the service you're in."

"Marine Corps." That wasn't so hard. He relaxed a little.

"How long?" she demanded.

"Ten years."

"That's quite a commitment." She drew in a breath and let it out. "Have you been deployed to a war zone?"

Tension shot up again. He nodded, his glance dropping to his empty mug. "Four times."

Sierra's brows drew together, and she reached across the table, laying her hand on his arm. "Thank you for your service."

The heat of her touch sent his blood burning through his veins. He didn't feel like he had done anything to be thanked for. While he was walking around on two perfectly good legs, Gunny couldn't even hold his newborn son in his arms, or hug his girls.

T-Rex shook off her touch and moved his hands to his lap. "My turn."

She nodded. "Shoot."

"How long were you married to your charming husband?"

"Seven years."

"Was he as abusive the entire time you two were married?"

Sierra glanced to the far corner of the room, her brows wrinkled. "He's always been demanding. I thought he'd mellow as we grew older together, but he didn't. Then he lost his job as a truck driver due to an accident a couple years ago. He was home all the time and I went to work. That's when he got mean."

"Children?"

She shook her head, her shoulders sinking a degree. "No. No children."

"By choice, or luck of the draw?"

"It just didn't happen. If I could, I'd have a dozen children."

"Do you come from a big family?"

She shook her head. "No. My parents died when I was six. I was raised in the foster care system."

"I'm sorry."

"Don't be." She smiled. "My foster parents were very good to me."

"Were?"

She sighed. "They passed away within months of each other five years ago. I miss them."

"No siblings?" he asked.

She shook her head. "You?"

T-Rex nodded. "I have a sister in Texas. She's married with three little boys."

Sierra looked at him with a smile. "They must love their Uncle T-Rex."

"I doubt it." He shrugged. "I don't see them often enough." Hell, he hadn't seen them since they were all in diapers. He made a mental note to visit his sister.

"Parents?"

"Retired and traveling around the country in a motor home." He shook his head. "They sold the home and ranch we grew up on and bought a motor coach. They never spend more than four months in any one place. Their goal is to explore every national park in the United States before they die. And a few dozen state parks."

Sierra leaned her elbows on the table and rested her chin in her palm. "Wow, sounds like a wonderful way to spend your retirement." A long strand of her blond hair fell forward over her cheek.

Without thinking, T-Rex reached across the table and tucked it behind her ear. He brushed his knuckles across her cheek, that same electric current sending shock waves through his system. He snatched back his hand. "Why do you stay here?"

She shrugged. "I love this town and most of the people in it. Minus one ex-husband. It's a great place to live and raise a family."

"But you aren't married and, from what you've just told me, you don't have family here."

She shrugged. "I'd love to travel, but I never considered doing it alone." Her lips twisted. "I'd want to share my adventures with someone else. I couldn't see myself standing at the edge of the Grand Canyon and having no one to share my appreciation for what I'd be seeing." Sierra laughed. "Sounds dumb, but that's how I feel. Besides, I was married from the time I left college until just a few months ago. We didn't have the money to travel. We barely had enough to pay the rent. So, there you have it. That's my pathetic life in a nutshell. The best part about it is working with the children. I love those kids."

"And they all love you."

"The little traitors were quick to switch their loyalties when you came through the door." She winked at him. "Why don't you have children?" Her eyes widened suddenly. "Wow, I don't even know if you're married." She pressed her hand to her lips.

He shook his head. "I'm not, and I don't have any children." Leaning toward her, he said in a low voice for only her ears, "Besides, I wouldn't have kissed you if I had a wife. Call me old-fashioned, but I believe you only kiss the one you're committed to."

Sierra sank back against her seat. "Whew. You never

know. I've been out of the dating scene for a long time. Heck, I don't think I've ever been in it. I married my high school sweetheart two years into college."

"What did you major in?" he asked.

"I would have majored in elementary education, but I didn't get to finish." She rubbed the third finger on her left hand.

"Why?"

"Clay thought college was a waste of time. He dropped out and got a job as a truck driver and we got married. When it came time for fall semester to start, he wouldn't let me go back. He said it cost too much, and what did I need a college education for anyway? He made enough money driving a truck to support us."

"And he lost his license."

She nodded. "Over a year ago."

"Seven years and no children. That from a woman who loves kids." He raised his brows.

"I wanted them." She shrugged and looked away. "They never seemed to happen. Can we talk about something else?"

"Sorry. I didn't mean to pry."

"It's okay. It was a sore subject in our marriage, and it still hurts."

"Then let's talk about what to order." He popped open a menu and perused the items he had yet to try. Soon, the waitress delivered a bison burger for him and a Southwestern chicken salad for Sierra. They spent the rest of the meal talking about the upcoming football season and who they thought would play in the bowl games.

When he'd finished the burger and fries, he ordered

another beer and sat back. "I'm surprised you know your college football teams."

She sipped from her wineglass and raised her brows. "Why? Because I'm a girl?"

"No," he hedged. "Because you're a woman. I thought most women disliked sports."

"That's a sexist remark."

"Guilty."

"My foster mother and father were huge football fans. We spent many weekends watching the games and yelling until our throats were raw." She smiled, her face softening. "I miss that."

"Was your ex a fan?"

She shook her head. "He liked hockey. Don't get me wrong. I love watching a good hockey game, too. But I missed watching football."

"He wouldn't let you watch football?"

"No."

"Jerk," T-Rex muttered just loud enough for her to hear.

Sierra laughed. "My thoughts exactly." For a long moment, her smile lingered. Then it disappeared altogether.

T-Rex found himself wanting to make her smile again.

"Speak of the devil." Sierra nodded toward the entrance and ducked her head.

T-Rex glanced in the direction indicated.

Clay Ellis strutted into the tavern, cocky as hell, sneering at anyone who dared to give a friendly greeting.

"Don't worry. He can't hurt you here," T-Rex said, clenching his fists beneath the table.

"I know. But he can make a fuss." She set down her wineglass. "We can leave now, if you want."

"I'd rather you finished your wine and I finished my beer and neither one of us lets him get to us."

She laughed, though it sounded less than convincing. "You're right." She lifted her glass and sipped. "I shouldn't let him get to me. I'm done with him." As she spoke, she lifted her glass. Her hand shook so much, the wine spilled onto her chest. "Darn. This was my favorite sweater." She dabbed at the stain with her napkin. When that didn't help, she looked up. "I'd better go to the ladies' room and see if I can get this out before it sets."

T-Rex watched as she left their table. His gaze switched from her to where Ellis leaned against the bar, flirting with one of the waitresses trying to fill a drink order.

As far as T-Rex could tell, Ellis hadn't seen Sierra.

"T-Rex, glad we found you." Caveman slipped into the chair Sierra had vacated a minute before. "We've been looking for you."

Kevin Garner, Ghost, Caveman and Hawkeye pulled up chairs around the little table.

"Uh, guys, I'm here with someone."

"Yeah?" Hawkeye, the army ranger of the group of military men, glanced around. "I don't see anyone else."

As one, all four men craned their necks, searching the room.

"Who is she?" Ghost asked. The Navy SEAL smiled, refusing to let T-Rex off the hook.

"Who said it was a she?" T-Rex drummed his fingers on the table, willing the men to leave before Sierra returned.

Caveman laughed. "You, by the way you're avoiding the question." The Delta-Force soldier crossed his arms. These men weren't going to give up until they got an answer.

"It doesn't matter." The only way T-Rex would get rid of them was to find out what they wanted. "What's up?"

"Charlie found the social media site the Free America group moved to," Ghost said. Charlie McClain was an old flame of Ghost's who moonlighted as a cybersnoop for the Department of Homeland Security.

"And?" T-Rex prompted to move the conversation along.

Ghost leaned closer, lowering his voice so that others couldn't hear. "There's been more noise about a potential takeover in the very near future."

"Any dates given?" T-Rex asked.

"No, just a general call to arms to stand ready."

"Great. And we're no closer to figuring out who's involved with the Free America group?"

"Our computer gurus, Hack and Charlie, said that anyone could have set up that group from a public library," Garner said. "The members of the group are using aliases, probably set up on public Wi-Fi systems."

T-Rex's fingers clenched into fists. "How much time do you think we have until they make their move?"

"We've known something was coming for the past couple weeks we've been here," Caveman said.

Garner, the team's leader, shrugged. "It could be a couple more weeks from now, or it could be any day. What did you find at the county records office?"

T-Rex pulled his wallet from his pocket and removed the notepad he'd used to record his notes. Then he brought up the photos of the maps on his cell phone. "Not much more than we already know. Olivia Dawson—" he glanced toward Hawkeye, who'd established a relationship with the woman "—owns this portion of land bordering the current pipeline easement." He pointed to the middle of the map on his phone. "On the north side of the easement is the national park all the way through the mountainous area. East of the Dawson spread, the land was recently sold to Pinnacle Enterprises."

"West of Dawson's ranch is owned by BRE Inc."

"Any idea who BRE Inc. is?" Caveman asked.

Garner's lips thinned. "Bryson Rausch Enterprises."

"The big shot in town?" Ghost asked.

Hawkeye's brows descended. "Liv says Rausch owns half the town. He offered to buy her ranch before her father's casket settled in his grave."

"I can't imagine the man risking a connection to the Free America group," Ghost said. "Why would he? He has plenty of money."

"I can't help but think what's happening with the pipeline is somehow connected with Free America." Garner stared into the distance.

"Wayne Batson admitted he was paid to kill the pipeline inspector," Caveman said.

"But he didn't share the name of the guy who funded him," Ghost reminded them.

"Hack hasn't found the money Batson claims he was paid."

"Unless he was paid in kind." T-Rex's eyes narrowed. "Do you suppose he was paid in weapons?"

"The weapons we can't find?" Caveman asked.

"Yes, those." T-Rex drummed his fingers on the table. "The ones that arrived in the boxes discovered in the Lucky Lou Mine."

Garner nodded, his own eyes narrowing. "Could be."

"We know Batson had a tactical training facility on his property and that he was training individuals there," T-Rex reminded them.

Leaning forward, Garner's eyes narrowed. "We can only assume they were members of the Free America group and Batson was one of them. But we have no evidence, and Batson didn't keep written or video records of those who came for the training."

"We all surveyed the site," Ghost said. "Watson had mock-ups of several buildings in a group, but we still don't know if they were generic buildings or in the configuration of the planned takeover target."

"We don't have much more than we had when we started." T-Rex slid the notepad over to Garner.

"I'll have Hack check into Pinnacle and continue digging into Rausch's business. He's in the process of reviewing Batson's computer. We hope to glean something from his contacts list."

T-Rex nodded. "What's the plan for tomorrow?"

"We could use some help in the office going through

any names Hack comes up with on the contacts list," Garner said.

Ghost raised a hand. "Charlie and I can help."

"I need someone to go interview a man called Leo Fratiani." Garner glanced at T-Rex.

"The other man who offered to purchase Liv's ranch?" T-Rex asked.

"Yes. We need to know his angle," Garner said. "Hack ran a background check on him. He didn't show up on any criminal, military or government databases, but he wants the Dawson place. That makes him a potential for funding Batson's murder of the pipeline inspector."

"Got anything on a Clay Ellis?" T-Rex asked. His attention spun to the bar where Sierra's ex-husband had been standing. He wasn't there. T-Rex sat up straighter, scanning the interior of the tavern.

"I don't have anything on Clay Ellis. Is he a person of interest?" Garner asked.

T-Rex pushed back from the table and stood so fast, his chair fell over backward. "Sorry. I have to go check on someone." He set the chair up straight and hurried toward the restrooms at the back of the tavern.

SIERRA HAD HURRIED to the ladies' room, angry with herself for spilling the wine on her favorite white sweater. She barely made enough money to pay rent, and she hadn't brought all of her clothes from the home she'd shared with Clay. Shortly after she'd left him, he'd told her he'd torched her things in the burning barrel. What she'd packed into the two suitcases was all she had left, all she owned.

Once in the ladies' restroom, she stripped out of her sweater, stuck the wine-stained portion under the faucet and rubbed to get the stain out. Perhaps the spilled wine had been a chance for her to get her act together. Her hands were still shaking uncontrollably. She rubbed the stain harder. She shouldn't let Clay get to her. They were divorced, and she had a restraining order. All she had to do was call the sheriff and tell him Clay was causing trouble.

The only problem with that scenario was that calling the sheriff had never really helped her situation. Any time she'd fought back against Clay's abuse, it had only made things worse. When she was still married to the man, she had gotten to the point she'd kept her mouth shut and faded into the woodwork.

Well, she'd be darned if she did it anymore. Leaving him had taken all of her willpower at the time. Since she'd been out of his house and on her own, she'd found her own self-worth. She refused to go back to being that coward she'd been for far too long.

She had her back to the door when it swung open.

Embarrassed at being caught standing in her bra, she clutched her sweater to her chest and spun toward the door, an apology on her lips.

Her words froze and her heart ground to a stop. "Clay, what are you doing in here?"

Her ex-husband stood in the doorway, his lip pulled back in a snarl, his dirty blond hair in need of a cut and a good shampoo. His gray eyes narrowed. "Coming to get what belongs to me."

Sierra jammed her arms into the sleeves of the sweater and dragged it over her head. "I don't belong to you, Clay," she said, her tone one of a parent explaining a simple concept to a particularly dense child. Once she had her sweater on, she slung her purse over her shoulder and dug her hand inside.

"You don't have your boyfriend in here to get in the way." He let the door close behind him and stalked her like a snake slithering up to its prey. "What are you going to do?"

"I'll scream."

He shook his head. "Won't do you any good. The band is playing now. No one will hear you." He reached out a hand toward her. "Come with me now and I won't be angry."

Her fingers curled around the hard plastic device T-Rex had armed her with. "I'm not going with you now or ever." She stood straighter, ready to take him on.

"Woman, you're coming with me, one way or another." He grabbed her arm and spun her around, slammed her back into his chest and clamped his arm around her middle.

Holding tightly to the stun gun, Sierra let her purse fall to the floor. "Let go of me, Clay."

"Or what?" He leaned close and whispered into her ear. "You'll yell for your boyfriend?"

"I don't need my boyfriend to fight my battles," she said through gritted teeth as she flicked the on switch.

"That's right. Come along quietly and no one gets hurt."

"No way." And someone was about to get hurt.

"Baby, you belong to me." He edged her toward the door.

Sierra dug in her heels. "I'm not going with you. This is your last warning."

He laughed. "Or what? You can't fight me. You're not strong enough."

"I don't have to be that kind of strong. I just have to be smarter than you. And that's not all that hard." She angled her arm backward and jabbed the stun gun into Clay's thigh.

He screamed like a little girl, shook violently and fell to the floor.

At one time in her life, she might have felt sorry for the man lying on the ground, completely incapacitated. But not anymore.

Sierra waved the stun gun at him. "Don't ever touch me again. Do you hear me?"

He lay there, his eyes wide, his body still twitching.

Flipping her hair back over her shoulders, Sierra tugged her damp sweater into place, picked up her purse off the floor and headed for the door. A woman with brown hair, wearing a leather jacket, stepped in as Sierra stepped out.

Sierra smiled at the brunette's horrified expression. "Don't worry, I'll notify the manager he needs to clean the trash out of the restroom."

The woman's lips twisted. "He must have deserved it."

"You have no idea." With a last glance over her

shoulder, Sierra left the restroom and plowed into a wall of muscles.

An iron grip descended on her arms, steadying her.

Shaken, she glanced up into T-Rex's face and sagged against him. "Oh, thank God."

He enveloped her in his strong arms. "What's wrong?"

The woman in the leather jacket who'd walked in while Sierra had walked out pushed out of the ladies' room, shaking her head with a smile as she passed Sierra and T-Rex in the hallway. As the door opened and closed, T-Rex had a chance to see what was inside.

His jaw tightened. "Ellis?"

Sierra held up the stun gun and grinned like the village idiot. "Couldn't have done it without your help. Thank you." She shook all over, but she'd never felt more empowered.

T-Rex caught her wrist, reached up and switched the device to the off position and then chuckled. "Glad it helped." He dropped the device into her handbag. "Are you ready to go?"

"More than ready." She gnawed on her bottom lip. "How long will the effects last again?"

"Sometimes as much as thirty minutes."

"I hate that he will tie up the ladies' restroom for all that time."

"I'll have someone remove him." T-Rex curled his arm around her shoulders and guided her back to the table where his teammates had taken up residence.

Garner stood and held out his hand. "Miss Daniels,

it's good to see you again." He frowned. "Is everything all right?"

T-Rex jerked his head toward the hallway. "Can you have someone clean up the dirtbag in the ladies' restroom?"

"Holy hell, did I miss a fight?" Hawkeye jumped up, grinning.

"Miss Daniels had a run-in with her ex-husband, Clay Ellis," T-Rex explained.

"I have a restraining order against him. You can call the sheriff and have him haul Clay out on charges of violating the order," Sierra said. What was the use of a restraining order if the man wasn't punished when he violated it? She'd hit him with a stun gun—how much madder would he get if he was hauled off to jail? Frankly, Sierra didn't care. Clay deserved everything he had coming to him and more.

Garner nodded. "Don't worry about the dirtbag. Just get Miss Daniels home."

"Thank you," Sierra said. For the first time in a long time, she felt like she had others, besides herself, looking out for her. With T-Rex's arm around her, the chill of being caught in the ladies' room by her ex began to fade.

The fact she'd taken care of herself gave her a surge of power, reinforcing her overall decision to get on with her life, without Clay Ellis. She'd been divorced for six months. Perhaps it was time to start dating.

A different kind of warmth spread through her, making her even more aware of the massive marine and the potential she'd felt in his kiss.

Chapter Six

T-Rex walked with Sierra back to the bed-and-breakfast, his arm firmly around her shoulders. He hated that she'd had to face Clay Ellis alone. But his chest swelled with pride over how she'd handled the man. Ellis would think twice before accosting her again.

The sweet day care employee who loved children shouldn't have to put up with an ex-husband of Ellis's low caliber. She deserved someone who could love and respect her. Someone who treated her like the beautiful, caring woman she was.

Someone like him?

He paused in front of her bedroom door and turned to face her. "If you need anything, just yell. The walls aren't very well insulated. I'll hear you."

She laughed. "Not very well insulated?"

Her smile was contagious and had his lips tilting. "You'll see." T-Rex leaned down and brushed a kiss across her forehead. "Sleep tight."

She stood for a long moment, staring up into his eyes.

He counted the seconds, praying she would go inside before he did something he might regret, like kiss her again. Lord knew kissing her a second time would only lead to more internal struggle than he was capable of resisting.

She moved, but not in the direction he expected.

Sierra leaned up on her toes, wrapped her hand around the back of his head and pressed her lips to his. She ended the kiss on a sigh. "I'd ask you in, but I wouldn't want you to think less of me."

"Sweetheart, I wouldn't think less of you. You impress the heck out of me." He leaned his forehead against hers. "The way you handled Ellis in the tavern…" He chuckled. "In my book, that makes you sexy as hell."

He was prolonging something he shouldn't even consider. The walls were thin. Anything they might get into would be heard by all of the guests.

As he thought about it, he couldn't remember seeing any other guests. The rodeo had left town, taking with it all of the out-of-towners, leaving Grizzly Pass feeling empty, almost deserted compared with the rush of people who'd been there days earlier.

Sierra and T-Rex might be the only visitors in the bed-and-breakfast. In which case, why was he worried if noises carried through the wall?

Then again, there was the issue of his being a career marine and confirmed bachelor. He wouldn't feel right playing with Sierra's emotions. She had enough problems dealing with her ex-husband.

"As much as I'd love to come in," he said, "I'm not sure that would be a good idea."

She nodded. "You're probably right. I'm a divorcée

with baggage. You really don't want to get involved with me while you're here. Although it's a little late for that. My ex thinks we are already involved. That, I'm sorry to say, will continue to cause you grief while you're in Grizzly Pass."

"I can take care of myself. And the fact you're a divorcée with baggage wasn't what I was thinking about." He brushed a strand of her blond hair back behind her ear. "I don't want to shortchange a beautiful woman who deserves more."

"Shortchange?"

He nodded, traced his thumb across her lip and resisted kissing where his thumb had been. "I'm only here for another week, maybe two or three. But then I'll return to my unit. I won't start anything I can't finish."

"Oh, I wasn't thinking of any commitment. I was thinking of practice." Her cheeks reddened.

He frowned. "Practice?"

"I haven't been on a date since high school. Spending time with you is like being on a date. I could use the practice." She laid her hand on his chest and stared at her fingers, not into his eyes. "I wouldn't expect you to stick around. And when you leave, I promise not to be heartbroken." Her voice softened, fading away with the last word.

He couldn't resist, he had to kiss her. She was too beautiful when she was embarrassed. T-Rex bent and skimmed his mouth across hers.

She lifted her chin and forced the connection to be more than a brief touch. Her other hand rose to cup the back of his head.

There was no going back. He crushed her body to his, the evidence of his desire pressing against her soft belly.

After plundering her mouth, he dragged his lips across her chin to suck her earlobe between his teeth. "This is insane," he whispered.

Sierra tilted her head to the side, giving him better access to her ear and to her neck. "Completely," she responded, in a breathy voice, curling her leg behind his.

Holy hell, what was he thinking? This woman was too recently divorced. If he took her now, he'd be taking advantage of her when she was at her most vulnerable.

Though he wanted to swing her up into his arms and carry her into the bedroom, he fought that urge, broke the kiss and took a step back. He breathed in short, tight breaths, clenching his fists to keep from taking her back into his arms.

She stood in front of him, her lips swollen from his kiss, her chest rising and falling as quickly as his. "I'm sorry."

"Why?" he asked.

"I must have done something wrong." She shook her head, her eyes glassy, a pucker on her forehead.

"You didn't do anything wrong. I'm the one who almost screwed up." He took her key from her and slid it into the doorknob. "Go to bed, Sierra. Sleep. I don't want to be your next mistake. Save yourself for a better guy who'll stick around."

Before she could say another word, he angled her through the door and closed it between them. It had to be one of the hardest things he'd ever had to do.

With leaden steps and tight jeans, he continued down the hallway to his room, entered, closed the door behind him and leaned against it. What had he been thinking?

Sierra Daniels was strictly off-limits. She'd been abused, for heaven's sake. Freshly divorced and vulnerable, she would only be hurt if he made love to her. As much as she tried to convince him that she needed "practice," she needed a lot more than that. She needed to learn to love herself before she loved another. Not that he was anyone to give advice on love and romance. He was one big failure in that arena.

Pushing away from the door, he grabbed his shaving kit and a towel and headed across the hall to the shared bathroom. A cold shower would help to douse the raging desire that had almost cost him his control.

Ten minutes later, he climbed out of the shower, dried off and wrapped his towel around his waist. With his shaving kit in hand, he walked out of the bathroom and almost ran over Sierra bent over in the hallway, collecting from the floor an array of shampoo and conditioner bottles and a tube of toothpaste.

"Sorry, I'll get out of your way." She shoved all the items into a torn plastic bag, gathered them to her chest and finally glanced up.

Her gaze started at his shins and climbed to the towel, pausing at the tent his instant desire had created.

T-Rex groaned. He'd need thirty minutes more in an ice bath to tamp down the intense heat that exploded inside when Sierra's gaze swept upward.

What sweet hell was this? He gripped her elbow and brought her to her feet. "Are you okay?"

"I'm fine," she said, her cheeks bright red.

"Good, because now I'm not." He turned her toward the bathroom and gave her a gentle nudge. "Go, before I forget how to be a gentleman."

SIERRA STAGGERED INTO the bathroom. The door closed behind her and she finally remembered to inhale. Then her breaths came in ragged gasps. She pressed a hand to her chest, willing her heartbeat to slow.

Seeing T-Rex in nothing but a towel had taken her breath away. The man had the broadest, most anatomically perfect chest of any man she'd ever seen in person or on television. But the evidence of his desire had captured her attention, shoving every other thought completely out of her head. He'd been hard for her.

Before she'd headed for the bathroom, Sierra had gone to her room, her hormones hopping, her libido so stimulated she hadn't been able to settle into a chair or in bed. She'd wandered around the room, counting the number of steps it took to get from one side to the other.

After ten laps, she'd forced herself to sit at the little desk and dump out the contents of her purse. She rearranged them and placed them back in the different compartments, assigning a specific pouch for the stun gun. She didn't want to waste time hunting for it the next time she needed to defend herself.

Once she'd completed her inventory and repacking of the items in her purse, she turned on the television in the corner and flipped through the channels. Nothing had appealed to her, or taken her mind off the man in the room next to hers. She turned off the television, grabbed the plastic grocery bag of toiletries she'd brought with her from her apartment, panties and a nightgown and headed for the bathroom across the hall.

She'd almost reached the door when the bottom fell out of the bag, spilling her shampoo, conditioner, lotion and toothpaste onto the floor. She'd dropped to pick them up when the bathroom door opened and… and… Sweet heaven, T-Rex had stood in front of her.

Standing in the bathroom he'd vacated, Sierra burned with the heat of her desire. Never in her life had she been that strongly attracted to any man. Not even during the early days of dating Clay. Yes, there had been a mild form of lust. But this was something entirely different. The feeling consumed her and made her lose focus on everything else.

Sierra shook herself, set her things on the counter and stripped out of her clothes, determined to push the man out of her thoughts. No man should have that much control over her thoughts and imagination. It could only lead to heartache and losing herself once again. She'd come too far in her self-realization to backslide now.

In the shower, she scrubbed her hair, face and body, trying to ignore the sensitivity of her nipples and the ache between her legs. She would not succumb to her desire.

T-Rex had laid it out for her. He wasn't staying. And he hadn't invited her to leave when he left. Not that he should. They were strangers, having known each other for only a few short hours.

She rinsed the suds out of her hair and turned the shower to its coolest setting. Anything to chill the heat inside her body. If she didn't get a grasp on her physical reactions to the man, she'd never get any sleep.

Dressed in her nightgown, her hair wrapped turban-style in the towel, she eased open the door. The hall-way was clear. A stab of disappointment assailed her.

"Idiot," she muttered beneath her breath. "Like he'd be interested in you. And you shouldn't be interested in him."

The door across the hall opened and T-Rex stood in the frame, wearing jeans and nothing else. "Did you say something?"

Her cheeks flamed. "No, just talking to myself." She scurried for her door. "You weren't kidding about paper-thin walls, were you?"

He chuckled. "No, I wasn't. The couple who'd been in the room on the other side of me were very loud in their lovemaking. I had a hard time facing them in the morning."

"Well, you don't have to worry about me. I won't be making a whole lot of noise," she babbled. "I don't think I snore, and once I'm out, I don't get up for any-thing short of a fire alarm."

"Good to know." His gaze swept her from her head to her bare feet, his eyes flaring as he skimmed over her bare knees and calves. "Good night."

His glance warmed her from the inside, spreading heat to her chest and lower to the juncture of her thighs.

"Yes, good night." She rushed through her door and closed it before she did something stupid like falling into the big marine's arms and begging him to make love to her. Wow, he had charisma in spades. How did women resist?

With little hope of sleep, she lay on the bed. The headboard rested against the wall she shared with T-Rex. If the walls were as thin as he'd said, he could hear her if she cried out.

After Clay had attacked her twice that day, Sierra felt more reassured having T-Rex on the other side of the wall. And she had the stun gun, should she need it.

For a long time, she lay in the dark, staring up at the ceiling. Sleep eluded her. She found herself listening for sounds from the other room, wondering if T-Rex was having trouble sleeping, too. The next thought that popped into her head was the big question: Did he sleep in pajamas or in the nude?

Sierra moaned, rolled onto her side and punched her pillow. This was not going to work. Thinking of a naked man would not put her to sleep anytime soon.

"Everything okay in there?" a deep, resonant voice said from the other side of the wall.

Sierra yelped and sat up.

"Sorry," he said. "I didn't mean to frighten you. I heard you moan and thought maybe you weren't feeling well."

Flopping over onto her back, Sierra pulled the extra pillow up into her arms and hugged it. "Good Lord, I can hear you as if you were in my room."

He chuckled. "Told you."

"You really must have gotten a blow-by-blow account of the couple's nights."

"Pun intended?"

It was Sierra's turn to chuckle. "If it fits…"

Quiet settled in again, but Sierra couldn't relax. It was as if she were clinging to an edge, waiting for another word from T-Rex to pull her back. When he didn't say anything, she couldn't remain silent. "Why did you join the military?"

"To get out of Texas and see the world." He snorted. "Only it turns out that it's not always the best part of the world."

"I can imagine." She picked at the pillowcase. "I know you said you're not married, but have you ever been?"

"No."

"You're a…good-looking guy. How have you gone all these years without getting hitched?" She bit her lip. "Sorry. If I'm being too nosy, just tell me to shove off."

"No. It's okay," he said. "First of all, I haven't met anyone who could put up with me."

Sierra laughed. "I find that hard to believe."

"It's true. I'm stubborn, cranky and hard to get along with on a good day."

"I get along fine with you."

"Second, after my first couple of deployments, watching other guys who had wives back home, I couldn't see myself subjecting a woman to the hardship of being married to a career military man. Many of my men would return to empty houses—their wives having moved back to their mamas, taking the kids with them."

"Some women are a lot stronger than you think. Surely you could find one who would be there when you got back."

"Yeah. *If* I got back." His voice faded to little more than a whisper. "Or *if* I came back in one piece."

Sierra's chest tightened. She could hear the strain in his tone. "What do you mean?"

"I wouldn't want to come back in a body bag. Or worse, a paraplegic. What woman wants to take care of her children and her husband for the rest of her life?"

"A woman who loves him more than life," Sierra answered.

"I couldn't put a woman through the heartache and demands of a life caring for an invalid."

Another long silence stretched between them.

Sierra broke it with, "You know someone like this, don't you?"

His answer was in the form of more silence.

"I'm sorry," Sierra said. "It must hurt to see one of your men so badly injured."

"Hurts even more that I can do nothing to make it better." T-Rex's voice was tight and hard. "He'll never walk again. He'll never throw a ball for his son. He'll never feel the softness of his wife's skin."

Tears welled in Sierra's eyes. "And because of this, you will never marry?"

"Yes," he said, his tone harsh.

"Did you ever think that maybe a woman would want to make the choice, to be the one to decide whether or not to take the risk on you?"

"It doesn't matter," he said. "I'd rather die than be a burden on a woman."

"Sometimes you aren't given a choice. Your friend

was given that choice. I'm sure his wife would rather have him alive than not."

"I told you I was terrible boyfriend material."

"Again, you weren't lying. Not because you're a member of the military. Most women can deal with that. You're terrible boyfriend material because you won't give a woman the opportunity to decide for herself if she's ready and willing to take the risk on you. You just avoid the situation altogether."

"Yes. Exactly."

"In the meantime, you're alone." Sierra's heart contracted. One of the reasons she'd stayed with her husband as long as she had was because she was terrible at being alone. Perhaps the death of her parents had made her less secure in her solitude. For the past few months of being single, she'd learned being alone wasn't all that bad. But she wouldn't want to be alone forever.

"I like being alone," T-Rex said.

"Because you've been alone for so long you don't remember what it's like to have someone else to share your life."

"I have my unit."

"And they are with you 24/7 when you're deployed, but they go home to their families when you're Stateside. Which leaves you alone again."

"I like it," he insisted.

"Uh-huh."

"I can choose what to eat for dinner. I don't have to ask permission if I want to go to a movie, and I can walk around my apartment naked, if I like."

Sierra laughed. "Yeah, but you don't have anyone to

talk to when you're down or someone with whom you can share the beauty of a sunset."

"I don't need any of that."

"No?" Sierra leaned up on her elbows. "What about children? Don't you want children of your own? A little girl or a miniature T-Rex to teach how to play ball?"

"No." His tone was hard and final. "What happens if I did have a little boy, and then I came back a paraplegic like Gunny? What then? My son wouldn't have a father to teach him the things a father is supposed to."

"Your Gunny is alive. He will be there for his son, to teach him by his words. He can hire a coach. I'm sure his son would rather have him than no father at all."

"I won't do that to any kid of mine. War's hell. I won't put a woman through the uncertainty. I won't have her waiting for the dreaded call or visit from the chaplain."

"If you love someone enough, you'll take whatever time you're given with that person," Sierra said softly.

"You've been reading too many romance novels. I'm surprised you still believe in love, given the fact you're divorced."

Sierra flinched and hugged the pillow harder, her eyes stinging. His words hurt. "For a long time, I thought I was the one who'd failed at my marriage. I stopped believing in love. It couldn't be real. It was just lust, and when that faded, you had nothing." Tears welled in her eyes. Those had been dark days in which she'd felt more hopeless than at any other time of her life.

"Look, Sierra, I'm sorry. I shouldn't have said what I said about your divorce."

"No, you're right. It took being away from Clay to realize it wasn't me. *He* wasn't capable of loving me. And maybe I wasn't capable of loving him. But I know I'm capable of love, and I'm not giving up on finding it." She held up her hand, even though he couldn't see it. "Don't worry. I won't look for it in you. You've been very clear on the subject. Now, if you don't mind, I'm tired and I have to get some sleep."

Silence filled the gloom, making it seem even gloomier.

"Good night, Sierra. I hope you find it."

I hope you do, too, she thought. *Then, you'll understand.*

Chapter Seven

T-Rex tossed and turned through the night. Sierra's words stuck with him, making it hard for him to clear his mind. For a woman who'd been in an abusive relationship, she was still optimistic about finding love.

As morning light edged through the curtains, T-Rex gave up on sleep, put on his running shoes and sweats and went out for a jog. Whenever he needed to think, he ran. He had a lot to think about, and there didn't seem to be enough time or road to ponder everything on his mind.

Number one was the last bit of conversation he'd had with Sierra. No matter how hard he tried to push it to the back of his mind, he couldn't. The last thing he needed to be thinking about was love. He was married to the corps. He was first, and foremost, a marine.

Any woman who dared to fall in love with a career marine was setting herself up for heartache and sacrifice. She would be left alone more often than not. Any children from the relationship would be raised by their mother. Deployments were a given, and they could be as long as fourteen months at a time. Gunny had missed more birthdays and dance recitals than he'd managed to attend. What kind of life was that for a woman, or children, for that matter?

Then why were so many of his troops married? Sure, some had deployed to come back to an empty house, their wives picking up and moving the kids back to their mamas. But there were those who kept the home fires burning and greeted their loved ones when they stepped off the planes. They were there with love in their eyes, truly happy to see their husbands.

Why couldn't that be him?

An image came to his mind of Sierra waiting at the airport or on the tarmac of a military landing strip, her blue eyes alight with happy tears, a pretty little girl, with her blond hair and blue eyes standing beside her, clutching her hand.

His heart pinched in his chest, forcing him to slow to a walk. He'd seen wives like that with their little ones gathered around their legs. Waiting for their husbands and fathers to step off the plane. The happy reunions always made him rethink his stance on his own bachelorhood.

Then he'd see a casket unloaded from the bowels of a plane, the widow and children of the fallen marine there to meet the transfer detail with the hearse.

No matter how much he longed for the love and comfort of having someone waiting for him at home, T-Rex couldn't do it. He wouldn't put a woman through that kind of heartache. He picked up the pace until he was running again. Anyone who would go willingly into a relationship with a career marine had to either be so in love to the point she couldn't think straight, or just insane. The worry alone would age the one left behind.

Again, he thought of Sierra, who still believed in love, despite having escaped an abusive husband. She deserved a man who would go to work and come home each day. A man whose job wasn't to kill, and in the process be shot at, have bombs lobbed in his direction or IEDs explode beneath his feet. She deserved an accountant, banker or rancher. A man who would always be there for her, who would always be home at night to protect her.

The thought of someone else coming home to Sierra made T-Rex's heart pinch even tighter. He pushed past the irritating pain and ran even faster. By the time he was almost back to the bed-and-breakfast, he was running full out. No amount of physical exertion was enough to push thoughts of Sierra from his mind. He might have to move out of the bed-and-breakfast to get away from her and the attraction he was feeling toward her.

As the bed-and-breakfast came into view, he slowed, winding down from the punishing pace. Whatever he did, he had to stay away from Sierra Daniels. She was everything he wanted but couldn't have. The sooner he accepted that, the better off he'd be.

Mrs. McCall was awake and setting the table in the shared dining room.

"Good morning, Mrs. McCall."

She glanced up with a smile. "Good morning, Mr. Trainor. You're up early."

"Yes, ma'am." He didn't bother to inform her that he

couldn't sleep because of one blond-haired, blue-eyed beauty on the other side of the wall of his bedroom. What good would it do?

Mrs. McCall laid out another napkin and placed a knife and fork on it. "How do you like your eggs cooked? And how many?"

"Two, over easy, and a slice of toast."

"Coffee?"

"Yes, ma'am. Black."

"It'll be ready in ten minutes. Just enough time for you to get a shower." She winked. "Would you happen to know when Miss Daniels will be awake?"

And why would Mrs. McCall think he'd know Miss Daniels's hours? Had she heard them kissing and talking?

"I'm awake," a soft voice said from the top of the staircase.

T-Rex's pulse stuttered and then raced as he turned to face the woman who'd been on his mind nonstop since he'd closed his eyes in an attempt to sleep last night.

Sierra descended the steps, her hand trailing along the rail. She wore a form-hugging light blue knit blouse the color of her eyes and a navy blue skirt. Her long, slender legs were encased in dark navy tights, emphasizing her tight calves and narrow ankles. She had her long blond hair loose around her shoulders.

The overall effect left T-Rex breathless, the desire he'd hoped he'd run off surging back in full force. "I'll go shower," he said through tight lips. He passed her as she took the last step down.

For a brief instant, their gazes connected.

T-Rex felt as if he'd been blasted by a bolt of lightning when he looked into her eyes.

Her irises flared, and she caught her bottom lip between her teeth.

Swallowing a groan, T-Rex jerked his glance away from hers and stumbled on the first step. Cursing softly beneath his breath, he caught himself.

Sierra touched his arm. "Are you all right?"

"I'm fine," he forced out, his arm on fire where her hand lay. He was freakin' great. The one person he needed to avoid was touching him, and he was going hot all over like a teenager in lust. Tearing himself away, he started up the steps.

"Is there anything I can do to help?" Sierra said behind him.

"Yes, thank you," Mrs. McCall responded. "If you could finish setting the table, I'll start cooking. How many eggs would you like and how do you like them cooked?"

"Two eggs, over easy, and a piece of toast would be nice, thank you."

Halfway up the staircase, T-Rex stubbed his toe on the riser in front of him. Had Sierra heard him order his eggs, or did she truly like hers just like his?

"Did you hear that, Mr. Trainor?" Mrs. McCall called out. "Just like you. You're making this easy. You're two peas in a pod."

T-Rex said something inane and continued up the stairs.

"Coffee or tea?" Mrs. McCall was asking.

"Coffee, definitely. Black," Sierra said in her soft voice.

At the top of the stairs now, T-Rex groaned. Could the woman be any more perfect? If she was a Denver Broncos fan, he might as well throw in the towel and ask her to marry him.

AFTER A RESTLESS night of very little sleep, Sierra had promised she wouldn't let herself get all wrapped up in T-Rex that morning. She'd been thankful she had the bathroom all to herself, without bumping into the man. If she was honest with herself, she had been a little disappointed that she hadn't seen him.

Determined to wipe him from her mind and get on with her life, she'd left her bedroom, ready to make it a wonderful day spending time with the children at the community center. Working with children always took her mind off her own troubles and made her smile.

Then she'd seen T-Rex at the bottom of the stairs, and all bets were off. He was right back front and center in her thoughts. Not that he'd ever left them. And he was all sweaty, his face and muscular arms glistening in the dining room lights.

Sierra's heart skipped several beats and butterflies fluttered in her belly. She could feel last night's kiss tingling on her lips.

And when she'd touched him… Holy hell, she was going to be sorely disappointed when the man left Grizzly Pass. She hadn't felt this excited by any man. Ever. Not even when she'd first started dating the captain of the football team in high school. That had been back when Clay was at the top of his game. He'd been nice to her and treated her like he really cared. She'd been flattered and thought she was in love with him.

But never had she felt the spark T-Rex set off in her by merely touching her.

As she set flatware on the dining room table, she listened for the sound of the water running in the shower upstairs and imagined T-Rex naked.

He'd told her not to get attached. And she had no intention of doing so. But what would it hurt to have a fling with the man? Sierra shivered and her core heated in anticipation of getting naked with T-Rex and making love.

He'd be so powerful in bed. All those muscles would be hers to touch, if only for a night. Then perhaps she'd get him out of her system and move on to finding a man she could fall in love with and who would fall in love with her.

She finished laying out the silverware and napkins and helped Mrs. McCall by bringing the toast and an insulated carafe of coffee to the table.

Mrs. McCall smiled. "Thank you for helping. The eggs are almost ready. I'll bring them out in a minute. Why don't you make yourself comfortable in the dining room?"

Sierra wandered out to the dining room. She couldn't hear the sound of water running. Her senses perked and her pulse sped. T-Rex would be down soon, and they would have to sit at the same table for breakfast.

How should she act? How could she look at him and not show how very attracted she was to him? Taking a deep breath, she purposely turned away from the staircase. She would not let T-Rex or any other man have that profound an effect on her. Letting her breath out slowly, she paused to stare out the window as the morning sun bathed the trees and other houses along the street in light. If she concentrated on the beauty of the world around her, instead of the marine in the shower upstairs, she might make it through breakfast without drooling.

The weatherman had predicted the morning would be clear and sunny. Later that evening clouds would roll in from the west. For now, the sunshine filled Sierra with a feeling of hope, and hope was a good thing when you were divorced, dirt-poor and somewhat homeless while your apartment was being rerooofed.

A dark pickup pulled up to the curb on the other side of the street.

As if a cloud descended on her spirits, the hope Sierra had felt faded, replaced by a heavy pall of anger and dread. "Damn him," she whispered, her hands shaking as she stepped back from the window.

Arms came up around her and a deep voice asked, "What's wrong?"

Sierra spun in T-Rex's arms and pressed her cheek against his chest. "Out there," she said, refusing to look again.

T-Rex stiffened. "Ellis." He gripped her arms and set her away from him. "I'll take care of him."

"No. Let the sheriff. I have a restraining order against him. If he gets any closer than fifty feet, the sheriff can arrest him."

"He's harassing you."

"He never liked to lose." Sierra stared up into T-Rex's face. "I'll call the sheriff."

"Do it. And if they don't show up and he's still there when we're finished with breakfast, I'll have words with him."

She smiled and touched his arm. "You don't have to fight my battles for me."

"Ellis doesn't have to harass you."

"Now that I have the stun gun, I can take care of myself." She stepped away and pulled her cell phone from her purse. As she hit the number for the sheriff's department, she left the dining room and entered the front living area.

"Sheriff's department," a woman's voice answered.

"This is Sierra Daniels. Is Sheriff Scott available?"

"One moment, please."

After a short pause, a deep, masculine voice came through the receiver. "Sierra, Sheriff Scott here. What's up?"

She sighed. "Clay's at it again."

"When is that boy going to get it through his thick head you aren't going back to him?"

"I don't know. But he's parked outside Mrs. McCall's bed-and-breakfast, where I'm staying. I didn't call, but I had two altercations with him yesterday."

"Sierra, you did right. We'll do something about it."

"I know. I just need to remember to call."

"That's right. We're here to help. I'll send a unit by," Sheriff Scott said.

"Thank you."

"Are you going to be okay?"

Sierra glanced across the two rooms at T-Rex standing by the window, staring out at her ex-husband. "Yes. I'm okay. I can protect myself. I just don't want him hanging around and scaring my landlady."

"We'll take care of it."

Sierra ended the call and joined T-Rex in the dining room.

Mrs. McCall entered, carrying their plates of steaming eggs.

As they settled in for their breakfast, Mrs. McCall asked, "Would you mind if I put the news on the television?"

"Not at all," Sierra answered.

"I'd like that," said T-Rex.

The bed-and-breakfast owner hit the remote for the fifty-inch television mounted on the wall in the corner of the dining room. She gave them a sassy smile as she adjusted the volume. "I love my big television. I occasionally open the dining room during football season. I love my Denver Broncos."

"I was here during your airing of the last playoff game." Sierra said. "The food was great, and the company was so much fun." It had been shortly after her divorce. She'd dared to venture out by herself and had thoroughly enjoyed the football game. "I'm a huge Broncos fan, too."

Beside her, T-Rex choked on his coffee.

"Are you all right?" she asked.

He set the cup down and covered his mouth. "Wrong pipe."

Mrs. McCall tuned in to the news station based out of Jackson Hole, Wyoming, the closest station to Grizzly Pass. "Look, there's Grady Morris on the steps of the state capitol."

"Isn't he the guy who was here a few days ago, campaigning for state senator?"

Mrs. McCall nodded. "He's been campaigning all over the state. The elections aren't far off and the incumbent is getting old, but he is a favorite." She turned up the volume.

A woman in a gray skirt suit raised her hand. "Mr. Morris, what's your stance on global warming? Will you vote for legislation to reduce greenhouse gases?"

The candidate stood straight, his gaze on the gathered crowd more than the female reporter asking the question. "I will study the situation and make the best possible decisions based on the scientific findings and what my constituents want."

"Great way to avoid the question," Sierra muttered.

"What about the pipeline running through the state and the southern border of Yellowstone National Park?" A dark-haired man, wearing a dark jacket, held out a microphone. "Will you put pressure on the federal government to put a stop to further expansion of the pipeline access?"

"I will stand by the people and do what's in the best interest of the people of Wyoming," Morris responded.

"Another nonanswer," Sierra noted.

"Is it true, Mr. Morris, that you were once on the Transcontinental Pipeline Inc. board of directors?"

Morris nodded, brows dipping. "Your point?"

"And isn't it true Transcontinental bought out Rocky Mountain Pipeline?"

Again, Morris nodded, his eyes narrowing slightly.

"And isn't Transcontinental in the process of negotiating their existing contract for the maintenance of the pipeline through Wyoming and for additional pipelines to pass, as well?"

"I wouldn't know," Morris responded. "I haven't been on the board for nearly seven years. Next question, please." Morris looked at the others in the crowd.

"Is it true Transcontinental is being investigated for failure to provide sufficient maintenance to the existing pipelines?" The man in the dark jacket wasn't going to let go of the pipeline angle.

Morris's mouth thinned into a straight line. "I'll take other questions from other reporters now."

The woman in the gray suit held up her hand.

Morris nodded to her.

"Mr. Morris, I'd like to know the answer to the other reporter's question. Is Transcontinental being investigated for failure to provide sufficient maintenance to the existing pipeline?"

"If they are, it should be available as public record." Morris straightened his suit coat and stepped down from the top step at the capitol. "If you'll excuse me, I have work to do."

"Mr. Morris, if Transcontinental hasn't been maintaining the pipeline properly, are the people of Wyoming in danger of a pipeline rupturing?"

"I don't have the answer to that question," he responded.

The woman in the gray suit followed Morris as he attempted to push through the crowd of reporters. "Will you, as a senator, make certain all measures are taken to protect the people of your state from a potentially disastrous situation with the pipeline?"

Morris didn't respond. The woman in gray turned to her cameraman. "There seems to be more than meets the eye on Grady Morris's connection to the Transcontinental Pipeline. I'll bring you my findings in the evening news." She signed off and the news returned to the station and the weather report.

"Mr. Morris has an uphill battle if he plans to be the next senator of Wyoming," Mrs. McCall said. "Too many people are unhappy about the pipeline running through our state to begin with. If Morris is in any way connected with the pipeline shenanigans, he won't get the votes he needs. And if Transcontinental thinks they'll put another one in with the first, they have another think coming. Ever since they bought out Rocky Mountain Pipeline, they've laid off everyone and quit maintaining the line. I'd be surprised if they don't get fined and booted off the pipeline altogether." Mrs. McCall grimaced. "Sorry. I'll step down from my soapbox now." She finished her tea and stood. "Can I get you anything? More coffee? Tea?"

Sierra held up her hand. "I'm full. Breakfast was great. If you keep cooking like that, I might decide to live here even after they finish the renovations on my apartment building."

"Sweetie, you're always welcome here. You're practically family."

"Thank you, Mrs. McCall." Sierra gathered her plate and stood.

Mrs. McCall paused on her way to the kitchen, staring through the window. "Now, what is the sheriff doing on our street so early in the morning?" She left the dining room and pushed through the swinging door into the kitchen.

Sierra's pulse sped up. She deliberately stopped beside T-Rex and piled his plate on top of hers. As she passed the window, she could see a sheriff's car pulled up against the curb where Clay's truck had been a few minutes before.

A smile curled her lips, and she felt a hundred pounds lighter. "Clay's gone," Sierra said.

"Even so, I'm following you to the community center today." T-Rex pushed back from the table and gathered the glasses.

"You don't have to," Sierra reminded him.

He shook his head. "No, but I want to. Can we not argue about it this morning?"

She twisted her lips in a wry grin. "Deal. And thanks." The smile he gave her spread warmth throughout her body.

And so, she had her escort to the community center. Clay wasn't there waiting to harass her, but Brenda was driving up as she arrived, and by the stupid grin on her face, she wasn't likely to let Sierra by without some good-natured ribbing.

Sierra hugged herself around her middle as she walked into the building. The man made her feel cared about and protected. No amount of ribbing would knock the smile off her face.

Chapter Eight

T-Rex waited until Sierra was inside the community center before he left. He didn't like leaving her with the possibility of Ellis showing up again and making a nuisance of himself. But he couldn't be there all the time for her. He had a job to do.

Just to relieve some of his anxiety, he stopped at the sheriff's office.

Sheriff Scott was standing at the front desk, talking to a deputy, when T-Rex entered. He finished what he was saying and turned with his hand outstretched and a smile on his face. "Mr. Trainor. Good morning. What can I do for you?"

T-Rex gripped the man's hand. "I wanted to thank you for sending a unit by the bed-and-breakfast this morning."

The sheriff's smile faded, and he released T-Rex's hand. "Clay Ellis needs a swift kick in the backside. The man can't get it through his thick, mean head that things were over between him and Ms. Daniels the day the judge granted her divorce."

T-Rex nodded. "That's the reason I'm here. I'm worried he'll try something."

The sheriff chuckled. "I heard from my guys that she got him good with a stun gun last night at the tavern. When he came out of it, he was madder than a wet hen."

"That's what I'm afraid of," T-Rex said. "He might see it as a challenge to catch her when her guard is down."

"You're right. I'll have a unit swing by the community center every hour during the day to make sure she's okay."

"Thanks."

"You and your team getting any closer to figuring out who's responsible for all the troubles around here lately?"

"We have bits and pieces, but not the full picture."

"That's about where we are. We think we know some of the players in the Free America group, but we don't have enough evidence to get the county judge to issue search warrants. Besides, we doubt they'd keep their weapons and plans in their houses. There are enough caves and old mines in those mountains to keep us looking for a very long time."

"Agreed."

"Well, keep us informed." Sheriff Scott clapped a hand to T-Rex's back. "We're here to help each other."

"You bet." T-Rex left the sheriff's office. He made his way to the Blue Moose Tavern and climbed the stairs on the outside to the temporary office of the Safe Haven operations center.

Ghost, Caveman and Hawkeye were at the conference table, staring at a map.

Garner stood behind Hack at the array of computer monitors. "Good, now that we're all here, we can get to work."

"What's the plan for the day?" T-Rex asked.

Their temporary boss pointed to two of the men. "Ghost and Caveman will continue to interview neighbors and friends of Don Sweeney to see if anyone saw other people coming and going from the man's apartment. Hopefully someone will come up with the name of the man who hired Sweeney to kill Olivia Dawson's father."

Sweeney had admitted he'd been paid to murder the rancher who owned the land bordering the pipeline. They still didn't know who'd paid him or if he had connections to Free America.

"I'd like to check Wayne Batson's place," Hawkeye said. "I feel like the sheriff might have missed something. The man trained people for combat, for heaven's sake. He's bound to have a bunker of weapons hidden somewhere on his ranch."

"I can help with the search," T-Rex offered.

Garner shook his head. "I have other plans for you. And I need to coordinate the search of Batson's ranch with the sheriff. They have the authority to search the ranch. No use getting hit with trespassing charges."

"After Caveman and Ms. Saunders were hunted like animals on Batson's ranch—" Hawkeye frowned "—I'd say we have a right to be there."

Garner nodded. "Still, we need to coordinate with the

sheriff. If he has people out there, you don't want to surprise them. With everything that's happened lately, they might shoot first and ask questions later. Not to mention the folks Batson trained on his ranch. They could still be using his facilities without our knowledge."

Unfortunately, Batson's computer information concerning people who'd been through his training camp had been programmed to self-destruct when tampered with. As soon as Hack had made his first attempt, the system shut him out and initiated a program to delete data files. Hack had turned off the server as soon as he'd realized what had happened. At that point the server had been sent to the state crime lab in the hope they could recover the data.

In the meantime, a shipment of approximately thirty AR-15, military-grade rifles had been sent to someone in the area. And they had yet to discover their whereabouts. Thirty semiautomatic rifles would do a lot of damage in a takeover.

Garner turned to T-Rex. "I have a special assignment for you. Today, I want you to tail Leo Fratiani. Our searches online haven't turned up much of anything. Find out if he's really on the up and up."

"Will do," T-Rex said.

Garner continued, "Then, this afternoon, I have a friend from the Wyoming Army National Guard flying in with a UH-60 Black Hawk helicopter. I need you to be available when he gets here. He'll take you up to scout the hills and valleys along and around the pipeline. Perhaps what we can't see from the ground, you can see from the air."

"I would think you'd want to be in that chopper," T-Rex noted.

"I do. Major Bailey and Lieutenant Strohm are on loan for the afternoon to get some flying time in. Unfortunately, I have an online meeting scheduled with my higher headquarters this afternoon that I can't miss. My boss wants a status on what's happening here in Grizzly Pass." Garner's lips thinned. "I'd like to tell him we've identified all of the members of Free America and found the person who funded the purchase of the AR-15s. As you all know, we're not there."

The men around the table were silent. If the others were like T-Rex, they took it personally that they hadn't found the source of the problems.

"We don't know if the troubles are directly related to the pipeline, or if someone is trying to throw us off." Garner turned away from the team and paced the length of the room and back. "The heavily armed Free America faction could be the real issue here. We know about the AR-15s, but we don't know what else they might have gotten their hands on. The sooner we locate the weapons cache and get a list of the people involved, the sooner we nail the ones responsible, and you can go back to your units."

"We're on it," T-Rex said.

Ghost nodded. "We want this resolved as badly as you. I'm from this area. I hate seeing it threatened."

"If Free America stages a takeover, anyone could be at risk. Look what happened to the local children. That was bad enough," Caveman said. "A nice old man was murdered, and all of those children could have died in that abandoned mine."

"Precisely why we can't let this drag on any longer. And with the internet hopping with Free America activity and forewarnings, we need to make it happen soon." Garner clapped his hands together. "Let's get to it."

Ghost, Caveman and Hawkeye left the office. Garner lagged behind. "Fratiani is staying at the Heartland Hotel. He likes to take his breakfast at the diner and eat lunch and dinner at the Blue Moose Tavern. What he does with the rest of his day, we don't know. He drives out of town."

"What's he look like?" T-Rex asked.

Garner turned to the man in the corner. "Hack?"

The computer guru had been sitting quietly, tapping away at his keyboard. He tapped some more, and an image popped up on one of his monitors of a man with dark hair and dark eyes.

"This is from his driver's license from the state of California."

"He's not even from Wyoming?" T-Rex stepped up behind Hack.

"No. He approached Olivia Dawson stating he was interested in purchasing her property, Stone Oak Ranch, for an investor. My inquiries indicate he works for a company called LF Enterprises. He's listed as the owner."

"Is he a broker?" T-Rex asked.

Hack nodded. "I looked up his license in the state of California. It's current and relatively new. He's also a licensed financial adviser. Also recent. Prior to those certifications, he worked for the pipeline industry."

"Okay, he probably knows his stuff and might have

an inside track on the pipeline dealings." T-Rex faced Garner again. "Do you want me to interview him, or tail him and observe covertly?"

Garner had joined him behind Hack. "I'd rather he didn't know you were on to him. If he's up to something, you might have a better chance of discovering what it is, if he doesn't know you're following him."

T-Rex nodded. "Will do." As he left the office and descended the stairs, he checked his watch. It was still early. He might catch Fratiani at the diner.

T-Rex hopped into his truck and drove the few blocks to the diner, got out and went in. It didn't take long to spot the man he was to follow that day.

Fratiani looked much like the picture on his driver's license, with his dark hair and dark eyes. He sat alone at a table with a cup of coffee, an empty plate and his cell phone in his hand.

T-Rex ordered a cup of coffee to go and sat at the counter mixing a dash of sugar and cream in the cup, though he preferred it black. He sipped the steaming brew and glanced over the rim of the cup.

About that time, Fratiani threw a twenty on the table and got up.

T-Rex gave him enough time to exit the building before he capped his coffee and followed.

The broker climbed into a four-wheel-drive Jeep and backed out of his parking space, holding his cell phone to his ear. He headed south out of town.

T-Rex jumped into his truck, settled the coffee in a cup holder and followed, keeping his distance so as not to tip off Fratiani that he was being tailed.

Three miles out of Grizzly Pass, Fratiani turned onto a dirt road. T-Rex drove past the road and didn't slow until he'd rounded a curve. As soon as he was reasonably out of sight, he turned around and headed the opposite direction, slowing as he rounded the curve.

As far as he could tell, Fratiani hadn't come out of the dirt road. His Jeep was nowhere in sight.

T-Rex pulled off the road onto another dirt road on the opposite side and drove far enough down it to hide his truck. Then he shifted into Park, leaped out and ran back to the edge of the road, hiding behind the brush, careful not to expose himself.

Nothing moved. After several minutes of close study, T-Rex crossed the road and entered the undergrowth paralleling the dirt road.

Moving in the shadows, he followed the road to a small clearing where Fratiani's Jeep was parked. Another vehicle was backed into the brush. All he could make out of it was the front grille of what appeared to be a pickup.

Fratiani stood beside his Jeep talking to a man who wore a jacket with a hood pulled up around his face.

From where T-Rex stood twenty yards away, he couldn't see the face of the man talking with Fratiani. Nor could he hear what they were saying.

Then Fratiani passed the man an envelope, said something in more strident tones and climbed back in his Jeep.

To avoid being spotted, T-Rex dropped low behind a tree and waited for the Jeep to pass before he dared glance around the tree. The man Fratiani had been talking with had disappeared, but the vehicle in the trees pulled out. It had a smashed right fender.

T-Rex recognized the truck as the one Clay Ellis had driven the previous day when he'd accosted Sierra at the community center.

What was Ellis doing talking to a land broker on a deserted road in the hills of Wyoming?

Ellis drove away, bumping past him on the rutted road.

As soon as Ellis was out of sight, T-Rex hurried back the way he'd come, using the road. Once he reached the highway, he paused long enough for Ellis's vehicle to disappear out of sight. Then he hurried across the highway, climbed into his truck and followed Ellis into Grizzly Pass.

When he came within cell tower range, he placed a call to Hack. "Check out Clay Ellis's bank accounts. I just saw him have a secret rendezvous with Leo Fratiani on a deserted road three miles outside of Grizzly Pass."

"On it," Hack said. "Where are you now?"

"Back in Grizzly Pass."

"Got word from Major Bailey he'll land in twenty minutes at the fairgrounds."

"That's sooner than expected," T-Rex said. "Did you notify Garner?"

"Couldn't get him. He's probably out of cell phone range by now. Garner didn't expect the pilot to get here at this time. He got away earlier than he thought he would. Will you be able to meet him at the fairgrounds when he lands?"

"I will," T-Rex affirmed. "In the meantime, I'm following Ellis."

"Right. I'll notify Garner when he gets back in cell phone range of the change of plans with Bailey."

"Until I hear differently, I'll go up with Bailey," T-Rex said. He caught sight of Ellis's truck at the far end of Main Street.

Ellis turned at the road leading to the community center.

Great.

Sierra didn't need Ellis disturbing her when she was around the children. Hell, she didn't need the man disturbing her at all.

T-Rex couldn't leave with the helicopter pilot when Sierra might be in danger, especially when her ex-husband could be up to his earlobes in nefarious dealings with a broker from California. Hurrying toward the community center, T-Rex formed a plan. He placed a call to the Mother's Day Out office.

Brenda Larson answered. "Grizzly Pass Mother's Day Out, how may I help you?"

"Miss Larson, this is Rex Trainor. We met yesterday evening."

"I remember. You're the big, tough-looking guy who scared off Sierra's low-life ex."

"Right. I need your assistance."

ONCE AGAIN, SIERRA was outside on the playground with the toddlers when Clay pulled into the parking lot. As quickly as she could, she gathered the children and herded them toward the community center before they saw Clay with all of his bad attitude and demands. She didn't need to traumatize the little ones two days straight. If Clay continued to harass her, she'd have to quit her job with the children. She couldn't risk one of them getting hurt physically or emotionally by Clay's bad temper.

Sierra had begun to wonder if she'd have to move out of Grizzly Pass to get away from Clay. She had friends here, but no family left. She had more reason to leave than stay. She didn't know what was keeping her in the small town where job opportunities were almost nonexistent.

She almost had the children to the door when Clay stepped out of his truck and shouted, "We're not through, you know."

Sierra didn't respond. Instead, she placed a hand on the child at the rear of the line and urged him forward. "Everyone inside for snack time."

"You shouldn't have hit me with the stun gun," Clay called out. He pulled a metal bar out of the back of his truck and slapped it into his palm.

Sierra's pulse raced. She could visualize it now. Having protected herself using the stun gun had done like she'd said it would. It had only made him madder and more determined to have his way. To top that off, he'd want retribution for the pain and humiliation. He'd take it out on her. If he got close enough to hit her with that bar.

Sierra had no intention of letting him ever lay another finger or anything else on her. But her stun gun was in her purse, hanging on a hook out of reach of little hands, inside the office. And she'd have to get up close to him in order to use it on him. "Get inside, now," she said to the children, her voice brooking no argument.

The toddlers all looked toward the man advancing on them. Some of them cried out, others dashed for the door and tried without any luck to pull on the handle.

Sierra pushed her way through them and grabbed the door handle.

Clay was halfway across the yard before another truck pulled into the parking lot, hopped over the curb and came to a skidding halt in front of Clay, almost hitting the man.

Her heart pounding, Sierra could have cheered when T-Rex dropped down out of the truck.

"Ellis, you're breaking the law," T-Rex said in a cool, even tone.

"The only thing I'll be breaking is you." Clay spun and went after T-Rex.

"Watch out!" Sierra yelled. "He has a steel pipe."

"Get the kids inside." T-Rex waved her toward the building. "I've got this."

Torn between helping T-Rex, who was no match against Clay armed with the pipe, Sierra had no choice but to get the children inside. She jerked open the door and ordered, "Go!"

Most of the toddlers ran inside, but a few clustered around her legs and kept her from moving forward. Eloisa sobbed, her arms wrapped tightly around Sierra's right leg. Marcus, a two-year-old boy, had a hold of the other leg, and a third child stood in front of her, blocking her path, bawling at the top of his lungs.

"Sweet heaven!" Sierra lifted Eloisa into her arms and grabbed Marcus's hand.

Brenda appeared just in time and snatched up the little one blocking the door. "Bring them into the gym."

Sierra followed Brenda inside. Once she had the toddlers in the gymnasium, she let go of Marcus's hand and peeled Eloisa's arms from around her neck.

"I'll take her." Brenda snatched the redheaded child from Sierra.

"I have to go back out and see what I can do to help."

"I called the sheriff. They are sending a unit."

Sierra didn't wait to respond to her coworker. She ran back out into the yard.

Clay and T-Rex were circling each other.

As soon as Sierra stepped through the door, Clay lunged for T-Rex.

Sierra smothered a scream and stood transfixed as T-Rex caught Clay's wrist and directed it downward, away from his body. The pipe hit the ground hard without harming T-Rex.

T-Rex gave the man a shove from behind, sending him stumbling forward. He righted himself, spun and swung again.

Ducking, T-Rex barely missed being hit in the head.

Clay had swung with so much force, when he whiffed air, he turned all the way around.

T-Rex planted a boot in the man's backside and shoved hard.

Clay went down, thrust the steel pipe out of his way as he fell and landed on his hands and knees. He scrambled to his feet and would have grabbed the pipe, but T-Rex beat him to it, kicking it well out of Clay's reach.

"You need to leave," T-Rex said.

Clay snarled and brushed the dirt from his hands. "I'll leave when Sierra comes with me."

"She's not going anywhere with you," T-Rex said. "She's with me now."

Sierra shook her head. "I don't want anyone hurt. Maybe I should go with him." She crossed the yard to where the two men stood.

"Now you're thinking," Clay said. "Come with me and no one else will get hurt."

"You mean, *you* won't get hurt." T-Rex slipped an arm around Sierra's waist. "She's not with you anymore. Leave her alone."

"She's mine until I tell her she's not anymore."

"Get over yourself, Ellis," T-Rex said, his voice low and threatening. "She doesn't love you."

"Sierra?" Clay stared at her through narrowed eyes.

"I don't think I ever loved you." Sierra swallowed hard and squared her shoulders, remembering every bit of the abuse she'd taken from the man who'd promised to love, honor and cherish her. The man had killed all of her illusions about what a marriage should be. "The first time you hit me, I knew I could never love you, Clay. Leave me alone."

Clay turned his glare on T-Rex. "You did this. She wouldn't have turned against me if you hadn't gotten in the way."

"I divorced you months ago," Sierra said. "Before Mr. Trainor was even in the picture."

T-Rex nodded. "Face it, Ellis, it's over. Learn to live with it."

A sheriff's vehicle pulled into the drive.

Clay shot one last, piercing glare at T-Rex. "It's not over until I say it's over." Then he climbed into his truck and drove past the sheriff's SUV without stopping or slowing down.

One of the sheriff's deputies got out. "Everything all right here?"

"It is now," Sierra said, leaning into the warmth and strength of T-Rex.

"Want me to go after Ellis?" the deputy asked.

T-Rex glanced down at Sierra, his brow raised.

Sierra nodded. "He needs to learn he can't treat me this way."

The deputy nodded. "I'll let the sheriff know. And let me know if I can help. I'm only a 911 call away." With that parting comment, he turned his vehicle around and left.

Sierra looked up into T-Rex's eyes. "Thank you for being here."

"My pleasure," he said, without removing his arm from around her.

She didn't want to move out of his embrace, but she had a job to do. "I guess I'd better get back to the children."

"I have an alternative proposal," T-Rex said.

Sierra's heart leaped. "A what?"

"An alternative to going back to work. I need someone to help me with a project I'm working on, but it requires that you come with me right now." He stared at her, his gaze unblinking, almost as if he were willing her to say yes.

When T-Rex looked at her with that level of intensity in his eyes, Sierra found him very hard to resist. "I can't leave," she said. "I'm working."

"No worries," Brenda called out from the doorway, still carrying Eloisa. "Take the rest of the day off. The babies are all down for a nap, and the toddlers are happy playing. I can handle them. Besides, there aren't that many of them, it being Friday and all."

"Are you sure?" Sierra frowned. "I can't leave you to handle all of them."

"I did it before we hired you. I can do it again." Brenda winked. "How many chances do you get to have a hunky man ask you to help him?" Brenda leaned forward and whispered in her ear, "If you don't take him up on it, I'll take your place."

A little stab of jealousy hit Sierra in the gut. She glanced toward T-Rex, a thrill of anticipation making her shiver from top to toe.

"You know you want to," Brenda whispered. "Besides, if you stay here, Clay may come back." She glanced at the children, just beginning to calm down after the second confrontation in as many days they'd had to witness.

A heavy weight of guilt settled in the pit of Sierra's gut. "I can't let this happen to the kids."

Brenda bit her bottom lip. "You didn't let it happen. Clay is responsible."

"Yes, but if I wasn't his ex, he wouldn't be coming to the community center, frightening the babies."

Sierra shook her head. "I'm sorry, but I'm going to have to quit until he settles down."

Brenda grabbed her arm. "No. You can't quit on me. The children love you."

"Yes, but I can't risk it. Clay might get more violent and hurt one of them. It's bad enough he's scaring them. The parents aren't going to put up with it for long. Heck, they're already telling me their children are having nightmares." Sierra straightened her shoulders. "No. I have to do this. I thought I could stay in Grizzly Pass, but I'm beginning to see it's just not going to work. Clay will never leave me alone."

Brenda frowned. "Why is he bothering you now? It's been months since your divorce. You'd think he would be over it and moving on."

"Sierra." T-Rex stepped up to the two women. "I have to go. Will you come with me? Or are you staying here?" He held out his hand.

Sierra stared at his hand as if it would lead her into an alternate universe, a place she'd never considered. Despite the fear of the unknown, she reached out her hand and took his. "I guess I'm going with you."

Brenda tightened her hold on her arm. "Just remember, you're loved and wanted back here. But if you find something better, I'll understand. Oh, and you can't get out of our tour tomorrow. I need you when we take the moms and kiddos to Yellowstone for our ranger-led activity."

Sierra hugged her friend. "Don't worry. I'll be here, bright and early."

Brenda's gaze shifted to T-Rex, and she smiled. "Take care of my friend."

T-Rex nodded. "I will." He tightened his hold on her hand and led her out of the community center. "What was that all about?"

Sierra sighed. "I can't work there anymore."

"Did she fire you?"

"No. I quit. As long as Clay continues to harass me, I can't be around the children." She glanced back at the community center. "I'll miss them."

"You should have had the deputy take him in."

"He'd just be out in a few days and even more annoying. He might harm one of those babies. I know if they were my children I wouldn't want me to be their caregiver. Not as long as Clay keeps coming around."

T-Rex nodded. "I get it."

"Even though we're divorced, he's still managing to run my life."

As the handsome marine held the door for her, Sierra climbed into his truck.

He rounded the vehicle and slid in behind the steering wheel.

"Enough of my troubles." Sierra forced a smile to her face. "What is it I'm going to help you with?"

"I need another pair of eyes."

"Another pair of eyes?"

"I'm going up in a helicopter looking for anything out of the ordinary in the hills."

She leaned forward, her heartbeat skittering against her ribs. "We're going up in a helicopter? I've never been in a helicopter."

"Then this will be a first for you. Are you up for the task?" He started the engine but waited for her response.

"Yes!" She laughed out loud, her entire body shaking with excitement. "When?"

He glanced at his watch. "In five minutes, if I can get to the fairgrounds by then."

Chapter Nine

While they'd waited for clearance for a civilian to go along for the ride in the UH-60 Black Hawk helicopter, T-Rex and the pilot, Major Bailey, and copilot, Lieutenant Strohm, studied several contour maps and the route of the oil pipeline. Some of the larger abandoned gold-rush-era mines were noted on the map, their locations clearly marked.

T-Rex waited, on edge, praying Major Bailey's commander would allow Sierra to join the search. He'd told the major she was part of Homeland Security's platform in Grizzly Pass. It wasn't exactly the truth, but T-Rex wouldn't have gone without Sierra. Not when Ellis would likely stalk her and possibly force her to go with him and hold her hostage who knew where and for how long.

Ellis needed someone to take him out behind a barn and beat some sense into him. Even then, T-Rex doubted the man would listen.

When the approval came through, T-Rex released the breath he'd been holding. He realized he'd be a whole lot more effective knowing Sierra was right beside him and not at the mercy of her abusive ex-husband.

Once off the ground, T-Rex stopped thinking about Ellis long enough to look out the side of the aircraft.

Major Bailey and his copilot were using the time in the chopper to log flight and training time. By flying through the hills, they'd get some much-needed nap-of-the-earth flying in. At the same time, they'd be flying close enough to the ground that T-Rex and Sierra could look for any signs of extensive road use, vehicles out on old logging or mining trails or people back in the hills where there normally wouldn't be any, especially when not in hunting season.

Sierra sat in the seat beside him, her eyes wide and bright, her hands gripping the safety harness strapped around her lap and shoulders. She looked at once terrified and excited.

T-Rex smiled. The woman might have been in an abusive situation, but she had a lot of gumption and a sense of adventure. She'd do all right once she got far enough from Ellis's influence.

What bothered T-Rex most was the fact he wouldn't be there to run interference against her ex-husband. He'd be out of Grizzly Pass just as soon as they fixed what was wrong in the area.

He leaned toward the open doorway and stared down as the helicopter neared the hills. Based on the map T-Rex had brought along with him depicting the route of the oil pipeline, they were getting close to one of the first points the pipeline inspectors would have checked. It was on the edge of the Beartooth Mountains in a grassy meadow. Nothing appeared out of the ordinary. The dirt road leading up to it was slightly overgrown with grass and bramble.

Flying a direct path, they entered a valley between two hills. The helicopter pilot followed the pipeline to the area where a pipeline inspector had been shot and killed since the military team had arrived in Grizzly Pass. Hovering between the hills, the pilot lowered the aircraft to fifteen feet above the valley floor.

The ground around the pipeline appeared somewhat disturbed. The rotor wash kicked up loose dirt, whipping it around, making it hard to see what was below.

T-Rex didn't know what he expected to find, but the area had seen one death and an attempt by someone to plant dynamite at the same point. Those facts alone gave them good reason to check it out again, despite the full investigation the state crime lab had conducted.

Nothing looked out of the ordinary on the ground so T-Rex redirected his attention to the hillsides rising up on either side of the valley.

"Anything?" he said into his headset.

"Nothing here," the pilot responded.

"Nothing," the copilot affirmed.

"I'm not sure what I'm looking for, but I don't see anything moving, or anything that appears out of place," Sierra said.

"Let's move on toward the border of the Stone Oak Ranch and the National Park," the pilot said.

T-Rex nodded. "Roger."

The pilot guided the aircraft upward and over the tops of several ridges.

From his bird's-eye view, T-Rex could see into the valleys. The aircraft moved slowly, giving them plenty of time to scour the hillsides looking for caves, mine shafts and roads leading into and out of the hills.

As they neared the hills near Stone Oak Ranch where Olivia Dawson's father had been murdered by Don Sweeney, T-Rex could see a lot more shadows against the sides of the hills, indicating overhangs and caves.

T-Rex leaned against his harness, trying to look out over the skids of the chopper. "Can you get closer to the caves?"

In response, Major Bailey tipped the helicopter and angled it nearer the caves, where he hovered in between two ridges.

"What's that?" Sierra said. "Are those vehicles?"

T-Rex leaned toward her and followed her arm to where she pointed at the side of the hills.

A truck was backed up to a cave. A shadow detached from the darkness of the cave, and a man dressed in camouflage stared up at the helicopter. He looked back to the cave and appeared to be shouting, not that they could hear him over the roar of the rotors.

A moment later, another man joined him, carrying a short tube. He extended it to double its length, settled it on his shoulder and aimed it at the helicopter.

"Rocket launcher! Get out of here!" T-Rex cried.

The pilot pulled back on the controls and goosed the throttle, sending them climbing higher, out of the valley.

"Brace yourself!" T-Rex reached over, grabbed Sierra's hand and squeezed it.

Something slammed into the back of the helicopter, sending it spinning around to the right.

"We're hit," the copilot shouted into the headset.

The pilot struggled with the controls, steadied the craft and pulled the nose upward as it rushed toward the side of a cliff.

T-Rex couldn't look away from the bare rock cliff they were rushing toward, as if he was mesmerized by his forthcoming death.

At the last moment, the chopper lifted up, skimming over the top of the ridge, the skids scraping against the hard surface.

Major Bailey looked around. "We have to find a place to put this baby down."

T-Rex looked around at the rugged terrain.

"It needs to be wide enough to allow for a sloppy landing."

"South. Go south toward Stone Oak Ranch."

"Those men who shot at us are moving," Sierra said, leaning toward the open door. "They're on ATVs."

"They're following us," the copilot confirmed.

"Can you get us farther away before you land?" T-Rex asked.

The craft shuddered and dipped. Major Bailey held on to the controls with both hands, his body straining. "We'll be lucky to land in one piece."

"Over there. On that knoll." The copilot pointed to a barren hilltop with a fence stretching across one side and angling downward into a valley.

"That's on Stone Oak Ranch," T-Rex said. "We could get help from the owner, Olivia Dawson.

"It will take at least an hour to hike down to her," T-Rex said. "It took thirty minutes to get to that point on four-wheelers from her ranch house."

"Those men on the ATVs might catch up to us." Sierra twisted in her seat, staring at the ground below.

As the pilot concentrated on flying the Black Hawk to the open knoll, the copilot put out a mayday call.

Twenty yards from the projected landing zone, the chopper sputtered, the rotor slowed and the descent came quicker than expected.

"It's going to be a bumpy landing," the pilot said.

T-Rex held tighter to Sierra's hand and gave her a tight smile. "We've got this."

No sooner had he said the words, the helicopter slammed into the ground and skidded across the knoll, coming to a stop near the other end, at the edge of a sheer one-hundred-foot drop.

Everyone remained seated until the rotors stopped moving and the pilot turned off the engine.

Then the pilot unbuckled his harness and turned in his seat to look at each person in the craft. "Everyone all right?"

The copilot nodded.

"I'm okay," T-Rex said.

Sierra grinned. "That was amazing."

Her infectious smile made T-Rex smile, as well. "Good job, Major Bailey."

"Thanks, but it would be even better if we hadn't been hit in the first place." He flung aside his harness and got out of the helicopter, stepping up to the edge of the cliff they'd almost gone over.

T-Rex helped Sierra out of her harness, slid out of his seat and held open his arms for her.

She let him help her out of the craft and onto her feet. Her glance followed the pilot standing a few feet away, looking down. "That was close." Sierra leaned into T-Rex.

He wrapped his arm around her waist and pulled her tightly against him. "Yes, it was." Too close.

The whine of small engines reminded him the men who'd lobbed a rocket at them were on their way through the hills to find them.

"What do you want to bet they will be armed?" the copilot said.

T-Rex nodded. "We need to get moving if we want to stay a reasonable distance ahead."

"I can't leave the aircraft here." Major Bailey backed away from the cliff's edge and joined them. "There's no telling what they'll do to it."

"The army can afford to lose a chopper. They can't afford to lose a trained pilot," T-Rex said.

The copilot nodded. "He's right. Without weapons to defend ourselves, we'd be sitting ducks."

"Were you able to contact the sheriff?" Sierra asked.

"We put out a mayday call but didn't get a response, so we have no idea if the call was heard." The copilot slipped his headset back on and sat back in his seat, fiddling with the radio dial on the control panel.

T-Rex glanced at his cell phone. No signal.

A moment later, the copilot got out of the helicopter, tossed his headset onto the seat and shook his head. "The radio is dead."

"Then we're on our own." T-Rex ran toward the other side of the hill and glanced down into a valley. Five men on four-wheelers were racing along a trail, headed their way.

T-Rex turned and almost ran into Sierra. "We have to get out of here." He took her hand and hurried back to the pilot and copilot. "We only have a few minutes before five aggressors top this hill. We need to get down off of here and to somewhere we can take advantage of cover and concealment."

"We don't want them to have the opportunity to shoot at us on the way down, so we'd better hustle." The pilot glanced around. "Are you familiar with the area? Do you know which way to the Dawson woman's ranch house?"

"Follow me." T-Rex led the way down from the hill, taking a trail barely wide enough for a four-wheeler. He'd been up there a couple of days earlier when he and the team had inspected the hill and the area around it, searching for a similar group of five marauders who'd given chase to Hawkeye and Olivia.

They had not been successful at locating the area from which they'd come. Numerous trails wound their way through the hills and mountains, weaving through the silent remains of a once-busy mining community back in the late 1800s. They'd spent a couple of days taking different trails, but they hadn't been able to find the men.

If they didn't get down to an area that provided cover and concealment soon, the attackers on four-wheelers would find them and pick them off, one-by-one. They hadn't hesitated in firing a rocket at a government helicopter, and they wouldn't balk at shooting four people.

They half walked and half ran down the trail, slipping on loose gravel. T-Rex worried Sierra would trip and fall over the edge. He held her hand, refusing to let her tumble to her death. Not on his watch.

As they neared the floor of a narrow valley, T-Rex paused and glanced up at the hill they'd just vacated.

The pilot and copilot had stopped to catch their breath. Each was bent over, hands on their knees. They'd pushed hard to get this far, and it hadn't been easy with the loose gravel and treacherous terrain.

T-Rex could hear the roar of the four-wheeler engines. He spun and grabbed Sierra's hand. She was winded and her cheeks were bright pink, but she gave him a brief smile.

"Are you all right?" T-Rex asked.

She nodded, glancing up at the hill they'd come down. Then she squared her shoulders. "Let's move. They're almost on us."

The engine noise grew louder as T-Rex led them toward a jumble of boulders lying at the base of an enormous overhang. If they could make it there, they'd have concealment and cover. It also might leave them trapped and outnumbered five to four. With no weapons but their minds, they'd have to come up with a plan. Either they would lay low and pray the attackers would give up and move on, or they'd have to fight back, barehanded.

Ten yards from the first boulder big enough to offer any kind of protection, the crack of gunfire echoed off the hillsides.

Dirt shot up next to T-Rex's feet. "Run!" he yelled, pushing Sierra in front of him. She picked up the pace, her feet flying over the rocks and gravel.

Another crack sounded, and the copilot fell to his knees.

"Damn. He got my leg." He tried to get up but fell back to the ground.

Sierra slowed and started to turn back.

"Don't stop. Keep moving," T-Rex ordered.

"But—" She hesitated. A bullet hit the ground beside her.

"Just go!" His pulse racing and unable to block the bullets from hitting Sierra, T-Rex flung the copilot over his shoulder and ran as fast as he could, weighted down by the man.

"Let me help," the pilot offered.

"Help by getting Sierra to a safe place."

The pilot nodded and ran to catch up to Sierra.

More gunfire echoed off the rock walls of the valley.

Sierra reached the boulder first and ducked behind, followed by the pilot. A few steps behind them, T-Rex made it to the boulder and dropped the man on the ground.

"How bad is it?" T-Rex asked.

The copilot gritted his teeth. "I think I can get around, but I might need a little help."

T-Rex nodded to the pilot. "You stand watch. Let me know how close they get."

Major Bailey nodded and eased his head around the opposite side of the boulder for a quick peek, ducking back as gunfire rang out. "They're standing at the top of the hill, their weapons aimed in our direction."

T-Rex pulled his knife from the scabbard strapped to his belt and tore the leg of the copilot's jumpsuit. He handed the fabric to Sierra. "I need long strips."

She quickly ripped the pant leg into four-inch-wide strips, wadded up one into a thick pad and pressed it to the man's wound. As she held the pad, T-Rex made quick work of wrapping the other strip around the copilot's leg. He tied a knot over the pad and helped the man to his feet.

"Think you and Sierra can make your way to the back of this stand of rocks?"

The copilot nodded.

Sierra draped the man's arm over her shoulder and wrapped one of hers around his waist. "We'll manage. But what about you two?"

"They're coming down," the major said.

"That gives us seconds to take positions and get ready to do what we can to protect ourselves." T-Rex shot a glance at Sierra. "Your job is to get Lieutenant Strohm as far back as possible and hide behind some really big rocks. If this turns into a shooting match, I don't want you two catching stray bullets."

She didn't move, her lips thinning into a straight line. "But what about you?"

"I can take care of myself." He nodded toward Major Bailey. "And I have backup."

Her brows dipped. "And no weapons."

"Can't help that," he said. "But you're wasting valuable time and putting the lieutenant in danger. Move!"

She jumped and started weaving through the huge boulders that had fallen from the side of the cliff, helping the copilot along as best she could.

Once Sierra was out of sight, T-Rex shot a glance at the major. "Sir, are you ready to play a game of cat and mouse?"

The pilot pulled a knife from the strap around his calf and nodded. "Let's do this."

T-Rex melted back behind the surrounding boulders and hunkered low. He circled back toward the trail where the riders were coming from and waited. They arrived in a swift procession, slowing as they reached the maze of boulders. Each man wore a black helmet and carried his rifle either resting in a plastic gun boot attached to the ATV or slung over his shoulder within easy reach.

After four of the five riders passed by him, T-Rex made his move. The last four-wheeler came abreast of where T-Rex was hiding. T-Rex leaped out, grabbed the man from the back of the ATV and dragged him behind the boulder, his neck in a headlock. Without the man on the vehicle, the ATV rolled to a standstill.

While the others were just coming to a halt, firing their weapons into the air, T-Rex tightened his hold around the man's neck, cutting off his air until he passed out.

T-Rex pulled the AR-15 rifle from over the man's shoulder and dragged the attacker's shirt off and down his arms, quickly twisting it into a knot around his wrists behind his back. It might not hold him long, but it had to be enough for the moment.

T-Rex grabbed the rifle and checked the thirty-round magazine. Then he eased up to the side of one of the boulders and opened fire, shooting at the ground near their tires, not giving them a chance to dismount.

The riders yelped, hit their throttles and raced around a bend in the trail and out of sight.

"Major, we have maybe a minute before they return on foot," T-Rex called out.

The major hurried toward him. "How the heck did you get that?"

"I borrowed it from the young man on the ground over there." He pointed to the man he'd jumped.

The attacker was starting to wake up. Still wearing the black helmet, he shook his head and cursed, struggling to free himself from the bonds of his shirt.

"The others will be back," T-Rex said, "but will probably sneak in. We need to make sure they don't get to Sierra and Strohm."

"There are only the two of us. How are we going to keep four men at bay?" Bailey asked.

"We have to keep our eyes open and be smarter than they are." T-Rex led the way through the boulders to the far end past which the riders had driven in their hurry to get away from the flying bullets.

T-Rex handed the AR-15 to the pilot and positioned him behind a large cluster of boulders. "If they come your way, don't wait for them to shoot before pulling the trigger. I guarantee they won't be as nice to you."

The major nodded and crawled down in between the rocks. "What about you?"

"I'll find them before they find me." He held his

knife in his hand and slipped in between the standing boulders, working his way through them to the point at which he anticipated the four men to breach the rugged array of rocks and giant fallen portions of the cliff. He paused, watching the trails leading back to him and the slope of the hillside.

The sun had made progress toward the jagged edges of the ridgelines towering on either side of the narrow valley. Before long it would be dark. The riders could be waiting for dusk to make their moves. Or not. At dusk, they would all be at a disadvantage.

T-Rex stood ready, straining his ears for even the slightest of sounds.

Chapter Ten

Sierra half walked, half carried Lieutenant Strohm deeper into the jumble of giant boulders, picking her way over the smaller rocks and around the larger ones. The sound of ATV engines moved closer until they had to be on the trail where she'd left T-Rex and Major Bailey. She moved as fast as she could to get Strohm out of harm's way.

Finally, the injured man ground to a halt. Leaning heavily on her, he whispered, "I can't…keep going."

Her back aching from the strain, Sierra looked around, searching for a place to hide and praying their attackers wouldn't see her or the lieutenant before they found one. "You can't stop out in the open. We need to get you hidden."

He agreed. Between the two of them, they got him wedged behind a pile of big rocks, completely out of sight to anyone passing by.

Moments later, gunfire echoed off the rock walls, and Sierra ducked low next to Strohm. Her heart pounded hard against her ribs as she knelt behind the boulders, wondering whether T-Rex and the major had been hit.

Then she heard the sound of engines moving away. Once the noise had faded, she counted to ten and slowly straightened.

The lieutenant grabbed for her. "What are you doing?"

"I have to see if they were hit. They could be injured and need help." She peeled the lieutenant's hand from her arm. "Will you be all right?"

"I'll be fine, but I'm worried about you," he said. "Your marine would kick my butt if I let anything happen to you."

He wasn't her marine, and the copilot was in no shape to protect her, but now wasn't the time for Sierra to correct him. She had to find T-Rex.

Easing her way back toward the trail, she pushed to the north, hoping to swing around and come from behind where she'd heard the ATVs stop. She grabbed a rock the size of her hand. It wasn't much of a weapon, but it was all she had in case someone attacked her or T-Rex.

As she neared the trail, she hid behind a boulder and studied the path beyond. It was empty. No one stood nearby or lay on the ground.

Then she heard someone grunting, the sound of gravel being disturbed and muttered curses.

Sierra eased back behind the larger boulders and followed the noise.

She had almost reached the source of the sound when she noticed a black helmet on the ground and a torn shirt. As she stepped toward them, she caught a flash of movement out of the corner of her eye. Before she had time to move or scream, a hand clamped over her mouth and an arm wrapped around her belly, trapping one of her arms to her side.

Heart pounding, she tried to remain calm. Whoever had her was bare-armed and smelled of smoke and body odor.

"You're coming with me," he whispered.

The hell she was. She flung her free hand with the rock up behind her, crashing it into the man's head.

He cursed, and for a brief moment, his hold on her loosened.

Sierra broke free, spun and kneed him in the groin.

He went down, his face turning a sick shade of green.

Her adrenaline still firing through her veins, she kicked him in the chin, sending him flying backward to land on the ground.

Sierra stood with her rock in her hand, breathing hard, ready for anything the punk might try next.

When he didn't move, she inched toward him.

The man was out cold.

Quickly, before he came to, she grabbed the abandoned shirt, ripped it into strips, rolled him over and tied his wrists securely. Then she tied his ankles. The jerk wasn't going to come after her or anyone else in her party, if she could help it. Wadding up the last piece of fabric, she stuffed it into his mouth.

Armed with her rock, she slipped back among the boulders, determined to find T-Rex and the pilot. What had happened to them?

It would be night soon, which would make it even more difficult to find them if they were injured.

She glanced up at the rocky hillside ahead of her and noticed a shadowy figure slipping down between the trees and rocks.

Was it another member of the gang of ATV riders who'd attacked their helicopter? She stood still, watching as the man made it to the edge of the boulder field carrying what appeared to be a military-grade rifle.

Where were T-Rex and the pilot?

The sun ducked behind the hills above them, casting the landscape into a deep, gray shadow. With adrenaline wearing off and no sun to warm the air around her, Sierra shivered.

Another shadowy figure followed the first, edging his way down the slope. Then another. That was three, plus the one she'd tied up made four. Where was number five?

Sierra stayed put, afraid to move and draw attention to herself. She had yet to locate T-Rex. Most likely he was hiding among the boulders, waiting for his chance to take down the attackers, one at a time. He wasn't injured or dead. Sierra refused to believe the combat veteran would have exposed himself to the gunfire.

Straining to hear footsteps or voices, she pressed herself back into a crevice and waited.

T-Rex HEARD SOUNDS from both in front of him and to the rear of where he stood. He was only mildly reassured by the fact that the man he'd knocked out behind him was unarmed. The men scurrying down the hill toward him still carried their AR-15s. He almost wished he hadn't given the major the rifle. If he had it now, he could have picked off the attackers as they worked their way down the slope.

Armed with only a knife, T-Rex's four-to-one odds were pretty lousy. He moved silently through the boulder field, easing from shadow to shadow until he was close to where the men would enter the rock-strewn area. His best chance was to get them one at a time. That plan would work only if the ATV riders split up.

He waited as the first man entered the field several yards away from him.

T-Rex backtracked and circled a huge boulder, praying he'd correctly anticipated the man's path. With his knife in hand, he listened.

The rattle of gravel alerted him to his quarry on the other side of the boulder. When the man in black stepped into view, he didn't see what hit him.

Neither did T-Rex.

He hadn't even touched the man, when he heard a loud thud and the guy dropped to the ground with a grunt and lay still.

Stunned, T-Rex glanced up to find Sierra standing with a big rock in her hand, her eyes wide, her breathing coming in ragged gasps.

T-Rex must have moved because Sierra's gaze shot from the man on the ground to him. She stifled a squeal and backed up several steps before she realized it was him.

A soft curse and the shuffle of gravel warned T-Rex others were coming. He shoved Sierra behind him. Then he took the man's arms and dragged him backward, hiding him among the rocks. He removed a knife from the man's belt and took his rifle.

The crack of gunfire filled the air nearby.

T-Rex grabbed Sierra and rolled her to the ground, throwing his body over hers. The shooting continued in spurts, very near to where they lay hidden behind the boulder.

At one pause in the firing, he thought he heard the sound of engines in the distance.

More shots rang out, and then another pause ensued. A deep voice shouted, "Vehicles coming! Get out! Now!"

The man Sierra had knocked out stirred, sat up and looked around.

"Move! Move! Move!" the same guy shouted, and more shots were fired in rapid succession from the semi-automatic weapons.

T-Rex pointed his weapon at the man sitting up and touched a finger to his lips.

The man took one look at T-Rex, rolled to his side and scurried behind a big rock.

"Don't let him get away!" Sierra urged, in a quiet, yet insistent voice.

"I'm not leaving you," T-Rex whispered.

"Then shoot him," she said.

"If I do, I'll give away our position."

"But he's getting away." She struggled beneath him.

T-Rex refused to let her up. "I'd rather he got away than you get killed."

When she tried again to get up, he touched a finger to her lips. "Shh."

She went still, her eyes wide, her chest rising and falling beneath his.

Heat filled him and raced to his groin. Sierra's soft curves beneath him and the adrenaline of the chase rushing through his blood had him hard in seconds. But now was not the time to have sensual thoughts about the woman he covered with his body.

The sound of feet moving through gravel came to them from so close, it had to be on the other side of the boulder.

T-Rex quietly rolled off Sierra and sat up with the AR-15 rifle in his hands. If the attackers found them, T-Rex would empty the magazine, protecting Sierra.

Major Bailey tiptoed into the gap between the rocks, the rifle T-Rex had given him nestled against his shoulder, his hand on the trigger. He turned, aiming the weapon at T-Rex.

T-Rex held up his free hand and whispered, "Don't shoot."

The man's shoulders relaxed. "Oh, thank God. For a moment, I thought you were one of them." He jerked his head toward the trail. "There are more ATVs coming up the trail from the south. The guys who were shooting at us scattered into the hills."

T-Rex climbed to his feet, reached down to give Sierra a hand up and pulled her into the crook of his arm. "We need to be ready in case they aren't any friendlier than the others."

The major glanced at Sierra. "Where's Strohm?"

"I have him tucked away pretty nicely. But I better

find him before it gets too dark to see." She started to step away from T-Rex.

He didn't let go of his hold around her. "We'll find him when we know for sure the ATV riders are gone and the new ones headed this way aren't here to harm us."

Sierra nodded.

The three of them eased up to the edge of the trail.

T-Rex insisted Sierra stay farther behind. He and the major aimed their weapons at the approaching vehicles.

Four ATVs rolled into sight.

T-Rex waited until he recognized the jacket of the man in front of the pack. It was the same jacket, with the Department of Homeland security emblem on it, Kevin Garner had worn that morning.

T-Rex lowered his weapon, raised a hand and stepped out of the shadows.

Garner leaped down from his four-wheeler and pulled off his helmet. "Holy hell, T-Rex. What happened?"

T-Rex glanced at the hillside where their attackers had run to. "You might want to step into the shadows. Up until a few minutes ago, we were under fire."

Garner's brows rose, and he joined T-Rex, the major and Sierra near the stand of boulders. He waved to the others, who all dismounted and joined them, removing their helmets.

Hawkeye, Ghost and Caveman crowded close.

"We got the mayday from the sheriff's office that your aircraft had been hit and was crash-landing in the hills," Garner said.

"Dude, you had us all worried," Hawkeye said.

"*You* were worried?" T-Rex chuckled. "You should have been on the helicopter." He clapped a hand on Major Bailey's shoulders. "This man did an incredible job landing the chopper." He shoved his AR-15 at Ghost. "But right now, we have an injured copilot we need to get to medical attention. Can you cover us?"

Ghost hefted the weapon in his hands, released the magazine, inspected it and slipped it back in. "Gotcha covered."

T-Rex turned to Sierra. "Think you can find him?"

HER HEART STILL racing and her body on fire from the pressure of T-Rex's pressed against it earlier, Sierra nodded and took off through the maze. She stopped a couple of times and studied the paths. Everything looked a bit different in the dusky light, but she recognized the landscape and moved on. Finally, she came to what would appear to the others to be nothing more than a pile of big rocks.

Sierra ducked between them and found the copilot, lying on the ground. "Hey, Lieutenant, I told you I'd be back."

"I swear you're an angel," he said, his voice strained, the pain making his mouth tight. His face was pale, and he struggled to stand.

"We could use a hand," Sierra called out, moving quickly to slip her arm around the man.

T-Rex stepped into the gap and looped one of the lieutenant's arms over his shoulder.

"Let me." Caveman entered the hiding place and

motioned for Sierra to move out so that he could get in and take Strohm's other side. They eased him out into the open.

Forming a two-man fireman's carry, T-Rex and Caveman transported the copilot to the trail.

After they settled the lieutenant on the ground, T-Rex straightened. "If he hasn't gotten away, we caught one of the guys who was with those who shot us down." He started toward the stand of rocks to the north end of the trail.

Sierra joined him. "He's not where he was before."

"No?" T-Rex frowned.

She shook her head. "But he's not far."

T-Rex's frown deepened. "And you know this because?"

She shrugged and gave him a twisted grin. "I have a mean arm when it comes to rocks."

"I've seen that arm in action." He chuckled. "It was pretty impressive."

They found the man where Sierra had left him bound and gagged.

"Are you sure you weren't a secret agent in a past life?" Garner asked.

She shook her head. "No, but I watch enough movies and television to know how to incapacitate the bad guy."

They pulled the gag from the man's mouth and dragged him out to the trail.

Now that she had time to study him, Sierra thought she recognized him. "Cody Rausch?"

The young man glared at her but refused to speak.

She shook her head and planted her hands on her

hips. "What will your father say when he finds out you've been shooting down government helicopters?"

He still didn't say anything, just continued to glare at Sierra.

"Fine. But you know the sheriff will be talking with you as soon as we get back to town."

Dusk had settled over the mountains, casting the group into a shadowy darkness.

A few minutes later, a rescue helicopter flew overhead, shining a bright spotlight down on them. The aircraft landed on the hillside above them, and the trained rescue team hurried down with a basket. They radioed back to the chopper to bring another.

Once they had the copilot and the bad guy in baskets, the rescue workers and the Safe Haven team carried the men back up the hill and loaded them into the helicopter. Major Bailey boarded the helicopter with his lieutenant.

Garner stood beside the helicopter to address his team. "I'm going with them to the hospital. I hope to be there when the sheriff interrogates Rausch. This might be the breakthrough we've been looking for. I trust you can get back to Grizzly Pass on your own?"

"We've got this," Ghost said.

Sierra wasn't as confident. Night had settled in. Thankfully, each of the ATVs had headlights, but the trails were treacherous in the daylight. They'd be downright deadly at night.

They waited while the helicopter took off, headed for the closest hospital, then the four men mounted the four-wheelers.

T-Rex tilted his head toward Sierra. "You can ride with me."

"I wasn't planning on riding with anyone else," she said, her words soft enough only T-Rex would hear. She slid on behind him and wrapped her arms around his waist. "I hope you know where you're going, because I don't."

He nodded. "I've been on this trail before. Though it was in the light of day at the time."

"We'll take it slow," Caveman said.

They left the boulder field. Caveman took the lead, T-Rex and Sierra behind him. Hawkeye and Ghost brought up the rear.

The night had turned cold, the temperature dropping close to freezing, even though it wasn't yet fall.

Sierra leaned close to T-Rex, absorbing as much warmth from his body as she could. By the time they reached the Stone Oak ranch house, she was shivering uncontrollably, her toes numb and her entire body exhausted.

Olivia Dawson met them at the gate and ushered them through, closing it behind them. "Come inside. I just happened to make a huge pot of beef stew. You look hungry and cold."

"Sounds like heaven," Sierra said, her teeth chattering. "Hi, Liv. Glad you're back in Grizzly Pass. I missed you." She hugged the rancher, glad to see the woman and the house ahead with the glow of lights welcoming them.

Sierra stumbled, her cold feet barely able to carry

her. She refused to give up now. Not when she was so close to a warm fire and food.

T-Rex came up behind her, scooped her into his arms and marched toward the house.

"I can walk," Sierra protested, though she didn't struggle. Being in T-Rex's arms meant she got to rest her body against his warmer one. She leaned her cheek against his chest and tucked her hands between them. "I don't think I've ever been quite that cold."

"We didn't go prepared for the possibilities."

She snorted. "Who would have guessed our helicopter would be shot down? Things like that don't happen in America."

His lips thinned and his brows descended. "Yeah, well, sometimes they do."

Caveman reached the door first and opened it for T-Rex and Sierra.

T-Rex entered and went straight for the living room, where he laid Sierra on a couch by a roaring fire and smothered her in throw blankets.

She laughed. "I think one will do."

"You might have hypothermia," he said. "You need to bring your body temperature back up." T-Rex tucked the edges of the blankets around and beneath her until she couldn't move her arms.

"Seriously. I feel like a mummy." She wiggled until she could get her hands and arms out. "I'm okay. Really." As if to belie her statement, she shivered violently. Her cheeks heated, and she shrugged. "At least I'm on my way to being okay."

When T-Rex dived for the edges of the blankets

again, Sierra touched his cheek. "I'm okay." She smiled up into his eyes. "Thank you."

He frowned and stood straight. "I shouldn't have brought you with me today. I got you involved where you shouldn't have been."

"I'm glad you took me. I've never flown in a helicopter."

"And I bet you've never crashed in one either." He tucked a strand of her hair behind her ear. "I hope like hell you never crash-land in one again."

"We have hot cocoa for anyone who wants some," Liv called out. She entered the living room swinging a sack of puffy white marshmallows. Hawkeye followed carrying a large tray filled with mugs and a pot of steaming cocoa.

After they all had their mugs filled with brew and a marshmallow or two, the men settled in the leather seats scattered around the spacious living room.

T-Rex paced in front of the fireplace, having sipped only once on his cocoa before setting it on the mantel. "That was too close."

"Now that we're all in the same room, tell us about it," Ghost urged.

T-Rex recounted what had taken place, from leaving in the helicopter to spotting the truck backed up to the cave. When he came to the part about being shot down from the sky, he was interrupted.

"They shot you down with a rocket?" Ghost exclaimed. "Holy hell, what kind of arsenal do they have?"

Caveman leaned forward, his hands clasped together.

"We need to get back up in those hills first thing in the morning."

"Hell, we need to have people on the roads, watching for any movement out of the hills." Hawkeye rose from his seat and paced the opposite direction of T-Rex. "They might decide to pack it all up and move it to an alternate location tonight."

"I'll coordinate with Garner and the sheriff. Who's up for a night shift?"

T-Rex raised a hand. "I'm out. I'm worried that now that Sierra's involved, she'll be targeted."

Ghost nodded. "I think between us and the sheriff's department, we can handle the night. But we need to be out looking tomorrow." He nodded toward T-Rex. "Except you."

Sierra directed a frown toward T-Rex. "I don't need you to look out for me tomorrow. I'm headed to the park at Yellowstone. I won't be anywhere around."

His brows furrowed as he studied her. "Alone?"

She smiled. "No. I'm going with my coworker, Brenda, and several mothers. We're taking some children to the park since they didn't make it there the day they were kidnapped."

T-Rex's brows dipped deeper. "Are you sure it's a good idea?"

"No one is going to kidnap half a dozen women in a couple of cars headed for the park. It's not like there will be a bus of children with only three adults. We'll be okay." She shook her head. "We can't stay home, afraid to get outside because of some band of troublemakers."

"I'll come with you," T-Rex said.

As much as Sierra loved having him around, she couldn't take him away from his duties. "You have a job. I'm not a part of that. We will be fine on our own, and the vehicles are already full."

"She's right," Hawkeye said. "Besides, we'll need all the help we can get if the hills are full of Free America homegrown terrorists."

For a long moment, T-Rex stared at Sierra. He didn't appear happy about her going off without him. But he didn't have a say in the matter. He'd be out of Grizzly Pass soon, and she'd be back to living alone.

A deep shiver shook her frame. A couple of days ago, she'd been perfectly happy to be alone.

Since she'd met T-Rex, everything had changed.

Chapter Eleven

After the hearty dinner of beef stew Liv provided, Ghost gave T-Rex and Sierra a ride back to Grizzly Pass and dropped them at T-Rex's truck at the fairgrounds. From there, T-Rex drove Sierra back to the bed-and-breakfast.

He used his key to open the front entrance. Low lights were left on in the hallway and the front living space for those guests returning late or wanting to relax in front of the dying embers in the fireplace.

Sierra passed the living area and climbed the stairs slowly, trailing her hand along the banister. She had to be bone tired after the stress of the afternoon. How many women held up so well after surviving a helicopter crash landing, being shot at and attacked by a man intent on killing her?

T-Rex was surprised and proud of how well she'd handled herself. He chuckled every time he remembered the image of her standing over that bad guy with a big rock in her hand. The woman had gumption.

When they reached her room, she paused and turned toward him. "Thanks again for saving me today."

"I think you have that backward. I should be thanking you."

She smiled. "I guess we could call it even."

He cupped her cheek in his hand. "You are an amazing woman."

She leaned into his palm and closed her eyes. "No, I'm an ordinary woman who did what she had to do in the face of adversity."

"You have your opinion, and I have mine." He brushed his thumb across her lips. "And right now, I want to kiss you so badly I can't resist. Tell me no and I'll leave you alone."

Sierra opened her eyes and stared up into his. "I'm not saying no." Her voice came out in a breathy whisper. She laid her hand on his chest and leaned up on her toes, lifting her chin.

T-Rex had no choice but to kiss those full, luscious lips. He couldn't have resisted had he tried.

His mouth crashed down on hers, and he brought his hands to her hips, pulling her close.

She parted her lips and met his tongue as he thrust inside her mouth.

T-Rex had never felt such an intense need to take this woman, to touch every part of her body and bury himself inside her. He caressed her tongue with his, twisting, sliding and loving the lingering taste of hot cocoa.

Her hands slid up his chest and around the back of his neck. Her calf circled his, and she pressed her sex against his thigh.

T-Rex groaned and ran his fingers up her back, buried them in her hair and tugged gently, pulling her head back. Then he left her mouth to trail kisses down the long, smooth line of her throat. Sweet beauty, her skin was so soft.

When he reached the rise of her collarbone, he paused and lifted his head to breathe and slow his pulse. That little pause allowed his brain to catch up and remind him who he was and who she was.

He was a marine, destined to return to his unit and deploy.

Sierra was a beautiful, desirable woman who'd been abused by her ex-husband. She deserved a man who would be there for her every day. A man who would shower her with the tender, loving care she so desperately deserved.

He wasn't that man.

He dropped his hands to his side and stepped away. "I can't do this."

She blinked her eyes open and stared up at him. "Did I do something wrong?"

He shook his head, every instinct telling him to take her into his arms and make sweet love to her through the rest of the night. But his brain couldn't allow it. "I'm not the right guy for you, darlin'. You deserve so much better."

"I don't want better," she said, closing the gap he'd put between them. "I want you." When she raised her hands to touch him, he grabbed them and held them away.

"I can only take so much. If we continue along this path, I won't be able to stop."

She smiled and shook her head. "I don't want you to stop."

"I could be gone tomorrow," he reminded her.

"Either one of us could have been gone today." She inhaled deeply and let it out. "Look, if it makes you feel better, I'm not looking for commitment. It's just that I don't want to spend the night alone. Not after all that happened today. You've been with me all day. Please." She held out her hand. "Don't leave me now."

He stared at her face and then down at her hand, and felt the walls of his resistance crumbling around him.

Finally, he took her hand. "I don't want you to regret what could happen between us tonight."

"I'll regret it more if we don't have this one night together." She lifted his hand to her cheek and gave him a soft, sexy smile that turned his knees to butter. "I need a shower. So do you." She didn't say more, just led him into the shared bathroom and closed the door behind them.

Once inside, she turned the handle on the shower faucet, tested the heat and then faced him. Her cheeks were pink, and she was chewing on her lip.

"I've never seduced a man before." She ran her fingers down the front of his shirt, pushing the buttons loose as she went. "I haven't been on a date since high school."

T-Rex dragged in a shaky breath and let it out. "You must be doing something right because I'm so turned on right now I can barely see straight."

She laughed softly and tugged his shirt loose from

his waistband. "Seeing straight isn't a requirement to-night. In fact, it might be a detractor."

When she reached for the button on his jeans, he put his hand over hers, stopping her there.

Sierra glanced up, wide-eyed. "What?"

He squeezed her hands gently. "Wait." He pulled his wallet from his back pocket and extracted two foil packets.

She smiled and shook her head. "I'm clean of any STDs and I can't get pregnant. But you're way ahead of me. I didn't even think about protection."

"For you more than for me. If there's even a chance of getting you pregnant, I wouldn't want to leave you to manage on your own."

She muttered something that sounded like *I'd take my chances.*

"What did you say?" he asked.

"I was married for seven years and never got preg-nant. It won't happen now. But I'm all for protection." She reached for his button again, worked it loose and then slid the zipper downward, taking her sweet time.

T-Rex gritted his teeth, ready to rip off his clothes and hers. But he didn't want to frighten her. She'd been through enough with her ex-husband. Being a Nean-derthal now would only reinforce all men were like Ellis. And he was nothing like her ex-husband. He cared enough about the women he had sex with to see to their satisfaction before his own.

But Sierra was testing his ability to hold back. When her knuckles brushed across his erection, he nearly came unglued. He captured her wrists in his and raised them above her head. Then he reached for the hem of her shirt, dragged it up over her head and tossed it on the counter.

She wore a lacy pink bra that framed her breasts beautifully. Unfortunately, it had to go in order for him to access the nipples beneath, puckering into tight little peaks.

Reaching behind her, he fumbled with the hooks. And fumbled some more. He couldn't seem to get the hooks to release. "I'm sorry. I'm way out of practice."

She laughed, tucked her arm up behind her back and slipped the hooks free. But she didn't remove the garment. Instead she cocked her brow.

T-Rex took it from there and slipped the straps from her arm, freeing her breasts. They spilled out and bounced a little in the process.

T-Rex cupped the rounded orbs in his palms and lifted as if weighing them. "Beautiful."

Sierra pressed her hands to the backs of his and inhaled, pushing deeper into his hold. "If we don't hurry, the water will get cold before we get in."

In seconds they were both naked and in the shower, laughing.

"Shh." Sierra pressed a finger to T-Rex's lips. He promptly sucked it into his mouth and bit down gently before releasing it.

"We can't have our landlady coming up to check on all the commotion," he said.

"No." Sierra leaned up on her toes and pressed her lips to his. "We can't," she said into his mouth.

T-Rex's laughter ended and his hunger built. He drew

her body against his and stepped under the shower's spray, letting it run over them both.

Sierra squirted body wash liquid into her hand and ran it over his shoulders and across his chest, rubbing until lather built and ran down his torso.

He returned the gesture, running his hands over the swells of her breasts, down to her narrow waist and across the flare of her hips. Then he bent to kiss one of her nipples, rolling the tip between his teeth.

Her back arched, pressing more of her into his mouth. He took it, sucking her breast, flicking the tip with his tongue until she moaned and dug her fingers into his hair and held him even closer.

When he'd had his fill of one side, he switched his attention to the other.

Sierra moaned and ran her leg up the back of his, rubbing her sex against his thigh.

"What did I do with those packets?" he asked, his voice as tight as his body.

She fished one out of the soap dish, tore it open and rolled it down over him, taking her time.

T-Rex growled and finished the job. Then he ran his hand over her buttocks and scooped her up by the backs of her thighs, wrapping her legs around his waist. Pressing her against the slick tiles of the shower wall, he kissed her hard, sliding his tongue into her mouth as his erection nudged her opening.

He lifted his head, dragging in a lungful of steadying air. "Tell me *no* now, if that's what you want."

"You're kidding, right?" Sierra shook her head and

eased her body downward, taking him inside her. "I want you. Please, don't stop now."

Her channel welcomed him, wet, warm and tight around him.

He eased into her slowly, all the way, giving her time to adjust to his girth. Once he was buried to the hilt, he asked, "Are you all right?"

"Oh, my," she said, her voice hitching. "More than all right. More, please."

He chuckled and pulled almost all the way out before reversing the direction.

"Harder," she whispered, wrapping her arms around his neck and tightening her legs around his waist. "Faster," she urged.

He thrust into her again and again, establishing a rhythm as ancient as time. But he held back, refusing to release. He wanted her with him when he did.

As the water grew colder, T-Rex steeled himself to withdraw and set Sierra on her feet.

"What? Why did you stop? I was almost there," she cried.

"I want you to enjoy this as much as I do," he said.

"I am," she said.

Still he rinsed them both, turned off the water and led her out of the tub onto the bath mat. With a warm, fluffy towel, he rubbed her skin dry.

Sierra returned the favor, lingering over his stiff erection. When she was done, she wrapped her towel around her body, while he wrapped his around his waist.

She took his hand and opened the door, poking her head out. "The coast is clear."

"My room or yours?" he asked.

"I don't care as long as we get there quickly." Tightening her hold on his fingers, she ran across the hall and pushed into her bedroom, dragging him in behind her.

T-Rex closed the door and twisted the lock. "Now I can show you how a lady should be made love to."

"I was counting on that," she said with a smile and let the towel around her drop to the floor.

SIERRA WATCHED AS T-Rex released his hold on his towel and the soft terry cloth fell, exposing the man's magnificent shaft, jutting out in front of him.

When he'd been inside her, she could barely breathe, he was so thick and...and...sweet love, he was so big. She couldn't wait to have him back inside her, filling that empty place she hadn't known ached for a man like him.

Taking his hand, she backed toward the bed. When the backs of her legs bumped into the mattress, she smiled. Oh, yes. This would be a night she'd remember for a very long time. She didn't want to waste a moment of it.

About to scoot her bottom up onto the bed, she was surprised when T-Rex swung her legs out from under her and laid her on the mattress.

She laughed. "I was getting there."

He stepped between her legs and leaned down to capture her earlobe between his teeth. "I know. But you were taking too long. I have plans for you."

She widened her legs and leaned back on her elbows. "Plans? Sounds tempting." Sierra lowered her eyelids to half-mast, her heart pounding at the deep, sexy way he was talking. What could be more exciting than what he'd already done to her in the shower?

T-Rex dragged his lips across her chin to capture her mouth, sliding his tongue alongside hers in a slow, arousing caress. He didn't pause long, working his way down the column of her throat to the pulse beating wildly at the base of her neck.

She slid her hands over his impossibly broad shoulders, amazed at how hard the muscles were beneath his taut skin. Every move he made flexed them and made her want to touch his body all over.

T-Rex captured one of her breasts between his lips and rolled the tip until it hardened into a tight little bead. Then he moved to the other and lavished his attention on it.

Sierra arched off the bed, pressing her breast deeper into his mouth. He sucked hard on it and let go, trailing his mouth down her torso, alternately kissing, nipping and tonguing her skin as he moved lower. When he reached the tuft of hair over her sex, he paused to look up at her.

She felt as if she were perched on the edge of a precipice, waiting for him to draw her over.

He touched her entrance with the tip of his finger, sliding it into the warm, wet channel. Then he dragged it upward, parted her folds and slathered that little nubbin of flesh that held the key to her ultimate release. Swirling, stroking and flicking, he toyed with her until she was a writhing, moaning animal, twisting in the sheets.

If that wasn't enough to make her crazed with lust,

he bent his head to her and flicked her with his tongue. There. In that very special place.

Sierra dug her heels into the mattress and came up off the bed, crying out, "Rex!"

He chuckled. "Like that?"

"Oh, my. Oh, my. Oh, my," she said, unable to form more coherent words when every nerve in her body was on fire with need. "Yes!"

Then he flicked her again and sucked her nubbin into his mouth, tonguing it over and over.

Sierra catapulted into the stratosphere, the tingling sensation graduating into lightning bolting through her from the molten core of her being to the very tips of her fingers.

As she rode the wave, she almost wanted to cry. This was right in so many ways. What T-Rex was doing to her was how it should always have been.

Before she came down from the incredibly beautiful high, she tugged on T-Rex's hair, urging him to come up her body and join her in the most intense pleasure she'd ever experienced.

He crawled up and settled between her legs. Then he kissed her and thrust deep inside her, filling her to full, prolonging her release to match his.

Again and again he thrust, until his body tensed, he thrust one last time and buried himself in her channel. His shaft throbbed inside her. He threw back his head and clenched his teeth so tightly his jaw twitched.

After a long, exquisite moment, Sierra floated back to earth.

T-Rex dropped down on top of her and rolled them

both to their sides, his arms around her, pulling her close. He stroked her hair silently and held her until his breathing returned to normal.

Sierra burrowed into his muscular body and rested her hand on his chest. She'd promised not to expect commitment from him. But she couldn't imagine going through life without ever doing that again. The man could have ruined her for all others.

Chapter Twelve

T-Rex woke before sunrise, warm, content and naked. Lying in a strange room with Sierra's body snuggled up against his was just about as close to heaven as he could imagine.

He eased his arm out from under her and stared down at the woman lying in the bed beside him.

Her blond hair fanned out on the pillow, and her mouth turned up in a sexy smile as if she was dreaming about making love. To him.

He bent to gently brush a kiss across her forehead. He'd never made love to a woman with such intensity and desire. And she'd responded in kind, her cries as free and powerful as her release.

Her ex-husband had been a fool. This woman was kind, gentle and caring. But the passion hidden beneath her beautiful and soft exterior was everything a man could dream of. The man fortunate enough to capture her heart would be a lucky person indeed.

The urgent need to relieve himself reminded him there was a world out there, and he'd be expected to join it soon. His only regret to the night before was that he'd have to get out of the bed and leave this woman for a day of hunting in the hills. He'd much prefer to remain in the warmth of her arms and make love to her all day long.

He slid from the bed, careful not to disturb her. Wrapping the towel around his waist, he left her room for his own, grabbed clothes and entered the bathroom. A quick, cold shower helped to reinforce his need to go to work, reducing his lusty thoughts enough he could think of the task ahead.

He would join the team in their search through the hills to find the cave with the cache of weapons. Unless the sheriff's department had captured them trying to leave the valley and relocate their store of rifles and whatever else they might have stashed away. He could always hope. Then he could stay where he was and spend the day in bed with Sierra.

But she had a job to do and a tour with the day care kids.

T-Rex sighed. Soon he was combed, dressed and ready to attack the day. When he pulled open the bathroom door, he almost ran into Sierra.

She stood in front of him, her hand raised to knock. Her beautiful long blond hair tumbled around her shoulders in wild abandon, but she had dressed in jeans and a long-sleeved blouse. Her cheeks turned a charming shade of pink, and she dipped her head. "Good morning."

T-Rex drew her into his arms and bent to nuzzle her ear. "Hey, beautiful."

"Ha. You're showered and shaved. I'm a mess."

"A gorgeous mess." He tipped her chin up and stared down into her eyes. "I wanted to stay in bed all day."

She sighed. "Me, too. But I promised Brenda I'd go with the moms and kids to the park at Yellowstone today."

"And you can't disappoint the kids." He bent to touch his lips to her forehead. "Need help scrubbing your back in the shower?" he whispered.

"Always." She cupped his face with her palm. "But you're all ready to go. I can manage on my own." She chewed on her bottom lip. "Will I see you at breakfast?"

He shook his head. "I have to meet the guys in ten minutes. That only gives me enough time to grab a cup of coffee." He frowned. "Are you sure you'll be all right at the park today?"

She nodded. "I'll be surrounded by the other ladies and the park rangers. Clay might be bold enough to attack me in front of a bunch of children who couldn't stop him. But surely he won't try anything in front of a bunch of adults."

"Yes, but he might try before you leave."

"I'll have Brenda pick me up in front of the bed-and-breakfast."

T-Rex nodded. "I'd like to be here to see you off." He glanced down at his watch. Eight minutes.

"Go." She touched his arm. "I'll be fine." Sierra grinned. "I'll carry the stun gun and a big rock, if it makes you feel any better."

He chuckled and pulled her into his arms, holding her tight. Then he claimed her lips in a kiss that felt like it could be their last.

Sierra wrapped her arms around his neck and returned the kiss, her breasts smashed against his chest, her belly pressing against his rising erection.

In need of air, he finally broke the kiss and rested his forehead against hers. "So much for cold showers."

She laughed, kissed him briefly and stepped out of his arms. "You have to go, and I need to get ready."

"Do you have my cell phone number?" he asked.

She shook her head.

"Give me your number." He pulled out his phone and entered her digits. Then he called it.

He could hear her phone ringing in her bedroom. "Now you'll have mine. Call me if you have any problems whatsoever."

"You'll be out in the hills and canyons. The call won't go through."

"I'll check my phone when I get back to town. I'll also text the number for Hack. He's always in the office. He can relay messages to me in the field. We'll carry radios to communicate."

She rested a hand on his chest. "Be careful out there."

He captured her hand in his, raised it to his lips and pressed a kiss into her palm. "You be careful at Yellowstone. I hear the buffalo can be aggressive."

Sierra snorted. "They are the least of my worries. I'll have half a dozen children around my feet wanting to pet them."

"You'll do great. Those kids love you."

She smiled. "I love them, too. Now, go, or we'll be here all day."

He turned and descended the stairs to the first floor.

Mrs. McCall held up a pot of coffee in the dining room. "Need one to go?"

"I'd love one," he answered.

"Everything all right?" Mrs. McCall asked as she handed him an insulated disposable cup filled with steaming black coffee.

"Couldn't be better." He took the cup and pressed a lid onto it. "Why do you ask?"

"I just wondered if you were tired this morning. What with all the racket last night." She didn't meet his gaze, but her lips curled upward in a smile. "That Sierra Daniels is a sweetheart. Always good to everyone. She certainly didn't deserve to be treated the way her ex-husband treated her."

"No, she didn't. And yes, she is a sweet lady."

Mrs. McCall met his gaze, her smile gone. "Sure would hate to see her hurt again."

T-Rex swallowed the piping-hot coffee he'd just sipped and nearly gagged on the heat burning its way down his throat. He sputtered and blew out a stream of hot air before responding to the older woman. "I'd hate to see her hurt, as well." Then, quickly, before the woman could give him more advice about Sierra, he left the dining room and hurried out the door to his truck.

Although he'd left the bed-and-breakfast, he couldn't seem to leave Mrs. McCall's words behind.

Sierra Daniels deserved to be happy. Though their lovemaking had been the result of mutual consent, T-Rex suspected it would leave her hurt in the long run. He'd leave, she'd be alone and her ex-husband would still be around to harass her.

A few days ago, all T-Rex could think about was leaving Grizzly Pass. Now all he could think about was what he'd be leaving behind. He no longer had the burning desire to return to his unit and seek revenge on the faceless enemy who'd crippled Gunny and killed other members of his team.

There were people right there in the United States who needed help. Innocents like Sierra and the children she was responsible for.

T-Rex had a lot to think about while he searched the hills for the homegrown terrorists.

SIERRA SHOWERED, DRESSED in a crisp, clean pair of jeans, a long-sleeved blouse and a sweater. After being so very cold the day before, she grabbed a jacket to take along, in case the temperature dropped or they were unexpectedly delayed in their return to Grizzly Pass.

She called Brenda, who agreed to swing by and collect her before meeting the other moms who would caravan out to the Old Faithful Visitor Education Center at Yellowstone. They had arranged for a park ranger to give the children a guided tour, explaining the ecosystem and the most interesting facts about the ancient volcano simmering beneath the surface. It would be a fun, educational trip for the children, one they'd looked forward to for over a month.

Too bad Sierra didn't feel much like going. She'd rather be out in the hills with the Safe Haven team searching for the men who'd shot down their helicopter yesterday. That wasn't exactly the truth. She wanted to be with T-Rex, whatever he was doing in the hills.

She eventually descended the staircase and joined Mrs. McCall in the dining room. They were the only two people at the table.

"Were there no other guests in the bed-and-breakfast last night?" Sierra asked.

The older woman shook her head. "No. Just you and Mr. Trainor. I expect a couple to show up some time this afternoon. But they're only staying the night before moving on."

Heat rose in Sierra's cheeks. If there were no other guests, had the establishment's owner heard the noises coming from her room last night?

Mrs. McCall reached across the table and patted her hand. "Sierra, sweetie, I've known you a long time. Your foster mother and I used to be in the same quilting club. I've watched you grow from a little girl with pigtails into the beautiful young woman you are now."

Sierra choked on the tea she'd been sipping and set the cup on the table. "Thank you, Mrs. McCall." She wondered where the woman would go with the conversation.

"I can see you are falling in love with Mr. Trainor."

Sierra gasped and shook her head. "No, Mrs. McCall. We've only known each other a couple of days. It would be impossible to fall in love that quickly."

Mrs. McCall gave her a knowing smile. "Sweetie, I knew I loved my Henry the moment we met. It just took him a little longer to realize he loved me, too."

Sierra's eyes stung. She blinked and looked down at her hand holding the teacup. "Really, I'm not in love. Mr. Trainor isn't going to be in Grizzly Pass for long.

When his mission is complete, he'll be on his way back to his unit."

"Sierra, it's not too late. You still have time to show him that he is capable of love. He doesn't know it, but he's halfway there now."

Sierra raised her glance to the bed-and-breakfast owner. "It's impossible. He's career military. He's leaving."

"So?" Mrs. McCall rose from her chair and collected the empty plates. "You have nothing holding you back. I'm sure your foster parents would have wanted you to get out of this little town, spread your wings and experience more of the world."

"If I wanted to, I could do it on my own." Sierra stood and helped clear the table, walking into the kitchen behind the older woman. "I don't need a man with me in order to experience the world."

Mrs. McCall nodded. "True. But if there's a special man, one who understands you, treats you right and loves you, isn't the experience richer?" She set the plates in the sink and turned to take the biscuit basket from Sierra's hand. "Think about it, will you?"

Sierra wanted to tell her she'd thought about all of those things and come back to the promise she'd made T-Rex. She wouldn't look for commitment. What they'd done last night was supposed to be a one-night stand. *The end.*

But she couldn't quite tack those two words onto what she was feeling. She couldn't believe last night was the end. Mrs. McCall was right about one thing. She still had time. Time to be with T-Rex until he left.

If he left without looking back, then she would add the two words to what they'd had and move on.

She might even decide to leave Grizzly Pass and see the world. Maybe there was a rich family looking for a nanny to travel with them. Or she could go back to school, finish her degree and find a job in another state as a teacher. The sky was the limit.

Sierra checked the clock. Brenda would be there in a few minutes, and she was still mooning over a man who'd made it clear he wasn't sticking around, nor was he the kind of man who needed or wanted a woman to follow him from post to post.

Straightening her shoulders, Sierra decided she'd take every minute she had with him and ask no more. In the meantime, she had a field trip to go on and she wasn't ready. She ran up the stairs to the bathroom, brushed her teeth and grabbed her jacket and purse. When she came back down, Brenda was pulling up in front of the bed-and-breakfast.

Before Sierra stepped out of the building, she checked for any sign of Clay. His truck wasn't anywhere in sight. Breathing a sigh of relief, she left the building and climbed into Brenda's SUV.

"Well, look at you all chipper this morning." Brenda shifted into gear and drove toward the community center. "How was your date with the marine yesterday?"

Sierra's cheeks burned, and she couldn't meet her friend's gaze.

"Oh, my God. You hooked up with him!" Brenda squealed in delight.

"What?" Sierra shot a glance her way. "I did not—"

"Oh, baby, don't even bother to deny it. Your lips are puffy, and you have a little beard burn on your cheek. At the very least you were thoroughly kissed. But the way you're blushing, it was a lot more than that."

Sierra gave up and sagged against the seat, a smile pulling her lips upward. "Yesterday was the best day of my life."

"Tell me all," Brenda insisted, her face animated. "Hurry, before we load up with kids. I want all of the lovely details."

"Well, other than the helicopter crash and being shot at, I'd say it went pretty well."

Brenda slammed her foot onto the brake pedal. "What?"

Sierra caught herself before hitting the dash. "You didn't hear? I would have thought the grapevine would have had it all over the county by now."

"You forget, I live alone."

"That never stopped anyone from spreading the most interesting gossip far and wide among the Beartooth Mountains." Sierra laughed and started from the beginning, giving a brief summation of what had happened up to the moment she and T-Rex arrived back at the bed-and-breakfast. "And that's what you missed."

"Oh, darlin', you're not stopping there." Brenda pulled up to the community center. "I want the rest. Give it to me. Quickly, because we're here and the kiddos are waiting."

"Sorry. We're being waved over." Sierra grinned and climbed out of the vehicle.

"Oh, that is so not fair." Brenda shook her head. "He must have been spectacular."

"Beyond," Sierra said, letting her smile broaden as she approached the mothers and small children who would be coming along for the field trip.

Sierra and Brenda would take three kids and two mothers in Brenda's SUV with seating for seven. Two other mothers would follow in a Suburban with another five children whose ages ranged from four to six.

The trip took only an hour and fifteen minutes when one drove the speed limit. But the roads were curvy. To avoid the usual carsickness, they took the curves very slowly and entertained the children with songs and games to keep them occupied.

When they rolled into the parking lot of the Old Faithful Visitor Education Center, the children were ready to get out and stretch their little legs.

"Why is the parking lot so full?" Brenda shifted into Park and got out. "I mean it's not even time for Old Faithful to blow."

Sierra climbed out of the vehicle and glanced around at the vehicles crammed into the lot and the vans with satellite antennas and the lettering of local television stations written on the sides. Then it came to her. "I forgot. Grady Morris is supposed to be here today for a campaign speech."

"Oh, yeah. Last night on the news, they said he'd have a special guest with him." Brenda tilted her head. "I wonder who it is."

"Based on the number of black SUVs and men in

black suits, it has to be a very important person," Sierra said.

The other two mothers and their children joined them. "Should we call off this excursion?" one of them said.

"It's awfully crowded," noted another.

"We're here," Sierra said. "We might as well check it out. Maybe our tour guide will get us out on the trails before this shindig kicks off."

The women herded the children through the parked cars, past several men in black clothing and black sunglasses, their jackets bulging. Probably with a weapon or two each.

The lobby was full of people, jostling each other. More men in suits and reporters with cameras and microphones.

"I've been here on a number of occasions when this place was teeming with tourists, but this is crazy," Brenda said.

Sierra nodded. "Let's just hope it's not as packed inside as it is out front."

They were disappointed to learn it was even more crowded in the center.

"Stay here," Sierra said. "I'll make my way to the desk and see if I can find our park ranger tour guide."

Brenda and the mothers backed the children into an empty corner and waited.

Sierra waded through the crowd to the desk and stood in a line seven people deep. By the time she reached the desk, she was ready to call the whole event off. The noise level had grown into a dull roar inside the building. It was giving her a headache and touch of agoraphobia. She didn't much care for large crowds.

"How may I help you?" The perky young woman behind the counter pushed a strand of hair back behind her ear.

"We made prior arrangements for the ranger-led activities."

The woman keyed into the computer. "Group name?"

"Grizzly Pass Mother's Day Out."

The noise in the room increased to a fevered pitch, and one of the counter clerks pointed. "There he is. The vice president of the United States."

Sierra spun in time to catch a glimpse of the vice president, flanked by Secret Service men, being hustled through the crowd from a back room and out the door of the building, leading to the geyser viewing area. The crowd outside cheered. Through the glass doors, Sierra could see Grady Morris standing on a raised stage, shaking hands with the vice president.

"You'll have Ranger Jared today," the clerk said, drawing Sierra's attention back to the counter.

"Is that really the vice president of the United States?" Sierra asked.

The young lady puffed out her chest, her eyes bright with excitement. "Yes, ma'am."

"Did you know he'd be here?" Sierra asked.

She beamed. "We didn't know until right before we left work last night. We all had to come in early and clean like crazy to be ready for him this morning. And they built the stage out by Old Faithful in less than two hours. It was amazing." The woman looked behind her.

"Oh, here's Ranger Jared. He'll take you to the exhibits room, unless you want to stand outside and watch the show first."

"No. The children are much too young to understand a campaign speech."

Ranger Jared glanced over the heads of the crowd. "I've never seen it like this. It's insane."

"You're telling me. Should we postpone and come back when it's not this crowded?" Sierra asked.

"No. No. This crowd won't be interested in the discovery room. We'll probably have it all to ourselves with everyone else outside. Come on back."

Sierra gathered the women and children and led them through the door where Ranger Jared stood.

He was right. The crowd had moved out to the geyser viewing area where the stage had been erected. Soon he had the kids engaged in learning about geysers, hot springs and more.

The children were happy to touch and explore the indoor exhibits and momentarily would be led outdoors to see some of the real deals on the trails.

Ranger Jared clapped his hands to get their attention. "If you will all step across the lobby into the theater, we have a little show we'd like you to see before we go outside. Follow me." He led the way back through the lobby and into the theater.

Sierra helped guide the small children into seats near the front of the room. Once they were all in place, she stood to the side, leaning against the wall.

The lights dimmed and the film began. It was all about the ecosystem of the park and how the volcano had come to be, how it had erupted and created a warm place for the animals to gather around during the cold months of the year. The narrator talked of the different species of animals that roamed the park, including bison, deer, elk, black bears, grizzly bears and the wolves that had been reintroduced.

Even Sierra was caught up in the video. The theater walls were soundproofed. The people outside the theater couldn't hear what was going on inside and vice versa. So she was surprised when someone burst through the door and yelled, "Get down on the floor and don't move or we'll shoot!"

With the doors open, she could hear the sounds of screaming and shouting and the crack of gunfire.

Sierra, her heart pounding, ran toward the children. "Get on the floor," she yelled. "Get down!"

Gunfire ripped through the theater.

"I said get down!" A man in a ski mask brandished a military-grade rifle in the air. "That means you, Blondie!"

The children screamed and cried. Most of them slid out of their seats and lay on the floor. One little boy sat petrified in his theater seat, too young to understand what was going on and too frightened to move.

Sierra dropped to her hands and knees and crawled to the boy, scooped him out of his seat and onto the ground, hunkering over him to block any bullets that might be fired in their direction.

"In here!" the gunman shouted. "Bring them in here!"

Sierra lifted her head high enough to peer over the seats at the upper end of the theater. Two men in business suits were shoved through the door by a group of men dressed in camouflage and ski masks.

"Down in front." One of the men waved his rifle at the others. "Take them down in front where we can see them. And turn on the lights. It's too dark in here."

A man in a ski mask kicked Ranger Jared in the side. "You. Get the lights on. Now!"

Jared staggered to his feet and hurried to the controls on the wall. He flipped several switches, and the lights grew brighter. As soon as he was done, he was shoved back down the aisle to where Sierra and the other women were hovering over the children.

The little ones sobbed, their cries getting louder with all of the shouting. It didn't help that one of the mothers was losing it in front of the kids.

"We're going to die. We're going to die," she kept saying.

"Lady, shut up, or you will," a man carrying a rifle said.

"Shh, Laura. We're going to be fine. Just keep your cool for the children," Sierra said.

Beside her Brenda shook, her teeth chattering. Not a week earlier, the woman had been in a bus hijacking. If anyone had a right to lose it, it was Brenda.

But Sierra couldn't, not when the children depended on her to see them safely home.

Chapter Thirteen

T-Rex met up with Ghost and Caveman in front of the Blue Moose Tavern. Garner hurried down the stairs, carrying what appeared to be two duffel bags.

"We're meeting Hawkeye at the Stone Oak Ranch and taking the four-wheelers from there."

"Whatcha got?" T-Rex asked.

"The armory." Garner laid the heavy bags in the back of his SUV. "M4A1 rifles, radio headsets and Kevlar vests. We're not going unarmed or unprepared."

T-Rex snorted. "Glad to hear it. I felt at a distinct disadvantage yesterday in the hills."

Garner's lips thinned. "We didn't plan on having a helicopter shot down."

"No, we didn't," T-Rex agreed and closed the hatch.

"How soon will the FAA be out to investigate the crash site?" Ghost asked.

"They're on their way now." Garner climbed into the driver's seat and twisted the key in the ignition. "Should be here before noon. All the more reason to find that cave and neutralize any bad guys before they stir up any more trouble." He glanced at the rest of them. "Are you coming, or not?"

The three men jumped into the SUV and held on while Garner sped out of town.

"What about the sheriff?" T-Rex glanced up at the hills. They appeared so serene, as though they couldn't possibly harbor a bunch of terrorists. "Any activity on the roads last night?"

"His men didn't see anything moving," Garner answered. "The one truck he stopped was a man on his way to the airport in Bozeman. No weapons stashed in his backseat or truck bed."

"I can't imagine them leaving their weapons cache in the cave." T-Rex shook his head. "Not after shooting down a military helicopter."

"The Army National Guard sent another Black Hawk. The pilot and copilot are waiting at the fairgrounds. The ship is armed to the teeth. The guard is angry about losing one of their birds. I barely got them to wait. I don't want to start an all-out war and get people killed who actually belong on the neighboring ranches. I told them to give us the morning to find the cave and attack it from the ground."

"I'm surprised they agreed," Ghost said.

Garner shrugged. "I had help from their higher headquarters."

"Will the sheriff's department be with us on this venture?" Caveman asked.

"They will. The sheriff, along with seven of his finest deputies and members of the Wyoming State Police, will be combing the hills alongside us."

T-Rex shook his head. "Sounds like this could turn out to be a goat rope."

"Can't be helped." Garner's hands tightened on the steering wheel. "We need the manpower to search the caves. If there are more than thirty AR-15s up there, it stands to reason there could be thirty men using them." Garner shot a glance at T-Rex in the front seat. "I'll take all the help we can get."

Caveman leaned over the back of Garner's seat. "How is everyone getting up into the hills?"

"We're taking the four-wheelers we left at the Stone Oak Ranch." Garner left Grizzly Pass and headed south. "The sheriff department has their own fleet of four-wheelers, and I have no idea what the state police will bring. All I know is we need to find these bastards and take them down before they hurt anyone else. Oh, and several of the folks we had on our list of possible members of Free America called in sick or didn't show up to work today."

"How'd you find out?"

"I had feelers out to their employers. They notified me as soon as the calls came in or the men didn't arrive on time."

T-Rex's hands balled into fists. Things could get real ugly real fast. "How many?"

"Nine that we know about, so far," Garner said.

"Sounds like they might be mobilizing," Caveman cursed. "Why couldn't we bring any of them in earlier?"

"We didn't have any evidence." Garner glanced in his rearview mirror at the men in the seat behind him.

"Ghost, you and Caveman followed some of them, and they didn't lead you anywhere but to their homes."

"Damned waste of time," Ghost grumbled. "If we could have interrogated them, we'd have had more to go on."

"What about Rausch? Has he talked?" T-Rex asked.

"The sheriff is meeting us at the ranch," Garner said. "Hopefully, he has news on that front." He glanced in his rearview mirror again. "If I'm not mistaken, that's him behind us now."

They arrived at Stone Oak Ranch and met Olivia at the house.

Several vehicles pulled into the driveway behind them, including four from the sheriff's department and three from the state police. They had trailers attached filled with four-wheelers.

Olivia and Hawkeye met them with contour maps of the area. They spread them over the hood of Garner's vehicle, and the team gathered around along with the law enforcement personnel. They determined the approximate location of the cave from which the rocket had been shot, assigned areas to each team and took off.

Because the Safe Haven team had been the most recent to visit the area, they led the pack.

T-Rex insisted on taking point. As he drove the roads to the narrowing trails up into the hills, he couldn't help thinking about Sierra. Was she all right? Had Ellis shown up that morning to cause problems? Or was her ex-husband with the Free America group, preparing to take over the world?

He wished he could be in two places at once. Alas, he couldn't and his job was exactly where he was.

As they neared the valley lined with caves, he slowed his ATV and pulled out a pair of binoculars. His team stopped even with him and did the same.

"Is that metal?" Hawkeye asked, pointing to one of the caves. "There. The third cave from the end. The one with the tire tracks leading up to it. Is that a metal ammo box on the edge of the entrance?"

T-Rex trained his binoculars at the third cave from the end of the valley. Just as Hawkeye had said, there was a metal ammo box lying on its side near the mouth of the cave. T-Rex dismounted, pulled the M4 rifle from the scabbard and waited for the others to catch up.

Garner organized the sheriff's deputies and state police into an assault team to follow the Safe Haven men into battle.

T-Rex led the charge, hugging the shadows of the trees, moving closer a little at a time. Soon he was standing below the cave in the shade of a lodgepole pine, staring up at an empty ammo can. Nothing moved on the trail or in the dimness of the cave. Nothing that he could see.

Ghost came up to stand beside him. "Anything?"

"I'd bet this was the cave. I'd also bet it's empty of the people who were there yesterday."

"Let's find out. Cover me." Ghost passed T-Rex and started up the hill.

T-Rex followed.

At the entrance to the cave, they paused, inching up

from the side, out of sight and range of anyone aiming a rifle their direction.

T-Rex poked his head around the side of the rock wall and peered into the darkness. Nothing moved. "Ready?" he said. "Cover me."

He took three steps into the darkness and felt something across his ankle. T-Rex froze and yelled, "Get back! This place is rigged!"

Since he hadn't triggered the detonator, he knew that if he moved his ankle now, he'd set off the explosion. He waited for Ghost to get back behind the safety of the rock wall. Then, taking a deep breath, T-Rex threw himself in that direction, somersaulted and rolled to his feet.

An explosion knocked him over and sent him tumbling down the hillside to the valley floor. He lay for a long time, his ears ringing, unable to take a breath. Dust flew all around him, dimming the light from the sun above.

Caveman appeared over him. "T-Rex!" He seemed to be shouting, but the sound barely made it to him. "T-Rex, breathe!" He pushed on his chest and forced air out.

T-Rex gasped and sucked in a lungful of dusty air. He sat up coughing, breathing as deeply as he could to fill his empty lungs. After popping his ears several times, he could hear better, but the ringing continued.

"They rigged it. They had a trip wire just inside the cave where you couldn't see it." T-Rex held up his hand. "Help me up."

Caveman grabbed his hand and pulled him to his feet. "Are you all right?"

"I have to be. If they aren't here, they have to be somewhere else. From what I could see before I set off the explosion, there were empty ammo cases, tables and chairs and maps on the walls."

"Could you tell what the maps were of?" Garner asked.

"No. I couldn't see that much. My eyes hadn't adjusted completely to the dark interior before the explosion." T-Rex covered his ears and pressed hard, hoping to readjust his eardrums. It helped, but he still heard sounds as if they were coming from the end of a long tunnel. And that damned ringing wouldn't stop.

Caveman and Ghost climbed the hill to the cave and pulled at a few rocks before shaking their heads and coming back down.

Sheriff Scott had joined them. "I'll see what I can do to get a crew out here to dig that cave out. There has to be something in there they're trying to hide. We might be able to pull fingerprints from whatever is left of the cases and ammo boxes."

Ghost pointed to the ammo box they'd passed on their way up before the explosion. "You might get something from that one. And you won't have to dig to do it."

The sheriff nodded. "I sent my men and the state police north following the trail to see if they find where they moved the goods. If you're up to it, you might want to follow. There are a lot of trails and roads leading into and out of these hills. Just because my men didn't see anyone on the roads last night, doesn't mean they didn't leave. But then again, they might still be holed up in an alternate location."

"We'll follow," T-Rex said. To him, his voice sounded as if he was speaking from a long way away. He started toward his four-wheeler.

Garner caught his arm and pulled him to a halt. "I think you should go back to the ranch house. You took quite a tumble, and that explosion probably didn't do your eardrums or anything else any good."

"I'm fine."

Garner held up two fingers. "How many fingers am I holding up?"

"Two." He frowned at his temporary boss. "Can we go now?"

Garner nodded. "Yes. But for the record, I don't like it. I think you should see a doctor."

"Later. We have a small army to stop."

They followed the others along the trail. Soon, T-Rex's head cleared enough to realize they were nearing the valley where the pipeline inspector had been killed.

As he rolled over the top of the ridge and came to a halt, he looked down at the trail leading to the bottom. The law enforcement officers were almost to the bottom. When they left the trail and drove across the valley floor, another explosion rocked the ground. Rocks and dust blasted into the air from the area around the pipeline.

The deputy in front of the pack flipped over the handlebars of his four-wheeler and landed a couple of yards away. The two ATV riders behind him swerved and flipped their four-wheelers. Those behind them stopped suddenly, leaped from their vehicles and ran toward the downed men.

From his perch high above, T-Rex stared down at the chaos and commotion. He glanced all around, from the top of the other ridge down the sides of the hills to the bottom. Nothing else moved. Not a single member of the Free America group stood around to watch the explosion here or at the cave. It was almost as if they'd known someone would come that way looking for them and they set up a smoke screen to hide what they were really up to.

Garner pulled his ATV up beside T-Rex and jerked the radio from the pocket of his jacket. "Garner here."

"It's me, Hack," the computer guy's voice crackled over the radio.

"Yeah, what's wrong?" Garner asked.

"Got trouble up north. You're wasting your time looking for your Free America group in the hills. They've staged their takeover."

T-Rex left his vehicle and crossed to where Garner stood.

"Where?" Garner demanded.

"At Old Faithful. They're at the visitors center. There was a campaign rally there today with Grady Morris. He had a surprise visitor with him."

"Who?" Garner asked.

"The vice president of the United States."

A lead weight settled low in T-Rex's belly. *Holy hell.* And then his gut twisted into a tight knot. "Sierra Daniels was going to Yellowstone today. They were supposed to be at Old Faithful today."

"Anyone else caught in the takeover?" Garner asked into the radio.

Hack replied, "Some women and little kids who were in the theater where they took the vice president. They think half a dozen women and half a dozen children were in there. Something like seventeen people are being held hostage."

"What's going on?" Ghost stepped up beside T-Rex.

T-Rex clenched his fists. "This whole effort today was a waste of time, a smoke screen for what they were planning."

"And what was that?" Ghost asked.

"They've taken hostages at the Old Faithful visitors center. The vice president is one of them."

Caveman joined them. "Vice president of what?"

T-Rex turned to his teammates. "Of the United States of America." He hurried toward his ATV.

"Where are you going?" Garner asked.

"Sierra Daniels was there." He threw his leg over the seat and started the engine. "I have a sinking feeling she's among the hostages, along with the children in her care. I'm going to rescue her."

SIERRA HUDDLED ON the floor with the other women, holding the little ones in her arms, trying to comfort them and keep them quiet. The armed men who'd taken them and the vice president of the United States hostage didn't look like they'd put up with much. Crying children would only make them angry and impatient.

They'd been held in the theater for over an hour without any idea of what the group was demanding. Some of the children had cried themselves to sleep. Others clung to the adults, hiding their faces from the bad guys. It wouldn't be long before they got hungry or had to use the bathroom. The crying would start all over again.

Sierra handed Brenda the little boy she'd been holding and stood.

"Where are you going?" Brenda asked, her brows furrowed, the strain of the takeover showing in the lines around her mouth.

"To find out what's going on and try to negotiate the children's release."

"You can't." Brenda grabbed her hand. "You heard them. They'll shoot anyone standing."

"You two, shut up and sit down," a voice said.

Another masked man entered the room behind the bossy one. "I'm taking over here," he said. "You can join the others outside in the lobby."

"I was told not to leave them," Bossy Man argued.

The man grabbed Bossy Man by the collar and shoved him toward the door. "Get the hell out! Now!"

Sierra recognized the voice and fought the sinking feeling in her belly. She'd heard that same tone too often over the past eight years. The man staring through the slits in a ski mask was her ex-husband, Clay Ellis.

Once the other man was gone, Clay started toward her. The other guard standing watch over the vice president and Grady Morris called out, "What are you doing?"

"Our leader wanted names of the hostages."

The man snorted. "He has the most important one.

No one tops the vice president except the president himself."

"Look here, young man." The vice president rose from the theater seat and took a step toward his captor. "Release us at once before this goes too far."

The man turned his weapon on the vice president and said in a cold, deadly tone, "Move one more step and I'll blow a hole right through you."

"You don't want to do that. Murder carries a lot longer sentence than kidnapping. In some states a murderer can get the death penalty. Don't go there, son."

"I'm not your son," the man spit at the country's second in command. "Don't tell me where to go or what to do. I know my chances of getting out of this alive are nil. Why should I care if I take a few people out with me?"

"Please, Mr. Vice President. Sit down," Sierra said. The last thing she wanted to see or have the children witness was the murder of the vice president or anyone else, for that matter.

The vice president backed up and took his seat.

Clay's counterpart aimed his rifle at Sierra. "Now, you sit down and shut up."

"Back off. I've got this one," Clay said. He walked all of the way down to where Sierra stood, grabbed her arm and dragged her away from the others. "Play your cards right and I'll get you out of here."

"I know it's you, Clay. That mask hides nothing from me," Sierra said, her tone low. "You can't let them do this."

"It's too late. We're in this now, and we're not going home."

"What does that mean?"

"Just what I said. We won't be going home from here. Once those in charge have their say in front of a billion Americans, we're going to scatter to the winds. I won't be going back to Grizzly Pass. And you're coming with me."

"Okay."

He squeezed her arm tighter. "Okay? Why the big turnaround now? Have a change of heart? Afraid of me at last?"

"I'll go with you. But I have one condition," Sierra said. This might be her only angle to get the terrorists to release the children. She had to play the card she'd been dealt.

"You're not in a position to demand conditions," he said.

"If you don't grant my condition, I won't go with you willingly. If you grant it, I will go with you and cause you no trouble."

His eyes narrowed in the slits of the mask. "What condition?"

"Release the children."

"No way. They're a bargaining chip."

"You have the biggest bargaining chip with the vice president of the United States. What more do you need? He draws more attention to the media than a handful of kids who will be screaming again as soon as they get hungry or have to go to the bathroom."

"Why should I trust you?" he said. "How do I know you won't go back on your word?"

"I'm not the one who lied and cheated in our relationship."

"You lied when you said until death do us part."

"I didn't lie. I was no longer married to the same man. He died somewhere in the past eight years. Whereas you lied when you said you'd love, honor and cherish me. What part of beating your wife is cherishing?"

His lips pulled back in a snarl. "If you weren't so damned mouthy…"

"It didn't matter if I talked or was mute. You hit me. And if I go with you again, you'll hit me again."

His eyes narrowed again. "So why would you promise to go with me, then?"

Sierra pushed back her shoulders and lifted her chin. "Because I care more for those children than I do for myself. They're just starting their lives. They deserve a chance to live them."

"I'm not in charge. I can't promise anything. But if it means you'll come with me without an argument, it might just be worth it." He shoved her back toward the women and children. "For now, sit down and shut up."

Sierra did as she was told, sinking onto the floor beside Brenda.

Clay walked back up to the exit. "I'll be right back."

"Yeah. That's right. Leave me with all of these hostages. At least give me enough bullets to take care of all of them."

Clay pulled a thirty-round curved magazine from a strap on his vest and tossed it to the man standing guard over the vice president. "Shoot them if they give you any trouble."

The man sneered. "Even your wife?"

Clay shot a killer glance at Sierra. "Especially my wife." Then he left the room, closing the door behind him.

If Sierra hoped to get out of the situation, she had to come up with a plan. She had no intention of going with Clay Ellis anywhere. The man was on a one-way path to hell, and he could damn well get there by himself. But she had the children to think of. If she could negotiate their release, she'd tell the devil anything he wanted to hear.

Chapter Fourteen

Thankfully, the Black Hawk waiting at the fairgrounds was large enough to carry the entire Safe Haven team and their weapons to Yellowstone National Park. The state police, county sheriff's department and the National Guard had been alerted and were on their way. Some of the county sheriff's deputies were there, herding tourists out of harm's way.

Garner was on the radio with Hack and the county sheriff the entire way there, keeping apprised of the situation. As they approached a field close to the Old Faithful Visitor Education Center, Garner turned to the others.

"There are approximately twenty heavily armed Free America members at the visitors center. Ten inside and ten outside." Garner stared at the four men. "Since they don't have a SWAT team available or on-site, I've asked if they would like for our highly trained combat team to be the ones to go in and neutralize the situation. Right now, they have a hostage negotiator working with the FA people."

"What do they want?"

"They want to make a big splash in the news. They've asked for news teams from the big networks. When they're done making their speech, they want helicopters to take them to the border of US and Canada. Only then will they release the hostages."

"Seventeen unarmed hostages and twenty bad guys armed to the teeth?" T-Rex shook his head. "Even they can't be serious. That's a transportation nightmare. And Canada will refuse to allow them in. They have to know they are on a suicide mission."

Garner's lips pressed into a thin line. "My bet is they'll wait until the news teams are in place and then they'll make their big announcement and martyr themselves and their captives."

"Should we wait and see if they can negotiate the release of the hostages?" Caveman asked. "We're not in the Middle East. If we go storming in, there could be civilian casualties."

Garner nodded. "If we go in, we have to go in stealth mode. We can't go in shooting from the hip and raising hell." He touched his headset. "Hold on. Hack's talking."

He bent his head and cupped his hand over his headset, nodding as he listened. When he glanced up, he smiled. "They've released eight children."

"Was that all of the kids?"

"The park rangers seem to think they were all part of a ranger-led group. There were eight children, six women and a ranger in the group."

T-Rex leaned forward. "Did they release any of the women?"

Garner nodded again. "Two women, identified as

mothers, were released with the children. They kept four of the women, the ranger, vice president and Grady Morris." His gaze captured T-Rex's. "They said they'd start shooting captives if they don't get those news crews in the next fifteen minutes. They'll start with the women."

T-Rex cursed and willed the helicopter to land faster. He understood the need to touch down out of range of the terrorists and potential rocket-propelled grenades. The Wyoming National Guard wouldn't want to risk losing another expensive helicopter through careless mistakes. But damn. Could they put the craft on the ground already?

His hand on the release clips of his harness, T-Rex counted the seconds until the helicopter skids kissed the dirt. He unclipped his harness, shucked his headset and jumped to the ground.

"T-Rex." Garner was right behind him with a hand on his arm. "You can't go charging in without assessing the situation and coming up with a plan."

"We can't wait until they start shooting the hostages."

"We have at least ten minutes before that happens. Ten minutes to get in and rescue them." Garner's hand tightened on T-Rex's arm. "We don't want to make them nervous and start shooting hostages sooner."

T-Rex drew in a deep breath and let it out slowly. Garner was right. "I won't let them kill Sierra."

"Or the vice president," Ghost added. "We don't want any of those people shot. We need to study the situation and come up with a plan."

His teeth grinding together, his jaw tight, T-Rex nodded. His teammates were right. "Time's running out. Let's get somewhere we can see what's going on."

The team grabbed the rifles Garner had packed into the duffel bag, checked the full magazines and slipped into the protective vests Garner had included. The rifles were equipped with silencers, which would come in handy if they wanted to take out certain bad guys and not alert the others. They were also given radio headsets for communication among the team members.

Meanwhile, Garner coordinated with the law enforcement team currently positioned in the parking lot. He informed them they would be swinging around from the side and to hold their fire.

"I'm having the law enforcement crew clear the parking lot. The helicopter pilot will move closer, providing a distraction while we move in from behind."

The team moved through the trees surrounding the visitors center on two sides. When they were close enough, T-Rex took the lead and crossed to one of the outer buildings separate from the larger main building.

"There's a man in the prone position on each corner of this end of the building."

"Can you sneak up on them?"

T-Rex studied all angles. He'd have to cross an area that would leave him exposed and alert the guards. He wouldn't make it without being seen. "I don't think so. If I step out now, they'll see me and open fire."

"That will alert the rest of them, and they might start shooting prisoners," Ghost said.

At that moment, three bison wandered past close to his position, heading toward the main building.

"Wait," T-Rex said. "I have an idea." He slipped the sling of his weapon over his shoulder and waited until the second bison was within five feet of him. Then he ran to get on the opposite side of the animal, hunkered low and walked with the big beast to the edge of the building, past the enemy guard on the corner. Once past the man, he left the bison and ran for the side of the building, hugging the shadows.

"Be ready," he whispered into his mic. He slipped his knife from the scabbard on his belt and crept up behind the man on the corner. He was almost on him when another bison loped out in front of the guard, capturing the man's attention.

T-Rex grabbed the guard by his boots, yanked him backward, out of sight of his counterpart, and slammed his head into the side of the building. The man fell limp to the ground.

T-Rex removed the bolt from his weapon and tied the guard's wrists with his own belt. Then he shoved the man's ski mask into his mouth. He didn't have much time.

A door on the side of the building gave him hope, until he tried it. It was locked. He shoved his knife between the door and the frame and jiggled it. He'd never unlocked a door like this before, but now would be the time to figure it out, since he was fresh out of hairpins or nail files.

He held his breath and jiggled the knife again. The lock sprang free, and the door swung open into a storage area stacked with boxes. Based on what Garner had briefed, the theater was on the end of the building he had entered. If he could get past the men on the inside, he might be able to sneak the prisoners out through one of the side doors. "I'm inside."

"The helicopter is on its way over. Ghost is making his move on the other guard."

"I can't wait. He can come through the door I left open. I'm going to check out the inside situation."

"Don't do anything rash until we're all inside," warned Garner.

T-Rex ignored Garner. He'd do what he had to in order to save Sierra. Glancing at his watch, he'd used five of the ten minutes he was working with. He inched his way through the storeroom to the door he presumed would lead into the bookstore or a hallway. He turned the knob and eased the door open toward him.

A man stood on the other side with his back to T-Rex.

T-Rex could see the lobby to the right. In his narrow view through the door, he counted four men armed with AR-15s standing to the sides out of range of potential snipers, all staring out toward the parking lot. The thumping of rotors could be heard as the helicopter hovered in the parking lot, making a slow landing to buy the team more distraction time.

T-Rex couldn't see anything to the left. He'd have to take a chance there weren't any other men close to the guy in front of him.

"I'm right behind you," Ghost whispered into his headset. "Invite the man in."

T-Rex reached out, slid his knife through the man's

jugular, wrapped his arm around him and yanked him into the storeroom.

Ghost was there to close the door behind him.

They waited for the call to go out to the others. When none did, T-Rex opened the door again.

Their attention still on the helicopter, the four in the lobby talked quietly among themselves.

"There's the helicopter." A tall man with a solid black ski mask watched as the helicopter hovered over the parking lot. "Where the hell're the news people?" one of them said.

"At this point, I don't care," said a man in a camouflage ski mask. "I just want to be on that helicopter and on my way to the border."

"Shut up!" The black ski mask guy shook his rifle at his teammate. "We aren't going until we get our message across. This is a call to arms to the people of this country. Or did you forget?"

"I don't see anyone else joining our team," said the man with the camouflage ski mask. "It's too damned hot to be wearing all of this crap."

"It's been thirteen minutes and we still don't have a news crew." Black ski mask man jerked his head toward the camouflage man. "Bring one of the women out. We need to show them we mean business."

The camouflage man turned toward T-Rex and hurried past to the theater. The other three men in the lobby redirected their attention to what was happening in the parking lot.

"There's a news van pulling in now," another man said.

"They better be connected with the national news, or we're not dealing," black ski mask guy said.

"Going to the theater," T-Rex said softly into his mic.

"The gang is almost to the building. We'll follow," Ghost said.

T-Rex stepped out of the room and tiptoed after the camouflage masked man, praying he wouldn't start a chain reaction that would get all of the hostages killed.

"I DON'T KNOW how you did it." Brenda hugged Sierra. "I almost cried when they let the children go."

Clay had managed to convince their captors to release the children and two of the mothers, who escorted the kids out of the building. That left four women, one park ranger and the two politicians. They kept them separated on opposite sides of the theater. Clay was in charge of Sierra and the women, while a more volatile man had his weapon trained on the vice president, Ranger Jared and Grady Morris.

"Poor Stevie and Gemma." Sierra's heart squeezed in her chest. "They didn't want to leave without their mothers."

"Yeah, but they're safe now."

"We hope." Sierra didn't know what had happened to them once the children left the theater. Clay had told them the children would be released unharmed.

In the meantime, she and the others were being held until the Free America group got what they wanted. What that was, Sierra didn't know.

After the children had been released, Clay stood for a moment talking to another member of the terrorist group. When that man left the theater, Clay walked down to where the women sat. He grabbed Sierra by the arm and yanked her to her feet, pulling her away from the other women. "I got your damned kids released, it's time you came with me." He dragged her toward the exit.

Sierra dug in her heals. "I'm not leaving until the others are released."

"You sure as hell are." His hold tightened on her arm. "You promised you'd come without argument if the brats were let loose." He shoved her up against the wall and pressed the rifle barrel against her throat.

Sierra didn't flinch, though the cool metal wedged against her neck made it difficult to breathe. "You heard me. Not until the others are released."

He sneered down at her, his face turning a mottle red. "So much for your word being good."

She snorted. "I learned from the best of liars."

He backhanded her so hard, her head snapped back and hit the wall. Sierra's ears rang and she saw stars, but she refused to pass out. "Besides, you can't just walk out of this now. This place has to surrounded by every law enforcement agency in the tristate area."

"I'll get you out. And we'll go far away from this hellhole."

She faced him, her jaw tight, her fists clenched by her side. "I'm not going with you."

For a long moment, Clay pressed the rifle barrel into her throat, his nostrils flaring. "Fine. You'll die with the rest of them." He shoved her toward the others so hard she fell to her knees.

Then he stood back and aimed his rifle at the four women, his eyes narrowed.

Sierra stood, squared her shoulders and joined the other women.

A moan came from the upper end of the theater.

Grady sat in a theater seat, rocking back and forth. "It wasn't supposed to happen like this," he muttered. "It wasn't supposed to happen like this."

"Shut up, Morris." The bad-tempered terrorist at the top of the theater hit Morris in the side of his head with the butt of his weapon.

Morris fell out of his seat onto the floor and curled into the fetal position, rocking and sobbing. "It wasn't supposed to happen this way."

"Hey." Bad-Tempered Guard got Clay's attention. "I gotta piss. When are we supposed to be replaced?"

"Hell if I know," Clay responded.

"I can't wait." Bad-Tempered Guard waved his rifle at the men. "Watch these three."

"Send someone else in," Clay said. "This is a lot of people for one guy to cover."

"So, you figured that out, did you? You didn't seem to think so when you left me alone a while ago." Bad-Tempered Guard snorted. "Seriously, shoot them if they look at you cross-eyed."

"Much as I'd like to do that, we can't," Clay said. "They're our tickets out of here. Without them, we're dead."

"We're dead anyway. You might as well take some of them with you." Bad-Tempered Guard left the theater.

Ellis moved to a more strategic position near their

prize catch, the vice president. Then he alternated watching the three men at the top of the theater and the women down in front by the stage.

Sierra figured Clay couldn't keep a close eye on all of them all of the time, and she assumed the primary hostage was the vice president. He'd be more concerned about keeping the vice president from making an escape than a bunch of women.

"How long are you going to keep us here?" the vice president asked.

Clay turned his head to study the vice president and the congressional candidate. "As long as it takes to get what we came for."

Taking her chance while Clay's attention was diverted, Sierra inched toward the stage where Ranger Jared had set out a display of the various types of rock that could be found in Yellowstone National Park. She selected two particularly heavy and dense rocks the size of her palm and hid them behind her back. The stun gun would have been better, but it was in her purse halfway up the theater on the floor somewhere. She couldn't risk going after it now. Clay might figure out that was what she was getting from her purse, since she'd used it on him before.

She moved back in place before Clay shifted his attention back to her. She caught his glance and let her gaze drop first. Let him think he had her cowed and she wouldn't fight back. They needed all the advantages they could get. If they were going to make a move, it had to be before Bad-Tempered Guard returned. Sierra didn't want to test his commitment to killing all of them if anything went south on their operation.

The next time Clay glanced away, Sierra handed Brenda one of the rocks.

Clay looked back again, his eyes narrowing. He stared long and hard at Sierra.

"Kind of hard to keep an eye on two groups, don't you think?" she asked.

He glared at her. "I have it covered."

"Would it be easier if we moved up to the others?"

"I'll tell you what would be easier." His lip pulled back in an ugly snarl. "You keeping your mouth shut."

Sierra held up a hand. "Hey, I don't want to get shot any more than anyone else. If that means making it easier on you, so be it."

Clay chewed on her words for a moment and then nodded. "You four women, move up here."

Sierra hustled the women up to where the men sat at the top of the theater, grabbing another one of the big rocks from the display on the stage along the way, careful not to let Clay see what she was carrying by moving close to the other women.

Once they were with the men, Sierra slipped one of the rocks into Ranger Jared's hand. Then with the other one gripped firmly, she edged her way over to Clay. "I've been thinking."

Clay glared at her. "I don't care what you think. You lied to me."

"That's what I was thinking about. I guess I was mad and wanted to get back at you for all the nasty, mean and horrible things you've done to me in the past."

"Where are you going with this? Because it's not convincing me I shouldn't shoot you."

"I don't want to die today. If it means leaving with you. I guess it's the only choice I have."

"Sorry, you had your chance. Now you're just one of the hostages." He jerked his head toward the others. "Get back with everyone else."

Sierra ignored his order and moved closer. If they wanted to get out of there, they had seconds to do it before Bad-Tempered Guard returned. "Clay, remember when we were kids and slipped beneath the bleachers to make out?"

"Where are you going with this, Sierra?" He pointed the barrel of the AR-15 rifle at her chest. "Get back with the others before I have to shoot you."

Sierra touched the tip of the barrel and pushed it gently to the side. "Don't you wish we could be that young and carefree again with our whole lives ahead and nothing to stop us?" She inched closer.

"There's no going back. You never loved me. I knew that the day we married."

She must have known it, too, but she shook her head. "We had it good for a while. We can do it again. If we try." Finally close enough to press her body against his, she wrapped one of her arms around his neck and leaned her breasts against his chest. Inside, she wanted to vomit. But on the outside, she hid her revulsion, thinking about the others in the room whose lives depended on her convincing Clay she still loved him and they had a chance at a life together. Which they didn't. No way in hell.

"Let's you and me get out of here. We'll start over." She kissed his chin and trailed her lips to his. "Let's leave now."

He crushed his mouth down on hers and dragged her body hard against his with his free hand.

Sierra raised her arm as if she would wrap it around his neck with the other. That was when she slammed the big rock to his temple, hitting him at the corner of his brow. Blood ran out of the gash into his eye.

Clay yelled and shoved her away, clamping a hand over the gash.

Before Clay could raise his weapon to fire, Sierra shoved the heel of her palm upward, catching Clay's nose, breaking it with a sickening crunch.

Since he was still standing and in the way of her freedom, Sierra kneed him in the groin. When he bent double, she slammed his head against her knee. "That's for all the times you hit me and I didn't know how to defend myself."

He fell to the floor. Out cold.

Sierra turned to the others. "Hurry! Let's get out of here." She headed to the other door at the top of the theater. The one opposite from the one Bad-Tempered Guard had gone through, and hopefully farther away from the men in the lobby.

Sierra was first to the door. She pushed it open enough to see into the lobby. Men in ski masks were shouting. She couldn't tell if they were shouting at each other or someone else. Sierra didn't care.

She pointed to a potted plant in the hallway away from the theater. Turning to Brenda, she said, "Make it to the plant first. Watch them. When they aren't looking, head for the exit at the end of the hallway."

The men were so busy yelling at each other, they weren't watching the theater.

Sierra touched Brenda's shoulder. "Go. I'll send the others. Help them get out."

Brenda nodded and ran for the potted plant.

Her breath caught in her throat, Sierra held it until her friend made it to the plant and then the end of the hallway and out the door.

She pointed to the vice president. "You're next, sir."

He shook his head. "Ladies first. Get them safe." He urged one of the mothers forward.

She shrank back, shaking her head. "I can't."

"Then come with me." The other mother grabbed her hand and dragged her through the door and down the hallway.

Once the two mothers were gone, the vice president touched her shoulder. "You're next."

She stood fast. "I'm last out. Go, Mr. Vice President. You're the big fish they have to negotiate with. If they don't have you, they don't have their bargaining chip."

"I insist," the vice president said. "Please, don't hesitate. The sooner you're out, the sooner the rest of us will go."

Grady Morris erupted from the floor. "Out. I need out." He ran to the door and out into the hallway without looking first.

A shout sounded behind Sierra. Bad-Tempered Guard ran into the theater from the other door. "Damn it! What the hell's going on?"

"Go!" Sierra shoved Ranger Jared toward the door.

Jared ran down the hallway, not bothering to hide behind the potted plant.

The vice president refused to budge when Sierra tried to push him through the door. Instead, he stepped between her and Bad-Tempered Guard, blocking any bullets that might be aimed her way. "Go." He shoved her out the door and turned toward Bad-Tempered Guard. "Don't shoot!"

Sierra had two choices: run or be shot.

She ran.

Footsteps sounded behind her, and gunfire echoed off the high ceilings.

"Stop, or I'll shoot," a voice shouted.

Sierra wasn't stopping. She was halfway to the outside door. She couldn't slow her momentum, even if she'd wanted to.

Another shot was fired.

Pain blasted through her calf and sent her falling flat on her face. Her head hit the floor, rattling her brain, making her vision blur.

More shouts sounded in the lobby. Men scurried, more shots were fired.

Sierra pushed to her knees and tried to stand, but pain ripped up her leg and made her fall back to the ground.

An arm reached around her and pulled her off the floor and locked her against a tense body. Her captor spun with her, facing the melee, and shouted, "Try anything, and I'll kill her!"

Pain knifed through her leg, pushing fuzzy gray fog

around her vision, but Sierra refused to pass out. Her vision cleared just enough to realize the men in ski masks lay littered across the lobby floor. Law enforcement personnel poured into the building, weapons drawn, ready to shoot anything that moved. In the middle of them stood a tall, dark, auburn-haired marine with wide hazel eyes.

T-Rex. And he looked scared.

Chapter Fifteen

T-Rex froze. A tall man in a dark ski mask held Sierra clamped to his side with one arm. In the opposite hand, he held a grenade.

"I've pulled the pin. If you shoot me, I'll release the handle. Sure, you'll kill me, but the woman dies, too."

T-Rex stepped forward, dropped his weapon to the ground and held up his hands. "Don't hurt her. She's done nothing to you."

"Yeah, well, she's going to get me out of here." The man waved the grenade. "If this goes off now, it will kill me, her and half of the people in this building. Do you want that?"

"No." Garner stepped up beside T-Rex. "No one will hurt you. What do you want?"

"I want that helicopter out there."

"You've got it." Garner turned to Caveman. "Get outside and clear a path to the chopper. Now!"

Caveman grabbed several deputies and ran out the door. Through the windows, T-Rex could see them clearing all personnel out of the path between the visitors center and the helicopter.

"I'll need escorts to make sure no one takes a shot at me and the woman," the captor said. "Consider it more collateral to ensure I make it to the chopper without dropping this baby."

"You've got it," Garner said. "I'll escort you myself."

"Me, too," T-Rex added.

"Then let's get going before the woman bleeds out."

That was when T-Rex noticed the pool of blood on the floor beneath Sierra. His heart pinched hard in his chest. He stepped forward, wanting to go to her and apply pressure to the wound.

But the man with the grenade was calling the shots. One wrong move and the wound wouldn't matter anymore.

"Let's go!" Sierra's captor yelled. He shoved Sierra forward, holding her close, the hand with the grenade held high for all to see and fear.

T-Rex feared all right. He didn't see any way out of this scenario.

Sierra stared across at him, a crooked smile on her face. "I tried to escape. I guess I didn't do so good."

"We'll figure this out. Don't worry," T-Rex said.

"Shut up and keep moving," said the man with the grenade.

"Wait!" a shout went up. The vice president emerged from the theater, escorted by Ghost. "Leave the woman. Take me."

The captor snorted. "A little late for heroics. I want in that helicopter in the next two minutes, or I'll let go of this grenade. And I don't care if it kills every last one of you."

"Please, don't. We'll get you to the helicopter," Garner assured the man. "Step this way. No one will hurt you."

"Damn right, they won't. Not if they want her to live."

T-Rex moved to stand on the other side of Sierra and the man holding her hostage. Between him and Garner, they walked the pair to the exit, striding slowly to avoid any misinterpretation of their movements.

Garner was first through the door, holding up his hands as he went. "Don't shoot!"

The parking lot in front of them had been completely cleared of all personnel. Many of the vehicles had been moved to allow the helicopter to land on the pavement. There was a line of cars in the handicapped spots between the visitors center and the helicopter.

Once T-Rex stepped through and moved to the side, the man with the grenade and Sierra emerged from the building. "Stay back at least ten yards," he said as he moved toward the parking lot and the helicopter.

T-Rex tried to think of a way to save Sierra. Perhaps if T-Rex threw himself at her captor and landed on the hand with the grenade, Sierra would be spared. He tried to calculate the amount of time it would take for him to close the distance between them and the number of seconds it would take before the grenade exploded. He couldn't risk it. If he didn't make it in time, the terrorist would drop the grenade and it would be the end of the terrorist, Sierra, T-Rex and Garner.

He'd never been faced with a scenario this important in his entire life. When Gunny had been hit, they hadn't known it was coming. They didn't have time to prepare.

Knowing what could happen was far worse. If that grenade dropped and he lived through the explosion, he'd forever wonder if Sierra would have survived if he'd chosen a different option.

He appeared to be faced with a no-win situation.

If the terrorist made it to the helicopter with Sierra, there was no telling what he'd do with her next.

T-Rex didn't want to think of the possibilities. He just wanted her safely away. Back in her room at the bed-and-breakfast, making love with him.

He wanted more time to get to know the brave woman and see if, as he suspected, they could be perfect for each other. He'd even consider giving up his military career to be with her. Anything. Just let her live.

SIERRA'S LEG HURT like hell, but she couldn't stand by and let this man get away with a government helicopter and possibly killing the pilot and copilot. As they neared the parked cars, she formed a plan in her head. It wasn't a good plan, but it was all she could think of. If she didn't do something quickly, T-Rex would try to save her, and then all hell would break loose.

T-Rex wouldn't let the terrorist leave the ground with Sierra. He'd do something horribly heroic like throw himself on the grenade. He was a good man with a lot of life ahead of him. He deserved to live it, not die taking one for the team or her.

Sierra couldn't let that happen.

In the time she had left, her mind flashed through what they had experienced together. It wasn't much, but their meeting and lovemaking had been intense and insanely satisfying. If only she had more time with him. If only she could have told him how she really felt about him.

If only she had another day to spend with T-Rex, she'd make the very most of it and savor it to the moment she died. All of this flashed through her mind and filled her heart, swelling her chest. Mrs. McCall had been right. In the couple of days she'd known T-Rex, she'd fallen for the big marine.

Sierra could imagine spending the rest of her life with such a man. Yeah, he'd be away a lot, and she'd be worried when he was gone, but she'd love him harder when he was with her. If only she'd had the chance to convince him he deserved to be loved and that he should give his lady love the choice of being there when he came home from war.

The walk toward the helicopter was slow due to her injured leg. She didn't have a chance of outrunning her captor. Whatever she did would require her to sacrifice herself to make it happen. Because, as the closest person to the man with the grenade, it was up to her to do whatever it took to keep T-Rex, Garner and the helicopter crew from bearing the brunt of a terrorist's plan. Thankfully, her captor had Garner and T-Rex back off to ten yards away from where they were. It would help with her plan if they had distance and cars between them.

As soon the terrorist marched her between two cars on their way to the helicopter, Sierra turned to T-Rex and dipped her head. Hoping he had caught her meaning, Sierra made her move and pretended to faint, letting her body go limp.

Her captor was thrown off balance and dipped with her weight. In order to balance himself and catch her, he bent and lowered the arm carrying the grenade as her body sank toward the pavement.

Then when she thought the bulk of the explosion would be sandwiched between the cars, she bunched her legs and shot up fast and hard, hitting her head beneath the man's chin.

He loosened his hold on her and the grenade.

Sierra dropped to the ground and rolled beneath a car. The world around her exploded, rocking the vehicle above her so violently she knocked her head into the undercarriage.

Blackness claimed her.

T-Rex HAD BEEN watching Sierra's face, worried she would bleed out before she even made it to the helicopter. Forced to maintain their distance, he was at a point with two vehicles between him and Sierra. He couldn't get to her fast enough to help her. He'd have to wait until they cleared the parked cars. But when her gaze darted to his and held, then she'd dipped her head, he knew she was going to try something.

He opened his mouth to shout *Don't do it*. But it was too late.

Sierra dropped toward the ground, as if she'd fainted.

"Get down!" T-Rex shouted as he ducked behind a vehicle. An explosion knocked him off his feet. A back flash filled his head of the Afghan village and the explosion that had crippled Gunny.

After the earth stopped shaking and the debris stopped falling, T-Rex rose from his position.

"Sierra?" he called out. "Oh, God, Sierra!" T-Rex ran around the front of the vehicle he'd ducked behind and nearly tripped over the hood of the next vehicle. It had been blown completely off the car. The top of the vehicle was mangled metal, and somewhere gasoline was leaking.

"Sierra!" T-Rex's stomach clenched as he looked between two horribly distorted vehicles to what was left of the terrorist. He held his breath, afraid of what he would find of Sierra.

She wasn't there.

T-Rex straightened and turned around. Had she been thrown clear of the vehicles? He didn't see her body lying anywhere close. "Sierra!"

A low moan sounded from beneath one of the cars.

T-Rex dropped down to his knees among the jagged metal and broken glass and peered beneath the chassis of what might once have been a sedan. A torn sleeve lay within inches of fingers. He reached for the fabric and nearly fell backward when it moved. A slim, feminine hand, marred with scratches and abrasions, reached toward him.

"Sierra?" He wrapped his fingers around hers and held on. "Oh, baby, we'll get you out of there. Hold on."

Garner arrived first, then Caveman, Ghost and Hawkeye. With the help of the other law enforcement teams, they lifted what was left of the mangled car off Sierra.

The emergency medical team that had been on standby moved in and pulled her out.

By then, she wasn't moving. Her hand had gone limp in his as they lifted the heavy vehicle.

T-Rex followed the EMTs as they loaded her onto a backboard. "Is she…"

"Alive?" One medical technician glanced up. "Yes. But we need to get her to the hospital ASAP and check her for internal bleeding. We don't know what damage she might have sustained due to the explosion or being crushed by the car."

T-Rex bent to kiss her forehead and whispered, "I'll be there when you wake."

Then she was loaded into a medical helicopter and transported to the hospital in Bozeman, Montana.

T-Rex watched until the helicopter disappeared, his heart leaving with it. "I have to get to the hospital."

"We'll have the Army National Guard helicopter take you in a few minutes," Garner said. "I want to go with you, but I also want to get an assessment of the situation here before I leave."

"I don't give a damn about what's here. I need to be there when Sierra wakes."

Garner clapped a hand to T-Rex's back. "And I promise, you'll be there, as soon as I get a status."

The team gathered around the terrorist who'd taken Sierra captive.

"Grady Morris is back in the building, spilling his guts, hoping for a plea bargain for information," Ghost said. "He's pointing his finger at this guy as the ringleader."

"Who is this guy?" T-Rex asked, reaching down to pull the ski mask off what was left of the man who'd almost killed Sierra.

Even before T-Rex removed the mask from the man's head, Garner spoke, "What do you want to bet it's Fratiani?"

T-Rex removed the mask. The man lying in pieces was Leo Fratiani, the land broker who'd tried to purchase Olivia Dawson's ranch after her father was murdered.

T-Rex shook his head. "Why?"

"He thought he could get away with it," Ghost said. "Morris says Fratiani was an engineer on one of the pipeline projects and was laid off when the work dried up. Since then, he's lost his wife to divorce and his home to foreclosure. He tried his hand as a land broker in California, but when he tried to acquire his own properties, no bank would give him a loan. His credit was crap."

"Then how did he get the money to outfit the Free America group with AR-15s?" T-Rex asked.

"Grady Morris," Ghost responded.

"The politician?" Caveman shook his head. "Why the hell would Morris get involved with someone as shady as Fratiani?"

Ghost answered, "He wanted to stir things up in Wyoming so that he could appear to be the man people should vote for to clean up what was going on, and put people back to work on the pipeline."

"Bastard," T-Rex bit out.

Garner glanced at Ghost. "How's the vice president?"

"Unscathed," Caveman said.

"The other hostages?" T-Rex asked.

"No injuries to the hostages, other than Ms. Daniels." Ghost chuckled and smiled at T-Rex. "Apparently, your girlfriend got them out before the shooting began."

Sheriff Scott joined the Safe Haven team and faced Garner. "I want to thank you and your team for helping us diffuse the situation. None of our people were injured in the process. Of the Free America group, we have seven dead, three injured and eight who gave up when the shooting started."

T-Rex turned to Garner. "Everyone is accounted for. Can we go to the hospital now?"

Garner faced the sheriff.

"We'll take care of everything here." Sheriff Scott nodded toward the waiting helicopter. "Go."

T-Rex met Garner's gaze.

Garner turned to Ghost.

"We can catch a ride back to Grizzly Pass with some of the sheriff's people," Ghost said. "I'd like to stay and help with the cleanup."

The Homeland Security agent nodded to T-Rex. "Let's go."

They jogged to the waiting helicopter. Within minutes they were in the air and heading to the hospital. Eventually, they were touching down near the hospital in Bozeman. The pilots of the Black Hawk had to return to their post, leaving Garner and T-Rex to find their own way back.

T-Rex didn't care. His number one priority was to be at Sierra's side when she woke. She'd taken the fall to keep anyone else from being hurt by Fratiani. The woman had guts and a heart as big as the skies in Montana. She was more than he could have ever wanted in a woman, and, by God, he would be there when she opened her eyes. She didn't have anyone else. And he needed to be the first face she saw.

It didn't make any sense. All the years he'd refused to give his heart to a woman, knowing it wouldn't be fair to ask her to stick around while he was off fighting wars. But for once in his life, he wanted someone to be there when he came home. He wanted that someone to be Sierra. Call him selfish, but he wanted that more than he'd ever wanted anything.

Sierra was strong, determined and had a big, loving heart. She deserved to be happy. T-Rex wanted to be the man who made her happy. If he had to give up his career in the Marine Corps, he would.

He was led to the emergency room waiting area, where he paced for the next thirty minutes while they evaluated and worked on Sierra. When the ER doctor finally came out, he glanced around the waiting room. "Family of Ms. Daniels?"

T-Rex raised his hand and hurried forward.

"Are you her husband?"

He didn't hesitate. "Yes."

"The bullet went clean through her calf. There was some tissue damage, but we expect she will heal completely. She's also got a concussion. Considering she was in the path of a grenade explosion, we'd like to keep her overnight for observation. Other than that, she should be able to go home tomorrow."

T-Rex released the breath he'd been holding. "When can I see her?"

"Now. She's been moved to a room on the third floor."

"Is she conscious?"

He smiled. "Yes, and she's been asking for a dinosaur. Maybe you'll understand. Not just any dinosaur. She wants a—"

"T-Rex?" T-Rex's face split into a grin. "I know what she wants." He shook the doctor's hand. "Thank you." And he ran for the elevator.

He found her room and knocked on the door.

"Come in," a feminine voice called out.

T-Rex pushed open the door and walked in.

A nurse stood beside the bed, adjusted the IV and turned toward T-Rex. "You wouldn't happen to be T-Rex?"

He nodded. "Guilty."

She stepped back so that T-Rex could see Sierra lying against the sterile white sheets. "This the guy you've been looking for?"

Sierra's face and hands were covered in cuts and bruises, but her smile shined, lighting the room. "You came."

"Wild horses couldn't keep me away." He crossed to the bed and lifted her hand to his lips. "Hey, beautiful."

Her cheeks turned a pretty shade of pink. "I'm a mess. And my ears are ringing."

"You're alive, that's all that matters."

Her smile slipped and she studied him, sweeping her gaze over him from head to foot. "You and Garner?"

He chuckled. "Alive and well."

Her shoulders slumped. "Thank God. I worried my attempt to escape would get others hurt."

"On the contrary. Your attempted escape saved lives."

"And your team?"

"All made it unscathed. It appears you are the only casualty."

"Figures." Her pout made T-Rex want to kiss her even more.

Still holding her hand, he sat in the chair beside her bed. "You know, I've been rethinking the whole military career thing."

She frowned. "Oh yeah? I thought you had it all figured out."

"That was BS."

Sierra's frown deepened. "BS?"

He grinned. "Before Sierra."

"Oh." She blushed and glanced down at her hands. "And now?"

"I'm thinking Wyoming might be a good place to live. As a civilian."

Sierra shook her head. "Are you out of your mind? You're a career marine. Why would you want to give that up?"

He brought her hand to his lips and pressed a kiss to her knuckles. "I believe there just might be more to life than killing the enemy."

She squeezed his hand. "But the country needs you."

"I'm finding that I need you, and I want to be a little selfish for once in my lonely, miserable life."

Sierra's fingers tightened in his, and tears welled in her eyes. "But you don't like commitment."

He lifted his chin. "It's a guy's prerogative to change his mind." Then he winked. "What do you think? If I could find a job in Grizzly Pass, would you consider going out with me?"

She shook her head.

T-Rex's gut clenched. He hadn't thought through what he was going to say to her, but when he'd asked her out, he hadn't expected no for an answer. "Why not?"

"I am not going to be the woman responsible for taking you away from the military duty you love." She pinched the bridge of her nose. "You do love being a member of the Marine Corps, don't you?"

He nodded. "Yes, but—"

"Then why give it up?" She stared into his eyes. "I don't have anything keeping me in Grizzly Pass. I've always wanted to see other places." She dipped her head. "Just not by myself."

"You'd follow me?"

She nodded. "If things work out between us, I'd follow you to the ends of the earth."

He lifted her hand to his lips. "What if I asked to stay on here for a few more weeks? You know, give us a chance to get to know each other."

She looked up through eyes swimming in tears. "I'd like that."

"If I can't extend my TDY with the Department of Homeland Security, I'll ask for leave."

"Then we have a date?"

"More than one, I hope."

"So the big, tough marine is opening his heart to possibilities?"

He nodded. "To you."

"What made you change your mind?"

"Babe, I've never met a woman who'd be willing to take a grenade for me. How can I not fall in love with you?"

She laughed out loud, winced and pressed a hand to her head. "Don't count on me taking too many grenades."

"Trust me, one was more than my heart could take." He leaned forward and kissed her lips. "Sierra Daniels, I think I'm falling for you. Is it possible to fall in love so quickly?"

"Captain Rex Trainor, I have it from a good source, it doesn't take long if you fall for the right person." She wrapped her hand around the back of his head and deepened the kiss.

This was where T-Rex wanted to be. With this woman, where she was. Whether in Grizzly Pass or at one of his duty stations. As long as she was there when he got home, he'd keep coming home.

Chapter Sixteen

"Gunny, I can't tell you how glad I am to hear you're going to get the feeling back in your hands." T-Rex stood at the railing of the wide wraparound porch at Stone Oak Ranch, staring out at the Beartooth Mountains and the bright yellow sun shining down on them. Life couldn't get better.

"You and me both. I'm working on the legs next. I want to be up and running by the time my son turns four and starts training for football." Sounds interrupted Gunny, and a moment later he said, "I have to go. My wife has a chore for me to do. You know the saying, *Happy Wife, Happy Life.* I'll touch bases with you later this week to see how the dates are going. Treat her like a princess and you'll win her heart."

T-Rex ended the call on the cordless phone.

"I'll take that." Liv Dawson held out her hand for the phone and handed him a bottle of beer. "Are you about ready for a steak?"

"You bet." He walked down the steps to the grill where Hawkeye was flipping steaks. "Need a hand?"

"No. I've got this. I've already been assigned grill

duty for when I retire from active duty. Liv is hopeless in the kitchen."

Liv handed Hawkeye a beer in exchange for a kiss. "I'm going to starve while you're gone."

"Six months. I put in my paperwork last night online. I'll be out of the army in six months."

"Then the real work begins. Are you sure you don't want me to sell this place and we both retire to a condo on the beach in Florida?" Liv slipped her arm around Hawkeye and leaned into him.

"Darlin', I love ranching. It's where I want to be."

"Glad to hear it." She stood on her toes to press a kiss to his lips. "Because there's a lot of work to be done and not nearly enough people to do it."

"CJ Running Bear is working out great. He's turned out to be an excellent ranch hand."

T-Rex glanced over to the teen sitting on the porch next to Lolly McClain, Charlie's six-year-old daughter. The young man had taken on a lot of responsibility and was helping his mother and siblings get back on their feet after losing his stepfather. "He's a good kid with a great work ethic. What if he wants to go to college or join the military?"

"We won't hold him back," Liv said.

Hawkeye nodded. "He deserves to follow his own dreams. But until then, he's agreed to help out on the ranch."

T-Rex went in search of Sierra. He'd last seen her helping Charlie McClain in the kitchen cutting up onions, lettuce and tomatoes for those who preferred hamburgers to steaks.

He found Charlie, but not Sierra. And Charlie was in Ghost's arms, kissing him.

T-Rex grinned. "You two need a room?"

Ghost broke the kiss and took a swing at T-Rex's shoulder. "We have a room, in a house we found online back at my duty station. Charlie and Lolly are moving in with me until I can make an honest woman out of her."

Charlie held up her hand, sporting a diamond ring on her left finger. "We're engaged," she said.

"That's wonderful!" Grace Saunders exclaimed and climbed the steps up to the porch to see the ring. "You three will make a great family."

T-Rex pounded Ghost on the back. The SEAL was obviously in love with Charlie. "And you're not staying in Grizzly Pass?"

Ghost shook his head. "I have a few more years before I can retire. Then we might consider returning to Wyoming."

"Until then, I can take my work anywhere there's internet." Charlie wrapped her arms around Ghost's middle. "Wherever Ghost goes, I'll follow."

Ghost kissed the tip of her nose. "Except when I deploy."

She laughed. "True. But Lolly and I will be waiting for you to come home."

T-Rex turned to Grace, the naturalist who studied the wolves of Yellowstone National Park. "What about you and Caveman? Are you leaving Wyoming to follow Caveman wherever the Delta Force takes him?"

Grace shook her head and smiled toward Caveman. "I can't give up my work. There's so much more to learn from the wolves we've reintroduced to the ecosystem here."

Caveman joined her and draped an arm over her shoulders. "I'm three months shy of my reenlistment. I've decided to leave the military. But I have a job waiting for me when I get back to Wyoming."

"He's coming to work for me," Kevin Garner called out from the horseshoe pit where he was playing against his wife, Kathleen.

Everyone seemed to have figured out where they were going. He couldn't be happier for the team he'd come to care about.

T-Rex looked around and finally spotted Sierra. She was coming toward him with a cookie in her hand. "Miss me?"

"You bet." He kissed her lips and then took a bite of the cookie. "You know, when I retire, I wouldn't mind coming back to Grizzly Pass. The place grows on you."

"I'm glad you think so." She leaned against him, fitting perfectly in the crook of his arm.

Together they stood at the porch railing, watching the sun set on the mountain.

T-Rex couldn't believe how lucky he was. He'd found the perfect mate in Sierra, and he didn't want what they had together to ever end.

Sierra was amazing. She'd taught him so much.

T-Rex finally understood that love was something you had to grab when you could for as long as you could. No regrets.

* * * * *

Don't miss the previous books in the
BALLISTIC COWBOYS *series:*

HOT COMBAT
HOT TARGET
HOT ZONE

Available now from Mills & Boon Intrigue!

"Ava, it's me, Faisal."

She hadn't heard right and yet she had. The voice, the words, even the shoes. It all came together. All of it was familiar. The fear fell away. She relaxed in his arms, her heart pounding a zillion times an hour.

"If I let you go, promise me you won't run," he said.

"It's a mistake to be here with me."

His arm eased and she slid down, landing on her feet and turning to face him.

The look he gave her was both intimidating and full of concern. "You could have died, running the way you did."

"But I didn't," she said obstinately as if her earlier fears had been based on nothing but her imagination. "It was a mistake to follow me," she repeated, for he hadn't responded the first time she'd said it. "Fai," she whispered. "You need to get out of here. Trust me."

"We'll get out of here together. It's what I do, protect."

SHEIKH DEFENSE

BY
RYSHIA KENNIE

First Published in Great Britain 2017
By Mills & Boon, an imprint of HarperCollins*Publishers*
1 London Bridge Street, London, SE1 9GF

© 2017 Patricia Detta

ISBN: 978-0-263-92898-3

46-0717

Our policy is to use papers that are natural, renewable and recyclable products and made from wood grown in sustainable forests. The logging and manufacturing processes conform to the legal environmental regulations of the country of origin.

Printed and bound in Spain
by CPI, Barcelona

Ryshia Kennie has received a writing award from the City of Regina, Saskatchewan, and was also a semifinalist for the Kindle Book Awards. She finds that there's never a lack of places to set an edge-of-the-seat suspense, as prairie winters find her dreaming of warmer places for heart-stopping stories. They are places where deadly villains threaten intrepid heroes and heroines who battle for their right to live or even to love. For more, visit www.ryshiakennie.com.

If you are reading this dedication, this one is for you.
You are the reason this book was published.
Thank you and enjoy.

Chapter One

"Son of a…"

The broken expletive was followed by a bang that seemed to echo through the bowels of the yacht.

Ava Adams's eyelids fluttered. Fitfully, she turned once, then twice. The yacht shifted and rocked in the waves. It had been a late night yesterday and the day before, not to mention the fact that this trip had been completely unexpected. She was dreaming—there was no reason to get up, not yet…not for hours yet.

Still, she shivered. Her sleep was skating on the edge of consciousness—what was reality and what was not were no longer clear. In her dream, she only knew that she needed to escape. She flung one arm out grazing the wall, causing her to turn to her other side.

She opened her eyes. She wasn't fully awake. She didn't even take in her surroundings before immediately closing her eyes again. But she couldn't shift as deep into sleep as she'd been. In fact, now with her eyes closed, her consciousness was heating up. She could see through the curtain of lashes. The moonlight drifted in a faint stream of light across the sheet that twisted around her waist. Her breathing leveled out and she fell asleep again. This time the sleep was even lighter than it had been before—more troubled. She didn't know how long she slept. She only knew that it wasn't long before she was again awakened. This time by sounds that she couldn't ignore. They were loud against the background of the once calm rocking of the boat. Her senses came awake, first noting the change in smell. She inhaled, long and slow. She'd done that often in the two days that they'd been anchored in this cove. She loved the hint of vanilla that was so pervasive and wove through the salty scent of ocean, of seawater. Oddly, the vanilla scent was gone.

"To hell—" a man's voice rose in a shout. It was a shout that seemed to be cut off as if forcibly stopped. He might have said something else. Words that jumbled in the scuffle and chaos of noise that preceded a crash, followed by another.

It was only a nightmare. It was a figment of her imagination. A result of the stress of stepping from one world into another; from academia into the world of a self-sufficient adult. Two weeks from today she was moving to Casper, Wyoming. At twenty-five and with a doctorate in psychology under her belt, it was about time. At least that was what she'd told herself. Her father had encouraged her to take all the time she needed. She knew that was a way of keeping her close, of keeping her dependent on him. Even though she had lived her own life, in her own apartment, paying as many of her college bills herself as she could with money she had made by occasionally tutoring other students, still she had relied on him. It gave him a chance to be the father he hadn't gotten to be when she truly had been a child. She'd allowed him that. For he'd become her parent in her latter childhood. It had been through marriage, but stepparent or not, she couldn't ask for a better father. Now they were making up for lost time. Thus, this trip. They both needed it—the time to be together. Life had gotten busy.

She hovered in the abyss between sleeping and wakefulness. But soon sleep was completely chased away as the shouts rose in volume. More disturbing was the absolute silence that followed. That brought her to full consciousness. She was still, hardly breathing, straining to hear. Were the voices real or only her imagination, or part of a dream? Seconds ticked by. She lay tense, unmoving. The conversation she'd had with her father earlier ran uninvited through her mind. Some, if not all, of the things he had said had been disturbing. He said he was concerned that his partner had gotten himself into a situation with fraudulent land sales. She'd begged him to give her details but he'd refused to say more. He had many projects and thus many people he'd partnered with and he hadn't given her a name. Instead, he told her that what he'd said and what was recorded in a Texan town would be enough, if it were ever necessary, for her to take evidence to the authorities.

What was going on? There was the sound of heavy footsteps, scuffling and another shout. Something banged above her, as if something or someone had hit the deck hard.

Besides herself, there were two other people on board. Her father and his business partner, a man she didn't know well. The arrival of Ben Whyte had been a surprise to both of them. They'd just been settling in for the night when he'd arrived on a small fishing boat.

The fisherman had dropped him off and left. Neither of them had expected him. This had been their vacation—she'd sailed here to Paradise Island, Bahamas, from St. Croix with her father after he'd issued the last-minute invitation. It had been peaceful until Ben had arrived. Almost immediately, she hadn't liked the tension that Ben seemed to generate. But the initial tension between him and her father later dissolved once they began telling boisterous sports stories. She'd retired for the night as they joked about the antics of a coach on the football field. But the joking she'd left less than an hour earlier was a far cry from what she was hearing now.

Things didn't sound too friendly anymore. A curse, a series of banging and scuffling sounds that echoed through the boat. She sat up, her heart pounding.

Another shout had her tense, clenching the sheet. One foot poised on the edge of the bed as she tried to decide whether this was dream or reality. Something crashed, a hollow bang like someone had hit a wall, or the floor. The sounds escalated in volume, an angry shout followed but the words were incomprehensible.

She grabbed her phone. The thought of calling for help crowded out the other possibilities. She wasn't sure who she would be calling or why. What would the local police do about a situation that was unknown even to herself? She needed to find out what was going on, if her father needed help, if…

Footsteps thudded over her head. Their heavy tread was oddly ominous when combined with everything that had preceded them. Then something else banged, a dull sound that seemed to echo through the boat. Something had fallen and hit the deck just a little to the right of where she now sat.

"What's going on?" she muttered. She flicked on the lamp by the side of the bed. Soft light bathed the room, chasing away the shadows but not the odd noises from above deck. She got out of bed. Blindly, she grabbed something to throw on. A silk wrap that she'd purchased only this morning with no intention of wearing here. It was a garment made for when she had a boyfriend. It was an enticing garment. Now, it was only the first cover at hand.

She stood there for seconds. The seconds could have been a minute, maybe less, maybe more. She considered her options. But her options were unclear in a situation that was as dark as the night around her. All she knew was that something was very off. The silence that had descended in the last seconds was almost as ominous as what had preceded it. A shiver ran down her spine as she left the room. She moved through the tight passageway, slipping past the galley, which was lit only by a thin streak of moonlight that streamed through a porthole to her left. Memory guided her to the narrow metal stairs that led above deck. She was afraid to turn on any more lights, for that might alert whoever was on deck. She wouldn't think of the fact that there might be strangers, a threat of some sort aboard the yacht. Her fingers quivered and the phone shook in her damp palm.

Only a few hours earlier she had been able to see through a porthole the shadow of the shoreline. Now, there was nothing but a dark, endless stretch of water. That was odd. But even more odd was the fact that the boat was rocking as if it were on open water.

She wished she'd grabbed her slippers, for the narrow passage was chilly against her bare feet. She could only hope that what she heard was nothing, a silly argument, a bit of a wind above deck that had knocked things over. But her thoughts were stopped midstream by another crash directly above her. She jumped and bit back a scream as she dropped her phone. In the dark she couldn't see it. She felt around. Seconds passed and then a minute, maybe two. It was futile. She couldn't waste any more time searching for the phone for above her something was terribly wrong.

She took the remaining steps two at a time. She pushed open the door onto the deck. She was met by a wind that seemed to come out of nowhere and wrapped a chill breeze around her, lifting the silk from her body. She held the wrap down with one hand and pushed forward, determined to find out what was going on, to put an end to it. Seconds seemed to become minutes. She stumbled and lost her footing on the rain-slicked deck.

Her breath caught in her throat when she stepped around the wheelhouse. The moonlight lit the deck revealing two men locked together, struggling. She froze and then she took a choked breath. She covered her mouth to block the involuntary beginning of a scream.

Time seemed to stop. She could almost hear the tick of her vintage, manual-wind wristwatch as she took in details. Blood stained her father's white polo shirt. But that wasn't what frightened her the most. Instead, it was the man who stood mere inches behind her father.

The moonlight revealed the face of the man. Ben Whyte. Like her father, Ben was in his late fifties. Now it was clear that her initial feelings about the man were not misplaced. The thought pierced her shock as she put her right hand over her mouth. She couldn't believe what she was seeing.

It wasn't possible.

Her brain, her feet—everything had frozen at the shock and horror of what lay ahead of her. Things like what she was seeing only happened on television. Not to normal everyday people like her and her father. And yet she knew her father wasn't normal. He was a wealthy philanthropist. But that wasn't the issue. Or was it?

The moonlight was glinting off the black barrel of the handgun that Ben had aimed at her father. The handgun's deadly gloss seemed to wink in the muted light of the deck. Worse, that same barrel was against her father's head. Time seemed to make the moment unendingly long when she knew that it was only seconds. She hadn't had time to think, to react, to recover from the shock. She could only watch this like it wasn't real, like it was happening to someone else. Because before she could move, her father twisted, grabbed Ben's gun hand and slammed it against the railing. Once, twice— the gun dropped and skidded across the deck.

"No! What are you doing?" Her voice seemed loud in the sudden silence. Vaguely, she realized that she hadn't shouted at all, that her cry had been no more than a whimper. She was behind and to the side of them and neither one of the men had seen or heard her. She glanced around the deck as if the answer to her father's plight lay there.

Unarmed, in bare feet and a silk wrap, with shaking hands, she was no one's hero. She looked around for a weapon, something to leverage her defense of her father. There was nothing.

Moonlight spilled over the surface of the water. She could see nothing but an endless tract of ocean around them. There was no sign of land, of Paradise Island or of the beautiful cove that they had docked in. They were in open water with no land in sight. But as much as that frightened her, the scene in front of her frightened her more.

One calamity had replaced another. Ben had her father by the throat.

"Dad!" This time the words crept past her frozen throat. This time the words weren't just her imagination. But still they were no help.

"Stay back!" Her father choked out the words with what seemed more willpower than strength, for she'd had to strain to hear him.

But rage flooded her and, despite her earlier doubts, she only knew that she had to join forces with her father. Take this threat down no matter what the odds. They could do it together, as a team—as her father always said they could. Of course, he'd meant much smaller, much less threatening situations than this. It didn't matter. This was life and death. It was, for whatever reason, them against him.

"What are you doing?" She flew at her father's attacker. The fact that the man had, a few hours ago, greeted her with all the cordiality of a long-lost friend, was now lost to her.

He was the enemy and she'd do anything in her power to stop him. Fueled by panic and a desperate kind of bravery, she grabbed his arm, trying to free her father.

"Let go!" she screeched. Her nails raked his cheek. Her actions were as desperate as she knew they were ineffective. There was no choice, there was only her and her father, who she feared would die without her help.

The punch hit her in the jaw and dropped her to her knees. She remembered nothing after that. She came in and out of consciousness. Minutes could have passed, even hours—she didn't know. The deck offered her its slick, rocking comfort as her face pressed against the cool surface.

As consciousness returned once more, the one thing that was clear was the silence. She struggled to keep her eyes open. Her head pounded and she lost consciousness again for a minute, a second—she wasn't sure.

This time when she came to she was groggy but able to sit up. As she did she saw the shadow of something against the wheelhouse. She tried to stand and slipped. Her hand caught her fall. She looked up, blinking, trying to clear her vision. She saw that Ben had somehow managed to get the pistol. But he had no chance to use it, for her father's arm came up. His arm smashed into his assailant, knocking him backward, sending the pistol flying.

"Go!" Her father waved. He glanced her way for just a second. Then, he was pulled back into a chokehold. His assailant had taken advantage of his brief distraction. Her father directed her with his eyes. Glancing to a place behind her. There was a life raft and she knew that he wanted her to leave, to leave him alone with his attacker.

"No!" she screamed, scrambling to her feet. She clenched her fists—her hands were empty. No phone. But something else caught her eye. It was the hammer her father had used earlier to fix the back ladder. She grabbed it.

Despite her earlier failure, she wasn't willing to give up. She'd do whatever it took to help her father. She wasn't thinking straight. She was unschooled in any sort of self-defense but desperate times called for desperate measures. Her attack could confuse, muddy the waters, give her father an opening. And with that her only thought, she charged forward. She was unaware of the breeze that lifted her short sleep T-shirt revealing her upper thighs. Unaware that the silk wrap had slipped off her shoulders or that it floated behind her. Her father choked as Ben crushed his throat with one arm. But she'd caught Ben's attention, she could feel his eyes on her and that was all she needed. She'd become the distraction and hopefully by doing that give her father enough of an edge to get free. Unfortunately, she could see from the look on his face that the only thing that stood between her and rape was her father. If her father died…

Ben looked at her with eyes filled with lust. He smiled in a way that held an ugly promise, one no woman would fail to recognize and one no woman would ever want. It made her feel dirty and terrified at once. She was frightened not just for her father but for herself. Too late, she realized her mistake. She should have put something else on, anything but what she had grabbed in her panic.

She'd never trusted him. She wished she'd told her father that. But it was too late. As if killing her father wasn't enough… It wouldn't happen. Her father wasn't dead and no matter how many times she had to remind herself of that, it wouldn't happen.

She raised the hammer and brought it down, catching Ben in the shoulder. He roared, releasing his grip on her father, reaching for her.

"Dad!" she screamed as she scrambled to get away from Ben.

Her father slammed Ben's arm into the wheelhouse.

He buried his fist in the man's midsection, throwing him off balance. Another punch hit him in the jaw and Ben gasped for breath. His third punch knocked Ben down.

"Run, Ava!" her father shouted and didn't give her a chance to consider before he had grabbed her hand. Together they ran, stumbling, propping each other up heading for the back of the yacht.

"Get in the life raft," he hissed in an urgent undertone. "Get out of here. I'll catch up. Once I…" His words were slurred. A tooth was broken and blood streamed from his mouth. His hair was wild and his eyes glazed. "Go." He was half lifting her over the edge of the yacht, giving her no option. She shook her head. Her fractured thoughts spun.

"Call Faisal!" her father said with a shove that had her landing in the dinghy. "Al-Nassar," he added as if she wouldn't know who he meant with just his given name. There was no other Faisal who had been in their life. But why call him now? Then she remembered— Nassar Security. There was no time for thoughts or justifications—there was no time for anything. They needed to get out of here. Already her father was undoing the ropes that attached the small craft to the yacht.

"No." She couldn't leave him alone. "Come with me!"

"This is the only way you can help me, kid." It was the pet name he'd always used for her, and still did despite her recent quarter-of-a-century status. He'd teased her on her birthday about how old she was and how old that made him.

Her eyes met his.

"Go."

"No." The word was strangled, panicked. As if she

had any choice. She was already below deck level and had to look up. "If you stay, so do I. I won't leave you alone."

He was so banged up. She couldn't leave him.

"I need you to go," he said firmly. "I can't be distracted trying to save you. I need to know you're safe."

It was his way of promising that he'd make it.

She knew there was nothing she could say to change his mind. Her teeth were pressing so hard into her lip that she tasted blood. And none of that stopped the shaking, the fear for both of them and for him especially.

"I'll be right behind you. I promise."

"Here." She stood up, fighting for balance as she reached up and handed him the hammer. She had to trust that he'd be safe. There was no help for it. He'd taken the option of choice from her. And she could see now that the life raft was so small it might sink under the weight of both of them.

He took the hammer, his fingers brushing hers, and at the same time pushed something into her hand. She didn't look but only closed her hand around the damp plastic.

"Call…" He wiped a trail of blood from his upper lip. His nose was bleeding, the blood mixing with that from his lip and trailing down his chin. "Al-Nassar. The number's there," he reminded her in a voice that was pitched only for her. Behind them she could see his assailant struggling to his feet.

"Go!" The word echoed like the needless repetition it was. She had no choice. Choice was the option that had been removed from her arsenal. Her father had decided. She would be safe and he would face… She couldn't think, didn't know. She only knew that she was alone.

"Dad…" That one word trailed, bottomless and hopeless. For there was nothing to say.

A gunshot had her on her knees with a scream as the raft rocked and threatened to tip. She clutched the rope lashed to the side. The raft settled enough that she could look up. There was no doubt that what she'd heard was a handgun. She'd heard them many times, on the firing range with her father.

Her head spun and she sat back down. When she looked up to where she had last seen her father, he was gone. Waves pushed against the side of the life raft taking it farther from the yacht. She needed to get to shore, get help. She pulled the engine cord, grimacing at the old-fashioned technology. Her father was usually the first to buy the newest and latest, except for the life raft. Its age was jarring in the scheme of everything else that was always so top-of-the-line. She yanked the cord again. Her arm ached and nothing happened.

Her father's last words seemed to spin in an endless reel through her mind.

Faisal. She had to call Faisal.

It was her last thought before she passed out in a heap in the middle of the dinghy.

BEN WASN'T SURE how it had happened. But he'd gotten lucky and landed in the water. He'd just missed hitting his head on the way down. He'd seen Dan fall overboard. But then he'd fallen in himself. It didn't matter, he'd planned to swim for shore anyway. He'd shot Dan first and he'd gone over a dead man. The yacht was on autopilot, its navigational system dead, heading somewhere out to sea. In other circumstances he might have laughed. It would keep the authorities occupied trying to find the boat.

There was only one threat left and that was the little witch of a daughter Dan had managed to dump in the life raft. There'd been nothing he could do to stop him. It had all happened so fast. He felt a twinge of regret. Now Dan was gone and the yacht was already too far away to be a consideration. He'd raised the anchor before the altercation began.

He swam toward shore. He'd locked in his mind in what direction and how far away they had drifted. Yet, the weather system was moving in faster than had been reported. It was a squall, and that and his aching shoulder had him gulping water and struggling as the weather worsened. Combine the weather with the fact that his clothes weighed him down, and it was rough going. He reached down, wrestling with the laces of his oxfords, finally managing to get them off and tie them to the belt loop of his pants. It wasn't supposed to go like this. He wished he hadn't had to kill Dan, but once he'd made the decision, he'd accomplished what he'd meant to. He'd shot Dan and he'd fallen overboard. Now there was only one problem he had to resolve before he could become a rich man. The one fly in the ointment was Dan's daughter. She wasn't supposed to be on the yacht. Yet, there she'd been like it was her right. He hadn't liked her the first and only other time he'd met her.

She'd heard too much and she'd injured him. Neither offense could be forgiven. A wave pushed him backward and had him swallowing water. He choked and flipped onto his back, resting, thinking. He had to get to shore and then he had to find Ava Adams, and when he did, the little witch had to die.

Chapter Two

The United States Coast Guard received the first distress call shortly before 0100 hours from BASRA. The acronym stood for the Bahamas Air Sea Rescue Association. A volunteer association, their resources were stretched with other cases and they were more than willing to request help. Two hours after the information was in the hands of the United States Coast Guard, that information was relayed to the Wyoming branch of Nassar Security.

It had taken that long for the connection between the owner of the yacht, Dan Adams, and Sheik Faisal Al-Nassar to be made. The connection came from the yacht owner's electronic log that had also provided their last location off the coast of Paradise Island. Dan Adams had included in the log his next destination and purpose. A meeting in Fort Lauderdale with Faisal Al-Nassar.

Faisal was told that the call for help was made on a cell phone. The call lasted exactly nine seconds and then had broken off and been too short to trace. It had been a male caller who had provided only two words, *Mayday* and *Ava*. Ava was Dan's stepdaughter's name and the other person aboard that yacht. There was no record of anyone else being on the yacht. The call had ended immediately after that.

Faisal couldn't believe that the father and daughter were missing. He was reminded of how long it had been since he'd spoken to Ava. While her father had remained in contact, he and Ava had lost touch. Still, the father and daughter were considered friends of the family. Now if it had been possible, Faisal would have left to begin the search immediately. But not only did he have to get to the Jackson, Wyoming, airport where they kept the company jet, the pilot had to ready himself and the craft for takeoff. They followed the twenty-minute rule. That was how long it took the pilot to prepare for takeoff.

Faisal glanced at his snowboard with regret. He'd just hung it up after waxing it and preparing it for a trip to Mount Hood in Oregon where there was enough snow to board throughout the year. Now that would have to wait. The thoughts of snowboarding were only a way of grounding himself, by thinking of what he loved, before being immersed in a case that was much too personal.

He brought his attention to the immediate as he called his brother Emir. Emir, the oldest in their family and the head of Nassar Security, was located in their head office, which was situated in Marrakech, Morocco. He knew without question that he could count on Emir to relay the plight of their old friend to the rest of the Al-Nassar family.

"Dan and Ava are lost at sea. The US Coast Guard is deployed as is the Bahamas Air Sea Rescue Association. Of course, the latter is volunteer. I'm on wing to fly to Florida," he said abruptly when Emir answered.

"What happened?" Emir asked. "They were on vacation. Last I heard they…" The words ended on an expletive.

"The yacht was last seen just off the coast of Paradise Island, Bahamas. It's since disappeared off the radar. When I spoke to Dan, he said he was heading to Fort Lauderdale earlier than planned. We had a meeting set up. A change of plans and then they disappear. Is there a connection?" Faisal asked. There was a raw edge to his voice that he made no effort to mute. "Look, I've got a plane to catch, I'll keep you posted."

"I'll let the rest of the family know. Dan stuck by us when everyone else thought expanding the business to the United States was a crazy idea. We'll stick by him now."

"Definitely," Faisal said, remembering all Dan had done. The Al-Nassars were an old and revered family in Morocco and Nassar Security was an established business in Marrakech. His family had been anxious to expand and it was partially because of Dan, who had lived in Wyoming at the time, that they had chosen that state. The rest, he knew, had been his own doing. He'd pushed the envelope with his siblings. He loved Wyoming and the wide open spaces. It was where he'd finished his degree. Fresh out of university, he'd been eager to be part of the new venture, especially if he could convince his siblings to choose Wyoming…and he had. He'd loved the new branch from the beginning, particularly because of the challenge. He'd known that in Wyoming his name and status as Sheik Faisal Al-Nassar would not open doors like it did at home. The idea had challenged and excited him. And despite the obstacles, his brothers had agreed—they'd all welcomed the challenge. And so Nassar Security had expanded. Dan had been a mentor to him in the early years.

During that first year of getting a footing in a new country, Dan had been the father that Faisal had lost too young. He shook his head as if that would dislodge memories. He'd never forget how special Dan Adams was to their family. Nor, despite losing touch with her, did he forget how special his daughter had once been to him. In fact, he was reeling more from knowing that Ava too was now considered lost at sea. His mind kept going back to the dark-haired beauty. He'd spent his last year of university with her. He remembered the jokes, the teasing and the parties, and he remembered something else—how she had made him feel.

Three hours later, from one of the Nassar Gulfstream jets, Faisal looked out the window. It was dark and cloudy in the minutes before the sun began to rise. His mind went beyond what he could see to the Atlantic where two people he cared for were now missing.

According to the United States Coast Guard, there had been only one call for help. It was thought to have come from the Adamses' yacht as that was the only vessel reported missing. They had heard a name but the call had disconnected. There hadn't been enough to give them a location, nothing. All they had was the name Ava spoken in a male voice.

He pushed back a strand of hair that seemed to have a mind of its own. He should get it cut but there never seemed to be enough time. He'd tried it short but that hadn't lasted. Ava had once told him that she loved his hair just over the tips of his earlobes and longer if he'd consider it. The latter wasn't a consideration but the former had stuck in his mind. He'd met her during his senior year in university and they'd become friends. They'd both grown up since then and gone their own ways. That part of his life was long over. At least that's what he told himself. Except today. He was again faced with the truth. He'd never forgotten her.

"We'll find them," he said in an undertone as if saying the words made them somehow more real. Maybe the words made his doubts of success smaller. While the Bahamas were close to the continental United States there was still a lot of ocean to cover. Without coordinates of any kind, they had only guesswork. Despite that and maybe because of it, he was not going to sit around waiting. Dan had planned to see him in Fort Lauderdale—it was up to him to make sure that meeting happened.

His thoughts went back to the last phone call.

Based on what they knew, the Adamses could be anywhere. They were no longer close to Paradise Island's shoreline. A search by the Bahamas Air Sea Rescue Association had already exhausted that option. Wherever they were, whatever had happened, the answers were on that yacht.

Ava Adams opened her eyes. Her head ached and something deep inside her hurt. That hurt was overshadowing the thumping that seemed to want to break her skull. Yet it wasn't pain. Not a physical pain but something more emotional. Fear. Anger. She didn't know what. Instead, she shivered. She was alone and she wasn't on the yacht. Where was she?

The yacht was gone. She had no idea what had happened to either it or her father. It had disappeared while she'd slipped out of consciousness. She had no idea how long she'd been unconscious. Nothing held any relevance, not time nor space—nor anything that had happened. All of it was a frightening blur.

The breeze ran light, cool fingers across her damp skin and she shivered. She didn't know how long she'd been unconscious, all she knew was that she was alone and there was no land in sight. Her head pounded and her vision was blurred. She couldn't see clearly no matter how hard she tried. She was fighting to remain conscious so that she could make that promised call to get help. Her father was counting on her.

The thought made her prop herself up despite her shaking limbs. She tried not to look at the dark water. There was only a thin layer of rubber and canvas between her and it. She couldn't think of it any more than she could contemplate the fate of her father. All she knew was that the yacht was gone and with it her father. She didn't know when it had disappeared or if her father was on board or if he was even alive. She struggled to sit up and the world spun. She took a deep breath and passed out.

The next time she came to, she could see that the sun was higher in the sky. It was behind her and she guessed that she might be heading west. She had no idea what that might mean about where she would end up. Or if she would end up anywhere except maybe at the bottom of the ocean.

Fear threatened to overwhelm her even as her gut knotted along with her fists. Her head spun and she had to fight not to black out again. She needed to think and yet she was fighting not to lose consciousness again. She needed to get help not just for her but for her father. He needed her. He was alone.

That thought collided with another. Was her father alive? She'd heard the gunshot as the life raft had slipped away from the yacht, carried by the ocean current. There had been silence after that as she'd drifted farther away.

The gunshot had echoed long after the actual event. The haunting reminder was like an omen. She could die out here and her father could already be dead. Those scenarios were ones she couldn't, wouldn't consider. Not anymore. She refused to think of him as anything but alive—just as she was determined to reach land, one way or another.

She took a deep breath and again she fought to sit up. The life raft rocked, threatening what stability it had as water sloshed in the bottom. She wasn't sure how it had taken on water unless it had been in those first moments as it had gone from the yacht to sea. The sea had been rough. It hadn't calmed much since then. It was cloudy and the breeze was picking up, only a bit of sun peeked through the otherwise dreary sky.

She had nothing. She looked down. She was virtually naked. The skimpy sleeping outfit had been a bad choice. Fortunately, her father had thrown his jacket over her. Who would have known that a trip that had begun as a lark would end like this?

It wouldn't end.

Determination shot through her chilled body. She had too much to do with her life. She had a new career that had yet to begin. Again she repeated that promise to herself and to her father. They would live. He would live. They had to.

Something cold pressed against her hip. She slipped

her hand under the waistband of her panties and pulled out her father's phone. She'd forgotten it was there.

Her heart stopped. She remembered that he'd handed it to her. It was a miracle that it had not dropped to the bottom of the dinghy, into the water that was gathering there.

She held it, the memory of her father handing it to her clear in her mind.

"Call Faisal."

She knew, as did her father, that if anyone could help them, it was Faisal. He headed the powerhouse investigative company run by his family, Nassar Security. At least he was in charge of their Wyoming branch.

The phone slipped in her damp hands.

"Sheik Faisal," she murmured. It was an odd thing to say, to even think. But in the chaos and panic of what had happened, she vaguely remembered what now seemed like so long ago. It had been her senior year of college when she'd first met Faisal. He'd transferred in for that last year. He'd been two years older but she'd been two years ahead of her grade. She'd skipped through grade school in six years instead of eight and skipped kindergarten altogether. Although, the latter didn't count, she'd been the standard age when she'd entered first grade. Odd memories drifted through her mind. Just the mention of his name brought everything back. She couldn't move, could only fight to remain conscious and all the while she remembered. She'd teased him about his title of Sheik, and he'd hated having it mentioned. It was strange the places her mind wanted to go when there was so little time. Consciousness could slip away as easily as it had returned.

She gripped the phone with the desperation of the survivor she now was. The phone and a man who had once been a friend, who she had once hoped would be more than just friend, were now her only hope.

The sun beamed down through a break in the clouds and instead of offering hope it only reminded her of the passage of time. It was a reminder that her and her father's chances of survival decreased with every moment that passed.

She swallowed heavily—the world was graying and beginning to spin. She shut her eyes, focusing on one thing, on remaining conscious at least long enough to get help, to contact someone, to…

Everything blanked out.

She didn't know for how long or what had happened in the time between awareness and when she opened her eyes again. Like before, all she could see was the ocean. She was in the middle of nowhere and drifting to who knew where. If she thought about it too much she might fall into the abyss and succumb to panic. Her hand slid on the slick bottom of the dingy where water was pooling and was now a quarter inch deep. She could sink if this continued. She took a deep breath. She had to remain calm.

She looked at the phone. It was still in her hand. Had it been there all along? How long had she been out this time? She couldn't remember. It didn't matter. What mattered was that no more time passed before she called. She pushed a button and the phone's screen lit up.

"Thank goodness," she said in a whisper with what seemed the last bit of strength she had. The wind pushed the struggling life raft in a half circle. As the raft shifted direction, she shivered. She didn't know how long she could stay afloat or where she was. She was dizzy, fighting to stay awake. She had to do this. She clutched the phone as if it were a lifeline, and in a way it was.

She looked at the screen, squinting as her vision blurred. Everything seemed to spin and then stop.

"No," she whispered. She couldn't afford to pass out, not before she made this call. Her stomach clenched and her hands shook harder at what was in front of her. But there was no changing the fact that the battery icon was red. Her hand shook harder. She needed to phone now, while there was still some power left. Instead she fainted.

When she came to, the phone was in her lap. She remembered the battery life as if that frightening fact had been etched in her mind. Hopefully there was some juice left and it wasn't too late. She knew this was her only chance. Without the phone, without this call and a connection there was nothing. Nothing but a hunk of rubber slowly taking on water stood between her and... She couldn't think of it. She had to remain positive. She had to get hold of Faisal. Her father's voice telling her to do that wouldn't leave her head. He'd suggested no one else, just Faisal.

She couldn't focus, yet she desperately wanted this horror to end. Despite that or because of it, she remembered another time, another place. Faisal. She'd been on the cusp of adulthood and he'd been her everything for such a short time. Now, again he was her everything but in such a different way. He was all that stood between her and death, between her father and death. This time she was counting on him like she never had before.

She took in a shaky breath, pushed herself gingerly

up and opened the contacts. She hit Faisal's number and the screen went black. The battery had run out along with every chance she'd ever had.

Her world started to spin. She tried to force herself to keep conscious and she couldn't. She slumped sideways as she blacked out. Her last thought was that she was on her own and she didn't stand a chance. But then the phone hiccupped back to life.

Chapter Three

Saturday, June 11—9:00 a.m.

It had been more than eight hours since the US Coast Guard had received the call from the missing yacht. And despite the time that had passed, they couldn't pinpoint where the yacht was. They assumed that the vessel's AIS, Automatic Identification System, a standardized system that would provide the identity, type, position, course, speed, navigational status and other safety-related facts about the vessel, was compromised. Whether that was due to criminal intent or was accidental was yet to be determined.

Faisal had checked the coordinates between Paradise Island and the continental United States. So much could affect the outcome. If it was foul play, that would change everything. If they were suffering engine failure, it could again change everything. And if they were moving under their own steam—doubtful—again, it changed everything. But with nothing to go on, they had to start somewhere.

He glanced over at Craig Vale, the only one of the Nassar team to make this trip with him. Craig was heading north after this to New York to meet up with other members of the tech team. But in the meantime, it was nice to have a researcher on the case. That so rarely happened. They were usually a distant voice via a phone or computer connection.

Faisal shifted his thoughts, focusing on what was ahead. He didn't like any of it. He was flying into a no-win situation. Yet, despite that, this was what he did and what he thrived on. He might not like it but his adrenaline was kicking in. The personal connection would no longer be at the forefront. In order for this mission to be successful he had to lead with his head, not his heart. It was no different than when his sister, Tara, had been kidnapped. He'd let his oldest brother lead the charge and he'd done the hardest thing he'd ever done in his life. He'd stayed here, managing their business thousands of miles away from that heartache. In the end, that decision had been the right one. Tara was home and safe.

He dropped the thoughts from his mind. Now, his mind was solely on this case. Rehashing probabilities and possibilities would get him nowhere. In a way, taking the thoughts from his mind, focusing on what was important, was like meditation, which was something he utilized at the beginning of every case. It was a practice he shared with his oldest brother, Emir, and Emir's wife, Kate, who had introduced him to it. It was something his whole family now practiced. It had made both their business and their family stronger and tighter as a result.

Thoughts of meditation fled as his phone beeped. It was only a notification that they were minutes from landing. He looked out the window of the private jet. Traveling by private jet was one of the many perks that came from wealth. It was also one of many he didn't give much consideration to. If asked, he would have admitted that he was privileged, lucky in the manner of his birth. It wasn't something he ever discussed or thought about. It was a fact that had always been. That part of his life, his family's inherited wealth and status, had been unchanging. He'd been born into wealth that had accrued over generations. It was what he'd always known. But it was this part, Nassar Security and his position as head of the Wyoming branch, that allowed him to play out his dreams of adventure. He couldn't imagine that anyone had a better life and there wasn't a day that he wasn't grateful.

Today was different. Today he faced a tragedy that could touch every member of his family. His phone rang, breaking into his thoughts. He froze and his heart leaped despite his training, which usually allowed him to maintain a cool facade. He held the phone for a split second for Craig to see. It wasn't a number he recognized. What unknown caller would phone now? He didn't believe in coincidence and yet he answered, praying to hear Dan's or Ava's voice.

Silence and something else. There was a sound that was as recognizable as it was disturbing. It was the sound of waves lapping against a dock or the bow of a boat.

Craig nodded, his blond ponytail bobbing where it skimmed over his collar. His nod confirmed the suspicion they had both had. His full pouty lips seemed at odds with a strong jaw. It was as if nature hadn't been sure if it was creating a tough guy or pretty boy. Either way, these conflicting traits belied his thirty-five years and made him look more like twenty.

They both held their breath, hoping the connection would hold, that they could get a trace.

"Hello," he repeated. "Dan?" There was nothing, only silence. The only surety they had was Craig's confirmation that this was Dan's number, but was it Dan? What were the odds that the search would begin on a lucky note? On finding a survivor before they'd even landed?

"Who are you? Tell me." He kept talking, hoping to keep the connection going.

He could hear something that sounded like the crash of a wave. It was different from the first one. This time it was rather like when one wave rolls down into another that is just building to a crest. It was a sound he was familiar with having spent time on a yacht with his family as a child.

He listened closely. He barely dared to breathe, as if even that might drown out other sounds, other clues. He heard what sounded like a soft breath. It wasn't much but what he'd heard sounded feminine. Feminine and indistinguishable.

The sound of water, the pattern of waves and the call of a seagull. Then there was nothing, only silence.

"Hello." He wasn't willing to give up. "Ava? Dan?" He didn't know if it was either of them. He was only taking a chance and betting on the odds against the fact that it could be anyone else. There'd been two people registered as leaving the dock in that boat.

He glanced at his watch and then over at Craig. As if to confirm his faith in him, Craig nodded and gave a thumbs-up less than a minute after the connection broke.

"I have the coordinates," Craig said.

Forty minutes later they landed. He left Craig to his own devices as he transferred to a sea rescue helicopter.

"I'd say it was good to see you, but unfortunately I can't—the circumstances suck," the pilot, Jer Keller, said. They'd flown together on a number of rescues. Jer was the same age as Faisal. He had married young and already had twin toddlers with his childhood sweetheart. But despite the differences in their home life, they both shared a passion for this. If Nassar Security hadn't existed, Faisal would have chosen a career in sea rescue. Getting the opportunity to be involved, as rare as it was, was usually a thrill. Not this time.

"At least we have hope that someone lived." He shook his head. Somehow the way he had pronounced those words sounded grim.

Sam Sanders, a blond man in his midforties, came up to them and shook each of their hands. He was an early retiree from the Coast Guard, an experienced member of Search and Rescue who had helped out as winchman in previous rescues.

"Sam," Faisal said and clapped his hand on the man's shoulder. "Wish we met under better circumstances."

Sam nodded in his quiet, rather stoic way. "Hopefully we'll be successful and you'll have use of me." It was pretty much the last thing he said for the duration of the flight.

They'd been in the air for five minutes when Faisal moved to the back where the side doors were open.

"Better view or just being hopeful?" Jer asked through his mic.

"Both," he said. There was no way to predict how this was going to turn out despite his hopes. All he knew was that there was a storm brewing. Already the air seemed heavier, more humid. It was the intensity of the feeling, not the humidity, that reminded him of

home, of Marrakech. But it had been a long time since
he'd been home for anything more than a short visit.
Wyoming was home now and humidity wasn't an issue.
Not like here. He could feel the air, thick and difficult
to breath. He loved the feel of open spaces, the small
population, the sweeping plains and the blessed winter.
The congestion of a city like Miami or the one of his
birth, Marrakech, overwhelmed his senses. He'd known
that since he was a boy. It was the reason why, for almost the last decade, he'd lived in Wyoming. It was a
vast state with a sparse population that fit his personality like nothing else. He loved the town of Jackson. It
was small, a good place to dig in one's heels. He could
never imagine going back. Big cities were fun in the
moment but anything more than a day or two and he
was antsy. Unfortunately he was here in Miami for as
long as it took to solve this case.

They'd been flying for well over an hour. Jer and
he had caught up on where each of them were in their
lives. For five minutes they flew in silence.

"Do you see it?" Jer asked.

"I do." He was hanging half out of the chopper.
Ahead of them and slightly less than fifty miles off
the coast of Paradise Island was a speck that didn't fit.
A minute later and it was clear that it was a small dark
gray dinghy.

"Bang on, Craig," he said as if the tech was actually present. His coordinates had been near perfect,
for the craft was only a mile away from where his tech
had tracked it. It was barely visible as it rose and fell
in waves that were growing larger with every minute.

"Raft," Jer said unnecessarily as he read off the coordinates. "We may have us a survivor."

The helicopter buzzed closer and it was hard to tell who or what they might be faced with. Faisal could only hope that there were at least two people in that life raft, the right two people—Dan and Ava Adams.

Tension mixed with excitement settled within the confines of the helicopter. The odds that this could be anyone else, considering even what little they knew, were remote.

"It's loaded," Jer said as he dipped the helicopter and lost altitude.

His gaze swept the area while never letting the life raft leave his sight. Dan and Ava had to be alive. He refused to accept another scenario. He looked at his watch as he estimated the hours they might have been in the water.

Faisal got into position to be dropped down. The flight suit he'd donned an hour earlier seemed both familiar and restrictive. He should have a wetsuit but he hadn't thought of that. Emotion had blinded him. He wiped perspiration from his forehead and let the adrenaline fire him up as it always did.

"One occupant," Faisal muttered a few minutes later as he slipped the harness on and prepared to be dropped. His heart sank. That meant that one of them might not have made it.

He wasn't going to assume anything. This could be Ava Adams or Dan Adams or it could even be someone else who had been on that yacht, someone he wasn't aware of. For now, he was focused on rescue, nothing more.

Whoever was in the raft hadn't moved. And it was impossible to tell from this distance if they were alive or dead.

Chapter Four

"We've got a survivor." Jer's overly enthusiastic voice seemed oddly disembodied as it came through the head-set.

Faisal didn't respond, not even to the whoop that followed Jer's statement. Neither were something that needed a response. Neither the enthusiasm nor the words that preceded it needed confirmation. They had all seen, as the waves rocked the raft, the movement within the small craft. But the move had been slight and gave no indication as to the condition of their survivor. Those thoughts ran through his mind as he focused on the details of his descent.

Sam turned and gave him a thumbs-up.

Faisal returned the gesture feeling pumped and optimistic.

The ocean was rough and the raft was clearly visible now. In fact, they were close enough to see that the survivor was alone, and that she was no longer moving. They could also see that her feet were bare. Her peach-colored wrap barely covered her torso and was the only spot of color against the dark gray craft and the stormy gray of the ocean only hinting at blue. Her dark hair spread like tangled clumps of seaweed around her. Her body seemed to rock with the movement of the water, rising and falling, offering no resistance. It was as if she were barely alive and, despite the movement they'd seen minutes earlier, that they might be too late.

Faisal pushed that thought away. He was poised at the open doorway, wanting to move into action.

"She looks in rough shape," Jer said as he turned the helicopter around, bringing it closer to the raft. He cleared his throat. They both knew that despite Jer's earlier enthusiasm, which was so typical of him, that what he said now only reflected his doubt that they had a survivor at all.

"We'll get her to Mercy in Miami."

"I'll let them know the status and give the Coast Guard a heads-up too."

"Possible survivor," he said for Jer's benefit so that he could relay the information. He only prayed it was true. If it were, they'd got here in the nick of time. She was in the middle of nowhere and way underdressed for the overnight conditions. Water in the life raft was causing it to list and that only caused more waves to crest the top of the small craft and fill it with more water. It was only a matter of time before this life raft sank.

They were closer now and it was clearer than it had been earlier that she wasn't dead. She'd moved. It had only been a slight, maybe involuntary action because she'd been still since but it was movement. Relief raced through him while at the same time he wished more than just the three of them were here to rescue her. If they'd had time they would have brought a medic with them. But the timing had been off and the swiftness with which they'd had to move out had prevented any of that. The only thing they could do was make tracks to the emergency room.

It was a fairly easy descent. What wasn't going to be easy was the landing. It wasn't something he'd done in a while but it wasn't unfamiliar, none of it was, not the work nor the pilot he was currently working with. Jer and he had worked together before many times and, despite his idiosyncrasies, he was one of the best.

Minutes later he was lowering himself toward the raft. He waved at Sam once as he gave a direction before twisting in the wind churned up by the helicopter blades. He angled toward the raft as much as he could but the conditions were against him. The wind was kicking up faster than he'd anticipated. The life raft was rocking in the waves. Despite Jer's expertise in keeping the helicopter in position, and Sam's with the winch line, it was taking all his skill to keep on target.

Already, he could see that this rescue was going to be much more difficult than they'd thought. They'd factored in as much as they could. While the wind had been part of that, there was no correcting for the force of the wind twisting him as he descended. That combined with a rough ocean had both the weather and the raft working against them. She'd moved only once since that slight movement almost ten minutes ago when they'd first spotted her. Had both times only been a figment of his imagination? Had it been only the result of the freefall of the raft as it fell within the trough of the waves? Yet he'd factored that, and they hadn't thought so at the time. Still, he wondered.

Dark hair streamed down her back. He was close enough now to see that she was slim and long legged, and while he shouldn't be sure without seeing her face, he knew without doubt who she was. And his heart pounded in response to that knowing.

He wanted to hurry the last few seconds up, get on the raft. But he couldn't rush, couldn't afford a mistake. Instead he took in details, as if that would take the edge off his impatience. She had little on, a silk cover that was soaked and covered nothing. What looked like a man's jacket was draped over her ankles like it had slipped down during the night. Her face was hidden from him by her hair. That was a concern for she was lying facedown. She could have suffocated against the rubber or drowned in the water that covered some of the bottom of the dinghy.

Ava. It had to be her. But if it was, this wasn't how he'd imagined their reunion. This wasn't how he'd imagined her at all. It had been five years since he'd seen her. She'd texted him a couple of times and he'd texted back and then they'd both gotten caught up in their own lives. They'd been friends and yet there'd been something else there. They'd both felt it and yet they'd never acted on it.

Ava. He'd never forgotten her.

It was odd to be thinking such things in the dark heart of a rescue. All his attention should be focused on landing in rough seas. Normally he would have focused but nothing about this situation was normal. His feet tentatively touched the edge of the raft and then lifted off. It was too small. He didn't know if it would hold both of them.

He had to try.

She moved.

Even in the awkward position he was in, relief shot through him. The wind twisted him yet again and he fought to come in at the right angle, to position himself with feet on the raft, not in the water. Either way, he'd get to her, but getting wet wasn't in his plan. At least, it wasn't the option he'd choose.

He pushed those thoughts aside. He needed to concentrate on the task ahead of him. He was hanging just over the life raft. As he determined how much of his weight the small vessel could take, she turned onto her side and opened her eyes. He put his foot down on the rubber to stop a slight spin. It was the last thing he did for over half a minute as he was caught in a memory he'd thought was long forgotten. It had been a youthful connection replaced by the reality called life and the space of five years. But the depths of those blue eyes reminded him that he'd never forgotten. The connection was brief. She closed her eyes again with a sigh as if she knew that she was safe even as she slipped back into unconsciousness. He couldn't waste time looking at her pale face or the full lips that were almost as pallid as the porcelain skin of her slim neck. There wasn't time to consider anything—she needed to get medical help. He went over her with quick hands and eyes. He made sure that there wasn't any injury that needed immediate attention, no blood or awkward positioning of limbs. There was nothing except an unnatural stillness that meant she'd slipped back into unconsciousness. A pass of his hand beneath her nostrils told him that she continued to breathe.

He had to get her into the helicopter and to the hospital as quickly as possible. The mysteries of why she was here and where her father was would have to remain just that. The US Coast Guard, the Bahamas Air Sea Rescue Association and a swarm of volunteers were searching the waters for the yacht. Hopefully Dan Adams was still on board and there'd be answers. If they found the yacht without him, despite having found Ava, the chances of succeeding twice were slim. The Atlantic was a big place and even now the waves were rough with weather reports saying it wasn't going to get any better. His focus returned to where Ava Adams lay unmoving with nothing but six square feet of air-inflated rubber to protect her from the elements. She wasn't even wearing a life jacket. That reality horrified him as he thought of all the possibilities and of how lucky she'd been. The Ava he knew was a poor swimmer. If she'd ended up in the water, she would have drowned in waves like this. She'd been lucky he'd arrived when he had.

It was five minutes before he had her harnessed and buckled against him. It had been awkward trying to balance on the dinghy and maneuver her into the harness. Now, he held her tight against his chest, his arm around her, her breasts pressed against his chest. It seemed inappropriate and wrong. And yet all he could do was hold one arm over the harness that held her and the other a safe distance away as he held the winch line. He looked up and signaled Sam to take them up. The roar of the helicopter blades and the crash of the waves below them made communicating impossible. The line twisted, and they turned, facing away from the empty life raft as the line slowly took them up.

She moaned and it was odd hearing her voice for the first time in so long. She opened her eyes. He hadn't expected that nor her unseeing gaze. It was as unexpected as the first time. This time her eyes held nothing but desperation and panic.

"Find my father." Her words were so low and breathy. It was like it took all her energy just to breathe.

"We will," he said. He held her tighter, her body damp and cold, and her curves pressed into him, teasing him in ways that he could not ignore.

His thoughts were blown away with her next words. "He'll kill him."

Chapter Five

He'll kill him.

With Ava safely in the helicopter, her words still echoed in his mind. Unfortunately, after that cryptic statement, she'd passed out. There was no clue as to who she might be referring to. The yacht had officially held two passengers, Dan Adams and Ava. Did someone want them dead? And if so, who?

They hadn't arrived a moment too soon.

Getting her into the helicopter was difficult, getting her on the stretcher, no easier. She'd been limp, and because of that, dead weight. She'd floated back into unconsciousness for a while after he'd gotten her into the helicopter and before he'd pulled up the rescue gear. A few minutes, not a whole lot more.

She grimaced and then squinted as if she couldn't focus. She wasn't looking at anything; in fact, her eyes were half-closed and hidden by long dark lashes. Her eyes opened a little wider but again remained unfocused on either him or anything else.

He remembered those eyes so full of intelligence and passion. He remembered the vivid blue piercing challenge of them and he remembered the vulnerability behind her shrewd intellect. Despite what he'd told himself over the years, he'd forgotten nothing about her. He pushed the thoughts from his mind. Irrelevant. He needed to keep her safe, get her warm and get her to the hospital.

The only assessment he could make was that she didn't seem to be seeing him. She wasn't looking at him or around him—instead it was as if she didn't see him or anything else at all. It was like she was asleep with her eyes open.

"What happened, Ava?" he asked in an undertone. Sam had moved from the winch just behind him up to the copilot seat beside Jer. Faisal was alone with Ava. Her misty blue gaze seemed to float past him, not taking him in or even her surroundings. She seemed to slip in and out of awareness. Her moments of lucidity were sometimes just moments of opening her eyes. She was unfocused as if nothing was part of her reality. He didn't expect an answer. He wasn't sure why he had asked the question. She was in a fragile state but at least now she had a chance. He hoped that they could say the same about her father, Dan Adams.

"Dad," she whispered as she closed her eyes. But that one word wasn't an answer, it only raised more questions.

"No, Ava. It's me, Faisal." He looked at the face that he remembered so well. The high cheekbones were pale, taut over the bones of her face. A few freckles that he hadn't known she had seemed to stand out against her pale skin. There was so little that had changed and yet so much. She'd been twenty the last time he'd seen her and he'd been twenty-two. For the majority of the years since then, he'd headed the Wyoming branch of Nassar Security. He hadn't forgotten Ava. He'd gone one way and she'd gone another. She'd continued with her schooling. He'd heard from Emir only weeks ago that she'd graduated with a PhD in psychology. Life had happened to them and their friendship had slipped under the radar for a time.

There had always been the promise of something more. But she'd been too young and he'd been with someone else. They'd been friends but always there had been the hint of something more. In another time, if he had been wiser things might have been different.

Seconds later, she opened her eyes. He was startled, for it looked like she had been crying. As if she knew, even in her half-conscious state, that she'd been the sole survivor. She closed her eyes again without having focused on him or on anything else in the chopper. It was like she was there and yet wasn't.

"How's she doing?" Jer asked.

"In and out of consciousness," he said.

"He killed him," she murmured a few minutes later as she opened and then again closed her eyes.

There was no point asking who. Sooner or later she would come to and then she would remember and be able to tell him what had happened. If it was too much later, they would find the information by other means.

He pulled another blanket over her. He reached for a third, rolled it and put it under her calves, thus elevating her legs. At least the fact that she'd shivered was evidence that she hadn't fallen too far into her unconscious state.

He needed to get some heat on her. More important, he knew that he had to get her out of the wet clothes that clung to her skin. The wet material was only chilling her even further and making the blanket useless. He pulled the blankets back, using one of them to shield what he could of her body. He peeled away the flimsy material. Her skin was damp. He tried to preserve her modesty. But there was only so much he could do. He left her panties on. They were damp too but what he'd done had been enough. At least she wouldn't arrive in the emergency room completely naked. Not that it mattered, but yet it did matter and he wasn't sure why. He tucked another blanket around her.

He put a hand on Ava's forehead. The contact sent a tingle through his hand as if there were still a connection between them. But there was nothing, all of that was over. It was stupid of him to think of that. Silly to remember something that had been nothing but a flirtatious friendship despite what he had wanted. It had been a long time ago. They were different people. He was sure she'd changed, much as he had. He regretted not following up with her. If he had then he'd know who she'd become, what had happened to the happy girl with the quick wit. He took his attention to the immediate. She was warm. There was a sheen to her forehead, like a fever might be developing. Her forehead was moist and not, he knew, from her time in the dinghy. He hoped she didn't have a fever but the heat he was feeling didn't bode well. It didn't matter. They would get her to the hospital and she'd be fine. It was the location of her father that was more disconcerting. For his fate was unknown.

"Dad," she murmured.

This time there was expectation in the way she said the word, as if she thought her father might make an appearance.

"Find my father," she said in a breathy whisper.

"It's Faisal," he said, hoping that his voice might somehow bring her back to consciousness.

He leaned closer. "You're alright." It wasn't a question but a statement meant to reassure her, to let her know that she was no longer alone.

She pushed him away but it was barely a tap as her one hand dropped and her other didn't even lift. Nor did she open her eyes. Her head moved to the side as if she were trying to do more but was too weak. "Kill…"

"What?" Sam asked.

"What the hell?" Jer's voice came through the headset. "What's she talking about? Kill who, what?"

"I wish I knew," Faisal said. His attention never left her face. But Ava had closed her eyes again as if that one disturbing word was too much. "Maybe something about what she's been through. Maybe nothing."

"Nothing. I doubt that," Jer replied. "*Kill* is a fairly intense word in any context."

"True," Faisal agreed.

"I've been in contact with Miami's Mercy Hospital. They're the closest and they're expecting us." Jer's voice came over his earpiece. "Contacted Search and Rescue too. They'll pass the info on that we've found Ava Adams."

Below, the ocean swept out around them but there was no sign of the missing yacht nor was there any sign of land. Wherever Dan Adams was, they could only hope he was alive and could hang on. The horizon stretched out in front of them and seemed to mock the fact that help was now minutes away.

BEN WHYTE ROLLED over and moaned. The sun was glaring in his eyes and he couldn't stand to look at it. He'd dragged himself to shore in the wee hours of the night.

He'd lost track of time during a swim that had seemed to go on forever. He hadn't realized that he'd been that far from shore. It was all supposed to be so much easier than it actually had been. The dispute and resulting fight should never have happened.

Dan Adams, he thought with disdain. The man was an idiot. He hadn't thought so only days ago, but it was clear now. Dan had signed his own death certificate by admitting what he knew and then confronting him with it. The Dan of the past would never have done that. He would have silently turned him in.

He looked behind him where he could see the distant rise of Paradise Island hotels and other high-rises. But on this strip of sand there was nothing. He needed to ferry over to the main island where the cruise ships were. From there he could slip on the below deck crew entrance on a ship heading for Florida. His hand slid into his pocket and pulled out a debit card and a small wad of soggy bills. He was taking a chance but he could use the card to get a ticket on the ferry.

He guesstimated that he'd swum for well over an hour before collapsing on this stretch of sand and passing out exhausted for the rest of the night. The only thing motivating him to stay alive was the fact that there was too much at stake for him to die. He was one transaction away from being a rich man and that idiot Dan Adams had almost ruined it all, him and his damn daughter. The meddlesome little witch.

He'd needed Dan. His reputation in their partnership was gold. The land didn't exist, at least not land owned by him, but by the time the damn foreigners found out about it, it would be too late. Except Dan wanted to pull out of the partnership.

He'd shown up on the yacht to give Dan one more chance. Ava Adams was never supposed to have been on board. Dan had told him he was going on a yachting vacation and he hadn't mentioned his daughter. Instead he'd mentioned the fact that his daughter had accepted a position—her first job. Supposedly it started in some forsaken Wyoming town in the next week or two. He'd forgotten the details. It had only amazed him at the time. Amazed him that anyone would want to live in that backwater. But she'd gone to school there and had been forever infatuated with Wyoming. All that aside, he'd never expected to see her. He'd never thought that she'd fly down to join her father. Dan had never mentioned the possibility.

His hand slid to his waist. Empty. He'd been armed at the beginning of this. Dan had hit him and for a minute his world had grayed and then, when he'd come to, he'd shot him and seen Dan fall overboard.

Now, Ava Adams, if she survived, at best she knew he'd killed her father, at worst she knew it all. He had no idea what her father had told her. What he did know was that he needed to close his last deal before the truth came out. But his Canadian buyer was already showing suspicion and reluctant to pay the balance of what he owed for that tract of land he was so hot to have. Time was of the essence, for he'd heard both impatience and a hint of disbelief in their last phone call. It was as if the buyer had lost confidence in the deal, in Ben's ability to facilitate the transfer. It was as if he sensed the truth. That couldn't happen, for the truth would destroy everything. Even without Dan's reputation backing him, he planned to close this deal. There was too much money at stake. One word from Dan's daughter and it would be over before he had a chance to leave. He needed that last payout and he needed it desperately. He couldn't chance the possibility that Ava Adams would reveal what she knew.

She needed to be dealt with immediately. But the grim reaper wouldn't deal out death by sleight of hand. If she wasn't dead yet, in order for her to die, he needed a gun.

Chapter Six

The flight to Mercy Hospital in Miami seemed to take forever. During the time in the air, Ava Adams had gotten worse. Her breathing was shallow. She hadn't regained consciousness since Faisal had stripped most of her wet clothes from her and wrapped her in thermal blankets. She wasn't shivering anymore but she wasn't moving either.

Now, seeing her like this, flirting with death the way she was, was killing him. It was like reliving another dark time when the life of someone he'd loved had been in jeopardy. Then, there had been nothing he could do. Here, there was still hope. He thought of that time. It had been a tragedy. His sister kidnapped. It had ended well. His sister was safe and completing her studies in the United States. Tara had intentions of joining Nassar Security in a full-time position when she graduated with her master's. He wasn't sure if he or any of his brothers were ready for that. He smiled at the thought, and his smile dropped as he looked at Ava. He pulled the blanket up, tucking it beneath her shoulders.

"How much longer, Jer?" he asked, although he already had the answer to that question. They were just words to fill the space, to make everything seem more normal.

"We're ten minutes out. How is she?"

"Unconscious," he said curtly. Nothing could make this normal and there was nothing more to say. Only Ava's thin breaths and her fragile pulse assured him that she was alive, that she was fighting to stay alive.

He had done all he could. The rest was up to Jer to get them onto the hospital helipad and Ava into medical experts' hands without delay.

"I've got this beauty flying her heart out," Jer assured him as if he'd read his mind. "We're only a few miles out now. She hanging in?"

"She's stable. Her breathing has leveled out. Pulse stable but a little faster than I'd like." He didn't like the way things were. For the truth was she hadn't regained consciousness in over ten minutes. Ahead, he could see the horizon open up on Miami. The city skyline appeared on the horizon and soon seemed to rise out of the ocean. Seagulls skimmed between sky and ocean. The slim stretch of sand became a dividing line between the endless stretch of ocean and the steel-and-glass highrises that pierced the sky. The high-rises gleamed in the sun, which had broken through half an hour ago. The expanse of steel and glass set as a backdrop to the timeless ocean was postcard material. But now he could only allow for seconds of appreciation. They would be landing soon. It was noon and it seemed like they'd been at sea for days rather than hours. But the thought that medical help was now within sight had him breathing a sigh of relief. Ava had been unconscious for almost the entire trip. Faisal couldn't have imagined this day during the fun party days they'd shared. When they'd danced on the edges of a friendship that might have been more. In a way they'd been a platonic couple with the suggestion of more, and yet, they'd never crossed that line. It was strange, because the spark had been there. But he'd had another girlfriend at the time and even though that girl hadn't been the love of his life, it wasn't in him to cheat on one woman for another. Things might have been different otherwise. Why he thought of all that now, he didn't know.

He'd finally broken it off with his girlfriend at the time but Ava was too immersed in her studies to see the truth of what he felt. And he'd never asked her out or admitted that he felt so much more. He knew now that saying nothing was a youthful mistake. But time and life had intervened. He was reminded of it all now and faced with how much he still cared.

He looked out the window and below the city seemed to have taken over the landscape. One minute they were on the edge of the city and the next they were targeting a landing strip on the back edge of the hospital. A stretcher and an emergency team were already waiting.

The landing was smooth. The hospital staff were as efficient as the last time they had done this over a year ago; only this time, the roof helipad was closed for repairs and they were forced to divert to the original pad at ground level located just outside the emergency entrance.

On the ground there was a bit of chaos as reporters and camera operators pushed forward. They'd arrived as the stretcher was coming off the helicopter and the camera operators were in their faces almost immediately. They seemed to know who Ava was and more importantly who her father was. As Faisal forcibly pushed back against the onslaught, cameras flashed.

"Do you know where Dan Adams is?" a reporter asked, pushing the mic in his face.

Faisal ignored him, trying to shield the stretcher and Ava with his body.

"Is his daughter, Ava, the only survivor? What happened to Dan Adams? Has he been found?"

The questions were rapid-fire and Faisal had to push forward, demanding that they move back and give the stretcher room. It was the first sign of how much local fame Dan's philanthropy with local boys' and girls' clubs and other charities had given him. Dan had started an organization that reached out to troubled children, and it had branches across Florida and the Caribbean, where he lived for most of the year. His celebrity status put a different spin on this investigation too. Dan by himself was highly regarded, but with the power of his philanthropy, he was a force that couldn't go unacknowledged. They weren't points Faisal had time to consider; instead he was hauling an in-your-face cameraman back by the collar.

"Move back, please. Miss Adams is unable to answer your questions right now."

"Dan Adams?" The questions continued back-to-back. "Is there any hope?"

"The search is continuing," Faisal said.

Frustrating minutes passed before the media finally moved back. They hadn't gotten the information they came for but it was clear that it was the best they were going to get.

As the media moved away and the medical professionals took charge of the stretcher, there was nothing more for Faisal to do. He stood there, his hands shoved in his back pockets as he remembered Dan Adams's words in what might have been their last phone conversation. "I need your help, Faisal. I may have a case for you. The likes of which, I don't know if you've ever seen."

He wished he'd questioned him more, but at the time he'd thought it better to meet face-to-face. He'd looked forward to hearing what their old friend had been up to since they'd last been in touch and he'd even imagined how that meeting would go.

He moved through the bustling medics and to the stretcher that Ava had been transferred to. Her pallid complexion looked almost waxen like a model in a museum. Yet somewhere behind that beautiful still face lay answers. Whether what she might know included the answers they needed to find her father remained to be seen.

What had happened on that yacht off the coast of the Bahamas? From the little Ava had said, it had been deadly. The danger lay in whether or not the events that had caused Ava to end up looking death in the eye in a rubber raft would follow her. He could only hope that the danger had died on that yacht. But assumptions were never safe and too often proved to be wrong. He couldn't live his life on assumptions; if he did he would have been dead long ago. Her father was still out there and he needed to be found, for him—for Ava. His knuckle skimmed her soft cheek, remembering better times, and his right hand went to the butt of his gun. He wasn't taking any chances.

Chapter Seven

Ava entered the hospital on a stretcher led by a physician and with an assortment of other medical personnel flanking her. Faisal felt a sense of relief and panic all at the same time. They were feelings that he'd had from the beginning of this mysterious rescue. He should be relieved that she was in professional hands yet he also felt a profound sense of loss that she was out of his. He strode down the gleaming corridor. He made his way past bustling nurses and doctors and other medical personnel moving quickly through the corridors. He wondered what had brought Ava and her father to this. What had they been doing on that yacht? And where was Dan Adams?

He knew none of it boded well. The United States Coast Guard were coordinating efforts alongside the Bahama Search and Rescue. So far, Ava was the only survivor. There was no sign of the boat or Dan Adams.

He strode through the hospital's doors as he followed the stretcher that carried Ava as if somehow keeping her in his sights would keep her safe.

"Mr. Al-Nassar," a nurse called. "A minute, please."

At first, he didn't slow his stride. He wasn't used to being called by such a formal name. The only thing more formal would have been if they'd used his real title of Sheik. Again, something he never used. It was a title that was more accurate than mister, for, like his father before him and his grandfather before that, he was born a Sheik. But none of that was him. He was just Faisal Al-Nassar to everyone he knew and everyone he dealt with. No one in the Wyoming office called him by any title. They called him by his first name. Here, it was obviously different.

"Yes," he said, turning around despite his thoughts on the formality of the address, the hesitation being so slight as to be unnoticeable.

"There's some paperwork that needs to be completed."

"I'm not her next of kin," he said shortly.

The stretcher carrying Ava had now disappeared behind the sterile-looking stainless-steel doors ahead of him.

"You're the best we have at the moment," the nurse replied. "If we're lucky she may come to long enough to sign consent herself. But in the meantime, if you could just give us what you know."

He took the clipboard and the pen she offered and filled out the forms as best he could. There were large gaps in the information he provided. He knew nothing of her medical history or, barring Dan Adams, who her next of kin might be. He couldn't tell them if she were allergic to peanuts or anchovies or neither. He knew her stepfather, Dan, because he was a friend of the family. He knew that her birth father had died when she was a toddler. When her mother had married Dan, he had acquired a ten-year-old daughter. Unfortunately, Ava's mother had succumbed to a debilitating disease and died a decade ago. Dan and Ava were close. As close as any family he'd seen, even without the blood tie. Dan had taken parenting seriously and Ava was his daughter in the full meaning of that word. He handed the clipboard back to the nurse. Most of what he knew would be of no use to the medical team working on Ava.

He went to security next, explained the situation and ensured that she had a private room with a guard on the floor. Next, he went up to the floor and spoke to the nurses' station, ensuring that media were not allowed near her. He wasn't sure the latter was enough. He knew how tenacious media could be, especially when they sensed there was a story.

"Of course," the charge nurse replied. "She's not the first. We've had other local celebrities."

He wasn't sure how Ava would feel about being called a local celebrity. There was a bit of a mix-up in that, for it wasn't she who was the celebrity but her father. For Ava, he knew the media's interest would be bothersome. She'd always been very private. To him, that explained why she'd taken a position as a psychologist with a public school in Wyoming. The pace was quieter but more important, it was far away from her father's success and the notoriety that came with it. She was low-key. He'd always loved that about her.

Five minutes later he was exiting the hospital. She was in professional hands. Hands that had assured him that she would be well taken care of. In fact, they'd made it clear that there would be no visitors until she was stable. He'd gone over the contact information with a hospital administrator who had assured him that he would be notified as soon as there was a change. He gave the information, knowing that it was unnecessary. Barring the worst-case scenario, he'd be in touch long before any of them needed to reach him. In the meantime, her father, Dan Adams, his mentor, was still missing.

But his mind was stuck on other words. *Worst-case scenario.* There would be no worst-case scenario. He would not allow that to happen. Despite the fact that they'd fished Ava out of the Atlantic on a mission that could have easily failed. Despite the fact that the odds were still stacked against them, he was determined that those odds could be beaten. They would find out what happened. Otherwise he would have failed because now it was her father and an entire yacht that were missing.

Outside, with the Florida sun beating down on him, Faisal looked at the phone in his hand. The one that had been found with Ava. It was white, a basic, no-frills model, reminding him that Ava had learned her low-key approach to life from her father. She'd always been too busy getting good grades to put much thought into lip gloss or fashion. She'd been, at least then, a basics-only kind of girl. But despite that, there'd always been a sexy kind of appeal about her. Another year of maturity under her belt and he could have fallen for her. And yet that wasn't quite true—he'd wanted her even then, but the timing had been off. They were unproductive thoughts that weren't relevant to the situation. All of that was a long time ago and none of it mattered any longer.

He turned the phone over, but it provided no answers. He moved off the sidewalk, out of the way of a man in olive-toned hospital scrubs, moving briskly toward the parking lot.

"Barb," he said into his own phone a minute later. A light breeze wrapped around him and gently rustled the leaves of a nearby tree. He'd just phoned Barb Almay who headed Nassar's research team. She was located in their Marrakech office where she provided research for both Nassar offices. He explained the situation to her and then asked, "Can you run a check on this number's call activity?"

"Of course," Barb replied. She was their head researcher and a technical whiz almost on par with Craig. Their team was good but as far as researching went, Barb was the best—hands down. Barb was originally from Boston and had been on vacation in Morocco over a decade ago when she'd met a Moroccan man and fallen in love. The story had a fairy-tale ending—they'd married and she'd stayed in Morocco. Now she called Morocco home and it was there where she had been discovered by his brother Emir, and hired as part of the Nassar team.

He slipped the phone into his pocket and moved from beneath the shelter of the palm fronds. Overhead it was a clear sky and a seagull dipped and soared as if there was nothing wrong in the world. It sent a chill through him as he thought of the woman he'd left behind, unconscious, to the care of experts. He thought of the man still lost somewhere on the Atlantic and it was all incomprehensible.

His phone buzzed. It was Mitch Brandt, a man he'd gotten to know in his initial search-and-rescue training when he'd been fresh out of university and still debating whether a career with the Coast Guard might be an option. In the end he'd finished the initial training only out of interest, when the chance to head a new branch of Nassar had been presented to him. Mitch had completed the training and eventually gone to work with the US Coast Guard. Mitch had promised to keep him as up-to-date on the search as he could. They were conducting the search from where the yacht had last been seen off the coast of Paradise Island and beyond into the Atlantic Ocean. Yet the oddity they had found, Mitch said, hadn't been on water but on land.

When Faisal hung up, a frown creased between his brows. Only yesterday evening, shortly after dark on Paradise Island, a local had reported an incident regarding a strange man hiring a fisherman to take him to a yacht that had anchored a mile from shore. The incident had been unremarkable until the news of the missing yacht had been leaked. They now knew that the yacht had belonged to Dan Adams. There had been two people on board. Dan Adams and his daughter, Ava Adams. The description of the mystery man indicated only that he was of average height, forty to sixty years old and Caucasian. A twenty-year age gap left a lot of room for guessing.

Two knowns and an unknown on board who, except for Ava, had since disappeared. She had been rescued and the other two had vanished along with the yacht. It was like something out of *The Twilight Zone*. He strode back to the helipad where Jer and Sam were waiting by the helicopter.

"What now?" Jer asked.

"You have to ask?" The question was redundant. The thought that they wouldn't take at least one more run wasn't even a consideration.

"I'm in," Sam said in that quiet, steady tone of his.

Thirty minutes later they were heading back out to sea, where they searched until just after dark. But there was nothing to be found. By mutual agreement and before exhaustion set in, they called it a day. Faisal sent an alert to the volunteer team coordinator to let him know the area they'd been assigned on their second pass was searched and empty.

"I can't believe Dan's still out there," Faisal said. "That we didn't find him."

"Not just him. There's the man with no name, as well," Jer said. "Guy shows up and a few hours later the yacht and its occupants go missing. Is there some kind of link between the two events? Seems rather co-incidental otherwise."

Faisal shook his head. He'd filled Jer in on the basics of the case, the search aspect anyway. "I don't know what that was about. Hopefully, Ava will be able to tell me something soon."

The lights of Miami's skyline lit the horizon. It was just short of nine o'clock in the evening. Faisal felt torn. He didn't want to end the search with Dan still out there but his heart was already back at Mercy Hospital afraid for Ava. Dan had an army of people looking for him; Ava had only him, or at least that's how it felt.

He pulled out his phone and placed a call. A minute later, he said, "Drop me at the hospital. The helipad is clear and there aren't any emergencies coming in." He'd just checked with the hospital authorities and, considering the circumstances, they were okay with a quick drop and leave. "You get home to your wife."

"She's not too happy with you," Jer said with a smile. He'd called earlier to let his wife know what was up.

"Doesn't matter what she thinks of me," Faisal said with a laugh. "She loves you, man. That's why you get away with murder. But you've made her wait long enough."

They'd already discussed the fact that Jer had commitments at home in Tampa. He had a wife and kids waiting for him and while his plans could and would be broken if Faisal asked—that wouldn't happen. Jer was a contract worker that he'd used often. He was also one of the best heli-pilots he knew. When this had all come down, he'd taken advantage of the resources he'd had in the moment. He'd contacted Jer only because they'd worked rescue before and Florida was his home state.

Sam, like Jer, had worked with him before on other cases and they were both based out of Miami. The rest of it, the fact that Craig was heading to the east coast anyway, had been a stroke of good luck. He'd known that if anyone could find out where that phone signal had come from and get to it in time, he could. He'd been right in thinking that and in doing what he had. He'd cobbled together the powerhouse team in minutes after hearing the news. They'd done what they'd set out to do. Now, there were search-and-rescue teams combing the area from both countries. But there was still no sign of the yacht or Dan Adams. He could only hope that he was still onboard, for then he stood a chance.

It was because of everything Dan had done for him and everything he'd been that Faisal had left Ava's side for the length of time he had. But if her father's life depended on it, he couldn't do otherwise.

"What's next?" Jer asked. The helicopter had just landed.

"I'm having a check run on the phone we found with Ava," Faisal replied.

"We're not heading back out?" Despite their earlier agreement, Jer sounded oddly disappointed. "I've got the rest of the night, man, if you need me."

"And Rene," he said, referring to Jer's wife, "will blame me when you don't come home at all tonight." He was fully capable of flying one of the company planes or helicopters if it came to that. "I'm going to wait. We've been out twice—had success once. Now I want to make sure Ava's alright."

"There's nothing you can do if she isn't," Jer said.

"True. But I don't like leaving her alone."

They were silent as a Jeep pulled into the adjoining parking lot.

"That's my ride," Sam said and a minute later he was departing with a nod.

"You knew her in college, didn't you?" Jer asked after Sam left, raising the subject with a worried look at Faisal.

"Yeah, we were friends. Her father and she were always considered family friends, no matter that I lost touch with Ava." The thought of how close they'd been and how easily it all came back at the sight of her was disquieting. "I'm hoping that Ava knows something. They've all the manpower they can muster on the search," he said, looking toward the Atlantic. "We've given it our all. Time for a rest. You might as well go home. You're supposed to be on vacation."

"Yeah, right." Jer grinned. "Rene has a list of odd jobs for me to do. More than I could get done in three weeks never mind six days." He shrugged. "Some vacation. In the meantime, I better get this bird home," he said, referring to the helicopter.

After Jer had left, Faisal received a call from Barb in their Marrakech office.

"I don't have a lot," she said. "But I thought you might want what I do have, for now anyway."

If the situation hadn't been so dire Faisal might have smiled. Barb often qualified her research as less than what she actually had. He waited for her to prove him right. "Let me have what you know," he said.

"As you know, the phone belonged to Dan Adams. That particular phone was on a pay-as-you-go plan. There wasn't anything unusual about any of it. What was intriguing though were the number of calls received from Vancouver. Over half dozen within three days."

"Vancouver, Washington?"

"British Columbia, Canada," she said. "I used some tech to unmask the private phone numbers and, as always, it worked like a dream. Interesting fact…a few actually—I don't have a name to go with the number, but I managed to get a location. Those calls were made from a Vancouver number in an area that, well, let's just say it's *very* wealthy. Many who live there are first-generation immigrants from China." She paused as if considering this seriously important. "So far that's all I have. I'm still working on the name of the caller."

He thanked her and ended the call shortly after that. As he hung up, he thought of everything that had transpired in recent days. Only three hours ago, in Fort Lauderdale, he was to have met with Dan. That hadn't happened. Now it might never happen. Fate had intervened in a particularly grim way. She had a harsh sense of humor, one he'd never much appreciated. He pushed that thought aside.

For now, they had nothing but tragedy on their hands.

Faisal clenched his fist. He'd lost too many people he cared about. He refused to let anything further happen to Ava and he prayed they found Dan.

But the facts weren't encouraging. And until either the yacht or Dan Adams was found, the only witness he had was an unconscious woman. His instinct told him that the answer to all this lay on that yacht. But the Atlantic was a big place to get lost in.

Chapter Eight

"Log the case as a code orange," Faisal said as he reported in for the second time to the home office in Jackson, Wyoming. Nassar coded all its cases in four categories from white to red. White was no threat to the investigator. Red was the most dangerous to client and investigator. Orange was the second highest rating. It meant that there was the possibility of danger to the investigator and an obvious threat to the client.

The whole case stunk. He didn't like the sound of the man who had arrived uninvited on the yacht just hours before tragedy struck. It was all too convenient, even easy, and that always spelled trouble. If it smelled like trouble—it was trouble.

He thought of their research team already working overtime and thought of how he'd be dead in the water without them. On both sides of the Atlantic, Marrakech and Jackson, Wyoming, their research and admin teams were the best. In fact, in the past, they'd had other companies try to lure some of their researchers away. The attempts had been unsuccessful. The benefits that Nassar offered its employees were unmatched, but then money had never been an issue for his family. He and his three brothers and sister had been born into wealth. Despite generous donations to charity, they became wealthier with each passing year.

At twenty-seven, Faisal was a wealthy man. It wasn't something he gave much consideration to, it just was. He had an accountant and an investing team who handled such things. He made sure his employees were well compensated. That was Nassar company policy. Their employees worked hard and without them, he knew his success wouldn't have come as easily or as quickly. That aside, with trusted employees in place, Faisal could stick to what he was good at and what he loved. He loved what he did—at work and at play. He played hard and he worked hard. Now, despite plans earlier in the week to learn to surf in Florida after his meeting with Dan followed by a snowboarding trip, he was back at work. It was clear that this case, wherever it was going to take him, was going to take some time.

His phone buzzed. He picked up before it had a chance to alert him twice.

"What's going on, Fai?" his brother Talib asked.

"Ava's been in and out of consciousness. But at least she's safe and being taken care of. She'll make it," Faisal said. After the almost six months that Talib had been in Wyoming, Faisal now wondered how he had functioned without him. Zafir had always shared his time between Marrakech and Wyoming. "There's no sign of the yacht. There are search teams out there now. Jer, Sam and I just got in from searching, although we brought Ava in early this afternoon." While he'd given a formal account to the office, he always liked to speak personally to his brother, if he happened to be in the office.

"Any word yet on Dan Adams?" Talib asked with concern in his voice.

"Nothing," Faisal said. "Nothing's adding up on this, T," he said. His middle brother, Talib had only recently relocated to Wyoming to raise his son, Everett, with his new wife, Sara. Talib was now his backup and had taken the helm as cohead. For Faisal, it had been a relief to have the pressure of being in charge eased. Unlike his other brothers, he would rather have more free time than more power and the responsibility that came with it. He and Talib were similar in that way. He believed that was because his mother had placed less restrictions on them as children and had insisted that a day was lost without a bit of fun. It was a concept he'd carried into adulthood. A jolt of sadness ran through him at the thought of her. He'd lost both his parents years ago in a tragic accident that only recently had been found to have a murderous twist. A case his eldest brother, Emir, had taken on had been the one that revealed the new information, which had threatened to destroy the family. But they'd made it through and their family had grown and become stronger. Now it was up to him to make someone else's family whole again.

"Dan Adams wasn't alone. Another passenger, an unidentified middle-aged male, as well as the yacht they were on, seem to have disappeared. There's no more information than that. Ava is our only witness and according to her attending physician, she's suffering traumatic memory loss. She was in bad shape when she came in. They did a preliminary assessment before I left. When I called a few minutes ago, I was told that physically she's coming around quickly but her memory is still not there. The Bahama Search and Rescue confirms the presence of another man—he was sighted by a local but they have no name."

"Wait a minute," Talib interrupted. "Zafir wants to speak to you."

A minute later his second eldest brother, and Emir's twin, was on the line. Zafir was vice president of the company and floated between the two offices.

"Do you need me there?" he asked. "I'm at loose ends before I fly home. I'll be back in Marrakech at the end of the week. Unless, of course, you're in desperate need of a hand."

"Not now. I'll let you know if this thing catches fire. Otherwise, I'll keep at it on my own. The United States Coast Guard and the Bahamas Air Sea Rescue and a bevy of other volunteers are out there. More volunteers than I've ever seen on a sea rescue."

"Alright," Zafir agreed. "The other agents are all working on cases and, as you know, Talib was just assigned one. But I'm all yours if you need me. For now."

For now.

They were words that they lived by, for circumstances in their business could change in an instant. And something in his gut told him that this one was about to do just that.

Five minutes later Faisal shook his head as he disconnected from his contact within the Coast Guard. There was no information since they'd last spoken. It seemed the only thing they'd been able to prove was what they already knew. The Adamses' yacht had disappeared without a trace. It was as if only Ava and the life raft they'd found her in remained as evidence that the yacht had ever existed.

It was just after ten o'clock in the evening when Faisal returned to the hospital. In his earlier phone call to check on Ava's status, he'd learned that she was going for a CAT scan. He was advised to wait a few hours until that and a variety of other tests were completed. Despite the leads he'd followed in the interim, he'd chaffed at not being able to see Ava sooner. But the physician he'd spoken to had encouraged him to give her some time. She'd been "through a trauma" were the physician's exact words and she needed a few hours of quiet and rest.

Anxious to see her, he took the stairs instead of waiting for the elevator. Even when he wasn't on a case and in a rush, he preferred stairs since he found elevators closed-in and claustrophobic. Besides that, the whole process, even with the latest and most swift of elevators, was still slowed down by the time it took humans to load and unload. He had no patience for that and so, as he usually did, took the stairs. He ran the six flights and arrived just as the elevator doors opened and a trio of medical personnel entered the floor.

At the desk, he stopped and waited as a pretty brunette finished a phone call before looking at him with a question in her eyes.

"I'm here to see Ava Adams," he said.

"Room 610," she said as if he needed that information.

"Is the attending physician available?" he asked. "I have a few questions." The physician he'd spoken to earlier had not been her attending.

Five minutes later he was striding down the hall, his

expression grim. What he'd heard hadn't boded well. She was fragile, awake and alert, if you could call still having no memory alert. She was on a secure floor in a private room, as he'd insisted. He'd thought that her youth and the vibrancy that he remembered would have her healing faster than what the physician said was normal progress. Nothing about Ava was normal. Despite what he was told, he had high hopes that she'd be able to fill in the many blanks.

"Ava," Faisal said as he leaned over the standard hospital bed's security railing. An intravenous machine beeped as it filtered medication into a line in her left hand.

She looked at him at first with puzzlement as if she didn't know where she was or who he might be. Disappointment coursed through him. If she didn't remember him, then what were the chances she was able to remember anything about what had happened aboard that yacht? Yet it was the former that bothered him. He'd never forgotten her and now it appeared she'd completely forgotten not only him but everything else in her life. The case slipped momentarily to the background.

"It's me… Faisal," he said as if maybe he'd read the expression on her face wrong, as if maybe there was still hope.

She didn't say anything and the hope slipped from his heart.

She didn't know him. He could see that there was no recognition in her eyes. He hadn't expected that. Somehow, he had hoped that under medical care she would have bounced back. Despite what he knew and what the physician had told him, he'd held to that belief.

"Faisal Al-Nassar," he said as if he were approaching

a stranger. And despite his formality all he wanted to do was comfort her, hold her and tell her that she was safe.

"Faisal," she murmured but there was no recognition in her eyes.

"We were friends," he said hating the past tense. He sucked back disappointment. They were friends now, at least he wanted them to be. Disappointment coursed through him. He'd imagined that she'd greet him with that lazy smile of hers and offer him a second chance, that he'd again be her everything. He mentally stepped back at the thought. Where had that come from? The thought had been as unexpected as the desire behind it. He'd never been her everything. Given a second chance with Ava, he'd take it. But they'd danced so far from that to where they were now, and back then they'd been only friends. She didn't remember him, the intimacy they'd shared, the intuitive knowing—all of that was gone. They'd both went their separate ways. But the truth was he'd never forgotten her. And now that she was back in his life, he wasn't planning to lose her again.

His thoughts were totally selfish. She'd been through hell and he was expecting her to react to his presence like she had a long time ago. That was the past. He needed to forget about what they had been, who they had been and deal with the now, the present. He was being insensitive, as his sister, Tara, would accuse him. But she was the member of the family who kept everyone in line. The only girl, she was his closest sibling and the family's heart.

"Where's my father?" Ava whispered, breaking into his thoughts and reminding him that he wasn't the only one with family. Her family was missing.

Where was Dan Adams? It was the question that

brought him back to reality, back to what was important. It was the question that was the crux of this case. Her words reminded him that there were more important things that needed addressing than old feelings between the two of them. He couldn't believe he'd even allowed those thoughts any purchase at a time like this. Did she know he was missing? How could she?

"You were the last person who saw him." He wanted to add the word *alive*. It was on the tip of his tongue but its shock value would do neither of them any good. "Is there anything you remember? Anything that might help us locate him?"

"Is he alright?" She struggled to sit up. The look on her face was pained.

He regretted bringing that look of pain to her. She'd had enough trauma and now he'd only added more.

"I don't remember," she said as she fell back onto the bed. She shook her head. "I can't remember." She clenched the sheet and again struggled to sit up.

"No." He placed a hand on her shoulder. "You need to rest. You've had a trauma, a shock. You were unconscious, you…"

"My father," she bit out. "We have to find him before he kills him."

Shock at her words rippled through him. She'd said the words earlier when they'd first rescued her. Somehow then they were less shocking, more easily placed into the context of her situation—perhaps even a hallucination. He could hear the fear in her voice.

Faisal frowned. "Who wants to kill whom?"

"I don't know," she said. "I can't remember. I just know that when he finds him…" The words trailed off as though she'd lost the energy to continue. She bit her lip, chewing on it before relaxing, but her eyes narrowed. It was clear that she believed every word she had said. "He's going to kill him."

She shook her head. Tears glistened and threatened to spill over.

She looked away, her hand clutching the bed rail and her heart monitor sped up.

"Ava?"

He wanted to take her in his arms. He wanted to make all of this go away and he could do neither of those things. He thought of the man with no name who had joined Dan Adams and Ava that fateful night. Who was he? Was he a threat to Dan? To Ava? Was it possible that he had something to do with the yacht going missing? There were too many possibilities that only seemed to increase every time he went through the questions. He hated to do this to her but she had been there. She knew. If she could only remember. "What happened, Ava?"

She looked at him, really looked at him, like she had in the past. Like she had when they'd danced together and laughed like friends and, he'd never admitted it to himself or to her but, he'd wanted so much more. That was half a decade ago—a lifetime. She shook her head and closed her eyes.

She was fading.

He ran a finger along her forehead, brushing back her dark hair. Her skin was damp. There were dark shadows beneath her closed eyes. She needed rest and she didn't need him haranguing her for answers. He was afraid to leave her alone and yet afraid to not be part of the search. He knew from the physician's report that she slept in short spurts and was awake at odd hours through the day. He sat with her the remainder of the night and she seemed to settle down as she slept through the night. This time it was he who slept off and on, watching her every moment he was awake.

He'd been on the go almost twenty-four hours, watching her, keeping her safe while he catnapped—this was his break.

In the early hours of the morning, he reluctantly decided to start his day. The hospital was beginning to come to life. He stopped at the nurses' station on the way out. There he was told that Ava had another lineup of tests that day. He knew she was in good hands at the moment. The search for her father was more in need of his efforts. Ava was safe. Her father was not. So he went out with one of the volunteer pilots that morning and through the afternoon. They searched an area the Coast Guard considered important. But bad weather, the yacht's failed equipment or the chance that the vessel had drifted far away from shipping lines could keep the craft off the radar. Despite the efforts of the United States Coast Guard, the Bahamas Air Sea Rescue Association and numerous other volunteers, there was still no sign of the missing yacht.

DAN ADAMS HAD been in and out of consciousness. There was one constant. Always the wet, hard surface pressed against his face. Sometimes the screech of a bird but more often the slap of waves against the bow awoke him. This time when he woke up the pain in his head and the light were blinding. He knew who he was but he wasn't sure where he was. That aside, he could only think of one person, his daughter, Ava. He remembered getting her in the raft. He remembered it swinging clear of the yacht. He even remembered it hitting the water. It was the gunshot that had thrown him backward. Now, his shoulder ached but the bleeding had stopped. He'd been grazed. When the bullet had hit him, he'd been thrown into the water. After the initial impact, he had struggled and trod water before he'd finally managed to pull himself up and onto the yacht by sheer will. He wasn't going to die, not with Ben still alive, a threat to his daughter. He remembered nothing after those traumatic moments.

Now, his mind was filled with worry for Ava. Was she alright? Had Ben gotten her too? For it was clear in his short periods of wakefulness that Ben had left him for dead, dead and adrift at sea. He wasn't sure but he didn't think that there was anyone else on the yacht.

"Av…" What should have been his daughter's name came out no more than a choked cough. It was strange, for one moment he knew she wasn't there and the next moment he thought she was, or maybe he just hoped. He couldn't speak, he could barely breathe and he was fighting to live. He turned on his side and coughed. Blood mixed with spit and sea water ran in a faded stream down the deck. He tried to sit up but his head spun and his ribs ached so badly he thought he would vomit again. He imagined his ribs were broken. It wasn't an improbable thought, for every breath was too painful to contemplate. Moving was impossible, he could barely tolerate the simple act of breathing. His head felt like it had been split open and as he slowly dragged his hand out from under his body and felt the side of his head, he could feel something warm trickling down his face. Blood.

His thoughts were cloudy and he shivered. The breeze off the ocean was cool and it seemed to chill his already damp skin. He tried to get to his feet once but his legs shook so hard that he lost his balance and crashed to the deck. But he'd been on his feet long enough to see that at least on the deck, he was alone, and around him there was nothing—only water.

Hours passed or it might have only been minutes.

He didn't know where he was or how long he'd been there.

Finally, he pulled himself off the deck, supporting himself on one knee, both legs too shaky to stand up completely. It had been hours, days even since he'd eaten or had any water. He needed to hydrate at the least so that he could live, for if he didn't Ben would kill Ava. If he hadn't already.

He reached for his phone.

Gone.

He remembered leaving it with Ava.

A feeling of dread snaked down his spine. He could only hope that Ava had contacted Faisal Al-Nassar. That hope was all that now stood between them and death.

Chapter Nine

Faisal strode toward Ava's hospital bed. He was relieved to see that, as the physician had just assured him, she was much better than the day before. Last night, when he'd sat with her, he'd been unable to tell anything of her alertness or change in status, for she'd slept through the night. His being there now seemed like it may have been more for him than her. He'd needed to know she was alright.

Now it was clearly different. She was awake and he could see that some of the vibrancy he remembered had returned. Her eyes had life to them and there was color in her cheeks. He smiled back at Ava as she gave him a smile of recognition. It was a relief to see her conscious and what appeared to be coherent. He came forward with long strides and took her free hand between both of his.

Her dark hair gleamed under the fluorescent lights. Her eyes shone with welcome despite the pallor of her skin and the beeping of machines that surrounded her.

"You're looking better than I expected," Faisal said. He let go of her hand and took a step back, not wanting to overwhelm her. At the same time, he realized that what he'd just said was slightly, if not completely, insulting. It wasn't what he had meant to say, not at all. But considering the circumstances he thought he might be forgiven. After all, he had saved her life. Unfortunately, he'd yet to save her father's. They weren't even sure that there was anything to save. That thought took any levity he might have felt at seeing Ava better completely away. "At least, better than yesterday," he added as if that made his faux pas any better.

Ava was sitting half up, propped by two pillows. And her smile was a surprise, considering what he'd said and how he'd said it. But then she hadn't been privy to his thoughts. And looking at her he doubted whether she had the strength to come back at him the way she used to. They had enjoyed their verbal sparring during their friendship. He was reminded again of how quick she had been, now that there was no answering repartee. It was unfair even as a thought, for he knew that she was in no shape for such things. She was physically fragile but still as gorgeous as ever. Her face was slimmer, her cheekbones more defined and her lips as they'd always been, full and naturally red.

He met the look of concern in her eyes that begged him for answers. But he didn't have any, not yet. And he had to quit thinking about how beautiful she was, how lush her figure was even in the hospital attire. Instead, he gave her a slight smile. "How are you feeling?"

This time, she smiled wanly as if sitting partway up with her head supported by pillows was almost too much for her. Beside her, the intravenous machine quietly beeped. He'd spoken to her physician, who had assured him that it was only a matter of getting her hydrated and then the intravenous would be discontinued. And at the speed she'd been recovering in the last few hours, she'd be ready for discharge in a day or two, at most.

"Fai," she said, her voice thin as she spoke in a whisper. There was a hoarse edge to the word, as if her throat was still raw from her experience. "I haven't seen you in a long time. Too long."

It was like yesterday and the day before had never existed. It was like she perceived everything in a different way than how it had happened. "The nurse said you saved me." The words were weak as if it was all she could do to get them out. She closed her eyes again, as if the light hurt or maybe the effort of keeping them open was just too much.

"I got you off the life raft, anyway," he said in a lighthearted way. He didn't want to act like the heavy, not in her state. Besides, this was the first true conversation they'd had since he'd rescued her.

She opened her eyes and smiled at him. "That's all?" she asked and her words were so quiet he almost didn't hear them. Yet there was an edge in her tone. Something that, this time, reminded him of the Ava he had known— quick-witted, sharp, never letting anything slip by her.

"What do you mean?"

"Always modest, you saved my life," she said with another attempt at a smile, but the smile didn't reach her eyes. "Thank you doesn't quite cover it."

"No thanks necessary," he replied. He felt like they were stuck in some impersonal chat loop. Where neither wanted to admit that they had anything more intimate than a general knowledge of the other. He wanted to ask her so many questions but he didn't want to tire her. He needed to start with the most critical. Instead she beat him to it.

"Where's my father? I need to see him." Her breathing seemed to both speed up and become more shallow at the same time. Her heart monitor sped up slightly.

"Ava."

Somehow her name was a substitute for the answer he couldn't speak, at least not to her. It was too bleak. But before he could say anything more she had slipped farther back into the pillows and closed her eyes as if it was all too much. A minute passed and then two. She opened her eyes and seemed to connect with him for a second before she shut them again.

He looked away from her as if needing a reprieve from the power of that connection. Her gaze seemed to demand that he get the answers she needed. It was ridiculous really, but that had been the Ava he knew, determined, smart—stubborn. Even now, it was as if she hadn't been to hell and back, and it gave him hope that her memory would return soon. As it stood everything hinged on her memory. Without it, he could have no idea how she had ended up in a dinghy alone in the middle of the Atlantic or who might be left on that boat. It was all a mystery.

He turned back. There was a shimmer of tears in her eyes and she clenched the sheet.

"Anything you can remember, Ava? The smallest bit of information could be helpful. I know things may be a little gray right now but your memory will return."

Silence lay heavy between them. A metal cart lumbered down the corridor and past her room. The noise was loud and grating.

He looked at his watch. It was large, oval faced with a black leather strap and a manual wind, a relic from another generation. He wound it as if just remembering the fact that time was slipping away and still they were not much further ahead. It was frustrating, especially when he guessed that much of what he needed to know was locked somewhere deep in Ava's mind. He put his hand over hers as if that would make everything better, as if somehow the contact would jog her memory.

"I have a watch like that," she said as if that was of paramount importance. "One that winds, I mean."

"I know," he said brushing his hand against the back of hers, feeling the soft skin and remembering other times. "I gave it to you."

Silence descended again. He waited, hoping for answers about that night, the night that mattered most. The night that had changed everything.

"I…" Ava whispered. She shivered as if the memories of that night, few as they were, were too much and too overwhelming.

He leaned closer.

The only thing they knew for sure was that there were three people on the yacht that night. Dan Adams, the registered owner; Ava; and the man who had arrived later. What had happened that evening? Had there been an altercation of some kind? What had been the catalyst for her to be in that life raft? Had her father been trying to save her from a sinking vessel or from something much more deadly?

Dan Adams might very well be the victim of foul play. But he had no evidence, and he'd yet to admit to Ava that her father was missing despite the fact that she'd asked. She was fragile right now and he didn't know what she knew or didn't know. All that aside, it was his job to protect her, physically, emotionally—the latter was impossible, he knew that but he'd do his best.

"Tell me, Ava, what do you remember?" He knew

he was pushing but if Dan was still alive they could well be running out of time. He didn't offer her a hint of what little he knew. He only hoped that she could re-member something of what had occurred between the time that she had ended up in a life raft and the yacht had disappeared.

"I wish I could tell you, Fai, but I just don't know." She shook her head. "I'm remembering the past." Her voice shook. "You—school, all of that. But what hap-pened on Dad's yacht—nothing."

He nodded, expecting that, as he'd been warned by her physician, and fighting for patience when he knew that time was imperative.

He sat down on the chair by her bedside, prefer-ring that to looming over her, which seemed to him to be slightly intimidating. He reached over and pushed a strand of hair from her cheek. Heat seemed to run up his arm at the brief contact and he pulled back as if he'd been burned.

"Fai," she murmured. Her free hand lifted as if reach-ing for him and then dropped. She shook her head. "I'm so sorry. I'm trying…"

"Don't rush it. It will come back," he assured her but he'd barely said that when her eyes widened.

"Ben…he was new. They did business together, he and my father. He was there. He wanted something. What it was, I don't know, or if I did, I don't remem-ber. Dad had a lot of irons in the fire, as you know. He couldn't seem to stick to one business venture at a time. I think at one point he was even invested in a car dealership. And, of course he was successful at them all. Maybe that was the trouble," she said with a hint of irony.

"So Ben was on board?" He forced the excitement from his voice. Now they were getting somewhere.

"Yes," she said, surprise etching her voice. "Now that you're talking about it, encouraging me to remember I mean…" She looked at him with a rather wispy smile. "I remember that now. He wasn't expected. At least I don't think he was. I met him once before, briefly. I remember that. He threatened…" She shook her head. "I'm not sure. I can't even remember his full name." It was the most she had yet to say and her voice was hoarse and barely audible by the time she got to the last words.

He was silent. There was little he could offer. Besides, outside opinion could change or even implant memories, somehow change her reality or how she perceived what had happened. He smiled, remembering her off-the-cuff psychology lessons all those years ago. He'd taken behavioral courses. But no course was as fascinating as seeing the passion in her eyes as she shared her enthusiasm for what made the human brain tick.

"Darrell Chan," she said unexpectedly.

"Who?" He leaned forward, the tension palpable. He knew that they were getting somewhere. "Was he on the yacht?"

She shook her head. "No."

"Who is he? How do you know him?" *Too many questions*, he chastised himself. He was threatening to overwhelm her and yet time had never seemed so tight.

She shook her head. Her lips were taut and her face was almost devoid of color. "I don't know."

Yet she'd given him the name as if it were the key to a national treasure. He looked at her. She was looking straight ahead as if she were deep in thought or more importantly, trying to capture her thoughts.

Two names. Two men. How did they fit together?

"Who are they?"

Again, she shook her head, her lips pinched.

"Do you know where either of them are from?" He hoped to at least narrow the names down geographically if nothing else.

She shook her head and began to look distressed. "Ben…" she murmured. "He had a gun," she said. Her voice was weak but determined. "And he said he'd kill him."

"Ben was there?"

"Yes."

"Was Darrell Chan there?" he asked. The repetition was only a precaution, a test on the blips of moments that she was remembering.

"No."

She shook her head.

"Ava," he whispered.

"Dad was going to report him," she whispered. "Ben," she said before he could ask. "He was so angry at my father."

Faisal leaned forward.

He stopped questioning her. She wasn't a prisoner and he'd almost begun an interrogation. He stood up, leaning over her and taking the hand that was free of the intravenous line between his. It felt soft and vulnerable against his skin. He thought of all she'd been through and tried with the small gesture to reassure her that he was on her side. That he was her friend and that… He killed the thought. There was no time to think of other things, of other longings, of other needs. And yet, in a delicate state of health or not, she still did things to him that no other woman could.

Ava was noticeably fading, her eyes were half-closed and her voice was trailing off.

Silence filled the room. Her eyes finally closed and her breathing was even. It was like she'd fallen asleep. He knew the pattern of this now. He waited, letting her gather her strength and, he imagined, weave together her fragmented thoughts.

Another minute. His patience was shredding and yet none of this was her fault. It was a ludicrous thought. The only thing he could give her was comfort and little of that, considering he couldn't bring back her father by his will alone.

"Ben," she whispered. "Whyte."

"Your father was going to report him?"

"Yes."

In the hallway, outside the closed door, another cart rattled past.

"Ben was there," she whispered. Her full lips chapped and pale. "That night…"

"On the yacht," he encouraged. It was information he already knew—at least he knew about the stranger. Now he had a name.

"Where is my dad and the yacht?"

He shook his head. He couldn't tell her this and yet he couldn't lie. "I don't know, Ava. We're searching for him."

A tear slid down her cheek. He clasped her free hand tighter wanting to take the pain of what he'd told her away. She shuddered and turned her face away; the seconds ticked by, but when she turned to face him it was like her mind was elsewhere.

It was then that Ava said, "Phony land. Big trouble," and then she passed out.

They were bizarre words and a simplistic way of

speaking that was not like Ava. It was as if she had taken a step backward after all her progress. But considering the trauma she had been through he supposed it wasn't unusual. Still he worried. He sat by her side and wondered how it had all come to this. Her dark hair hung in lackluster tangles that framed her face. He arranged her pillow so that she was raised to the angle the physician had recommended.

The monitor began to beep a warning. Her blood pressure had just dropped. He hit the call bell and rolled her onto her side, propping her in that position with one of the pillows. It was one of many things he'd learned in his emergency medical training when he'd certified for sea rescue work. Before he could get to the door to shout for help, two nurses were in the room. They assured him that the physician was en route. He was directed to the hallway with an efficiency that would have impressed him at another time.

He hung back in the corridor until she was again stable. What was clear in the aftermath was that there would be no visitors of any kind for the next few hours. The attending physician had been adamant.

He could deal with that. There were things he needed to do now that she was safe once again. No thanks to him, he thought rather ironically—he believed that it had been his questions that had upset her and brought her close to another medical crisis.

He was left with the sure knowledge that time was running out.

"WHAT DO YOU HAVE?" Faisal asked as he answered his phone. He'd just left Ava's side and was about to put in a call with the new information when Barb's number showed as the incoming call. Barb didn't call unless she had something. She'd been with the company long enough that minor research was immediately dumped to one of five other employees. Interestingly enough, they were all women. He wasn't sure what that might mean, if anything.

"I have a name of someone else on Dan Adams's yacht that night. Ben Whyte," she said briskly. "It isn't much but I thought that I'd at least give you what I know so you have something to go on."

That was part of what made Barb great in the office. She was aware of the pieces that needed to link together to make a case work. She was always one step ahead of the investigators in the field, getting information to them quickly and efficiently. She'd unearthed the most difficult piece of evidence in record time.

"Ben Whyte was picked up on the beach of Paradise Island. The identity pickup was just good luck. Anyway, goes like this. The local fisherman who took him out said he dropped a driver's licence. State of Florida," she said before he could ask. "He found it later at the back of his boat but by the time he had a chance to return it, Ben was gone. He turned it in to the local authorities but it wasn't really of much interest until now."

"Ava just confirmed that he was on board. Interesting turn of events."

"So she's conscious?" Barb asked.

"Most of the time," he replied. "She said that a man named Ben Whyte joined them later." He remembered that she'd also said that it was unexpected. "If he's connected with Dan he may have spent some time in the Caribbean where Dan lives part of the year. Just a guess but…"

"I'll get what I can on this Whyte character," Barb said before he could ask. He could hear her clicking away and knew she was digging answers out of the internet. He waited. Sometimes she was so quick that there was no point ending the call, she would only end up calling back.

A minute passed and then two. He'd learned a lot in the field, working on so many cases that involved a mystery. Two of the things he'd learned were determination and patience.

"Several people by that name but only one who has recently been in the Caribbean," Barb said as if there had been no break in the conversation. "Not sure if there's any relevance, but he changed his name thirty-six years ago from Tominski to Whyte."

"No criminal record?"

"None that I can find. Not sure why the name change," Barb replied. "But I'll let you know what else I find. By the way, I'm still working on your Vancouver connection."

"Look into land transactions and also a man by the name of Darrell Chan. I know I just keep piling it on."

"I love the challenge," she laughed.

"That's good because there's more. I remember Adams talking about some land speculation. I didn't think anything of it. But then Ava said something that was odd. 'Phony land.'"

"Phony land?"

"I know, strange. And then she said big trouble."

"The mind works in mysterious ways, especially when it's been through a shock," Barb said.

"True," he agreed. "It's got to mean something. I know that Adams wanted to meet about land. In fact, he said that it was nothing he wanted to talk about over the phone."

"Interesting," Barb replied.

"Exactly," Faisal agreed. "See if there's anything recent, and then go back as far as you have to. Use all three names, Adams, Tominski and Whyte."

"Done," she replied. "And stay safe," Barb demanded. She had been with them for so long she was like family, watching out for each of them, worrying from the safety of the office.

"I will," he said, ending the call and thinking only of how his safety was secondary to finding Ava's father. He needed to find Dan Adams soon for he sensed that time was running out.

Chapter Ten

Sunday, June 12—9:30 p.m.

Ava took a deep breath as the nurse left her room. She had bounced back in the last few hours. She knew that from the way everything seemed clearer rather than a confusing cloud of sound. She also knew she was better by the fact that she didn't want to constantly sleep and, most telling of all, she was now remembering big chunks of previously forgotten events.

Faisal had been here again and just left. She admired and appreciated his dedication. Something came alive within her just knowing that he was near. But there was something she needed to do without him. He'd just left—that meant that he wouldn't be returning again for at least a few hours. She'd encouraged him to get some sleep but she knew that he would get the minimal necessary before returning to be with her. She'd demanded that he stay at the hotel and at least get a night's sleep. She'd finally gotten that promise out of him.

The machine on her left beeped but the one on her right was quiet. It was only a blood pressure machine, which the physician had just used, assuring her that her blood pressure was normal.

Ava was remembering things that she hadn't told Faisal, things she hadn't told anyone. Truthfully, she'd remembered none of it when he had asked. And if she had, she didn't know if she would have told him.

Faisal.

She'd once fancied herself in love with him. But she'd been young, what had she known about love or life or any of it for that matter? She pushed the thoughts away. The past didn't matter. She knew that she kept returning to it because it was the only clarity she had, that and a gut instinct that she had to get out of here. She also knew that she couldn't involve anyone else, for to do so would be to place them in danger. Even Faisal couldn't know what she planned, for despite what he did for a living, it didn't make him invulnerable. She needed to get out of here, alone. It was on her shoulders to put a stop to this. She didn't consider the irony that she didn't know what she needed to stop. All she knew was that if she didn't succeed both she and her father were in trouble. That is, if her father was still alive. The thought choked her and tears trembled on her lashes.

She shook her head. She couldn't think like that. She'd survived and her father would too. She clung to what she did know. One place and a memory that were branded in her mind. She didn't know what they meant. She only knew that she had to get to that place to find answers.

But her emotions were raw as she thought of the feel of her hand in Faisal's. Her heart felt like it stopped at the thought of him. He was gone. She hadn't seen him in five years but she'd thought of him often. She tore her thoughts from Faisal and to what she needed to remember. A tremor ran through her. Her father. The last time she'd seen him was when she'd been in the life raft. She remembered a feeling of panic of wanting to reach out and help. He'd been on the yacht and then she'd lost sight of him and remembered only the feeling of horror and helplessness that had enveloped her. Where was he now?

She could remember that the doctor had told her that her memory would come back. She remembered studying about memory. She remembered studying a lot of things. What she didn't remember were the last hours on her father's yacht and they were the most important hours of her life. There were things she remembered—what she had told Faisal for one. But there were other memories that seemed to fade in and out. Things she knew were important and she hadn't told Faisal because they'd faded too quickly. She knew in her gut that knowing that time, reclaiming that last bit of her life might provide the one clue that would save her father's life.

She shuddered. She remembered everything that had happened at the hospital during the times she had been conscious. It was only the time before that, on the boat, that was in question.

She knew with a surety, that her father's reputation needed to be saved. She also knew that Faisal had been searching for her father. She had to help him and to do that she knew she had to go back to where it had all begun. She had to do it alone. She couldn't endanger anyone else.

She was certain of that, that and the face of a man she could now see in her memory. The threat to her father's life, the name of the town. All of it was engraved in her mind and all of it culminated in a strange little place, and a strange phrase. She'd heard him say it, Ben Whyte, her father's partner. She'd overheard him on the yacht when he thought he was alone. "A little piece of hell in the heart of Texas," she whispered. Whoever threatened her father, the secret to it all began there. Both her father and Ben had confirmed it.

She'd already shared with Faisal what little she remembered, including the names her father had given her. She couldn't share this new memory. She shook her head as if reaffirming her thoughts. He couldn't be involved. Already she and her father had been marked for death and it appeared only one of them had survived. She choked back a sob. Alive, dead, she was unable to hold a conviction either way on her father's plight. All she knew was that she needed to stop this before any more people died.

She'd had solid food since this morning but they'd left the intravenous in to keep her hydrated as an extra precaution. The physician had spoken of having it removed today or tomorrow. Considering the time, she guessed it would be tomorrow. She couldn't wait. She looked at the intravenous tubing, at the needle in the back of her hand, took a breath and yanked. A sharp bite shot up her arm and then the needle dropped to the sheets along with a trickle of bright red blood. She took an end of the sheet, pressing it to the back of her hand and with the other hand she fumbled for a tissue. This was proving to be a messy endeavor. She didn't want to leave a trail of blood behind her. She pressed for a minute and then lifted the tissue. The wound was weeping more than bleeding. Good enough. Her legs shook. She took a deep breath and then another. She could hear voices in the hall. She lay back down and pulled the thin blanket to her chin.

The door opened.

She closed her eyes, sensed a presence and then heard the door click and opened her eyes. She was alone.

She waited, one minute and then two. She didn't have many minutes to waste. Her father needed her. And whoever wanted her dead would not stop. She wasn't sure how she knew that, but she knew that her being near anyone endangered them. She needed to get out, get to Texas and get her memory back. For it was only then that she could stop whatever evil had been set in motion that night on the yacht.

She pushed the door slowly open. The hallway was quiet. She slipped out turning left past an empty staff room where she slipped in and saw the strap of a purse in a drawer. Someone had forgotten to lock up her purse or meant to come back quickly. She didn't think. She'd never done this before but she was desperate. Two minutes later she was out of the room with fifty dollars in her hand and was heading for the emergency exit. On the way down the utilitarian stairs she stopped at each floor. Three flights down there was a floor that appeared to be more for supplies than patients. It was there that she found a pair of scrubs and a pair of shoes. She changed right there in the empty, open hallway. It was her last stop before emerging on the bottom floor and into a back parking lot. She took a deep breath. Her heart pounded. She knew only one thing. She had to get out of here, out of Miami, out of Florida. Her memory was coming back and with it fear. She had to get far away, for there was one thing she knew for sure. The man on the yacht, Ben—wanted her dead. While her memory didn't give her all the facts, her gut told her that he would stop at nothing. She also knew that finding the evidence her father claimed existed was up to her—she was her father's last chance.

Chapter Eleven

Miami, Florida
Sunday, June 12—10:45 p.m.

Ava had ridden two city buses and fallen asleep on the second. Fortunately, she'd told the driver where she wanted to get off. Now, in a drugstore almost ten miles from Mercy Hospital and across the street from the intercity bus station, Ava looked in a small cosmetic mirror above the eyeshadow display. It was the first time she'd seen her reflection since this ordeal had begun. She grimaced at the tangled hair, the pallor of her face and the dark circles under her eyes. She was a mess. If nothing else, she needed to take a brush to her hair and add some life to her face with some cold water. But the only thing she could get here was a brush and maybe a tube of lip gloss. Then she remembered her financial state and dropped it all from her list. A finger combing was all she could afford for now. Later she'd wash her face in a public restroom.

She sighed and turned away from the mirror. Despite everything that had happened and maybe because of it, she was forever indebted to Faisal. It was partially because of his generosity that she had enough money for a bus ticket to Texas. But Faisal was always very liberal with money, generous with his friends and those he cared about. She remembered that from her college days. Then, he'd paid for everyone's meal on more than one occasion. And, when he'd thrown a party, he'd paid for all the food and alcohol, even though he didn't drink. He'd always been about what everyone else wanted, what made them happy and so he gladly shared his resources with others. To say he had deep pockets was an understatement. His first gesture when they spoke had been to make sure that she'd had enough money for snacks or books or whatever she might need, including a meal in the hospital cafeteria if it came to that. It was one hundred and fifty dollars. While he'd never know where her thoughts had gone when she'd seen the money, she remembered the guilt of taking it. She also remembered the desperation that didn't allow her to quibble over his offer. Normally, she'd never have agreed but there was nothing normal about this situation. She was in deep trouble. She would never have turned to Faisal without her father's suggestion, but she believed in her dad. When, in the heat of panic and trauma, her father had steered her toward Faisal, she'd never questioned it. Then it had been different, a desperate situation. But now, she could only think that Faisal was the boy she had gone to school with. There was no way she would involve him in the unidentified trouble she found herself in. It was bad enough that she might be in danger. She wouldn't have him in danger too. He'd rescued her and that alone was enough.

Despite what Faisal had given her, her funds were low. She could get to where she needed to go in Texas but she was going to be eating little once she was there.

She'd needed more money. What she'd done to get it wasn't her. She grimaced at the thought of what she'd done, stealing money from someone's purse—she fully intended to pay the woman back with interest.

Theft. Her stomach clenched at the thought. But there was no going back. A change in shifts with the hallway temporarily clear had given her the opportunity to escape. She'd planned all of it. Evening was a slack time. Even her security took a break. With patients settled, medical staff tended to take their breaks, as well, and the hallways emptied.

From here on in she was in survival mode. She had to conserve what she had for the bus ticket out of here. She was ready to hit the road. She had a place in her memory but no purpose. She only knew that there were answers there and that she needed the memories to save her father or at the least salvage his reputation. A sob rose and stuck in the back of her throat. This was all so difficult. She wished she hadn't had to run from Faisal. He'd been so good and yet his presence had also brought back so many other memories. And her presence only put him in danger. She couldn't think of any of this right now. Instead, she focused on collecting her meager supplies. She bought water and energy bars. But as she went to the counter to pay, her vision blurred. She had to lean on the counter to get her equilibrium. But despite her efforts, the items still dropped from her hand onto the counter more forcibly than she might normally have intended.

"You alright, honey?" the clerk asked in a drawl that reminded her of where she needed to be and that time was slipping away. The clerk's hands were on her full hips and her face was heavily wrinkled and, despite what appeared to be too many years worshipping the sun, seemed to emanate motherly concern.

"Fine," she muttered. But she looked away as the world spun. She clung to the counter and took a deep breath. The world righted again.

"You're sure? I have daughters your age. I'd hate to think that if they were in trouble, someone wouldn't help them."

She couldn't take this much sympathy. She was either going to cry or pass out. She could do neither. This was all on her. There was no one to lean on, including this kind stranger. Instead, she took a deep breath and was finally able to meet the eyes that looked at her with so much concern that she almost wilted and burst into tears. She couldn't do that. She pushed back from the counter. She had to stand on her own two feet if she wanted to fix what was endangering her family. If she could only remember more.

"I'm fine," she repeated like a skipping vinyl record. "Really. Thank you."

The clerk looked at her for a second longer as if assuring herself of the truth of that and nodded as she rang in her items.

Ava took a five from her pocket. The money felt treacherous and wrong in her hand. A minute later, she left the store with the few things she'd bought in a plastic bag over her arm.

Her thoughts went to Faisal. He wanted to help. She wanted to trust him but she didn't want to hurt him. Somehow she knew that what she faced was better handled alone—without risking anyone else being hurt, like her father.

Would he try to follow her? Knowing him, remembering what she knew of him—she knew he would. At least he would try. That was why it was important he didn't find out where she was going. She had no connection to Texas, there was no reason to believe she'd go there. It would be over before anyone could find her. There was something else that nagged at her. Her memory stalled. It needed to come back faster and there was nothing she could do to change that. She remembered her studies on amnesia. She'd never thought to apply that small part of one semester to real life, especially to herself.

She remembered that Faisal had mentioned something about her father on his last visit, but her memory had still been incomplete. Now, her returning memories only made the danger that much more palpable. Ben Whyte. The thought of him and what he'd done made fear run through her body so strongly that she wanted to throw up.

She needed to think yet somehow her most powerful resource was silent—all cylinders not a go. It was the worst time to be intellectually limping. She was running out of time to come up with a plan. Worst of all she needed to remember what it was that threatened her very life and what drove her to a little Texan town seemingly in the middle of nowhere.

She moved around the drugstore and to the parking lot. Two bins sat side by side. Could she be lucky enough that at least one of them was a used-clothing bin? There was no one near the bins and the lot on that side wasn't well lit. It was perfect cover. With a bit of luck no one would see her. She hurried over.

"It is," she murmured seeing the charity name on the bin. She raised the lid. The bin was full, another bonus. She could reach quite a bit of the clothing, at least what was on top. If it weren't this full, she would have been out of luck. Instead, she yanked out an oversize beige sweater. She dug as far as she could reach and pulled out a beige canvas bag. Beige seemed to be her color tonight. She dug some more and found a pair of jeans, much too large. She tossed them back and dug, finding a T-shirt. She looked down at her scrubs. They were brown. She had a matched set. There was no one around. In front of her were office buildings. It was after work hours and other than cleaners, they were quiet. She imagined that unless the odd cleaner looked out at just the wrong moment, it didn't matter if she changed here, no one would see her. Behind her was the drugstore, the side that faced her was windowless. She moved between the two bins and tore off the top that matched the scrub pants and replaced it with the T-shirt and then the sweater. She put her water and granola bars in the bag and put it over her shoulder. She tossed the shirt she'd been wearing into the bin. She didn't look great but she blended in with the general population a lot better.

She hurried back around the corner of the drugstore and across the street to the bus station. There, diesel fumes tainted the air and luggage littered the sidewalk. The fumes from the buses waiting beneath the lights that lit the area like daylight threatened to choke her. Half a dozen buses idled on the tarmac and only ten feet from her a wiry, gray-haired man was loading luggage into a bus's underbelly. Someone jostled her and she shifted away. The area was quickly becoming crowded with people as departure and arrival times intersected. Her heart pounded and she fought to look normal, like a young woman heading cross-country in a pair of scrub pants and a sweater. She looked down-and-out for sure but she was also boarding a bus in an area of Miami that couldn't be called well-off. A bus pulled in, next to one that was pulling out.

There was so much she didn't know. If she'd had access to a computer she would have checked her father's email. She knew it was a critical piece but instinct told her that her answers lay in a Texas town of negligible size and it was imperative she waste no time getting there.

She took a breath, fighting for normalcy. Yet nothing was normal. She was running on instinct. Still choking in a gray fog of memory loss, she was following her gut and it was screaming *run*.

She went inside to purchase her ticket.

Outside again, Ava coughed from the fumes and her eyes teared. She fumbled in the pocket of her scrubs for one of a handful of tissues she'd stuffed there before leaving the hospital. She knew, despite her change of clothes, that she looked a wreck. She'd tried hard to blend in but she'd been to hell and back, and she was still wobbly on her feet. To her right a black woman with gray hair stopped short, looking at her with what seemed like concern. Then she scowled. Ava turned away, her heart skipping a beat. She didn't need attention, sympathetic or otherwise. She moved a few feet away, putting distance and more people between her and the curiosity of the stranger.

She pushed deeper into the crowd. She was thankful the woman whose eye she had caught only minutes ago had disappeared into the queue for a bus marked Chicago.

A middle-aged woman in jeans and a blouse, who also had sunglasses perched on her head as if she were making a fashion statement, glowered at her. Ava drew herself up taller. She shifted tactics. The way to fit in was to believe you belonged here, that everything was right and that was the aura she'd exude. She'd read that somewhere. This was something that she could never imagine happening to her. And yet it was. She was fleeing from a trouble she couldn't remember. She only knew that she needed to get out of this city. It wasn't safe and it wasn't the place where she would find the answers she needed, answers that would save her father.

In the meantime, she had to look like everything about her and her situation was normal. It was the appearance she had to portray even though she ran a risk of standing out even in her toned-down outfit.

Loud voices had her turning her attention to her right where a couple was arguing. She turned away. The crowd continued to jostle this way and that. It was her best defence, remaining out of sight hidden amid numerous people.

AN HOUR LATER, near the back of the bus and seated alone, at least for now, Ava took a deep breath. She went over the most recent events. It was a joy to savor the memories she did have. She couldn't believe her luck. But she'd whisked through purchasing a bus ticket and boarding the bus without a second look. Whether it was the late hour or whether identification wasn't needed, she didn't dwell on her good luck.

The memories were coming back and she wished for the first time that they weren't. They were hard and fast and intense, and they were worse than she could ever have imagined.

She was a witness to attempted murder. Her hands shook at that thought, not so much at the knowledge, she'd always remembered that, it was the details that were slowly coming back. The sounds of the scuffle, the gun blast were clear in her mind. She'd already been in the raft but too far away. The waves had taken her twice the distance away. Finally, the vast ocean and the darkness had blanketed the distance between them and she'd been alone.

They'd been attacked that night on the yacht. Their attacker had never meant for her to get away. Her father's desperation in those last moments had made that obvious. Now, her father might be dead and that was something that she couldn't change. She needed to focus on what she could change, saving his reputation before the man who may have killed him stole that too.

FAISAL LOOKED AT his watch. It was just prior to midnight. The helicopter's spotlight showed nothing but the swell of waves. There was nothing to indicate that the yacht or any of its occupants had ever been here. He finger-combed his hair. His head ached from lack of sleep. He hated the thought of leaving Ava alone but he'd been assured that she would sleep through the night. That reassurance had galvanized him to go out on one more search. He'd hoped that, of all the searchers out here, he would be the one to find Dan Adams. It was ridiculous thinking. He'd had more than his share of luck when they'd found Ava. An hour later, he and the pilot agreed to call it a night.

Other volunteers took over where they had left off,

combing the ocean for what was really a tiny piece of flotsam in a vast ocean. It was five in the morning before he was back in his suite, which seemed empty and hollow. He lay down to grab a few hours' sleep before going up to the hospital to see Ava. She'd been scheduled for an X-ray first thing that morning, so there was no need to go in until that was complete. He managed three hours before his phone rang. He looked at the number and knew that everything was about to change.

Chapter Twelve

Monday, June 13—6:30 a.m.

Ben Whyte couldn't believe how easy it had been. He'd slipped in the crew entrance of a cruise ship heading from the Bahamas back to Florida. While at sea, a news report had confirmed that Ava Adams had been found floating in a life raft in the Gulf Stream somewhere off the coast of Miami. He didn't get the specific details because they didn't matter. He was almost giddy with relief. He controlled himself long enough to hear the rest, which only confirmed what he knew. She was thought to have been a passenger on the yacht owned by Dan Adams. The report also provided the information that Ava was at Mercy Hospital in Miami. It was all he needed.

He'd known it was a crazy idea to kill her here. He knew that he should wait for a better time. But desperation had driven him when he'd slipped by hospital security and gone up to Ava Adams's floor. Luck was on his side when the staff at the nurses' station were distracted by a doctor's arrival. He was able to slip by the station unnoticed. Within a minute he had made his way down the hallway.

When he'd entered Ava's private room, she was sleeping. Her face was turned away from him and her long dark hair covered what he might have otherwise seen of her face. He'd stood staring at her for a minute.

He took a deep calming breath and slipped the pillow out from beneath her head. She shifted in her sleep. Then he settled the pillow over her head, shifting the pillow to her face and pressing down as she woke up and began to scream. The sound was muffled by the pillow. Her struggles quickly waned and he easily held her down. Eight minutes later he was able to open the door and calmly walk away.

Dead, just like her father. He smiled.

As he walked down the hall, heading back to the elevators, he could hear the murmur of voices from the nurses' station. He paused and then kept walking. He had nothing to fear. He was a visitor like any other. But his heart pounded despite his mind's reassurances and he slowed his pace while he was within earshot but out of sight of the nurses' station. He was curious as to what they were saying.

"Stole fifty dollars from me." There was an edge to the speaker's oddly soothing husky voice. It was a sexy, morning-after voice and reminded him how long he'd been without. "I can't believe it. I wouldn't have thought it was her but she left a note." The woman laughed. "Promised to pay me back. Signed it Ava Adams."

"And took off just like that?" the other laughed. "I kind of like it. An escapee."

More muted giggles.

"They didn't waste any time filling her room."

"No. We're maxed out on patients this week. Had one in the hallway. An unacceptable situation."

Damn it, he thought. Was it possible? Had he killed the wrong woman? A shiver streaked through him. He'd killed only twice in his life before this. But both times had been justified. Now he wasn't so sure. Had he officially become a cold-blooded murderer, killing someone for no reason? A shudder ran through him. He'd become just like his brutal father, who had let his emotions, especially anger, rule his actions. He'd disappeared from his life, sentenced to jail, after killing a man in a barroom brawl. Ben had been six and glad to see him go. His father was the reason that he'd changed his name from Tominski to Whyte as soon as he reached the age of majority.

He wouldn't think of that—instead he had to focus on the now. He had to force himself to breathe, to calm down and to take a closer look at his surroundings, to act normal.

"I wonder if they'll find her?" the other nurse mused.

"I doubt if they'll look but I'd sure like my fifty dollars back."

"I can't believe that Ava Adams just slipped out of here—past us."

He walked faster, keeping his eyes ahead and only stopping at the elevator. He stood there like any other visitor, waiting for the elevator to arrive at his floor. Except he hadn't pushed the button.

"The authorities weren't called," the woman with the husky voice said.

"Fifty bucks is fifty bucks."

Neither of the nurses were looking his way.

He turned and headed to the stairwell without another thought to the woman he'd just killed. Ava was still alive and he needed to find her. He pushed open

the door to the stairwell and felt the rush of cool air like
a calming balm. Behind him, at the far end of the hallway where he'd so recently come from, he could hear
hurrying footsteps and agitated voices.

He knew what that was about or at least he could
guess. They'd found a patient dead. But they wouldn't
know it was murder, not yet. He'd be long gone by the
time that information was known. He'd propped her
back on her pillow, leaving her lying there, still and
not breathing. Nothing would show, at least not immediately, that he had leaned on that pillow with a good
portion of his weight nor that she'd had no chance. She
was doomed from the beginning. And she wasn't Ava.

Ava Adams needed to die and she needed to do it
soon. He took the stairs at a run as if flying down the
fire exit, possibly breaking his neck, would somehow
take Ava out sooner.

Monday, June 13—8:00 a.m.

WITH HIS THOUGHTS on Ava, Faisal answered his phone
with a more abrupt hello than normal.

It was Colin Vanstone. He was the hospital administrator. Faisal had had a few conversations with the man
since Ava had been admitted. This time, Colin began
the conversation without his usual niceties.

"I don't know how it happened. Ava Adams has left
the hospital."

"What do you mean 'left'?" It seemed like time
stopped, like he wasn't making sense of what the man
was telling him.

"She's no longer here. But I can assure you that she

was definitely not discharged. In fact, considering the shape she was in earlier, I'm surprised—"

"When? Where?" Faisal punched out the abbreviated questions as he cut the man off. He could feel the plastic of the phone creak under the pressure of his fingertips. He eased his grip.

"I'm sorry—"

"I don't need your apology," Faisal cut him off. "Give me the details and quickly."

He listened as the administrator relayed the few facts he knew. The facts turned out to be nothing more than a bed check that had turned up an empty room. There had been no sign of Ava anywhere on the floor. That was hours ago. Faisal couldn't believe it. Ava was missing. It was nothing that anyone had predicted or, in his defense, could have predicted. She wasn't in shape to run. She had shown no signs of that, only a worry about her father. He'd judged all of it wrong. This changed everything, in a way that was unthinkable. In fact, from what he could see, the case—what there was of it—was majorly compromised unless he could find her. And he'd better find her fast.

"I'm not sure how she escaped," Colin Vanstone admitted. There was a sheepish edge to his voice. "Although, even the security you had in place took breaks."

"Escaped." He frowned. As if she was being held prisoner instead of being kept safe. *Escaped.* Despite everything that had happened, the thing that was highlighted in his mind was the word *escaped.* It left an ugly taste in his mouth. Escaping was for convicts not for someone like Ava. She'd been a voluntary patient in an American hospital, not a dangerous criminal. All that aside, the thought of her alone on the streets of a big city like Miami in her state was inconceivable. She had no money, no transportation, no nothing and a faulty memory.

"It seems she disappeared several hours ago. The room has since been filled…"

"Filled?" There was a harsh edge to the word. He couldn't believe any of this.

"I wasn't notified until…" His voice trailed off as if he had more to say and yet was reluctant to add whatever it might be.

"What the hell?" he spat out, skipping over what only appeared to be a lame excuse. "How did you let her get away?" He paused, realizing that what he had said had been contradictory to his thoughts about escape, but it didn't matter. What mattered was finding her. "When did it happen?" He had more questions that he wanted to ask. But there were only so many answers he was going to get, and none to the question of where she had gone. He was ready to move now. To get her back. He wasn't sure how this had happened. He'd never thought she'd run.

"Considering the circumstances, I discharged the security."

"Discharged the security…" His voice was slow and deadly as his mind tried to wrap itself around the massive screwup that had happened.

Faisal bit back his next comment. He didn't need to waste time on judgments.

"She was seen going down the corridor, alone. Last evening."

"Yesterday?" He couldn't filter the anger from his voice. This was unbelievable. He wanted to hurl the phone and go after her immediately. But that would be ridiculous. He needed the facts, he needed control.

"A volunteer saw her, they had no reason to question her, or, for that matter, report it. In fact, he wouldn't normally be there that late but he'd brought a magazine up to a patient. Then the ward clerk found the note…"

"What note?"

"She borrowed fifty dollars. At least that's what her note said. Opened an unlocked cabinet and took a fifty from one of the nurse's bags." The administrator cleared his throat. "I'm not sure how it happened. She wasn't under guard but—"

"She was your responsibility," Faisal snarled. He couldn't believe this, the why of it—nothing gibed. Where had she gone and why had she run? Had she felt threatened?

"What kind of shape was she in?" he asked. There were so many concerns here, not least of which was Ava's physical health. He remembered how she'd been when he'd last seen her. Weak, still confused and lying down.

"When she was last seen by a nurse at 9:30 p.m., she was awake and alert but her memory was still shaky. That's what the last charting reveals." He cleared his throat. "They'd given her solids but hadn't taken the intravenous line out."

"What are you saying?" He could only picture the needle providing sustenance directly into her vein—it had still been in. That meant…the thought dropped, it was an ugly visual.

The administrator cleared his throat as if his next words were difficult or at least reluctant. "She pulled it out and not well. There was a trail of blood on her bed sheets."

"She was bleeding?"

"Nothing major, the wound will naturally seal itself within a matter of minutes. Usually we apply pressure in the form of a cotton pad and a light bandage. I wouldn't worry about that."

"What do you propose I worry about?" Faisal asked. He'd left money for her in case there was something she needed at the gift shop, or for a meal at one of the hospital kiosks. He'd been generous in what he'd left— now he realized that he might have been too generous. He'd facilitated her escape. Like a fool, he thought as he fought the urge to hurl the phone. Instead he clenched his fist and directed his ire at the man who'd just given him the news.

"Seriously, this has never happened. When we've had patients in a hurry to get out of hospital care we've been able to convince them that it wouldn't be in their best interest," the administrator said as he skated over the damning words.

"Why not this time?"

"She gave no hint of her intention."

Smart, that was Ava. She'd kept silent and used that as a cloak to slip out under the wire. She'd obviously remembered something that she hadn't revealed to him.

Darn her, stubborn as he remembered, except now the playing field made the deception on her part all the more dangerous.

"I can't believe it happened. I mean the hallways are empty at times but this time it wasn't just the hallway that was empty but the nurses' station too. She literally lucked out."

She outsmarted you, he thought. It wasn't surprising. He remembered how wicked smart she was. She had gone on for an advanced degree long after he'd kicked formal education aside for a chance to work in the field and take the helm of the Wyoming office of Nassar Security.

His mind returned to the present. She might have some resources but she wouldn't have much. And she had no clothes. He couldn't imagine that she'd get far considering what she had available for a wardrobe. "What was she wearing?" Faisal asked, thinking of the sleepwear that he'd rescued her in and the equally inappropriate hospital gown.

"I couldn't tell you."

He should have expected that answer. "She couldn't leave in a hospital gown," he said, trying to keep the edge out of his voice.

"True but in a hospital it's easy enough to get your hands on a pair of scrubs. It's the norm to see them anywhere in the city—people coming and going from work. I'm not saying that's what she did, however."

Unfortunately, it was a valid point, Faisal thought grimly. The various hospitals and medical facilities in the city employed a huge network of people. Many of them dressed in the classic scrubs, from physicians to nurses and even students. It wasn't an uncommon sight even outside hospital grounds.

"There's more," the administrator said.

"Get to the point," Faisal growled.

"That patient, the one placed in her room, has since passed on. A tragedy. A young woman admitted for possible gall bladder surgery died before we could help her."

The blood seemed to roar in his ears. He wasn't sure if he was hearing right. "Ava's room was filled and that patient has since died?" he repeated the facts as he understood them. He wasn't sure how this could happen.

"Yes, it appears that way. An autopsy has been ordered. She was only twenty-eight and this was completely unexpected."

"What did she die of?"

"We don't know," Colin replied. "Could be a number of things. An aneurysm for one. It's rare but not unheard of."

"Foul play?" It had to be asked. Faisal was frustrated and not done with this man. Had Ava been the target?

"It's possible but doubtful." There was a slight hesitation in the way he said the words, as if he didn't quite believe them.

"Was there anyone around, anyone suspicious-looking?" Faisal didn't keep the impatience out of his voice. The man's methodical tone was driving him crazy.

"One of the nursing assistants saw a man at the elevator shortly before the body was found. Nothing was thought of it. He could be a visitor."

"What did he look like?"

"Middle-aged. Gray-streaked dark hair. Caucasian. Average height. She only saw him from the back."

"Anything else?" he asked and his gut told him that everything about this was wrong. Not just the murder, which was beyond wrong, nor the fact that Ava had disappeared, but there was something else, something even more deadly.

"The next patient was moved in immediately after we discovered the first patient, Ava, missing. The room was cleaned an hour after the discovery but the name hadn't been reassigned. It was still marked Ava Adams," the man said gravely. "I don't like what that might imply. The body is just being removed now," the administrator said in a regretful tone of voice.

Faisal's entire body was tense. His senses were on high alert. This information changed everything. The woman in Ava's room was dead, murdered, he was sure of it. Within hours of her leaving…it was beyond hope that the intended target had not been Ava.

The question was still who had killed and why, and more important, where was Ava now? And why had she run?

Five minutes later, Faisal disconnected with less information than he'd like. But considering everything that had happened, he doubted if the woman who had died in Ava's room had expired from natural causes.

Faisal clenched his fist. He sat for a minute staring silently into space. He could have been anywhere. He didn't see the elegant decor of the suite. He couldn't believe that Ava had regained her strength and potentially her memory and then coasted out of the hospital with an ease that bordered on the ridiculous. He needed to find her, like yesterday, and before someone else did.

Chapter Thirteen

It was less than an hour since Faisal had received that fateful call that Ava was missing. Now he looked long and hard at the face of the young woman who lay dead on the cold steel of the examining table. Her hair was long, almost to the middle of her back. She was brunette and a few years older than Ava. After that, the similarities stopped.

He'd insisted on viewing the body in the hope that the similarities would somehow give him a much-needed clue. Now he didn't know why he'd bothered. It was depressing and frightening all at the same time. Looking at her frightened him for Ava and saddened him for the deceased woman's family.

"She may have been asphyxiated," the coroner said.

He listened as the coroner went into some detail on why he believed that could be a possibility.

"Her eyes are bloodshot. Classic sign of asphyxiation."

A chill ran through him like none he'd felt before. He'd stood in this position many times but never had he felt the haunting fear that the person before him could have been someone he knew and loved. He almost took a step back. That thought combined with the cold steel and sharp smell of disinfectant that depersonalized death was almost too much. This wasn't Ava but someone had loved her.

Regret and anger snaked through him as he thought of how this young woman had died unnecessarily, how it could just as easily have been Ava on that slab. The reality was as disturbing as it was unthinkable. Whether they could prove it or not, he was sure that this woman had died of unnatural causes. It wasn't right or fair. And he knew it happened much too often. He'd thought of adding a branch of investigations geared solely to violence against women. He'd seen too much of it in his work. But now wasn't the time for such considerations.

Five minutes later, Faisal was heading across the hospital parking lot to a charcoal 1967 Mustang he kept in Miami for his rare visits to the city. He slipped behind the wheel and leaned back against the plush leather, the keys in his lap, his arms crossed and a frown on his face.

A woman who supposedly should have been Ava was dead. The fact that the decedent had been in Ava's room and Ava was still the registered patient indicated that Ava was the target. Now there were questions that needed to be answered, and quickly.

Where had Ava gone? He tamped down the panic he'd felt at losing her when he'd only just found her. He had to stick to facts.

She'd come here for a vacation with her father before starting her working career as a clinical psychologist with a public school in Wyoming. But none of that gave him the answers he needed. She'd flown out of Casper, Wyoming, where she'd leased an apartment. It was interesting that she'd stayed in the state where she'd studied, at least for her first four years, and where they'd met. It was far from her father's residence in the Caribbean. But as much as he knew she loved her father, tropical life had never been for her, she'd said so often. So Wyoming, the end of school and the beginning of a career, was where her life had been until just a week ago when she'd joined her father in St. Croix for a voyage to the Bahamas. Now, her father was missing and she'd fled. To him, it was clear that she knew something and that she didn't trust anyone to help her. That pained him but he couldn't dwell on it. How he felt had no relevance to helping Ava.

He reviewed the facts, running them through his mind in record speed until he hit on what he considered to be key questions. Did Ava's secret threaten her father's well-being or his business? Yet her father was missing, possibly already dead, and still she'd run. Was it a threat that had frightened her? Did she know something? What had caused her to leave the hospital?

Whatever Ava was after, he was sure it was major and he was also sure that it was linked to the death in her room. He'd left the morgue with more questions than answers and an unspoken confirmation that Ava was no longer safe. She'd run and he thanked everything he cherished for that. If she hadn't, she'd be the one in that morgue.

Still, the fact that she'd run left him with questions. Why hadn't Ava turned to him instead of running? For whatever reason, she hadn't trusted him.

He opened the car door and stepped out. Despite the feeling of urgency, he had no direction. He needed to think this through. The door shut and he pressed the key fob, locking the door without a backward glance.

His mind went back over the case, of what he knew

and what he might have missed. A yacht with what they could only assume had two men on board had disappeared. The Coast Guard had no answers and the vast Atlantic was hiding its secrets well. What had happened? What had Ava seen? He stood with his hands on his hips for a second, looking right, left and behind him as if on the quiet street there might be an answer. But all he saw was a pretty girl in a sundress walking a white poodle. Her long blond hair had stripes of baby blue. He'd like to tell her to dodge that salon the next time she had her hair done. It was a lighthearted thought amid the gravity of what had happened.

Faisal stared across the street where high-rises hid the vastness of the Atlantic. Somewhere beyond Miami's crowded docks lay a deadly secret. A secret that may already have killed.

FAISAL STOOD ON the sidewalk outside of Mercy Hospital considering his options. Ava's father's final destination had been Fort Lauderdale. He looked at his watch—it had been over an hour since he'd been told of her disappearance and it had been longer than that since she'd made her escape. From what he knew she might have had all night and had definitely had most of the morning. He'd like to grab the hospital administrator and shake sense into him. Instead he clenched his fist and tried to put himself in Ava's position.

What was in Miami for her? He couldn't think of anything. Where would she have gone? Her identification was missing, along with her credit and debit cards. The only money she had was the one hundred and fifty dollars he'd given her and the fifty dollars she'd lifted.

Two hundred dollars wouldn't get you far, not if you wanted to sleep and eat.

A city bus lumbered by and stopped. He waited with the others at the stop and once inside, spoke to the driver. Two minutes later he stood on the curb. He now knew that there was a bus that went from the hospital to the intercity bus depot. It stopped here every fifteen minutes and arrived at the depot with one transfer. Ava could have been out of the hospital area within fifteen minutes of exiting the building. If that were true, she could be long gone. The problem was that, even if he was right, he didn't know where she was headed or why. He didn't know if a bus was the answer but it was a place to start.

Five minutes later, he was again behind the wheel of his Mustang. He put the car in gear and with a screech of tires headed toward the depot. But an hour later he was ready to ditch the conversation with the man at the security desk. He was sun-bronzed and wrinkled with age, sun or both. He looked like he'd been working far too long. Worse, he refused to reveal any information. Instead, he stated that it was an infringement of traveler confidentiality and his oath of employment. Faisal doubted if he'd taken any oath of employment but whether he had or not, it was clear the conversation was going nowhere. He turned away in frustration but the feeling of eyes on him had him turning around. She was a plump woman somewhere between forty and fifty-five. Her brown hair was bobbed in an efficient shoulder-length style and she had a suitcase by her side. She seemed to be giving him the literal once-over—like she was deciding if she should trust him or not. Her lips tightened and she let go of the handle of her suitcase. It was as if she'd made her decision.

"I may know what you need," she said. The words sounded ominous and hollow like something from an old murder mystery, much like the tattered Agatha Christie in her hand.

He almost turned away—she could be an eccentric looking for a little excitement in her day. Judging from her flowered dress and the way she seemed at home, as if hanging around a bus depot was what she did, there might be a good chance of that. Yet his instinct told him to listen, and experience had taught him that evidence could come from the most unlikely places.

"I saw her, you know. The woman you're looking for." She put the book down as he closed the distance between them. "Gorgeous woman, at least I think she could have been but she looked sickly, frightened even. I didn't speak to her. She left here late last night." She looked at her watch and then sheepishly back at him. "I suppose I've lost track of time."

There was something about the fact that she never quite looked at him, and the way the ticket attendant had looked at her with disdain that made him doubt that the woman was a credible witness.

"Me, I'm headed here and there," she said vaguely, as if he had asked. "She got on a bus to Fort Lauderdale." She frowned and leaned forward. "You don't believe me?"

"I never said that." He'd put no thought into her last words other than Fort Lauderdale was where he had planned to meet Dan Adams. It was possible that Ava went there to find answers. He met the woman's bloodshot, brown eyes. The determined tilt to her chin seemed to say that she was going to make it despite her circumstances. "It's true. I don't know what her ticket read but that was the bus she got on. Hard woman to forget. If I were younger I might have been mighty jealous."

"Anything else?"

"Fort Lauderdale, like I said." She shrugged. "I'd love to go myself but funds are…" Her voice trailed off.

Faisal peeled off enough bills to get her across the country. "Here," he said simply. "Treat yourself to a trip."

Her eyes lit up as she took the money almost reverently. "My daughter lives in Chicago," she said simply. "I'll go there." And for the first time, there was purpose in her expression that made Faisal feel that she might not be the only one whose luck was about to change.

Reluctantly, he moved away. He looked at his watch—it was nearing noon. She could already have been there and left the bus depot heading for another destination. Enough time had passed. His phone buzzed.

"Zaf," Faisal said as he answered. "Things have changed direction here." He went on to tell Zafir how the occupant of Ava Adams's room had died, possibly murdered by suffocation. "One thing is clear—if it was murder, the murderer thought they were taking out Ava. The records hadn't been switched over, some foul-up at the front desk."

"So if it's murder, the murderer didn't know what Ava looked like," Zafir said thoughtfully.

"He knew alright. Thing is the victim had long dark hair and was close in age. If her head had been turned…"

"A case of mistaken identity."

"Unfortunate," Faisal said, "that anyone had to die. But what I have out of all of this is that the description the administrator gave of the man they think is the murderer matches Ben Whyte. He was the second man on the yacht that night."

"You're assuming he's alive. It could be a long shot but on the other hand, if he is you've got yourself a suspect."

"This case is not like anything I've seen before."

"I won't disagree with you there. My question is, what are the chances that Dan's still alive?"

"Not good," Faisal said grimly. "That's why, considering what's just happened, I'm focusing on Ava. Her safety is paramount. This death, it makes my skin crawl. Who would want to kill her?" He moved the phone to his other ear as he collected his thoughts and a breeze pushed a strand of dark hair across his eyes. He pushed it back impatiently.

"She knows something," Zafir said and there was a dark edge to his words.

"You're right about that. She had some traumatic memory loss when I saw her but eventually that's going to go away. Meanwhile, we've upgraded to a red," he said. He thought of the danger to Ava, which would also shadow him as he'd do anything to protect her. He'd do it for any client—but for her... He paused.

"Go out of touch—"

"And you'll send help," he interrupted. "Meantime, I'm heading to Fort Lauderdale."

"Dan Adams's intended destination."

"Exactly. But not just that—I had a tip at the bus station. Ava may be headed there."

He ended the conversation shortly after that. The longer Ava stayed missing, the more Faisal worried for her safety. Especially now that he knew there was a killer on her trail, and she was running out of time.

Chapter Fourteen

Fort Lauderdale, Florida
Monday, June 13—3:00 p.m.

Despite what Faisal had been told, there was no evidence that Ava Adams had gotten off at Fort Lauderdale. And there was no information to be found at the bus station in Fort Lauderdale. The man at security was no more helpful than the guy in Miami. In fact, he appeared to be more interested in the sandwich he was chewing than anything Faisal had to say. It took all Faisal had not to yank the sandwich from his hand. But instead he had to take the high road and walk—there might be information to be had, but it wasn't here or in this moment.

He stood outside for a moment and considered what he knew. Ava Adams had vanished. No one had seen a dark-haired, slim woman in scrubs. Faisal had asked every potential witness—the ticket agent, a number of other employees and a bus driver. No one had seen her. But it was possible that she'd disguised herself. Even a simple disguise, hair tucked up, a cap of some sort. The ditching of the scrubs—that is if she'd passed a clothing donation bin or similar such options. Providence could present all sorts of opportunities that one wouldn't notice in other circumstances. Desperation was a strong motivator.

His phone buzzed.

"What do you have, Barb?" He knew there was an edge to his voice but frustration did that. Whether Ava had been on a bus heading through Fort Lauderdale or whether she hadn't was still a question. As it stood, Ava had disappeared, leaving him concerned and beyond frustrated.

"Darrell Chan was the Vancouver man Dan Adams was in contact with a few times in recent days. He actually wasn't that hard to locate—I hacked into Adams's email and phone records and found him. Not too difficult to put two and two together. In fact, I think Ezra could have done it," she said, referring to her five-year-old daughter.

Despite the seriousness of the situation, there was a smile in her voice. Besides her efficiency, that was the other thing that made Barb so great to work with—her ability to add humor to any situation, even some of the toughest.

"I don't know, Barb, Ezra's smart but you're giving her a little too much credit," he said with a slight laugh that surprisingly, despite the situation, came naturally.

"Watch it or I may require babysitting duties again," she laughed. It was a standing joke between them that in a pinch a few years ago she'd brought Ezra to the office. He'd been in the office he used in Marrakech that day and the little girl was fascinated by the record player he kept on the filing cabinet. He'd spent the last hour of the day sitting on the floor with her tapping out the beat of "Smoke on the Water." Barb had found the two of them there and never let him forget it.

"Tell her we'll have another go next time I'm in Marrakech," he said.

"I tell her that and she'll be begging you to show up next week. She's smart but her patience needs some work."

Faisal laughed. It made some of the more difficult aspects of his job easier to have staff who knew him well enough to know when he needed just a moment of light diversion. A smile or a laugh to release the pressure before he exploded from the stress he was under, this time to save a woman he loved. And just like that his lighthearted mood dissolved into the turbulence of self-realization. His fist clenched the phone so tightly he threatened to crack the plastic. Love. He didn't love Ava, he couldn't. It wasn't true and yet his heart told him that it was.

Barb continued, unaware of the revelation that had just broadsided him.

"This thing just gets bigger the more I dig. I've hacked one email that Chan sent. He seemed to be under the impression that Dan was partnering with Ben Whyte on land deals in a southern rural area of Texas. Chan had already paid Whyte for one property and had reservations about the second. This all happened in a very short period of time. Thirty days. Interesting thing is that there's nothing filed online in the county land registry to verify any of this."

Faisal shook his head at what Barb was implying. But there was no denying the fact that Dan had mentioned land transactions when he'd called. At the time, the call had been brief and he hadn't gone into details. Still, he'd been surprised at the idea. Dan had never dealt in land before, not that he knew of. But real estate wasn't illegal and he hadn't given much more thought to it.

"Go on," he said as she paused as if waiting for confirmation from him.

"Here's what I have on Chan. He immigrated to Canada from Hong Kong while it was still part of Great Britain. Before it became an administrative region of China. As you know that all happened in 1997."

Faisal bit back a comment. He'd learned that it was quicker to let Barb say what she had unearthed without interrupting.

"For a decade or more prior to 1997, wealthy Hong Kong nationals were acquiring property in countries around the world as part of an exit strategy. The Canadian cities of Vancouver and Toronto were hotbeds for wealthy Hong Kong citizens to acquire real estate. Chan invested in real estate and owns numerous properties in Vancouver, mostly commercial."

"Anything else?"

"Not yet."

"Thanks, Barb," he said as he disconnected, smiling at the needless lecture on foreign affairs. But that was what made Barb so good. She never assumed you knew and she never wasted time asking the question if just flipping the information off would take less time. His mind switched to Chan. He wondered, since Chan lived a short flight away from Texas, whether he'd made the journey to verify his purchase or, more interesting still, whether he hadn't.

He wondered if there was a connection to what had happened on the missing yacht—a shady business transaction didn't seem likely. Dan Adams had always been a straight shooter.

He replayed in his mind everything Barb had said about Darrell Chan. The man had long since obtained a Canadian citizenship and established roots in the country. Considering the price of Vancouver real estate and the number of properties involved, Darrell Chan must be a very rich man.

An hour later, with all possibilities exhausted in Fort Lauderdale and no new clues as to Ava's whereabouts, he stood in the penthouse suite in the Nassar-owned hotel. Faisal contemplated everything he knew. He hated this part of the job, when he was forced to wait, to gather information before moving forward. When his phone buzzed, he grabbed it.

"I had to dig hard for this," Barb said. "Looks like Chan was fleeced."

"Fleeced?"

"He was sold a piece of land that was never going to be transferred as the seller didn't have ownership. Chan paid millions for a large tract of so-called ranch land. I found all that in a trail of emails in which he claimed Dan Adams was responsible as the seller."

"Unbelievable. I'm betting that's what the phone calls between Darrell Chan and Dan Adams were all about."

It looked like Dan Adams had been speculating in land, an area that he'd never shown an interest in before. In fact, he'd reacted with disdain the one time the subject had ever come up. Now he appeared to have done an about-face. More disturbing was the fact that there was evidence of fraud. Dan Adams had neither the heart nor the need to steal. Something much more sinister was going on. But despite knowing all that, he was stunned into silence. He could only listen to what Barb had found.

Sales of land in southern Texas. Purchases where no land had ever changed hands, nor would it. Ranch land sold to foreigners—*the perfect patsies*, he thought. They would arrive to discover there was no land and by the time they did the perpetrator would be gone. Dan Adams's name was on every deed. None of it made sense.

"Interesting thing," Barb said, "I've found no official record."

He hung up with a sense of foreboding. Something wasn't ringing true about any of this.

Monday, June 13—9:00 p.m.

THE GRIND OF the road, the sleepless night, all of it had exhausted Ava. She'd been on this bus for hours and there were hours left to go. The rest breaks had only made her wary and they proved more tiring than being on the actual bus. There, she was constantly vigilant, afraid that someone had followed her. Now, she slouched back in the seat trying to get comfortable. It didn't help. Despite cat napping through the journey, her head ached and her back hurt. The slight curve of scoliosis in her lower back ached as it always did without regular exercise. The nagging pain was the least of her problems.

On her head was a worn Chicago Cubs ball cap under which she had tucked her long hair so very little showed. She'd found the cap on the ground by the Miami charity clothing bin she'd raided before getting on the bus.

She didn't think about who might have been wearing the cap before—couldn't. She was in survival mode.

A middle-aged man looked back at her from his place a seat ahead and across the aisle. There was a question in his eyes as if something about her bothered him. She knew her appearance was off, that she might appear lost or homeless in her worn, ill-fitting clothes. She hoped at worst she only looked down on her luck. She broke eye contact. Her psychology studies had taught her that the connection between strangers was fleeting. Memory happened when it was highlighted by an unexpected event or accentuated over a period of time or through repetition. She'd leave him nothing to remember. His ego and the memories that supported them were more relevant to his sense of self than she was.

She tapped her foot. The sneakers she was wearing pinched her feet, but there'd been no choice. They were the closest to her size in the hospital locker room. She felt bad. Someone would be going home in her work shoes.

She ran the back of her hand across her eyes, sweeping away dust, sweat and the remnants of the tears that the thought of her father always brought on. The air-conditioning seemed to barely move the air and the heat was cloying. She lurched in her seat as the road got rough for a minute and then settled into its regular rhythm. They'd encountered a detour only an hour ago and the ride had become slow and bumpy as they took a narrow, paved side road.

She looked out the window but there was nothing to see but the occasional sweep of blacktop, a road sign lit up by the headlights and darkness. She thought of Faisal. He'd been at the hospital every day, sometimes for hours. Once, she wasn't sure, but she thought he might have stayed the night. She remembered waking up in the night and seeing him there watching her. He had made her feel safe, feel like it would all work out, that her father—she turned her head to the window. She couldn't think of her father. It was all too grim, too seemingly hopeless. There was only his memory that she had to preserve, to make right. To ensure that his reputation and the charities he supported would remember him as the outstanding and upstanding man he was.

She tore her mind from the grim thoughts and instead her thoughts returned to Faisal. Seeing him again only reminded her of how much she'd missed him and of how much she still cared. It had been difficult not to tell him of her new memories, not to trust him. But that was the problem, she did trust him and she didn't want to place him in danger. Despite the years they'd been apart, she cared about Faisal too much. It seemed like both yesterday and so long ago since she'd seen him. Over the last few years, he'd never been far from her mind but her studies had been more important. At least that was what she had told herself as the years had slipped by. But he'd never left her heart. The hard truth was that she'd lost track of Faisal but she'd never forgotten him. She'd picked up the phone so many times to call him but she'd never known what to say. It had all been so long ago. A time when she'd felt things for him that she shouldn't have felt for a friend. They were feelings that she'd had to hide, for then Faisal had a girlfriend. She imagined it was the same now. He'd matured into an extremely handsome man.

Emotions aside, the smart thing would have been to trust him. He'd rescued her and she knew he was an investigator. Protecting people was his job. Knowing that didn't change how she felt. She couldn't involve him. She didn't know what she was up against and neither did he. Her father was more than likely dead. The thought of that again brought tears to her eyes. She couldn't jeopardize anyone else no matter who they were or what they did for a living. The only way to stop this was to uncover whatever it was that her father claimed was hidden in the small town where she was headed. She needed to go into her father's email, which he had shared the password for, just in case. But there'd been little time and no computer easily accessible, at least so she'd thought at the time. Her mind hadn't been clear then. The email was important, she knew that. It was the first thing she'd check when she arrived.

"Just in case something happens to me," her father had said after giving her the password to his email.

Something had happened. She wiped away a tear. The only good that had happened in the last hours had been the return of her memory.

"Miss," an older woman said in a muted, nighttime voice as she stretched her arm across the aisle and held out a small packet of tissue. "You look troubled."

"I'm fine," Ava said, glancing briefly at the woman who had gotten on the bus at the last stop over an hour ago. The last thing she needed was attention of any kind.

The woman shook her head as if she were reading between the lines and seeing everything that Ava was trying to hide. "It will get better. No hardship lasts forever. You'll see."

"Thank you," she managed but the woman's compassion had almost caused her to break. She couldn't allow that to happen. She had to get it together. It was all on her and in getting to a small town in the middle of nowhere. To save her father's reputation she needed to be there. But to be any help at all, she needed to get it together as quickly as possible.

Two hours later, she was thanking the Fates that brought strangers into your life. For the woman turned out to be a lifesaver. Her name was Anne Johnson and somehow she made the fear, without ever knowing that it existed, manageable. She talked about her family, of mundane things—her sister who was waiting for her. Her voice was the kind that was soothing, a Southern drawl that was filled with life experience. She spoke briefly of her four grown children.

"All of them older than you," she said. "Six grand-children so far."

The conversation went on—one-sided as it had been from the beginning. Eventually it faded as the night thinned, and as dawn broke they reached the stop that was Anne's. She felt a sinking feeling in her gut as Anne got up, grabbed her overstuffed flowered carryall and reached over to squeeze Ava's shoulder. Her smile was wide in her dark, round, rather plain face.

"You'll be okay," she assured. "And if you're not, you know where to find me."

Where to find me.

The thought that she might have to do that. That she might need Anne's help. That fear found her and rode with her the last miles until a small town in Texas glimmered in the distance, offering hope with a good dose of fear.

Chapter Fifteen

Faisal put a call in to Aaron Detrick, an undercover operative with the Royal Canadian Mounted Police, or RCMP. He'd gotten to know Aaron when he'd had a case over three years ago that had involved a suspect crossing into Canada. Aaron and he had worked each side of the border to keep his client safe. That work had provided him some insight into the Canadian system and a fantastic contact in law enforcement.

He left a message for Aaron to give him a call.

Ten minutes later the phone rang.

"Aaron," he said. At any other time he would have been pleased to connect with him again. It was only distance and busy lives that had kept them from becoming better friends.

"You had a request in about Darrell Chan?" Aaron asked after they'd put in an abbreviated version of pleasantries. "I assume this is a secure line," he said without question.

"You know it," Faisal replied. "I was wondering if there's any record on him. Anything at all."

"Surprised that you ask. We've been trying to tag him for a long time. The guy is strange. Not in a personality type of way but in the way he dances between good and bad. He's made millions in Canadian real estate, is one of those types who's seen as a good guy, but is actually someone who will kill if you get in his way. The force," he said, referring to the RCMP, where he served as a detective sergeant, "has been trying to nail him for half a decade now. But he's slippery. He runs a mega real estate enterprise. He immigrated with money and has made another fortune in Vancouver. I expect you know the details of that."

"No. Actually, I'm just starting to get an idea of what he's about," Faisal replied.

"In the past he's run into a few glitches in business, shall we say. Deals that aren't quite what they seem. In two cases that we know of for sure, the people suspected of the crime against him have died. Not at his hands and not by anyone we can pin. There's a widely held belief within the force that it's the work of hired killers."

"Hired by Chan?"

"That's what I'd like to say we know but there's no evidence linking the killings to him. The way things came down, when you apply logic—well, in my opinion, it points straight at him. Without evidence, he continues to get away with murder. And he does it by hiring hit men, basically scum, but murderers nonetheless."

"Dangerous only when crossed."

"Exactly," Aaron said. "So what's going on there?"

Faisal explained what he knew. He told him about the calls that Chan had made to Dan Adams. "There's no evidence to say there's any wrongdoing," he was quick to add.

"Except for the fact that Dan Adams is missing. Of course, that's not saying anything," Aaron said. "I ran a CPIC on Chan, like you asked, and it came up clean," he said. He referred to the Canadian Police Information Centre's database. The database held criminal record information on Canadian citizens. This wasn't the first time that Faisal had asked for such a favor.

A few minutes later, he hung up.

Later with the lights of Fort Lauderdale spread out like a rich blanket beneath him, in another penthouse suite much like the one he left in Miami, Faisal checked the weather report. That's when things went from bad to worse. For now it appeared that the coast of Florida might get the brunt of Hurricane Dexter.

Tuesday, June 14—6:30 a.m.

AVA TOOK A deep breath as the bus passed the sign for Tristan, Texas, population 2,001. It would be a relief to get off the bus. But arriving at her destination was overwhelming. Her stomach heaved as she faced what felt like the moment of truth. She tried a trick she'd learned a long time ago, diverting her thoughts to something inane. She wondered who the "one" in the population sign was. Was it the most recent birth in town, maybe the only one this year? But the lighthearted thought didn't change her mood or the dark reason she was here. Once the bus came to a stop, she stood up, feeling underdressed and underprepared. She was darn close to helpless. This was the last place she knew her father planned to visit before he left for that fateful yacht trip that… She wiped the corner of her eye with her forefinger. She couldn't think of the fact that her father had more than likely died at sea and his reputation was about to be destroyed if she wasn't successful. It all seemed so surreal, everything that had happened these last few days. She felt like she had been moving in a cloud.

She remembered what her father had said on the yacht about Ben. He'd told her how he had backed Ben financially in a bid to help him get a footing in a real estate business. Ben was a man he'd met through his church, a man who was down on his luck or so he'd thought until he'd discovered that Ben was lying to him.

She grabbed her bag and dispensed with her thoughts. She needed to focus as she took her first look at her new temporary residence. The bus depot at Tristan was nothing like the one in Miami or any of those that had followed. It was small and worn, the paint peeling from the wall of the waiting area. As Ava stepped off the bus, the first thing that hit her was the heat. The temperature had soared since yesterday. Barren land with scrub brush stretched out to the north and south. In front of her were the worn edges of Tristan. The sign for a Flying J truck stop was visible about a half block away, along with a couple of motel signs. When she looked behind her, she could see a stretch of dry, desert-like prairie. She knew that the answer to what had happened on that yacht lay in this little community in a faraway corner of Texas.

She needed money. What Faisal had given her, what she'd taken—guilt made her pause—was almost gone. She needed more. This time she'd acquire it through a job. That meant short-term, menial labor.

She swung the mostly empty canvas bag over her shoulder and stepped out of the station. She blinked as the sun beat down on the blacktop. Her view of the town from here wasn't much. Trailers crowded together on one side. Commercial buildings with wire-fenced yards, cars in one, tires in the other. A number of motels just ahead, all low-rise, peeling paint, low-end. It was exactly what she needed. She headed toward the last in the row.

"This isn't going to be the Marriott," she murmured to herself as she remembered vacations her father had taken her on. He'd always been generous that way, taking her on no-expense-spared holidays throughout her life. She shook her head. She lengthened her stride. The sooner she got settled, the sooner she could help her father. Hopefully save him, she thought, clinging to the hope that he lived. But the odds of that were slim. Now there might well be only her and Ben, the man who wanted her dead. If she wanted to live, she had to find the evidence that he'd kill to hide.

Chapter Sixteen

Tristan, Texas
Tuesday, June 14—9:30 a.m.

As Ava stepped into the quiet confines of Tristan's only library, she was hit by the haunting edge of nostalgia. The smell of books reminded her of academia and her career that had yet to begin. It reminded her of her past studies, of everything that in the last few days had seemed lost. In fact, in the face of her new reality, they *were* lost. There was only the nightmare that she somehow had to wade through without getting anyone else hurt. Despite that thought there was something…someone, actually, who emerged out of the ashes of pain—Faisal. Ironically, now when she needed him most, she'd turned her back on him. But she'd had no choice. She'd cared about him too much. She'd thought about him too often through the last years when school had occupied her life in a way she knew few other periods of her life could. It was strange how psychology had turned her into an old soul with a knowledge that someone her age should not have. Again, she was diverting herself and her thoughts, and ultimately her need for Faisal. She'd never forgotten him and now she'd run, leaving him behind in the hopes of keeping him safe.

She pulled her thoughts from the past and from Faisal with difficulty. She had to face the present and the unknown if she were to stop whatever evil had taken out her father and could very well hurt others she loved. She had two names. She knew Ben Whyte had tried to kill her father. She also knew that the evidence for the land deal that implicated her father was filed here in Tristan—at least that's what her father had told her. The second name was Darrell Chan; she knew nothing about the man, except that her father had said in the event of tragedy to tell the authorities about him. She had— she'd told Faisal. She regretted that. It endangered him by giving him another degree of involvement.

She pushed the thought from her mind. On a back table a stack of books sat beside a thin, gray-haired woman who glanced up once from the computer terminal and then returned her attention to the computer.

"Can I help you?" The librarian smiled and Ava tried not to stare at the woman's thin lips, which were generously coated with red lipstick and stood out like a slap in the face. Her hair, bobbed at the ears, was a no-nonsense cut. That look clashed with the lipstick's attempt at glamour but her blue eyes smiled with a vibrant youthfulness.

If her problems had been simpler, the look and the attitude would have made Ava feel at home. As it was, she was on edge, well aware that she had little time. There was so much to do and it was already midmorning. She still had to find a job. The twenty-five dollars she had left weren't going to carry her far and she needed to eat. Her stomach growled as she thought of food. She'd had little of that. A loaf of bread and a jar of peanut butter had been her only purchase this morning and the groceries were tucked in the canvas bag over her arm.

Ava Adams had disappeared in favor of Anne Brown. It was a plain name that suited her current situation and had been inspired by the woman who had been so kind to her on the bus.

"I'd like to buy some computer time."

"No charge," the librarian said. "The town is trying to get more people online. The locals are notoriously cheap and sometimes I think that half of them might really believe in the rise of the machine. *The Terminator*, loved that movie," she said in response to what Ava knew was a slightly blank look. "Look, sorry, too much information." She gestured to two terminals, one that was occupied, the other free. "Help yourself. Call me if you need assistance."

"I will, thank you," Ava said. She went to the terminal, which was in a far corner of the library away from both the librarian and the woman who seemed to be the only other patron in the library.

She pretty much knew that she was fishing in the dark. But she had nothing else but the knowledge that this place was the beginning of it all. What beginning that might be she didn't know. Hopefully, there was some clue to it all in her father's affairs. She opened his private email account. She'd told her father often enough to kick the email and move into more secure messaging methods but he'd been old-school that way.

He'd hinted that he was ready to take her advice two weeks ago. That was when he'd given his account password to her. It had been a casual mention, as though saying nothing would ever happen but he wanted to tell her anyway. He'd said that if something happened to him, she should access his email. At the time she'd thought that it was only because he was close to hitting a landmark birthday, shortly after hers, and he was feeling his own mortality. Now it meant so much more.

As she clicked through the various emails, she felt less like she was intruding into her father's private life than she'd thought she would. There were more business-related than private emails. They were emails concerning various meeting results, a response from a birthday greeting to a woman she knew had acted as his assistant.

Five minutes in she was frowning as a name kept reappearing. Darrell Chan had sent her father a number of emails in regard to ranch land he had purchased in the area.

The correspondence was antagonistic, about a complaint that didn't seem quite clear. They were messages that seemed mired in secrecy as if there was a code being used. None of it, including the land mentioned, made any sense. Her father was a man who had been involved in a variety of businesses in his day. But he'd always had a particular loathing for real estate ventures. It had something to do with his own childhood growing up with a father who was what he liked to call a slumlord. As a result, or so he claimed, he had no use for investing in real estate. Therefore, land transactions weren't something her father would be involved in— until now, apparently.

A shiver of foreboding ran down her spine. She'd never felt so alone. And for a second and then two she let her mind wander to a place of safety and that took her immediately to Faisal. She wished she could talk to him. More than that, despite her actions, she wished he were here. She remembered the way he had looked at her the last time she'd seen him. She could have melted into his arms but she hadn't acted on that or even admitted it. In truth, she hadn't been in any condition to act on such feelings. She pushed the thoughts from her mind. What she felt for Faisal had no place here.

She opened another email. There Darrell clearly stated that he wanted his money back. It seemed that he was beginning to believe that he'd been duped. She scrolled down. There was nothing else, no further correspondence. Nothing sent by her father, nothing received. And the date of the last email was the same as that fateful night on the yacht.

"What did you get involved in, Dad?" she whispered. Whatever it was, Ben Whyte and that ill-fated night on the yacht were now looking like they might be the climax of a deal gone terribly wrong.

A few minutes later she closed the account and after asking the librarian where land deeds were registered, she was directed to a small office down the street. A half hour later she left that office realizing that this was much worse than she imagined.

"Fai, what would you do?" she murmured as if he were by her side. Her father's name was signed on the transfer of the very land that Chan had insisted he'd been sold. Worse, the signature in her father's name was not his, it was forged. She was sure of that. She'd seen her father's signature often enough. Now, she clutched the copies of two land transactions that the clerk had given her. She was exhausted and she still had to fulfill her last promise to her father—to stay alive.

Chapter Seventeen

Fort Lauderdale, Florida
Tuesday, June 14—11:00 a.m.

Faisal's phone buzzed.

"I've been digging into land deals in rural Texas," Barb said. "Like you asked."

"Did we confirm my suspicions?"

"Not exactly. What I did find was that Dan had a number of calls in recent weeks from Ben Whyte. He was calling from a small Texan town—Tristan. So I checked into the place. It's a going-nowhere-fast kind of place. Stopover for truckers and such heading for bigger centers. Nothing much goes on."

"Strange," Faisal replied but his heart sped up slightly as it always did upon receiving a major clue. His gut told him that was where Ava had gone. His logical mind told him that he had no other options, no clue, no direction. He had to follow the clue he had or remain in a state of inertia. The latter was no more comprehensible than it was feasible. The problem was that he was pretty sure Ava wouldn't be using her own name but he had no idea what she was calling herself now. He had to go back to the bus depot and see if somehow repetition would provide the break he needed. The only thing he could do was ask employees, fellow passengers even, whoever might have seen her. But none of the passengers would know her name, so that only left employees. And so far, he'd struck out in dead-end Fort Lauderdale. It was beyond frustrating. He needed someone who remembered her boarding the bus. So far he hadn't received that break.

"Also, one other thing. I've had an eye on Darrell Chan," Barb said, breaking into his thoughts. "He's landing in Hong Kong International Airport as we speak. Seems our boy is flying the coop while he can."

"Interesting."

"That's not all," Barb said with barely a pause. "I've got evidence that he bought more than one tract of land near Tristan, Texas. A huge spread. There's no evidence of a monetary transaction other than a small initial deposit."

"Who did he purchase it from?"

"There was nothing about the sale online. The only evidence I have is an email from Darrell to Dan."

"I wonder if the land even exists."

"I wondered the same," Barb replied. "False deeds, pretty easy stuff. Hard part, from what I can see, is not getting caught. Darrell Chan was promised acres of land. Oil rich, at least that was what it was advertised as and all of it in south Texas. That's what I'm getting from hacking into more of Dan Adams's emails, but, like I said, none of this is registered in online records."

"Damn," he said shocked at what she said. "I can't believe it." In fact, he didn't believe it, at least not that Dan was voluntarily involved. He believed a lot of things but something like that of Dan, no.

But opinion wasn't proof and he'd need proof to nail Dan Adams's killer to the wall.

Any proof he needed was in Tristan, Texas. He clenched his fists at the thought that if Ava was there she was alone and without his protection. He needed to get there as soon as possible.

This time when he contacted security at the Miami bus depot, he got action. Security agreed to check the video. Thirty minutes later he knew that a woman matching Ava's description had been there. Her ticket would take her to the small southern town of Tristan, Texas. The estimated time of arrival was five hours ago.

He hung up shortly after that. He dashed the back of his hand across his forehead before grabbing his go-bag. He'd never felt anything so urgent in his life as the need to reach Ava. The story was piecing together quickly and he liked none of it. What he believed was that the truth had come out that night on the yacht and Ava had been witness to it all. He needed to get to Tristan, Texas, without delay.

Two minutes later he had the chopper on alert. Fifteen minutes after that he was preparing to board.

BEN WHYTE STUCK out his thumb and an hour later realized that getting another ride would be a long shot. The semi driver had just dropped him off. The hours on the road hadn't been kind. He no longer looked safe, nonthreatening. He was scruffy-looking, a middle-aged man with an after-five shadow and a wild look in his eye. No one else was going to pick him up. He ran his fingers through his hair, took his mind from what he couldn't fix, such as the beginnings of a beard, and plastered a goofy smile on his face. His lips ached from the effort and he couldn't bring a smile to his eyes but a few cars slowed, hesitated and then changed their mind and sped up. A few minutes later, he had success. A battered blue Cougar, a dream car for a car enthusiast, slowed down and pulled over. He eyed the Cougar, thinking of the possibilities. It was a car that one would fix up, that… His thoughts broke off as he concentrated on the smile, focusing on making the smile reach his eyes. The man who'd stopped for him might be a decade younger. He had artfully disheveled hair and a carefree look in his dark eyes.

He smiled, all the while thinking that soon he could quit with the idiotic smile that was killing his facial muscles. His lips actually hurt from the effort but it had paid off.

"You need a lift?"

"I do," he said calmly as he opened the door and slipped in knowing that this time he needed to take control. He was too close to his goal. No more sitting in the passenger seat and watching the miles go by. He didn't need a witness this close to his goal.

Ten minutes later he was at the wheel. It had been surprisingly easy. There was truth in everything getting easier with practice. This time he hadn't felt anything. It had been rather unreal. There'd been little blood in the kill. A sharp whack with the wrench he'd stuffed into his bag earlier. He followed the assault with a second blow just to ensure that he'd done enough frontal lobe damage to kill the driver. A bathroom break on the shoulder of the road, five minutes into the ride, had given him the opportunity. He supposed the element of surprise had given him the advantage but Eric hadn't been much of a fighter. By the time he'd realized—seen the wrench Ben held in his left hand that he'd conveniently picked up at the gas station—it was too late. There'd been a panicked look in his eyes when he'd realized what was coming down. Now, the seat was wiped clear of any blood with a jacket he'd found in the backseat. He'd thrown that into the ditch along with the body of his Good Samaritan.

There's no such thing as do-gooders, boy. It always turns out wrong. That had been one of the last pieces of advice offered by his father. It was the best thing that no-good piece of crap had done for him.

"No such thing," he repeated as he cranked up the radio and tapped a hand against the wheel as AC/DC's "Highway to Hell" beat at top volume. He floored the vehicle. He needed this deal done before the buyer became suspicious and Ava spilled what she knew. If she knew what he suspected she did then there was only one place to be, Tristan. That's the only place where the records were accessible for they weren't online. But no one was going to access them, he'd make sure of that. Then, once it was done and Ava Adams was dead, he was getting the hell out of town. He would be out of the country before Darrell Chan put a hit out on him.

Now he had to get to the place he'd once called home, back to where it had all started and where it would all end. He couldn't get there fast enough. Everything he was, everything he'd be—it all rested in Tristan, a little piece of hell in the heart of Texas.

Chapter Eighteen

Tuesday, June 14—4:00 p.m.

Thank goodness for small towns, Ava thought as she briskly pulled the sheets off a bed. She loaded them onto her cart that was sitting just outside the door. The roar of diesel was a reminder that this town might be small but it was also a stopover for truckers. Fleets of them passed on the side roads as they took a break before heading to the bigger centers. She mused about how in a city she would never have been hired without any credentials. That was a good thing as she couldn't haul out her list of academic accreditations. None of her diplomas would do her any good here. Fortunately, in this small town in the south of Texas no one had given a thought to asking her for identification. They needed the help and she needed the employment. She'd never worked in the service industry. She'd been lucky. Her father had insisted she keep her mind on academics, and with the exception of her tutoring, a salaried job, no matter how part-time, was not a consideration.

Not wanting to arouse suspicion, the story she had told the motel owner of her reason for a lack of belongings was one of tragedy. Her home had flooded following a torrential rain. The disaster that followed caused her to leave her rental unit behind. She'd managed to leave the place unnamed and vague, rather like her memory had once been. The woman who managed the motel had asked no questions, only expressed sympathy. She'd felt beyond guilty about that but she had no choice. She'd make up for every shady thing she'd done when it was all over. That is, if she lived to see the end of this.

She'd been hired at noon and outfitted by one o'clock. It had been a stroke of luck when the woman who would have worked this shift had gone home sick. She'd even been given an advance on her paycheck. She'd had to ask and churn out an addendum to her hard-luck story and, frighteningly enough, that hadn't been too difficult. With a little tweaking, her real story was every bit the hard-luck case, so she wove bits of it into the story she'd already told. In fact, the story was so good, she'd surprised herself at her desire to keep embellishing. It wasn't a habit she was going to keep once this was over. In fact, she was surprised that the story had worked, that the woman who ran the motel had agreed to a small advance in exchange for her beginning work immediately. It wasn't much, but it was something.

BEN WHYTE'S HEAD hurt like hell and anger coursed through him. He eased his grip on the steering wheel when his knuckles started to ache. He'd get that little witch who could ruin his plans.

He needed Darrell Chan to pay up for the land he'd signed on to buy. It was the biggest deal ever and the one he needed in order to be able to call it quits. Once he had the money he would leave the country and everything else behind. He didn't need Dan Adams's interfering daughter ruining it all with something as simple as the truth.

It was here, in this out-of-the-way place, that all his dreams would come true. That's what he'd thought only weeks ago and then Adams had done what he hadn't anticipated. He'd thought their partnership was solid and he'd been proven wrong. Adams was never supposed to find out the truth and yet somehow he had. He'd had no choice but to take him out. With Adams out of the way, he hadn't expected another piece of flotsam—his daughter. By the time he'd realized that Ava Adams was on board, it was too late. Adams managed to get her off the yacht and out of his hands. She was a fly in the ointment and he wasn't sure what she did or didn't know. But if Dan had told her anything, he would have told her where the evidence could be found and that was here in Tristan. He had to make sure she wasn't here and if she was, he had to find her. If she was here, he was betting that she hadn't gotten farther than the outskirts of town.

He pulled down a service road, passed a filling station and then a junkyard piled high with rusted cars and assorted farm implements. Like many small towns where businesses had been shut down, a cluster of metal and pipe from projects long forgotten sat abandoned along with gas stations on either end of town serving travelers that never made it to the town center. A police cruiser drove slowly by, the officer glancing at him curiously. He nodded but didn't smile. He'd found eye contact and a friendly, but not too friendly, demeanor worked best with the local authorities.

He turned left into the rutted and worn blacktop

of the motel's parking lot. He'd been to three others like it. But this time as he walked out of the administration office, he knew that he'd hit gold. It wasn't the same name but there weren't a lot of twenty-something women checking into motels in this town, not that matched her description. She was here. He touched the gun hidden beneath his shirt. He'd gotten not just a car but a gun when Eric had picked him up. The boy had been sheer gold.

Ava Adams, the name was like nails on a chalkboard. She knew too much and she was too smart. She was lethal in her own way and she needed to be removed just like her father had been. Unfortunately, he didn't have any time to drag it out, to have any fun. It was a shame because he wanted her in every way a man wants a woman. He wanted just one shot at her before she died.

Chapter Nineteen

Tristan, Texas
Tuesday, June 14—6:00 p.m.

Close to Tristan, Texas, and still in the air, Faisal received a grim lead. The radio was playing and a news report came on. One of the top stories was about a man being killed after picking up a hitchhiker. Motorists were advised to be on the lookout for a middle-aged Caucasian male about five-ten...

The report went on. Faisal had heard enough. His gut told him that the hitchhiker was Ben Whyte. But the interesting thing was that he'd murdered and stolen someone's car while hitchhiking.

He couldn't believe what he was hearing. He phoned the Houston Police Department and asked to speak to Detective Morris. Rex Morris was another law enforcement officer he'd dealt with before. He was open-minded as long as you didn't try playing any games with him. Even though it had happened outside Rex's jurisdiction, ten minutes later he had the details he needed. The death had been particularly violent. A wrench, wiped suspiciously clean of even a fingerprint, had been found in the ditch. The coroner had been on the scene and was convinced that the bludgeoning marks were fairly indicative that the wrench had been the weapon. In the meantime, the authorities would lift whatever DNA they could. Unfortunately, there was nothing solid to go on. All they had was a description of the vehicle the victim had been driving and an APB was out. He gave a brief description to Rex of the case he was on. They hung up with an agreement to notify each other if the vehicle was found. There was nothing else. He had to take the tip he had and run with it.

His phone buzzed.

It was Barb with the information he'd asked her to follow up on. Ben Whyte's mother's location. She'd found Evangeline Tominski's address and phone number in Chicago. He knew that this wasn't going to be an easy call and he was proven right minutes later. The woman sounded worn and beaten like she'd been a victim. If he could have painted a picture of the trajectory of her life, he guessed that it would have been done in gray with splotches of red—dull with moments of great trauma. It was sad and disheartening. Listening to the story of someone beaten down all their life was one of the few things that made him regret his career choice.

She'd opened up as soon as he'd told her who he was and that he was looking for her son. He listened patiently as she told him that her son, Ben Whyte, had supported her with an occasional check that he mailed to her. She said many things, many of them irrelevant but some very relevant, including how she was terrified of her son. She muttered that he was violent and had beaten her up many times. She said that she was afraid that he'd turn worse, kill even, just like his father. She then mentioned that some of it was her fault. She hadn't left his father even when he'd pushed the boy down the stairs in a fit of rage. Her son had limped ever since. And still she'd stayed until her husband had turned that anger outside the family and been jailed for murder. It had been an entirely disturbing telephone conversation. Sometimes, there were aspects of this business he detested. This conversation was one of them.

Knowing what had shaped Ben Whyte gave him a clearer picture of who he was dealing with. He bet that Tristan, Texas, had drawn him back because that was where Ben Whyte had spent the majority of his miserable childhood. It was a rural area of southern Texas surrounded by nothing but flat arid land. Familiarity had drawn the man back.

He shook his head as he mulled over the details of the call. Ben Whyte hadn't had a chance. He'd come out of the ashes of an abusive childhood deeply scarred. It was urgent that he find Ava immediately. Ben Whyte was an unpredictable, troubled man. Not only that, but if what his mother said was true, like his father, he had no love of women. A woman-hating man with a grudge. He shuddered at the thought of it.

Thirty minutes later, Faisal had the chopper pilot drop him five miles from Tristan town limits. In a town this size, the arrival of a helicopter wasn't going to go unnoticed. He had a vehicle waiting for him. It was a basic silver SUV that blended in with all the others. It was the perfect choice—mass-produced, dull and mundane. It was exactly what he needed to remain under the radar. While the town was a good size, it was still small enough that a stranger would eventually be noticed by someone.

His mind went over all that had transpired. What did

Ava think she was doing? She'd phoned for his help and now fled it. He'd considered possibilities including that somehow she might have had a heads-up on the man who had killed the patient after her. Hospital surveillance hadn't told him much more than that he was an average-sized male who had kept his face carefully hidden from the surveillance cameras. So far, he appeared to be working alone.

His phone buzzed. This time it was his contact within the Canadian RCMP, Sergeant Aaron Detrick. "There's a bit of information I thought you ought to know. I was just speaking to one of the other officers who had worked undercover on the case we discussed. Chan has a couple of go-to men, basically killers for hire he uses. It's not often. I think, rather ironically, like I said before, Chan considers himself a good guy."

"Some good guy," Faisal said, and then he regretted the interjection. Aaron tended to be a bit long-winded if given any kind of encouragement.

"There's one name that came up just recently, Dallas Tenorson. He's been arrested a number of times. Violent acts, a brutal beating during a robbery, road rage, but nothing to keep him locked up for any length of time. Except, we were sure he was behind a killing last spring. Cause of death, gunshot to the head. One shot took the victim out cleanly—that doesn't happen often. It had hit man written all over it, between that and a clean crime scene. No one was ever convicted. The evidence was just too thin. But the interesting thing is that the man who died had been up on charges for rape. He raped Chan's daughter. She committed suicide immediately after the rape."

"A tragedy," Faisal said, thinking of the girl.

"Chan never missed a beat," Aaron said.

"He's tough," Faisal said with a hint of sarcasm.

"And more importantly smart, but he tripped up this time. We were able to ID the last hit man he used but we've got no evidence to pin on Darrell. We have suspicion based on recent activity and a witness who insists they'll commit suicide before they admit what they know on the record. So unofficially, like I said, his name is Dallas Tenorson. He's been in and out of juvie, is from a broken home—the classic story. His record from juvie has been purged so now there's no record, nothing to prevent him from moving freely around the country or across borders. He has a passport. Now thirty years old and has never held a steady job. So how is he surviving? Contract work, if you get my drift."

Faisal's laugh was dry. It wasn't a drift but a slam in the head. Everything he'd heard up until the hit man's description had been enough to make him sick. This Dallas—he deserved what he got. Up to no good and destroying other people's lives. Faisal wouldn't mind being the one to take him out. He pushed his thoughts aside. Instead he said, "I'm guessing that you've got nothing to pin him with."

"No evidence. We know he's transient and smart enough to cover his tracks. There was no paperwork found for the two previous hits, no electronic trail—phone trail, nothing. They had to have met in person but there's no witness either. We had a guy undercover, but he didn't get close enough to nail him, just close enough to make some pretty valid assumptions. Anyway, I'm telling you this so you can keep a watch out. I've sent you a picture too. Should be on your phone now. That's pretty much all I can do. Anything else and

I'll be stepping over a line. Trouble with the law," he laughed. "Okay, it wasn't funny."

Faisal chuckled. "Not really, but thanks for the effort, man."

After Faisal disconnected, he wondered what else there might be. He knew he was lucky in his line of work to have established such a connection. He could only be grateful for what he got.

From everything he knew and from what Aaron had told him, he knew that time was running out. Chan was on his way to Hong Kong and, if he followed his former pattern, being crossed, in this case defrauded, meant he'd put the pins in place. Someone was going to die and he'd bet that someone might be Ben Whyte. But with Ben potentially on Ava's trail, that left her in the middle.

He just hoped and prayed that he hadn't arrived too late.

Chapter Twenty

Faisal took a room in a run-down motel on the outskirts of town. That was where he began his search for Ava. As far as choice there wasn't any. It appeared that all the motels on the edge of town were run-down. But it was there that he'd be less noticed. It wasn't unlike other towns. The only exception was that Tristan was more worn—more forgotten.

Finding Ava was critical. Ben might be here too but his priority was making sure Ava was safe and literally out of the line of fire. He ached to see her but despite the small size of this town, it might not be that easy.

He was dressed down and the vehicle he'd rented was a few years old. And after the last few days running between searching the water and going to the hospital, his after-five shadow had turned into stubble. He was not unlike many of the scruffy men he'd seen in the nearby Flying J. Or the two men he'd seen enter the diner next door. If someone was going to remain unseen, the best thing to do was remain on the fringes. The people who didn't fit, and those that had secrets, congregated there. He'd seen these types of places again and again while working a variety of cases across the country. They were places where secrets could be hidden. Knowing that, it was the logical place to start. And it was really only a place to set up his home base. He doubted if he would be spending much time in this room. The best way to start searching for Ava was by questioning the people who lived here. Someone had seen her. Someone knew who she was and he'd find that someone if it took all night.

Ava. He'd never forgotten her and he knew now that he never would. He only hoped that he could find her, that she was safe, that if she were willing, he could hold her in his arms again.

But he'd no sooner dropped his small duffel bag on the worn double bed in the grim little room than a gunshot sounded outside blowing any of his hopes aside. He was on his feet and his Glock was in both hands. An engine revved. Glass crashed and someone shouted and then there was silence.

The silence didn't last long. It was soon filled with a woman's voice and a string of curses. Her shouts filled the parking lot. He pulled the ratty curtain back and could see a woman standing in the fading evening light with her hands on her hips only six feet to the right and in front of him. It looked to him like she was the aggressor. As such, she didn't appear to be in immediate danger. She hurled a bottle onto the pavement. Shards of green glass scattered in every direction and glinted under the light of a nearby parking lot. Ten or so feet away, a biker with black leather chaps and a faded red bandanna on his head shook his fist at her; in his left hand he held a handgun. He could guess now what had happened. There'd been a fight and now the gun was being used as a scare tactic, nothing more. Still, he didn't like it. The woman, no matter how worn out she looked or what her occupation, didn't deserve that kind of treatment.

Faisal opened the door to his room and stepped out. It was clear now, from the gestures of the biker as he left the lot, that the shot had only been meant to frighten and not harm. It was also clear that the woman, now that she had thrown the bottle, was unarmed. It had been the biker who had shot in the air.

"Ma'am, are you alright?"

The woman's eyes were wild, her hair in tangles. She was wearing a faded yellow wifebeater shirt. The cotton sagged and her dark nipples were clear against the thin fabric. *Wife beater.* He grimaced. But as much as he hated the term for the sleeveless T-shirt, here it seemed troublingly appropriate. But despite her revealing and worn-out attire, her legs were positioned in a fighting stance. Her hands were in fists and her arms were rigid at her side.

Oblivious to his words, she told him where to go in words he had no respect for.

The woman turned her attention to him. "I'm not interested in you either. No man is getting anything free. You want…"

"No." He cut her off. "I'm not interested."

"Not good enough for you, boy?" she asked. Her double chin quivered and her brow wrinkled. She ran a hand through her hair, which was platinum blond with mud-brown roots.

"You're beautiful, ma'am," he said. Flattery was a powerful tool to manipulate people. He thought that maybe she deserved a compliment—he doubted if she got any from the looks of her and this place. This area, this hotel, all of it, didn't attract the kind of people who were into niceties.

"You'll do," she said with a smile. "Flattery and chivalry will get you everywhere," she said in a tone and with words that hinted at more sophistication than the earlier incident and her appearance indicated.

He held his phone out to her with a picture of Ava. "Have you seen this woman?"

She paused. "Yeah," she said thoughtfully, chewing her bottom lip. "She was here this morning, asking for work. I run this joint in case you're asking. Not that it's much." She shook her head. "Anyway, as far as rooms, we've got none but the Blue Moon down the road does. I told her to go there." She looked at him with more street wisdom than real smarts. "For a fifty I'll give you a bit more." Her eyes roved over him.

Faisal couldn't help himself, he gave her the fifty. "Treat yourself," he said gruffly. He hoped if nothing else, the money would keep her off her back and give her some dignity, at least for one night.

He turned and headed for the SUV. He needed to get to the Blue Moon and he needed to do it, like, yesterday.

AVA WAS EXHAUSTED. She'd gone from a hospital bed to cleaning rooms in the space of less than two days. The evening sun had just set as Ava turned out the light and slipped into bed. Despite being physically drained, it was still early and she couldn't sleep. Instead, she was plagued by thoughts and possibilities. She'd learned that land transactions were not immediately filed online in Tristan if at all. In the land registry's dismal and tiny office, the woman in charge was good-natured and after paying the fee she requested, was more than willing to give her a photocopy of the deed and transfer documents for the land her father had told her about that fateful night on the yacht. In fact, she'd given her copies of two land transfers—the second had come as a surprise but it too had her father's forged signature.

Now she had the evidence that at least the signature on the piece of land in question that Ben Whyte was selling wasn't her father's. Tomorrow she'd turn what she had over to the authorities. Today wasn't an option as the county sheriff's office was in the next town and she wasn't sure if she wanted to hand this over to the local police office which consisted of two officers. When she'd asked the librarian about them she'd been given a lackluster review.

She hated being here, hated everything about this place. The sooner she could deliver what she'd found to the authorities, the sooner she could get out of here. She didn't feel safe here, not in this shoebox of a room, not in this town. Her breath came in on a hitch as she thought of Faisal.

She could hear his voice like he was here, low, deep and confident. She remembered how he'd told her that she was safe when she'd been in the hospital. And she'd felt safe not because of where she was but because he'd been there. She never should have left him or tried to do this on her own. Now she longed to hear his voice. She needed him and yet she'd run from the help he'd offered. She'd done the right thing, she reassured herself. As much as she longed for him, this was on her.

She lay on her back, staring at the ceiling. Too tired to get up and too distracted with her whirling thoughts to sleep. A car pulled up. She tensed. Instinct told her to leave the light off, as if she sensed something wrong.

There was a knock on the room to her right and then silence. There was no one there. That room was empty.

Who did they want?

Who were they looking for?

She felt like a kid holding her breath at the scary part of a movie. Instead of holding her breath she was remaining still, quiet, listening.

The footsteps crunched on the gravel. That meant they were coming closer. It was a strange fact she'd noted on arrival, that the end units had gravel stalls while the rest of the parking lot was paved. It was like the pavers had run out or became exhausted by the project before completion. Either way, she'd seen it as an odd little bonus. It made detecting someone nearby, especially in a vehicle, somewhat easier.

She sat up, swinging her feet to the ground, thankful that she'd slept in her T-shirt and scrub pants.

She couldn't stand another minute without finding out who was there. But when she peeked out the peephole, there was nothing. The peephole had a limited range though. She took a step back. Her heart pounded as if instinct was again telling her what her other senses couldn't, that something was wrong.

A bang on the edge of the parking lot, as if someone had hit a metal pole with a large heavy object, had her biting back a shriek and jumping away from the door. Could it be gunfire? But that was insane—or was it? She remembered her employer mentioning something about a nearby gun range. That explained it. A sigh of relief raced through her. But she had to make certain. She pulled the faded blue cotton curtain back a few inches and peeked out. She could see nothing, the lighting was too weak. She thought of her exit strategy.

If there was a problem, the front was already compromised. The bathroom window was small but she could fit; she'd already checked out that option. There wasn't a threat, she told herself through gritted teeth. *Relax.*

She squinted as if that would allow her to see more than what the filmy light of the one parking lot light and her outside unit light allowed. The parking lot was half-empty but the motel was only half-full. It turned out that had worked in her favor, for she'd only had to work a partial shift to finish up what another employee hadn't. Physically, she couldn't have done more. Traveling here had taken what little energy she had.

The motel sign sent a thin bluish stream of light across the parking lot, from the north side. Nothing moved. She took a deep breath and let the curtain drop. Then she retreated to the bed, where she perched as if she might need to leap up and run.

Seconds and then minutes ticked by.

She began to relax when she heard footsteps again. Again, they seemed close to her room. Then they stopped. Somehow the silence was more frightening. Again, she moved to the window, glanced sideways and crouched down, peering over the window ledge. What she saw frightened her. A man stood in the faint light. He was maybe fifteen feet from her front door. A car door banged. His back was to her, facing the parking lot before he moved away deeper into the lot. Then he turned. She knew that profile, that large, rather hooked nose was distinctive. The light outlined him perfectly.

Ben Whyte.

Her mouth went dry and her hand shook as she dropped the curtain. Did he know she was here? In this room? Had he discovered that Anne Brown was Ava Adams?

She stood up. She looked at what stood between her and danger: a weak safety chain, an economy lock and a cheap flimsy door. Again, she crouched down, trying to keep out of sight. She nervously lifted the curtain, an inch, then two. She peeked out the window. Now she could see the shadow of what looked like a man crouched low and moving from the fringes of the parking lot directly toward her. He was coming in at a different angle, not walking upright as if he had honest business but rather as if he was sneaking in. Whoever he was, this was someone different.

Her heart raced and her mouth was dry. None of this boded well. She hadn't been comfortable from the beginning and had slept in her clothes as if prepared to run. Now her fear had been validated.

She backed up and spun around, heading for the bathroom where the small window led to the back alley.

She needed to get out fast while she still had the chance.

Chapter Twenty-One

Faisal had stopped in the office of the Blue Moon Hotel. The office was separate from the row of units that sat diagonally from it. He'd walked in from the street, not wanting to call attention to himself or alert anyone to his presence.

He walked into the office prepared to face whoever was manning this operation with all the charm he could muster. A woman lifted her head from the desk, looked at him with rheumy dark eyes and smiled. Her disheveled bleached blond hair was giving him déjà vu, for it reminded him of the manager's style in the hotel he had checked into. He pushed that thought aside. He needed information and he needed to concentrate to get it.

"Can I help you?"

Her round, out-of-shape body leaned over the counter, spilling her large breasts literally onto the counter. He kept his eyes on her face, ignored her disappointed look and smiled his most charming smile.

"Beautiful night," he said.

"It is."

And from there he turned on the charm. It was a gift that he rarely used but one that came naturally. Ironically, he'd used it twice in the space of an hour. He gave his full attention to the woman on the other side of the counter. By the time he was done with his "feel good," "you're the greatest" routine, he'd asked the questions he needed to and gotten the answer to each of them. She readily identified Ava from a picture.

"She checked in this morning. Poor thing needed work. She covered an afternoon shift," she said, her eyes roving over him. "She's in the end unit."

He left the office with a smile and a quick salute and headed away from the units she'd pointed at. He'd seen movement he couldn't identity, and putting himself into a possible line of fire was no way to help Ava.

He moved quietly along the fringes of the parking lot of the Blue Moon Motel. It was dark and there was no traffic on the road that skirted the motel that he now knew Ava was staying at. He crouched down using the darkness as cover. He paused for a moment to take stock of the situation. He gave himself a minute and then two, for he was hidden behind a boulder that looked like it had been placed there in an aborted attempt at landscaping. Ahead, the lot was dimly lit by a light on one side and the blue light that thinly streamed from the motel sign. The place was run-down, the motel itself painted a faded and dismal gray. Ironically, that fact was at complete odds with what one might expect given the motel's name—Blue Moon Motel. The only thing blue was the annoying sign that cast blue tendrils of light across everything.

His attention turned toward the movement he saw by the end unit. It was the bulky shadow of a man. He had a picture on his phone, thanks to his RCMP contact, of the hit man but in the muted light from this distance, he wasn't identifying anything. A shadow moved farther away. The bulk indicated it might be another man. The first man was nearer the building, while the other man was yards away, putting him on the edge of the parking lot. A gunshot echoed through the night and he hit the ground near the sidewalk, where he immediately rose to his haunches and moved behind the hood of the nearest vehicle.

Dallas Tenorson or Ben Whyte or both could be here or not and it was all supposition. The only thing that was for sure was that a gun had been fired. He was pretty sure it had been from the man nearer the motel units aiming for a second one in the parking lot. But the man at the fringes had not fired back. That in itself was an interesting fact.

The information he'd received confirmed that Ben Whyte was in the area. Could one of the two be Ben? If it was Ben, he had the home advantage. These were his childhood stomping grounds. He knew every bit of this land. He'd known that the land deals had been nothing but worthless contracts. He'd known it all, for this was where they'd been inked. It was here that they had fleeced enough buyers to make Ben a rich man if he could just cash in on his last deal.

He crouched down. He had his gun out and in one hand. He wasn't expecting to shoot anyone, not yet. He hoped not ever, but then he always hoped that. He squinted. He could see the shadowy figures, one moving in on the other. He wasn't sure what was going on. His priority was keeping Ava safe, and to do that he needed to get her out of there as quickly as possible.

One man moved closer to her door. Too close for his liking. He knew who it must be. He could see the off-kilter way he walked, as if one leg couldn't quite support the weight that was expected of it. He knew why he walked that way. One of the unit lights near the end clicked on and then immediately off but it was enough to see the distinctive profile that was Ben Whyte.

Faisal shifted his Glock, feeling the comforting weight. He had no sympathy for either Dallas Tenorson, a man who seemed to spend his life contracting to kill, or Ben Whyte, his intended victim. If the second man was Dallas, then there was no way he could take him out without giving an open path for Ben to kill Ava. Ava's room remained in darkness and he could only wonder if she was awake or asleep. Was she spooked by the earlier gunfire? There was always the chance that she'd open the door and make herself vulnerable. He could try to take at least one of these men out but neither were close enough for a clean shot.

It was too dangerous. He couldn't risk trying to take either of them out and alerting the other to his presence. Instead, he had to sneak around them and get Ava out before he addressed the other two. To do that he was going to have to go around back. He could only hope that, like every motel built in this style, there was a window in the bathroom. He thought of fire codes. He didn't know what the damn fire codes were—he could only pray. If there wasn't a window... The thought dropped. He wouldn't think of that and would just have come up with a new plan then if it came to that. He began to make his way around the building, moving quickly before the explosive situation in front of him blew up.

A movement ahead. Ben Whyte was five yards from Ava's front door. There was no more time to consider. He had to move. He ducked down behind a worn-out van with chipped gray paint. Another shot was fired and the man on the fringes of the worn parking lot dropped. The shot was masked by the sound of a semi pulling out on the edges of the commercial district of town.

He couldn't get a clear shot from here. With his gun in both hands he moved quickly and quietly to the back of the building. He slipped around the building with his back to the wall, watching for movement in the darkness broken only by a yard light over fifty feet away.

Two minutes later he was outside Ava's back window. He gave the signal that they'd used so often, what seemed like forever ago. He waited. Nothing.

He tapped on the window again. One, two, three—same as he had so many years ago when he called her out in their university days to whatever party had been going on. He hoped she remembered. Hoped that she realized the danger and got out before it was too late. Before he needed to do something more drastic that could compound the danger she was already in.

She had to remember. But he couldn't assume anything, couldn't make that mistake, for Ava's life was on the line.

Chapter Twenty-Two

Someone or something was tapping on the bathroom window. Ava bit back a shriek. She was blocked in. She'd heard what sounded like a gunshot in the parking lot and she'd kept low after that, afraid to look out or to somehow draw attention to herself. Now there was someone at the back—her only escape hatch. Her tiny sanctuary had just become her trap. Her heart pounded and she was glad she hadn't had a chance to eat much or she was sure fear would have her heaving it all. She was poised in the doorway of the bathroom to run and there was nowhere to run to.

She couldn't breathe and her heart was racing.

That familiar tap again. The tap that had meant so many other things so long ago. Was it her imagination? Wishful thinking? Or divine providence? It didn't matter if it was none or any of them. She had no choice. She had to take the chance. It could be anyone or it could be him.

She didn't need any other motivation. She didn't care who was in the alley. Fear skated over everything her rational mind told her, and she knew that she had to get out.

Her hands shook as she balanced on the tub. She

pushed but the window seemed stuck. She pushed again. Her nail ripped. She didn't stop. Finally, the window opened a crack and with a heave she pushed it all the way up. The faded, blue-checked curtain fell across her face and she pushed it aside as she boosted herself up. Fortunately, the window was big enough that she was easily able to slip out of it without bodily contortions. She dropped to the ground just as she heard the crack of wood splitting and knew that the door to her room had just burst open.

She landed hard and stumbled. She reached out as if intuitively she'd known all along that someone friendly was here, someone who would stop her from stumbling or face planting. That was only wishful thinking. She had to get out of here if she wanted to live.

"It's me."

A man. Her heart was pounding so hard that she thought her chest would burst.

She bit back a scream, backed up and turned to run. She'd give it her best. She wouldn't die from lack of trying. Instead she ran straight into the solid wall of a chest and strong arms that held her tight. There was no escape. She was doomed and if it weren't for the arms holding her, she was sure she might have expired from fright.

She tried to twist away and at the same time she tried to make herself smaller, to slip out of the iron grip that held her. Her heart was beating so fast and so loud that she thought she might die just from that alone. Fear raced through her and at the same time anger was building. The adrenaline rush was more from anger than fear now. She'd live through this or die trying. She raised her foot to bring it down on the beige canvas high-top sneaker. *Not an ordinary shoe. Designer.* The words ran through her mind but didn't connect with what that meant.

"Ava."

She twisted and managed to sink her teeth into his hand. A curse and then she was turned roughly around to face him.

"Damn it."

The grip loosened and she was free. But the freedom only lasted a few seconds before he had her again. This time by her waist, her feet off the ground, she was held tight against him.

She kicked backward and clipped his shin.

"Ava, it's me… Faisal."

She hadn't heard right and yet she had. The voice, the words, even the shoes. It all came together. All of it was familiar. The fear fell away. She relaxed in his arms, her heart pounding a zillion miles an hour. The danger she had anticipated replaced by a danger that had a different meaning, different depth.

"Fai?" she said, even though the familiarity of the voice validated the truth.

"If I let you go, promise me you won't run," he said.

"I wouldn't—"

"I'd catch you anyway," he cut her off darkly.

"Let me go," she said. "I won't run." That part was true, for she had no vehicle and no place to run to. "But it's a mistake to be here with me."

His arm eased and she slid down his hard length, landing on her feet, as she turned to face him.

The look he gave her was both intimidating and full of concern. "You could have died, running the way you did."

"But I didn't," she said obstinately, as if her earlier fears had been based on nothing but her imagination. "It was a mistake to follow me," she repeated, for he hadn't responded the first time she'd said it. "Fai," she whispered. "You need to get out of here. Trust me."

"We'll get out of here together. This is what I do—protect."

"I know," she whispered but she really wasn't quite sure she did. She knew about his company, even knew about his position but she'd never imagined any of this. She wasn't sure any layperson actually could.

"It's dangerous," she said as if he'd said nothing at all. "Being with me."

"I can take care of myself, Ava, and you. You need me. Maybe more than you realize."

Something deep inside told her that he was right. That it had been a mistake to come here alone. "There's someone after me. He'll kill—"

"Let's get you out of here. This place has been compromised."

A gunshot seared the night and overrode the other sounds. She bit back a scream.

"Damn it."

He grabbed her hand without another word. They were running down the narrow overgrown alley, where trees grew wild and uncontrolled by a gardener's clippers. Their branches reaching beyond the confines of the yards they grew in, crowding the alley. He boosted her over a fence, through a yard cluttered with aged vehicles. A dog barked. The sound muffled and slightly ominous as if there was something the dog could see and they couldn't.

She ran as if he were her only salvation. And she

supposed it was true. She'd be dead if Faisal hadn't been here. Her father had died and she knew that she was next on the list. She clung tighter to his hand and wished she could go back to a place in time when she'd never run from him in the first place. She couldn't protect him. It had been foolish of her to try.

BEN COULDN'T BELIEVE IT. Darrell Chan had tried to take him out.

Despite the advice he'd given Chan, despite how convincing he'd believed he'd been, Chan hadn't listened. He'd told Chan that purchasing land in this area would be slow going. Tristan wasn't a big place and the land-registry process moved like everything else—slowly. He'd told Chan that it was best not to delay paying the purchase price since that would grease the system's wheels and get everything moving faster. Apparently, Chan hadn't believed him, about anything. The deal had fallen through.

He ducked behind a car and could see the man Chan had sent after him was still moving. He'd thought he'd gotten him minutes ago and had gone for the little witch in the interim. That had been a mistake. He rubbed his shoulder. He'd almost got it then.

He narrowed his eyes, watching. He knew who he was up against. He'd done his research. The loser was a hired killer. Chan had used him before; he was good. But he wasn't that good.

Ben moved diagonally. He was in the open but he was low and it was dark. A shot hit close enough to kick up dirt and make a pebble clip his wrist. He bit back a curse and put his mouth on the wound.

Damn it, he thought with a snarl. He flattened himself to the ground by the back tire of a van and watched, waiting. The loser had taken his last shot. He'd picked the wrong man to try to take out. He hadn't spent hours at the range for nothing. This guy was done.

He dropped to his chest as he had a brief visual and then nothing. He inched forward, both hands on his gun, his eyes combing the half-empty lot, searching for him. The one who saw the other first was the one who would come out of here alive.

There'd be one more shot.

It would be his.

Movement.

Running. The slap of sneakers on pavement. A shadow of a man.

He took aim and fired. Once, twice.

Someone would hear him.

Damn it. He didn't care. He shot again.

His target fell.

It was time to get the hell out of here.

Chapter Twenty-Three

"How did you find me?" Ava gasped as she was literally dragged by her hand. She knew that Faisal was pacing himself, that he was holding back. She was running full tilt, giving it her all. But she was no runner. She needed to stop for breath. "Those were gunshots?" she gasped. "What's going on?"

"Keep moving," he gritted. They'd already jumped one broken fence. Now, he was almost lifting her over another listing three-foot fence that backed yet another property.

There was no time to answer anything. They needed to get out of the area. They ran for a few more minutes, taking them another block away before he stopped.

"You're alright?"

"I need to rest," she gasped.

She looked at Faisal and saw that he had a gun in his hand. The sight of that did nothing for her pounding heart. This was unbelievable, unthinkable. She'd known Faisal's work could be dangerous but somehow she'd never imagined this. She couldn't fathom it. Instead, she looked around. The street they were on seemed quiet, deserted. Across the street was a steel Quonset and she remembered another time and something else her father had said.

"You're remembering," Faisal said as his dark eyes scanned her face.

She nodded. "My memory is back."

"Can you go any farther?" he asked. "You can tell me everything later. And I can tell you what you need to know, what I've found out."

"He wants to kill me."

"I know," he interrupted. "But someone's been sent to take him out. I don't know which of them is going to walk out of that parking lot. But we're going to be as far away as possible."

"This is beyond what I thought."

"Way beyond."

"What else do you know?" she asked.

"More than you think," he replied. "But right now I need to get you to safety."

FIVE MINUTES LATER Faisal had left Ava in the driver's seat of the SUV he'd rented. He'd made sure all the doors were locked. And he'd given her strict instructions that if anyone but he approached the vehicle, she should take off and never look back. He didn't think that would happen. Where she was, in the parking lot of a local fast-food restaurant, couldn't be any more well-lit and, therefore, any safer. "If you feel threatened in any way, drive. Don't analyze it, just go. Head for Ballad," he said mentioning the next town twenty miles west of Tristan where the sheriff's office was located. "Promise me you won't hesitate. You'll just go and report everything to the sheriff there."

"I promise," she said.

He'd left her there. It was the best place he could come up with in a time crunch. He had to go back. He'd run all the way back, daily sprints making the run easy. Five minutes later, he stood on the fringes of the parking lot outside the motel room that Ava had called home for not quite a day. A man lay sprawled on his back ten feet from the lone parking lot light. Otherwise, the lot was empty of people and dotted with the same vehicles that had been there fifteen minutes ago.

He moved carefully forward, crouched down to approach the body. He assumed it wasn't Ben. He needed to be sure. The body was lying faceup. He beamed a small flashlight at the figure that was obviously dead. The man matched the picture of Dallas Tenorson. Wiry, early thirties, dark hair and he guessed about five foot eight. He went through the man's pockets. No identification but he didn't expect any. The hit man had come to take Ben Whyte out and instead Ben had taken him. He didn't feel anything for him. These types of men were desperate, dangerous, from hard backgrounds, and they lived and died by violence. To them, a life was only as good as the coin you could lay on it.

He moved silently across the parking lot, keeping low and out of sight. He could see the flicker of a television through the window in one room. He thought of the gunshots, not many admittedly but still enough to have attracted attention. A dead man in the parking lot to cap everything and still it had brought no curious bystanders from their units. Everyone was caught in their own melodrama whether real or spoon-fed to them through the television screen. Beyond them was undeveloped land and a shooting range. You couldn't have picked a better place to take someone out. Ava had set herself up perfectly without even realizing it. But then how could she have known? The shooting range was hidden. It was behind the dilapidated warehouse that sat diagonally across from a commercial lot. He'd seen it himself only because he'd driven a back road in that took him past the facility. So gunshots wouldn't be unexpected in this rough area near a shooting range. It was a shooter's nirvana.

Five yards from Ava's room he could see that the gravel had been disturbed with what looked like a footprint. He thought of the dead man. The same fate could have befallen Ava if he hadn't been there. The thought of it made him sick. The door was cracked and he only had to push gently for it to open. Inside, the bed cover had been thrown across the room and there were towels scattered on the floor as if they'd been thrown in frustration. There was nothing else, no personal belongings, nothing left behind to give any indication as to who had been here.

On a hunch, he lifted the mattress and there was an envelope. He picked it up and looked inside, quickly thumbing through the papers and seeing that they pertained to land transactions. Ava had been busy.

He stepped back outside where he made a call to the local authorities and asked for the chief of the local police department. Davis O'Connor was a man he'd contacted earlier. He liked to be prepared for such things. You never knew when you might need police assistance, especially in his field. He had been proactive this time too and had made sure that the law knew who he was, but not precisely what he was about.

Now they had a murder and he knew they wouldn't be returning to Miami, at least not immediately. There was the hurricane warning affecting flights into the area. But more importantly, this had to be reported. It was pretty much a given that the police would want them to hang around. A fair enough request as long as he could keep Ava safe.

He'd thought this was a targeted hit. It was about Ava. He hadn't expected what he found when he entered the main office. There, the same woman who had eaten up all the charm he could throw at her now lay in front of the check-in counter on her back, a bullet hole in her chest, blood covering her blouse. Her eyes were open and she looked rather surprised. He squatted down. He knew what the outcome was before he did it—he took her pulse anyway.

"Sweet hell," he muttered as he strode out of the office.

Faisal could hear the sirens now. He jogged back to get Ava. The police would want to speak to her too. He slipped into the passenger seat leaving her in the driver's seat. He put a hand over hers as she reached as if to turn the key and start the vehicle. Her bottom lip quivered and he moved closer putting his arm over her shoulder, offering her comfort with his touch and protection always.

"You came back for a reason, Ava. What was it?" he asked softly.

"Dad told me to read his emails and I did when I got here to Tristan. Darrell Chan said that he had proof that Dad had sold him land, that his name was on documents he had in hand. Dad claimed he'd never made such a transaction."

"Your father had no interest in real estate but his name carries a lot of weight."

"Exactly," she interrupted. "But Chan had documents with Dad's signature on them. Dad told me the proof of his innocence was here, in Tristan."

"He told you to come here?"

She looked rather sheepish. "No. He told me to tell you."

"And you didn't." Anger ran through him at how she'd endangered herself.

"I'm sorry, Fai." Her voice trembled. Then she straightened her shoulders and turned to look at him. "But I found the proof to clear his name. The signatures on the transactions filed in Tristan are forged. I know Dad's signature. I need to go back and get the evidence."

He shook his head. "Is this it?" he interrupted her as he pulled out the envelope he'd taken from her hotel room.

"Yes. They're copies of both land transactions that Ben filed with forgeries of my father's signature. The last one was what was going to make Ben Whyte rich."

"And where Darrell Chan balked."

"Yes," she murmured. "Dad planned to come here and collect the evidence himself but if he couldn't, if something happened, he wanted me to tell the authorities or you what had happened and where the proof was. That's what he told me before the argument, before…" Her voice broke.

"Ava," he said, his eyes never leaving hers.

"I'm okay," she said. "Ben didn't know that my father was onto him. He arrived unexpectedly that night on the yacht, I'm not sure why."

"And your father somehow revealed what he knew or more likely Ben guessed," Faisal said. "Ben probably didn't know that Chan had already contacted your father."

She shook her head. "No and Dad didn't tell him, not then. Not while I was around."

"From what I can see, this land doesn't even belong to Ben or your father," Faisal said. "It was a fake transaction from start to finish."

"Unbelievable." She shook her head. "I think my father confronted Ben that night. A stupid move on his part," she said with sadness laced through the words.

"Faisal Al-Nassar?" The sheriff's deputy called out fifteen minutes later as he approached the motel office which the local police had now cordoned off with yellow tape.

"Yes. That's me," he said, coming forward with his arm outstretched. They shared a firm shake. Ava was at his elbow like a silent shadow.

"Hell of a mess. We're not used to murder in this town," Davis said as he came up beside the deputy a few minutes later. There was something that sounded like strain in his voice.

Faisal had told the deputy what he knew only minutes ago and Ava had added what she'd heard along with what she had found at the land registry office.

"We'll be interviewing the other guests, seeing if anyone saw anything." Davis tipped his cap. "You say that one was a hit man?"

"Yes." He gave him Aaron Detrick's number. "He has the information on that. I know if there's any way for them to pin something on their suspect they'll be more than grateful to you."

"RCMP you say. Be a first—never worked with a foreign government," Davis said with an off-kilter smile.

Faisal almost smiled at that. He doubted if he'd be working much with one now. If the case crossed borders it would be more than the police in this little town would see but rather the county sheriff, who had already stepped in, would be involved.

The police officer's phone rang and he walked away to take the call while the deputy had moved on to examine other evidence. Two minutes later, Davis came over to where Faisal stood beside Ava. Her arm brushed his side as if touching him somehow gave her some solace.

"There was a sighting of a middle-aged man matching the description of this Ben Whyte just five miles outside of town. He was heading north." He looked at Ava. "The sheriff's office is on that. I think based on that, you're more than likely safe. Let me know what hotel you change to but stick here in Tristan. That's an order." He looked at Faisal. "Barring an emergency, I'll need you around for at least the next twenty-four hours." He shook Faisal's hand. He'd offered him a different level of respect than he would any other witness as soon as he'd learned of Faisal's connection to Nassar Security.

But no matter what had transpired, the truth was that Ben Whyte was still on the loose and Faisal wasn't so sure that he'd accomplished what he'd set out to do. Factoring out the manager of the motel who had been an unfortunate casualty, one man had died as he'd tried to take out another. Ben Whyte had lived. He'd been just outside Ava's motel room when Faisal had removed her from danger. The one thing that was clear was that Ben Whyte's work wasn't finished and that meant only one thing. He'd be back.

Chapter Twenty-Four

"Fai," Ava murmured.

She insisted on calling him by that abbreviated version of his name, one that only some of those closest to him used. Every time she did, it was like she had touched him with the heat of a lover's hand. It was outrageous, ridiculous. And he wanted to tell her to stop calling him that as much as he wanted her to call him that every day of his life. Few, except his brothers, called him by that name. He seemed swamped with nostalgia as he drove. He remembered the first time he had met her. He'd been enthralled with her. He would have dated her if he hadn't liked her so much, and if he hadn't been dating someone else. There were so many *if*s. None of his romantic entanglements at that time had turned out well. He didn't want to wreck a good friendship. That's what he'd told himself then. But the truth was that she slightly intimidated him with her drive to succeed. He'd never met anyone like her. And at the time, he'd been too young to appreciate her maturity. That combined with her drive gave her that edge. It was an edge that, for a young man, had been frightening. And he'd have died before he'd have admitted he was frightened of anything. That had been a long time ago. His thoughts shifted.

Two people had died, a man and a woman. He was used to it. She wasn't.

"You're alright?"

"Fine," she replied with a failed attempt at a smile. "At least I will be given time."

He knew that. If anyone, any layperson, could come back from this, it was Ava. The thought dropped. Thirty minutes later they stopped at a gas station with a small grocery and picked up a few things to have a casual meal. They had ready-made sandwiches and potato salad along with disposable plates and cutlery.

"Is that your stomach I hear?" Faisal asked. They had just settled into their new room in another place. It was an end room on the first floor of a hotel on the other side of town. He was putting potato salad on paper plates. The small counter was crowded with a coffee-maker and a microwave, leaving little space to work. He banged his hand once on the coffeemaker almost sending the carafe flying. He picked up the bottle of juice he'd bought from the motel vending machine and poured them each a glass. He took a plate and a glass over to her.

"Thanks," she said with a smile.

He made a second trip to get his own sandwich and drink. He made himself comfortable in the only other place to sit besides the two beds—an overstuffed, yet harder-than-rock faux leather chair.

She looked at him, her bare foot tucked under her legs as she stretched out on one of two twin beds. Her smile was contagious, whimsical and yet amused—

a sign that even amid trouble and tragedy, life would eventually go on.

She took a bite of the sandwich. "Heaven," she said with a smile.

It dawned on him as he saw the slight shake of her hand and the ravenous way she bit into the sandwich that she hadn't eaten recently. "When was the last time you ate something that was cooked?"

"Something that wasn't peanut butter—is that what you mean?" she asked. "There wasn't any time to get groceries or, more accurately, I was too tired to hunt for anything better," she said before he could reply. She shook her head with a wry smile. "I guess that the last time, factoring out hospital food—" she grimaced "—was that night on the yacht."

"Ava, I'm sorry. And you've got nothing more than another sandwich, I'll—"

"No." She stopped him. "This is all I need for now. Promise me a good breakfast tomorrow and everything will be fine."

"Deal," he said with a laugh that was more expectation than amusement.

They ate in silence for a minute.

He finished his sandwich and came over to sit on the corner of the bed near her. She didn't look at him but instead wiped her mouth with a napkin. The sandwich had been thick with roast beef, lettuce and mayonnaise. A dab of mayonnaise was still on the upper corner of her mouth. He wiped it gently away. "I wish I could say that I won't ask you any more questions, knowing how much they upset you. But unfortunately—"

"You have no choice," she interrupted. "Don't feel bad. It needs to be discussed, figured out. Dad's name needs to be cleared. His name was used to steal millions of dollars and if he hadn't stumbled on the plot, it would have been much more. Ben Whyte used his good nature, convinced him he was helping a friend and then took advantage of him. First it was just financial support but then he forged his signature on land deeds. He was selling land that he didn't own and using my father's reputation to validate himself."

She was standing now, pacing.

He got up, taking her hands in his. "Ava. I'm so sorry you had to go through any of this."

"It's almost over, isn't it?"

"It is," he assured her.

She looked at him with wide, troubled eyes. "I missed you, Fai," she murmured.

"Why did you run? You know I would have protected you."

She shook her head. "I'm sorry. I didn't want you hurt, I…" Her gaze traveled to his waist where his Glock was holstered. "I should have known better. I regretted it later. If I could undo…"

"You doubted me?"

"Never…I…" She shook her head. "I don't know what I was thinking."

"It was a stupid mistake, sweetheart."

"Sweetheart," she repeated and looked up at him with a troubled frown.

"Promise me you'll never do that again."

"I hope I never am in such a situation, ever," she said instead.

"You won't be," he said grimly, his hands settling on her shoulders as he drew her closer. "I'll protect you always, Ava," he said in a low growl as his head bent and his lips met hers. At first the kiss was soft and hesitant, then it deepened and his tongue teased her lips to open. She felt so soft and vulnerable as he held her but he knew that was an illusion. He'd seen her strength. She'd proved it before and in spades these last few days. She was everything he'd ever imagined and more.

His phone rang.

He held her tighter.

The phone rang again and he reluctantly let her go.

"I'm sorry," he said after he'd seen the number display. "I need to take this. I'll be just outside."

"I think I'll run a shower," she said looking slightly bemused.

He wasn't sure what his brother Talib was calling about, but it would be something important. His timing couldn't have been worse.

He opened the door and stepped outside. The parking lot was dimly lit, similar to that of the Blue Moon Motel. He supposed it was a way of saving money. They weren't making a lot based on the price of the rooms. The Blue Moon. The comparison was like a warning running uncomfortably through him.

"Faisal?"

What Talib said next had his full attention.

"Coast Guard just reported in. They've found a Caucasian male on a yacht. He was found by an American container ship. The yacht drifted into the shipping lane. The man is alive but unconscious. They haven't made an identification yet, but…"

"There's a good chance it might be Dan Adams," Faisal said with a note of relief. "The IMO number matches," he said referring to the International Maritime Organization number on a boat's hull that identified it for the lifetime of the craft. "I'll keep it quiet until we have something for sure. There's no point in getting Ava's hopes up."

"She thinks he's dead?" Talib asked the question, which was more of a statement.

"Yeah. I haven't dissuaded her. There's too much at risk. Ben Whyte is still on the loose, and only four hours ago, the manager of the motel Ava had checked into was killed, as was Dallas Tenorson. He was hired to take out Ben Whyte."

"Bugger," Talib muttered. "This case is one ball of ugly."

"We're wrapping it up," Faisal said. "If the survivor turns out to be Dan, that will just be the icing on the cake. In the meantime, once the police have investigated and the weather improves on the east coast, we'll be moving on, heading back to Miami. We're hanging here in case we can provide the police with any more information. Ava's memory is back. I hope that what she remembers fills in any remaining gaps we have.

"Evidence points to the fact that Ben Whyte double-crossed the wrong man." He went on to explain to Talib what had happened earlier in the Blue Moon parking lot.

There were still questions. After he hung up with Faisal he strode the length of the lot. He stood there for a minute, breathing as if fresh air alone would give him the answers he needed. His mind went back to Darrell Chan. They knew that he was in Hong Kong at the moment. But they also knew that he had the resources to reach anyone he wanted anywhere in the world. The question was if he had the motive to do so. From what they'd gathered he did. Ben Whyte was still alive. It was only a matter of time before Darrell Chan hired some-one else to take him out. That is if he hadn't already.

He headed back to the room but stopped when he saw that the door was open. He'd closed the door but he hadn't locked it. He'd been right outside, there had been no need to lock it. He should have locked the damn door.

There was a scuffling noise inside and then a small gasp. He'd recognize that voice anywhere—Ava.

He pushed open the door without hesitation. He used the element of surprise as his gun was already in both hands, ready for use.

"What the hell?" Faisal stopped dead at the sight in front of him. Ava was being dragged backward by the sinewy tanned arm of a man who had a gun to her head.

"Come any closer and she dies."

"There's no need for this," Faisal said calmly as he watched Ben Whyte and prepared himself for any un-expected moves. The man didn't know him and yet he wasn't asking who he was. That didn't bode well.

"I thought I could just kill her and end this, but that's not true anymore is it?" Ben snarled.

"If this is about money, I can give you what you want and more."

Ben cursed, dropping one expletive after another. "Liar. You don't think I know that you want me dead."

"I'm not lying. I can get you out of the country a rich man. That's what you want, isn't it?" The words were difficult to say when what he really wanted to do was launch himself at the creep who held the woman he loved. The thought blazed through his mind with-out hesitation. It was overridden by his outrage over the situation she was in and his fear for her life. And, as a result, he skated right over the fact that a truth had again been laid bare if not in public, in his own heart.

Ben moved back, his grip on Ava's neck causing her to choke and clutch his arm with both hands as if she could pry the sinewy limb from her neck.

"I guarantee—a million dollars on the table. You walk out of here a free man." He'd throw the damn money in a bag along with this piece of scum and drive him out of the country if necessary. At least that's what he'd tell him. In the end, he would drive him straight into the arms of the authorities and a jail cell, or kill him if necessary.

He deliberately tried to keep his eyes from Ava who had nothing but a towel around her. Her hair hung wet along her face and dripped down the towel. A long strand ran down the side of her neck. He pulled his attention away from her.

"I'm an Al-Nassar, we have…"

"I know who you are," Ben snarled. "Chan would have given me ten."

"I can easily do ten million," Faisal said as if this was nothing more serious than a game of poker.

He could feel his heart pounding. The stakes were higher than he could have imagined with Ava's life on the line. He was seriously making this up as he went along. He was using anything that was believable. Anything that would get Ava out of this man's arms and safe. That was all that mattered, and he'd say anything he needed to up until then.

He tried not to look at Ava, but it was difficult. She was right there. Looking frightened and courageous all at the same time. He wanted to tell her it would be alright, but he didn't know himself how this would turn out. There was still a good chance she could be injured or worse. He needed to play this right and play it well. And he didn't have much time to do it. It was a tight situation. He'd never been in any quite like it, at least not with someone he knew, someone he cared about. He forced his attention from Ava and to her captor. It was the only way.

Ben looked at Faisal in an odd way, the gun clenched in his hand, his grip on Ava's neck every bit as tight. But the expression on his face had changed. He was assessing Faisal now, slotting him into a different category.

Silence. Seconds ticked by.

"You're playing me," the man snarled. He took a step back, again roughly yanking Ava by the neck with him.

Ava bit her lip. A trickle of blood appeared, telling him how hard she was fighting for control. Her eyes met his as she tried to communicate with him. He could see fear and something else, something that told him that she was alright. They'd make it out of this, but he'd have to kill the bastard to do so. He just needed the opportunity. Her look told him everything he needed to know. She was in and on board. He had everything he needed except for a plan.

"Ben." It was time to get personal here. "The deal is brilliant."

"It is, isn't it?" This time his voice was captivated not by anything Faisal had said but instead, he suspected, by his own words. A narcissist at his worst, Faisal analyzed.

It was almost impossible not to look at Ava but he had to stay focused. He had an advantage; Ben's gun hand was wavering. His face was flushed. These were all signs that he was weakening. He could take him out.

It would be risky, but he only needed one chance and he'd kill the no-good son of a desert dog. He wasn't sure if he could give Ava any kind of signal. He hoped she was following along, that she was on the same wavelength. He had to depend on that, on her wits.

A dog barked outside, distant, maybe a block away. Then a horn sounded and Ava jumped. It was all he needed. He had to take the chance. Otherwise, he knew deep in his gut that the outcome would be bad. He'd seen Ben's desperation. He knew the make-or-break of the situation and knew that with any more leeway, Ava was dead.

He gave her the look—subtle, just a flick of his gaze to his right. It was a signal to move where he indicated. Instead she stood there. She seemed paralyzed in place before sinking her teeth into Ben's hand. His grip loosened and she slipped away.

Faisal shot—aiming with all the skill the hours at the range had given him. Yet, all the while he wondered how things had come to this. To Ava standing, half-dressed, seemingly in shock. Her face white, her black hair long and wild, only the towel wrapped around her. He registered all that as he watched the man fall, as blood ran onto the floor and it was clear that whatever danger he presented was over.

Still, he needed to get her out of here. The dead man was too close to Ava. She'd survived the first trauma but the second was threatening to do her in. She was shaking. He pulled her tight against him, his arm over her shoulders, her head on his shoulder.

"It's over," he whispered into the faint rose scent of her hair. He felt her quiver against him. "Let's get out of here," he said, and this time he meant they were taking the chopper and getting the hell out of Texas. Sheriff's orders or not, they were out of here. He'd put in his report and then hit the road. The Lone Star state had offered enough challenge, for the time being anyway.

She looked up at him as if finally realizing what had happened as she looked at the body and her lips tightened.

"Is it over?"

"He's dead."

"He wanted to kill me," she murmured as she wiped tears away with the back of one hand.

"Ava…" he began, reaching to take her into his arms. To comfort her, to…

She pushed him gently back. "It's alright. I'm fine. I suppose we need to call the police—again." She drawled out the last bit.

"Again," he agreed. "This time I lay odds we'll be taken down to the station."

She smiled wanly at him. "It beats how I spent the last few minutes. I think we'll both survive."

"Let's get you away from this," he said.

"Let me get dressed," she said.

"I'll get your clothes," he said. There was no way he was letting her step around the body to get her things in the bathroom. Instead he did it for her and stood with his back to her and between her and the corpse as she dressed.

A minute later she was dressed and ready to go. He had her hand and it felt like he would never let her go. And even while doing that, he was on the phone. The police needed to be informed.

"Do you think we'll ever know what happened to my father?" she asked softly.

Faisal looked at her as they leaned against the rental, waiting for the authorities. "I don't doubt it," he replied.

"I wish Dad had…" She choked, unable to finish her thoughts. And they both knew what that last word that she couldn't say was. She wished that her father had lived.

There was nothing he could say. He didn't want to offer her false hope. There was still a chance that her father hadn't survived. Everything was still too volatile. Chan was still on the loose and Dallas Tenorson might be dead but he was only one of a number of hit men Darrell Chan could have hired. This case wasn't closed yet, not by a long shot. Danger still lurked.

Chapter Twenty-Five

They had just finished giving their report at Tristan's police office where two deputies from the county sheriff's office had remained on site. Both Faisal and Ava had told the men what they knew. It was close to midnight before they were able to leave. Faisal opened the door of the SUV and Ava slipped in.

They'd just received the news from Talib that Darrell Chan was still in Hong Kong. On a tip from the RCMP, he was detained by Chinese authorities on conspiracy to commit murder. As well as a possible second-degree-murder charge. If everything went as planned, he'd be facing justice in either a Canadian or an American court. The authorities from the countries involved would be negotiating that. Whichever country's court he landed in, the odds were that he wouldn't be a free man for a very long time, if ever.

"It's odd… Darrell Chan was rather a silent criminal," Ava mused. "Not someone you'd fear on the street, but don't cross him. Dad would have appreciated…" She couldn't say any more; tears threatened.

He took her in his arms. "Ava," he murmured against the soft fragrance of her hair. There was nothing more to say, no certain news that would bring her comfort.

"Dad was taken advantage of," Ava said. "He was so mild-mannered."

"Which is what Ben counted on. He had a plane ticket for Thailand leaving in the next week. One way."

"Then why did he want my father…"

"He needed to convince his last client. Your father has a reputation of being aboveboard and honest. That information is easy to learn. He's a local celeb."

She considered that for a moment. "I never quite thought of it that way."

"If the deal with Chan had gone through, Ben would have had enough money to end his illicit career. This part of it is only a guess, but from what I'm getting from my Thai source, he'd already rented a property in northern Thailand for the next month using his grandmother's maiden name. What he planned to do after that is anyone's guess."

"What's yours?" Ava asked softly.

"He was going off the grid. Disappearing and living out his life. We more than likely wouldn't have heard from Ben Whyte again. But I don't think that means he'd stop. Con artists are a strange bunch."

"They're proud of what they do."

He looked at her with a smile. "Exactly. It's not just a way to make money, but an art."

"Rather a twisted way to look at things," she said with a smile.

"There are more twisted things in this world than either of us can dream of," he said, the look on his face serious.

"Crazed things," she said with a sad look on her face. "This has been the vacation from hell. I can't believe we ended up in a little town in the bottom end of Texas."

"Tristan was the perfect place to hatch such a scheme. Small town surrounded by scrub brush and ranch land. The kind of place where the town's kids just want to escape. I've never seen such a down-and-out place. Ben had spent enough time there growing up that what he described to the buyer, the pictures, all of it was real. What wasn't real was the actual sale."

JUST BEFORE MIDNIGHT, Talib called. "How are you holding up?"

"Fine. It's Ava I'm worried about," he said.

"What I remember of Ava, she'll be fine. She's strong."

"What's up?"

"I have some news. The autopsy report on Kelsey Willows, the woman who took Ava's hospital bed," he clarified. "The report is back and strongly hinting at foul play. One of the cleaners saw a man he's confirmed is Ben Whyte from a picture enter the room just before her death. It's looking like murder."

"I suppose there'll be no resolution on that. Too bad."

"In a way," Talib said. "But Ben Whyte's dead and that can't be anything but a good thing."

"True," Faisal replied.

"This went all the way to the heart of Texas," Talib said. There was a hint of a smile in his voice. "There's other news, Faisal, and that's why I'm calling. They've identified the survivor I mentioned earlier. The Coast Guard just notified me. It's Dan Adams."

Minutes later, Faisal was giving the joyful news to Ava.

"Your father is alive," Faisal said. "He's weak but he's going to make it. He's en route to Miami now."

"Alive," Ava whispered. She could barely fathom the words. It was everything she had hoped for and nothing that she'd expected. "How?" She shook her head. "Never mind. It doesn't matter, what matters is that he's alive."

"And I heard he asked for you," Faisal said.

"He's conscious?"

"Amazingly, yes," Faisal said. "Your father's a survivor. I don't know anyone else who would have survived an attack and then over four days at sea. He was very lucky," he said seriously. "The yacht was reported by a container ship when it finally drifted into shipping lanes."

Ava reached for Faisal's hand, her palm grazing his. The heat of his skin on hers offered her the strength she needed. But still the questions remained. Her father was alive but was this nightmare truly over?

Mercy Hospital, Miami
Wednesday, June 15—2:00 p.m.

FAISAL STOOD BEHIND Ava in the doorway of the hospital room. Her father had been airlifted off the container ship that had found him. Faisal and Ava had left Tristan early this morning by helicopter.

They'd landed on a nearby private airstrip and he'd hired a driver to bring them here. He wouldn't leave her alone. It was too emotional for her. And that aside, he was invested too. This man was important to the family but, more important, he had to be here for Ava. The possibility that she might lose her father had been devastating for her. Now she hesitated in the doorway of his room as if she couldn't imagine after everything she had been through that this could be real.

He put an arm around her waist, giving her support even as he urged her forward. They slipped by the un-smiling security. Faisal's unconcealed handgun empha-sized the seriousness of all that had transpired. Whether this was over or not, Faisal wasn't taking any chances.

"I can't believe it, I hoped…" She looked up at him with tears in her eyes.

"It's him, Ava. I promise you. He lived."

She leaned for a second against him. It was as if she were gathering strength. She reached up to gently run her fingers down his cheek before taking a step away from him.

The man had his back to them. He was emaciated and his hair was grayer than Faisal remembered. Dan turned the wheelchair around. The distinctive features, the piercing brown eyes were exactly as he remembered.

"Dad!" Ava's voice was weak and seemed to break, even on that single-syllable word. But Faisal knew the word meant so much. She'd told him less than twenty-four hours ago that she thought she'd never be able to say it to him again. It had been her worst fear and her worst nightmare.

Faisal watched the two of them embrace and mar-veled at the fact that Dan Adams had lived. The yacht had drifted into the shipping lane and that appeared to be the only thing that had saved him. It had made him visible, or at least more visible for he'd still needed a passing ship to rescue him. But luck had held and some-how the yacht's trajectory had missed the worst of the hurricane. The Florida coast too had also missed the brunt of it. All in all, considering what had happened to get him in the situation, Dan Adams had been lucky. He'd survived the injuries that Ben Whyte had inflicted on him. In a nightmare of days and nights he'd still managed to survive.

For a minute there was silence as Ava hugged the man she'd called father for more than half of her life.

"I thought you were…" She couldn't say it. She choked on the word.

"Gone," he said with a half smile.

"Yes." She smiled, relieved at how things had turned out. "I thought I'd never see you again. What happened? Are you alright?"

Dan looked at her sadly and Faisal stepped in to put a hand on Ava's shoulder as she knelt by her father. "Give your father some time."

"No," Dan said firmly as he looked at both of them. "I'm fine." He reached out, his arm bare and thin, the dark hair standing out against the pink and blistered skin.

"Why isn't this wrapped?" Ava said, her attention drawn to the arm as Faisal's had been.

"They're leaving it for now. Don't worry, honey." Dan's laugh was hardly a laugh at all but instead a dry sound that seemed to scrape from somewhere deep inside him. "I'll live and that's the main thing."

Ava made a small choking sound and wiped her eyes with the back of one hand. She stood and Faisal's arm went around her waist. She looked up at him.

"I'm okay," she reassured him.

"How did you ever get involved in anything so shady?" She looked at Faisal. It was a question that had remained unasked between them, for her father had always been a law-abiding upright man and to be involved with someone like Ben was incomprehensible. "An error in judgment?" she asked.

"It's over," Dan said with a weak smile. "Ben was a man who needed a helping hand, or so I thought. He took my intentions all wrong. That night on the yacht was desperation on his part." He shook his head. "It was my fault. Like a fool I told him that I couldn't go along with his scheme. It wasn't just men like Chan who were getting fleeced, he was taking hard-earned money from people who had little savings. Either way you looked at it, Chan or no Chan, rich or poor, it was criminal. But I should never have told him I was going to report him." He shook his head. "I can only say my anger got the best of me. It was an incredibly stupid move."

"How'd you find out what he was doing?" Ava asked.

"It was when Darrell Chan contacted me. It was clear then that something was up. He was the one that told me that he'd purchased land and had a deed with my signature on it completing the transfer. But it was his doubts about that second piece of land that had him contacting me in the first place and revealed this whole mess."

"Land was being sold by Ben Whyte that wasn't owned by him. Using your name on land you had no claim to or no knowledge of," Ava added. "Land he had no right to sell. Unbelievable."

"Forged deeds," Dan said. "I discovered that he was using my reputation to validate his scheme and selling tracts of land that he didn't own, and forged my signature on two transfers. It was at that point that I knew that I had to do something. But I still thought that I could talk sense into Ben." He shook his head.

"You set up a meeting with me to have it investigated," Faisal said.

"Exactly. I wanted to make sure my suspicions were right. I'd always planned to notify the authorities," her father said softly. "I just waited too long to do it."

"Ben took out the navigation and computer system. There was no way to track you," Faisal said. "How did you survive getting shot and then knocked overboard?"

"I was lucky enough to grab a rope on the way down. Although I still ended up treading water for a bit. And Ava—" he looked at her with a slow smile "—had left her window open. I finally managed to crawl in there. I found her phone and called for help, but I wasn't connected long enough to trace." He shrugged. "I suppose it wouldn't have mattered anyway, the yacht was drifting. I can't tell you what happened immediately after that. It was the last thing I remembered for hours. When I came to, I crawled to the upper deck. Literally crawled," he said as his hand brushed against the bandages on his thigh and he glanced at his right leg, which was in a cast. "And again that was the last thing I remember for a long while. I was in and out after that. I was just lucky they found me when they did."

"Oh, Dad." Ava put her arms around him. "We were both lucky. I don't know what I would have done if I'd lost you."

She let him go and took a step back.

"But there's more?"

"I'm afraid there is." He shook his head. "What happened is my fault."

"Dad, no…"

"Ava, listen," he said. "I shouldn't have gotten involved. I should have called the authorities immediately," he said. "I'll regret that until the day I die. I made a mistake," Dan said. "You could have died."

"I didn't," Ava said. "You're an honorable man."

"A stupid one who should have played along, at least I should never have…"

"It's okay, Dad," Ava said. "We all lived through it."

Dan was quiet for a minute. "I'll be going home after all this." He looked at Ava as if waiting for her to join in. "How about a short vacation before you start…"

"My new job," Ava finished as she shook her head, taking both her stepfather's hands in hers. "I can't, Dad. No more delays. I know you'll be okay and I'll visit at Christmas, I promise. But for now, I need to get my own life going in Wyoming." She looked back at Faisal.

"I see," Dan said softly.

"Dad…"

"No, sweetheart, I really do." He looked at Faisal and a silent understanding seemed to pass between the two men. "I'm tired. Maybe you two could come back later to visit." He looked back as a nurse entered the room. "Besides, I won't be here that much longer. My doctor said they had plans to discharge me."

"That's right," the nurse said with a smile as she overheard the last part. "I heard you'll be discharged in a few days."

"It can't happen soon enough," Dan said with a smile as he looked at the arm Faisal had around his daughter's waist.

Chapter Twenty-Six

Friday, June 17

"I hate to leave him," Ava said.

It was two days since they'd found her father and he was well on the way to recovery. She'd spent time at her father's bedside but she'd also spent time with Faisal. He'd offered her a suite in the luxury hotel his family owned and that he called his home away from home. But she'd spent more time with him than in the suite he offered, as they made up for the time they had lost. They'd laughed together and they'd seen a different side of Miami, a more laid-back, romantic side, as they strolled the beach at sunset and had supper in a quaint café they discovered by accident one day.

Now, the late afternoon sun streamed in through the picture window as she sank into the thick luxuriousness of a mint-green leather couch. When they'd left her father after learning he'd been found, she'd felt at peace for the first time in days, knowing that he was safe. Now, she glanced around the Nassar company–owned penthouse suite in Miami. It was luxury with a toned-down touch. Classic rock played in the background and reminded her of Faisal's love for seventies-era rock. Five years ago, she'd shared that love with him at parties and even a few lazy evenings like this. But she'd been twenty then. It seemed a long time ago. She held a cup of tea, a soft blanket over her shoulders as she tucked one foot beneath her and stretched the other leg out. "Dad's been through a lot and when he's discharged he'll be going home alone…" Her voice trailed off and her lips tightened. "I don't like it, but…"

"You can't be late to start your own life." He cupped her chin, his eyes looking into hers. "You have a career to begin, a life ahead of you, a new job waiting. Your father knows that."

"I know." She smiled as he dropped his hand and put his arm around her shoulders. "I can't wait for that, at least I couldn't until all of this."

"It will be fine. The excitement for your career will come back. The memory of this trauma will fade."

"Will it?"

"I promise," he said with a low growl in his voice.

"Still, I owe him—"

"You owe it to him to be happy," Faisal said, looking at her with a smile. "You heard what the doctor said, he'll be discharged soon," Faisal assured her as they sat in the Miami penthouse suite. The suite belonged to the Al-Nassar family but was used primarily by him. "You need to start your own life, your own career," he repeated as if saying the words in a different way would somehow make them more real to her.

"How did you get so smart? You're right. That's exactly what my father would want." She lowered her teacup and looked at him with a sheen of tears in her eyes. It was all so much to comprehend and yet she still felt she owed her father.

"He wants nothing but your happiness," he said.

"I know you're right. He's said it often enough to me."

"It's what every parent wants. I know mine did and I know Dan does too," he said.

She looked at him and saw something else in his eyes, a hint of nostalgia, sadness even. She put the tea down and took both his hands in hers. "I'm so sorry, Faisal. You lost your parents when you were a teenager. And here I am thinking of going off, of leaving him—"

"Ava, quit dramatizing," Faisal interrupted with a smile. "My parents' accident was tragic but it has nothing to do with any of this. Sure, I'd change it if I could, but even so, no parent would hold back their child. That's what kids do, grow up."

She looked down at her hands and smiled at the fact that they looked so small, almost lost in his. He seemed to notice not at all. Instead he pulled her against his chest, his arm going around her as if he was never going to let her go.

"I think it's time we began thinking about our own lives, our own family."

"What do you mean 'our'?" She looked at him with a frown, her beautiful eyes troubled.

"Don't deny that there's something special between us. There always has been."

She met that statement with silence.

"I know we were apart…"

"Five years," she said with a hint of regret. "I thought of you often."

"I love you, Ava. I always have. And now with you in the same state, there isn't even geography to separate us."

"That never separated us," she whispered.

"No, you're right. It was our youth."

She turned her face up, an invitation she'd wanted to offer a long time ago. He took it as easily as she'd dreamed in the past. He leaned down and kissed her with all the passion of the unsaid words that lay between them.

"Come with me," he said thickly. He led her to a bedroom hidden down a hallway of soaring ceilings and skylights. The skylights dusted sunshine along the mellow wood floor. The floor reminded her that he had told her all those years ago that he was restoring old flooring he'd obtained from a demolished church. The old and the new wove together to make the suite breathtaking. On the floor by the sprawling bed was a woven Moroccan wool rug, its colors a dark, muted brown that was accentuated with patches of cream. Overhead a skylight streamed light into the room. Against one wall was a stereo system with a collection of vintage vinyl records lined up on either side. She didn't see any more after that. Instead, she let him lead her to the downy seduction of the bed, which seemed to fill the room with a promise.

It was she who pulled him down onto the bed as she fell backward, playfully testing whether it was as soft and as inviting as it looked. But it was his firm lips on hers, his readiness against her that took all her playfulness to the next level. Their clothes disappeared in their roughhousing of play and desire. An hour later they lay naked in each other's arms.

"This is how it was meant to be," she whispered. "I hear Wyoming calling."

"Just Wyoming?" Faisal said with a laugh.

"For the moment, yes," she said with an answering laugh. "I love you, do you know that?"

"I should hope so," Faisal said. "I don't want to lose you again. I only hope you feel the same way."

"You won't be given that option," she said with a smile in her voice.

He leaned over and kissed her, hard and deep, and yet briefly. When he rose up on an elbow, he looked into her eyes. "You're everything to me, do you know that, Ava? I love you," he finished before she could reply.

Tears glistened in her eyes as she reached up to draw him to her. "I wish every moment of our life could be like this," she said.

"Like what?" he asked thickly.

"Spent together."

He ran a thumb along her collarbone. "That sounds perfect to me. Any way we cut it, we'll be together…"

"Forever," she finished. "It's everything I want, Faisal."

"We'll be married," he said as he plopped down beside her.

"What kind of marriage proposal is that?" she asked with a giggle. She turned over on one elbow so they were nose to nose. Chest to breast, and despite how erotic it all was, for a moment they were serious.

"Ava Adams, would you do me the honor of being my wife?"

"Forever and always," she replied as her lips met his. And the kiss seemed to last forever.

When the kiss finally ended, they lay shoulder to shoulder. The air-conditioning caressed their heated skin and Ava thought she might have reached nirvana. It was then that Faisal reached under the pillow and brought out a box. "To seal the deal, my love."

"Are you always going to be this romantic?" she said with what she knew was a loving, yet sarcastic edge to her voice.

"Open it," he said with only a small hint of the Al-Nassar command she'd teased him about when they'd been together at school.

She opened the box and saw a ring that was like none she'd seen before nestled in a satin bed. She wouldn't even ask how he'd gotten it so quickly. She was quickly learning that it was the Al-Nassar way. Instead, she could only look at it with damp eyes. The band was delicate strands of gold that appeared to be braided together. The heart-shaped diamond sparkled in its setting. The ring truly reflected the love he'd so recently admitted.

"It's beautiful." The words weren't enough and yet that was all she could say. "It's unique, romantic..." Tears threatened. She had no words to explain how she felt. It was a moment she'd never dreamed of despite how she'd always felt about Faisal. He'd been everything. He was everything.

"You're everything," she said as if he would know what she meant.

And the look in his eyes told her that she had said it all.

"It represents my love and the love of family."

"You mean children?" she asked, looking into his dark eyes.

"Maybe or maybe just the love of those we allow into our lives."

"That's beautiful, Fai," she said, leaning over to kiss him.

He pulled her closer. His eyes looked deeply into hers. Then he kissed her, long and hard and hot. The kiss lasted a minute and then two before it ended. She looked at him with all the love she was feeling, the ring clutched in the palm of her fisted right hand as if she would never let it go.

But a few minutes later she watched as he slipped the ring onto her finger. A ring that was unique and rare, much like the man she'd always admired and loved and had now agreed to marry. It was a ring fashioned from love, hope and a promise.

Outside the sun shone even brighter as it offered all the hope and warmth of the promise of their future together.

* * * * *

Check out the previous books in the
DESERT JUSTICE *series:*

SHEIKH'S RESCUE
SHEIKH'S RULE
SON OF THE SHEIKH

Available now from Mills & Boon Intrigue!

Join Britain's BIGGEST Romance Book Club

50% OFF your first parcel

- **EXCLUSIVE** offers every month
- **FREE** delivery direct to your door
- **NEVER MISS** a title
- **EARN** Bonus Book points

Call Customer Services
0844 844 1358*

or visit
millsandboon.co.uk/subscription